LIPSTICK ON THE HOST

LIPSTICK ON THE HOST

Aidan Mathews

Secker & Warburg
LONDON

First published in Great Britain 1992
by Martin Secker & Warburg Limited
Michelin House, 81 Fulham Road, London SW3 6RB

Copyright © 1992 Aidan Mathews

The author has asserted his moral rights

'Train Tracks' was first published
in *20 Under 35* (Sceptre).

A CIP catalogue record for this book
is available from the British Library
ISBN 0 436 27422 1

Set in 11/13 Bembo
by Deltatype Ltd, Ellesmere Port, South Wirral
and printed in Great Britain
by Clays Ltd, St Ives plc

for Lucy, for later

CONTENTS

TRAIN TRACKS

Timmy leans across the arm-rest of his window seat and tells the airhostess that he's sick. He might have told the cabin steward, the one who brought him the magnetic chess set with the missing bishop ten minutes before, but he didn't; he may be only twelve, twelve and a bit, but he's learned already from his mother and his sister that secrets are best shared with women.

The hostess smiles at him. Her smile is brisk, professional; her eyes are tired. A little fluid is oozing from her left earlobe where the pearl stud ought to be. He wonders whether it's tender, remembers his sister having her ears pierced by the ex-nun on her thirteenth birthday. Did the Germans take the earrings as well as the gold fillings from the men and women they killed in the camps he couldn't pronounce?

'Sick?'

'A bit.'

'In your head or your tummy?'

'In my stomach,' he says.

'Maybe you drank that Coke too fast. Would you feel better if you put your seat back? Or if you got sick? Sick into the bag.'

'No.' He has already stowed the sick-bag and the in-flight magazine and the sugar sachet from the lunch that was served, in the pocket of his school blazer as souvenirs of the flight.

'We'll be in Dusseldorf soon,' she tells him; and she reaches across the other, elderly passenger to rumple his hair with her red fingernails.

Now that she's touched him, he has to confess. He hopes the other passenger won't overhear, but the man seems to be asleep, his mouth open, a dental brace on his bottom teeth as if he were a child again, and a slight smell of hair-oil from his button-down collar.

3

'I can't go,' Timmy tells the airhostess. 'I've tried to go ever since I woke up at home this morning. I tried at the airport, in the departure lounge, and I've tried twice since the plane took off, but I had to stop because I was afraid that there'd be other people waiting outside. And it gets more sore all the time.'

She laughs; it's meant kindly.

'That's only constipation,' she tells him. 'It'll pass. And now you know how women feel when they're having babies.'

She begins to move away as the elderly passenger comes to.

'I could report her,' he says to Timmy. 'I could report her for saying things like that.'

Timmy doesn't answer. Instead, he stares out the window, tilting his glasses slightly on the bridge of his nose to bring the countryside beneath him into sharper definition. What do women feel when they're having babies, and why is it wrong to say so? His stomach tightens again, the pressure to pass a motion makes him gasp.

'Are you all right?'

'Yes. Thank you.'

The elderly passenger in the next seat holds a Ventolin inhaler to his mouth, and sucks sharply on it. After ten or fifteen seconds, he exhales again slowly, as if he were blowing invisible smoke rings. He glances at Timmy.

'The good life,' he says.

'Were you in the army during the war?'

'Yes. I was.'

Timmy's delighted. He puts the bottoms of two pawn pieces together, and their magnets meet precisely.

'In the commandos?'

'In catering.' The boy's face falls. 'Don't despise it. An army marches on its stomach.'

But Timmy looks away at the window. Far below him, he can see a river that must be the Rhine, a thin tapeworm the colour of concrete; and near it a road, perhaps an autobahn, a relic of the Reich. But where are the train tracks? Surely there must be train tracks between Dusseldorf and the city of Krefeld where the Sterms have their home. After all, there are train tracks everywhere in this strange, sinister land; and the train tracks lead from

4

the cities through the country to the concentration camps, and everybody knew that they did, knew at the time, and said nothing.

The boy thinks of the depots, of the huddled deportees. He thinks of the chemists, the teachers, the mezzo-sopranos, squeezed into stifling cattle-trucks, sealed carriages; men with beards who had lectured in anatomy, artists and actresses whose dressing-rooms were lavish with insect-eating plants from Argentina; people who could talk in three languages, yet who had to pull their dresses up or their trousers down and squat over straw while the train roared towards the watchtowers.

'Would you like to see the cockpit?'

The hostess beams at him. She seems revived. Or is she coming back because of what the elderly man said? Could she lose her job because of him?

'No, thank you.'

'Don't you want to be a pilot when you grow up?'

He looks at her, at the weeping earlobe, a wisp of brown hair black at the roots.

'No,' he says. 'I want to be a Jew.'

She frowns, the elderly passenger turns to stare at him; and the plane begins its descent.

His classmates troop through the shallow chlorine pools back into the men's dressing-room. They peel off their swimming togs, and wring them out over the basins, excitedly chattering in this vast wooden space with its lockers like baskets. One of them whistles the theme song from *The Monkees*; another pushes a hair-clip up his nostril to scrape out a scab.

'I'm dying for a drink. Water, water.'

One of the boys, pretending to be thirsty, lets his tongue loll. A taller child volunteers the tiny pink nipple on his chest, and the thirsty one nibbles greedily at it.

'There you go, my child. Suck away.'

Timmy twists his regulation gym shorts, twists and tightens them until the last little strings of water drip down on to the floor. He'll have to wear them again on the bus journey back to the school, because he forgot his togs today, for the third time in a single term. As a penalty, he has to write out the Our Father twelve times, once for each year of his life.

'Into the showers! Into the showers! Quickly, quickly!'

It's Mr Madden, standing in the doorframe, shouting. He's carrying the large Tayto crisps carton where he puts the boys' glasses and watches for safe-keeping while they're in the pool. Timmy hurries into the shower, jostling, being jostled in turn, the hips and buttocks of the other boys grazing against him. He lifts his face to the hard hail of the water.

'Do it now, Hardiman. Come on. Do it now.'

One voice, two, then many, all of them. Timmy joins in, though he doesn't quite know what it is that Hardiman must do. The boy beside him lifts his wrist. There's a phone number written on it, a five-letter phone number; it looks like a camp tattoo, it looks like –

'You all have to pay me sixpence. All of you.'

They nod solemnly; they're hushed now. Hardiman folds his arms across his chest, and stares at his penis. One of the boys stops the shower; the others surround Hardiman to shield him from the door. Outside they can hear the shrieks of the prep class, dog-paddling on their yellow floats, and a distant whistle. Timmy wishes he had his glasses. Things are blurred without them. He has to squeeze the edges of his eyelids with his fingers in order to make anything out.

'You look a bit Chinese that way,' says the boy beside him.

'Do I?'

'A bit. Listen, Tim, when you go to Germany next week, will you bring me back some Hitler stamps?'

'Any moment now,' says Hardiman; and, sure enough, his penis begins to grow: slowly at first, then more swiftly, it stiffens, straightens, and stands up. The boys stare at it in silence, at its beauty, its lack of embarrassment.

'And I didn't even have to stroke it,' says Hardiman. 'Most people have to stroke it. But I can make it big just by thinking.'

'Thinking what?' says Timmy. 'What do you think?'

'Never you mind,' Hardiman says.

They've left the airport, arrived at the station, boarded the train and found a compartment, before Timmy has an opportunity to examine Frau Sterm closely. Modest and mild, she doesn't much mind such inspection. Instead, she smiles benignly out the window, watching the long, low barges on the river.

'The Rhine,' she tells him. 'The Rhine.' And she laughs, laughs because this strawberry-blond boy is looking at her so seriously, as if she were an ichthyosaurus or some other creepie-crawlie in the Natural History Museum where she brings her own son, Claus, on rainy Saturdays. She laughs, and lifts her hands to her forehead to flick back her fringe. The two boys will hit it off, she thinks: they're different, and difference, despite what universities may say, is the fountainhead of friendship. That was the aim and outcome of these programmes, a pairing of peers, of boys whose fathers had fought as enemies but whose sons, she thinks, whose sons will build rabbit hutches together.

Timmy's intrigued by the hair under her arms. He's never seen it before. Neither his mother nor his sister have anything like it. He hasn't even come across it in the *National Geographic* or in his father's large, forbidden volume called *Diseases of the Breast*. Is it restricted to Germans or to German-speaking countries? Or is it found in Italy and France as well? Frau Sterm doesn't seem shy or secretive. After all, she's wearing a sleeveless dress. Besides, Europeans are different. In Spain, his sister wouldn't be allowed out without an escort; in Greece, she'd have to wear a black frock if her husband went and died. The world is peculiar.

'Are you afraid?'

She grins at him, showing her teeth. She has many gold fillings. If she were a Jew when she was little, they would have torn the gold out of her mouth with mechanics' tools. But she can't be Jewish, and not because the Jews are dead now, but because she's married to a man who served in the Wehrmacht, to a man who got frostbite in Russia. So perhaps the gold is from a Jew, perhaps it's migrated from one mouth to another; perhaps it was used to the sound of Lithuanian, to the taste of kosher sweetbread, and now it hears German greetings, and chews sausage.

'No,' he says. 'I'm not afraid.' And then, because he can't bear her to look at him without speaking, he decides to tell her about the presents.

'I have duty-free bottles for you,' he says. He can't remember what they are; his parents chose them. 'I have a model airplane for Claus. I have a Heinkel, a Heinkel bomber. There are a hundred and fifty bits. Do you know Heinkels?'

'Yes,' she tells him. 'Yes, I know Heinkels.' She becomes silent again.

Timmy's got to go to the toilet. It's the same problem, the need to shit something strong and solid that seems stuck inside him, the inability to shift it. He leaves the compartment, squeezes past a woman holding a hat-stand like a stag's antler in the passage-way. He excuses himself as the two of them manoeuvre, excuses himself and wonders whether she'll think he's English, and, if so, whether she'll hate him, remembering perhaps a charred torso under masonry.

'Thank you,' he says.

'You're welcome.'

In the toilet, he's alone. The seat is plastic, not wooden like at home. And the lever for flushing is attached to the cistern behind; it doesn't hang from a chain. Timmy lowers his trousers, studies his underpants to ensure that they're not stained, but they are, slightly. How is he going to clean them without Frau Sterm finding out; and if she does, what can he tell her? His mother's warned him twice, three times that a boy is judged by the state of his shirt-collar and the condition of his underpants. He sits and strains, sits and strains. He feels behind him with his fingers, between his cheeks, to where the tip of the shit is wedged, but he can't pass it. The pain is too much.

The toilet is dry. Timmy can see down through it, though there's a loop in the exit pipe. Sleeper after sleeper after sleeper, thin strips of gravel and grass, a whirling monochrome, a rush of field-grey greyness. They would have seen the same, the ballerinas and the butchers, their eyes pressed to the chinks in the shoddy wooden goods trains.

The boy tears the identification tag from the lapel of his blazer, the one with his name and flight number on it, the one the airhostess with the red fingernails had written. He holds it over the bowl for a moment, feels it flap in the uprush of the breeze, and then he lets it go.

8

★

'*Voilà*,' says Mr McDonagh; and he whisks the sheet away. '*Voilà*. That's German, I think, or maybe it's French.'

Timmy fumbles with his glasses, blows the short hairs from the lenses, and puts the glasses on. Mr McDonagh has followed his father's instructions to the letter. His hair is more closely cropped than it's ever been before. He looks denuded, ridiculous. His cheeks flush pinker.

'I was only obeying my orders,' Mr McDonagh says.

The customer in the next chair chuckles.

'Jesus,' he says. 'You look like something that walked in out of the camps. When is it you're off anyway?'

'In three days.'

'Bring us back some reading material,' says the other man. 'Will you do that?'

'A bit of culture,' Mr McDonagh tells Timmy. 'The Rhine maidens out of Wagner.'

'*Die grossen Frauen*, more like. Do you know what I'm getting at?'

Timmy shakes his head.

'Leave him be,' says Mr McDonagh, blowing quietly on Timmy's bent neck. 'The child's a holy innocent.'

Timmy peers up at Mr McDonagh's reflection in the mirror.

'The boy I'm going to,' he explains. 'His father was in the German army. He was in Russia. He got wounded there. It was the same year Mum and Dad got married. So while he was sheltering behind some tank during snowstorms, my parents were on honeymoon down in Parknasilla, except that the hotel was full of priests. Isn't that strange?'

'Not really,' says Mr McDonagh. 'Priests had a lot of money twenty years ago.'

'Do you remember the invasion of Russia, Mr McDonagh?'

'Do I remember the day I got engaged? Of course I do. I was in the army myself at the time.'

'Where? Whereabouts?'

'I was stationed in Limerick. I was in the Irish army.'

'Who did you want to win?'

'The Allies, of course. I wanted the Allies to win. But . . .'

9

'But what?'

Mr McDonagh cleans his glasses with the end of his navy-blue tie.

'I wanted the Allies to get a bloody good thrashing first. After what the British done to us.'

The boy looks down at his lap, around at the floor. Thick tufts of his own hair litter the lino. It was strange to think that your own bits and pieces, toenails, fingernails, follicles of skin, strands of hair, an assortment of your own bodily parts, could be sorted out and swept away, like dog-dirt or a broken salt-cellar. And it was still stranger to imagine the small, sodden mounds of human hair that the barbers of Belsen and Buchenwald had shaved from schoolchildren, from tots whose first teeth were still intact, from teenagers who cycled bikes without holding the handlebars.

'What about the Jews, Mr McDonagh? Did you know about the Jews?'

'Ah, the Jews,' he says, shaking the sheet he has taken from Timmy. 'The Jews. A very versatile people. Sure, every second actor is a Jew; and they're all over Hollywood. What happened to the Jews was such a pity.'

The other customer clears his throat. A soft ball of phlegm sits on his under-lip.

'There's some lovely Jewish women as well,' he says. 'Not so *grossen* now, but every bit as *frauen*. Now why the fuck wasn't I born in Munich?'

Frau Sterm shows Timmy round the house. She shows him the kitchen, the living-room, the study where Herr Sterm works on his legal cases, the narrow ground-floor bedroom for any visitors. He doesn't notice much at first, because the whole house has a strange smell he can't identify. Aerosol sprays are new to him; back home, the maid cleans the bookshelves and the table-tops and the brass canopy over the fireplace with sponge and spittle, the elbow-grease of ages. Here it's different, a bright, brittle world.

'You like it?'

Frau Sterm lets the bed down by pressing a catch. It emerges from the wall and folds away slowly to the floor. Timmy's never seen one like it before, or the double-glazed windows that overlook the front lawn, a lawn without a fence or a stone wall to protect it, a lawn that slopes unselfconsciously to the public pavement.

'Yes,' he says. 'It's very nice.'

She stretches out her hand to him.

'Come. I have more to show.'

The boy follows her back into the kitchen. There's a low whine, like the noise of a mosquito, from the overhead light. The skeleton of a fish sits on the draining-board. Across at the window there's a bowl piled with grapes and pale bananas, but when he looks more closely he finds they're made of glass. And beside him on the polished counter he can see a weighing scales with the brand name Krupps, loose flour in a circle round its stand. He has seen that name somewhere before; he can almost retrieve it, but not quite.

'I have a letter for you,' she tells him. 'A letter from your family. It was here two days.'

Timmy takes it, tears it open. It contains one sheet of paper, paper so thin it's almost transparent. The writing is his sister's.

Dear Timmy.

It is now about nine o'clock, and I am going to bed. You are already asleep upstairs, and Mummy is choosing your trousers for the journey. It is strange to think that when you read this, you will be in the land of Hansel and Gretel. That is why I am writing.

I will go to the shop each Wednesday, and collect your comics, so that when you come home again in ten weeks' time, you will not have missed anything. Isn't that typical of

Your Adorable Sister.

Frau Sterm is folding laundry at the other end of the kitchen. Timmy thinks that it's kind of her to have turned her back while he was reading his letter; it's the first thing she's done that has made him less panicked and petrified. If only the smells were not so different, if only there were one smell which reminded him of the hot-press or the scullery at home. He wants to sit down straightaway and write to his sister, telling her that he travelled on a jet plane without any propellers, that he saw strange magazines at the kiosks in the airport, magazines with sneering women sticking out their bottoms; that he lost his German phrase-book somewhere between Dublin and Dusseldorf, and he can't remember how to say that he's having a lovely time; that there's a weighing scales in the kitchen, made by Krupps, and weren't they the same factory that built the crematoria; and that he's tried, and tried, and tried, but he still can't go big ways.

Frau Sterm pounds the kitchen window very precisely with a twisted kitchen towel, and a bluebottle staggers for a moment around the juices of its stomach before dropping to the ledge. But the blow has activated the sensors on the ultra-modern burglar alarm system. The bell wails through the house like an old-style air-raid alarm. Timmy cannot hear her at first when Frau Sterm tries to explain, and anyhow she hasn't the words.

'I understand,' he says.

His father tucks him in, brushes a few shavings of wood from a pencil off the side of the bedspread. Timmy puts his sketch-pad down. They kiss. His father switches off the light.

'I can always talk more easily in the darkness. Why do you think that is? I often wonder.'

Timmy doesn't say. He works himself more comfortably into the sheets. And waits.

'About this trip. You mustn't be frightened. People are kind the world over. You'll see. That bloody Italian you have for Latin's been filling your head with all sorts of nonsense, just because his brother got a bayonet in the bottom somewhere in Sicily. And the comics you read are no better – Boche this, Boche that, Boche the other. Officers with monocles, infantry like wart-hogs. The Germans are no better and no worse than anyone else. Do you believe me?'

'Yes.'

'Most of the music I play is German. Don't you like Mozart and Mahler? Don't you like Beethoven?'

'Yes.'

'So you see. Herr Sterm's a lovely man. If he seems a bit . . . remote, well, that's the way Germans are. Until you get to know them, of course. Then it's party-time. You remember playing

12

mushroom billiards with Herr Sterm last year, over in Connemara, and how he let you win all the time. Now I never let you win, not if I can help it.'

His father moves towards the door, a dark sculpture in the soft light from the landing.

'Remember this. To begin with, the Germans didn't invent anti-semitism; they inherited it. And who did they inherit it from? I'll tell you. They inherited it from the different Christian churches. That's who. You couldn't say these things ten years ago, or people would think you were an out-and-out Communist. But now with the Vatican Council going on, folk are finding out that a mouth is for more than sucking spaghetti.'

'Yes.'

'If anyone annoys you, just tell them this: in the middle of 1944, the Allies precision-bombed a munitions factory outside Auschwitz. Precision-bombed it. Pulverised the whole complex. But they didn't bomb the train tracks leading to the camp. They knew perfectly well that the camp was there; they knew perfectly well what was happening inside it. Flame-throwers turned on pregnant women; newborn babies kicked like footballs. But they didn't bomb the train tracks. And now after twenty years, they talk about preserving the otter.'

The door swings open.

'I had a patient this morning. On the table. He was different.'

'Why?'

'He died. He died on me. I had to . . . rip open his ribcage. I had to hold his heart in my hand, and pump it with my fingers until it started to beat again. I worked his heart with my own hand, something I use to pick my nose with.'

He stretches out his hand.

'Want to touch it?'

'No.'

His father grins.

Timmy stands up, holding his shorts with one hand at his knees, and turns to stare into the toilet-bowl. He has finally managed to empty his bowels. It has never taken longer to do so, never been so distressing before. His bottom aches. He wipes it gently, inspects the paper before he discards it. It only partly covers the massive turd lying in the shallow bowl. The sheer size of it fascinates the boy. How can there be room for such a thing inside one's stomach?

But he mustn't delay. He's been inside the bathroom for almost fifteen minutes. Frau Sterm may come knocking. He presses the plunger firmly, and blue water gushes down the rim of the bowl. It swirls in a frothy fashion round the turd, spitting and bubbling; but then, slowly and silently, it ebbs away, it drains and disappears, it leaves the brown, bloated mass where it is. Timmy tugs the lever desperately. Nothing happens. The cistern is empty. It may take minutes to fill again. He hoists up his shorts, buttons the fly, washes his hands, runs them through the stubble on his scalp. Where is Frau Sterm? How long has he been now? How long? The room may be smelly. He opens the window, scatters toilet water on the cork floor. How long?

The cistern has filled again. It must have, because the noise of gurgling has stopped. Timmy forces the lever, more slowly this time, and again the blue water cascades in. He waits, he watches it settle. The waters clear.

The turd has not budged.

The boy runs out of the bathroom. There's a door to the left-hand side, but he hasn't been shown the rooms upstairs. Perhaps it's where the Sterms sleep; perhaps Frau Sterm is in there now. He stops, starts towards it again, reaches it, peers round the door. It's a child's room, a boy's room, Claus's room. There are Disney transfers on the walls, a beachball in the corner, a thin Toledo sword; and on the floor immediately in front of him, there's a model train-set, stacked train tracks, little level crossings, carriages, tenders, engines, miniature porters and stokers.

The boy listens. He can hear nothing. He leans forward, snatches a long length of train track, and rushes back to the bathroom. He locks the door, listens again. Then he drives the train track fiercely into the huge shit, working it this way and that, stabbing and slashing at it until the motion begins gradually to disintegrate. But he doesn't stop. He pounds and pummels, pounds and pummels again. At last, at long last, he's satisfied; he adds another mighty jab for good measure, and flushes. Piece by piece, fragment by fragment, the turd is swallowed up, swept down.

Timmy begins to cry; but he can't allow himself, not yet, not now. There's still the train track, the train track. How long has he been here now? He fumbles with the tap, turns it full on, holds the track beneath its blast of water, picks at the particles of shit with his fingernails; but it's no use. The thing is sodden, it stinks, he can't clean it. He stands for seconds, staring at the toy piece; then he rushes out of the bathroom, down the stairs to the ground floor, and stops, straining for a footfall, the least sound. Where is Frau Sterm?

When he reaches the garden, he hurls the track with all his strength into the air and over the low wooden stockade behind the rhododendrons and the raspberry bushes. It lands among rosebeds in the neighbouring garden. Timmy has thrown it with such force that the muscle under his armpit hurts him. Now he can let himself cry.

'I won't hurt you.'

Timmy is standing in his pyjamas in front of his mother. It's late, the last night before he leaves for Germany. His bag is packed.

'I put a scapular inside the suitcase,' his mother says as she takes his penis out of his pyjamas. 'Do you know what a scapular is?'

'No.'

His mother pulls his foreskin up and down, up and down. She tries to be very gentle.

'A scapular will protect you,' she says. 'My mother gave me a scapular when I went on my honeymoon with Daddy.'

'Did it protect you?'

She laughs.

'What protection did I need?'

Timmy decides to tell her.

'I had a dream last night. A dream about you. I was sitting in a deckchair somewhere, and a whole herd of cows walked up to me. Their udders were dragging on the ground. They wanted to be milked.'

'And did you milk them?'

'Yes. I milked them with my bare hands, on to the grass. There was no end of milk.'

'And where did I come in?'

'You didn't. But I felt the way I always feel when I'm with you.'

His mother kisses the tip of his nose. She slips his penis back into his pyjamas.

'I want you to ask Frau Sterm to do that for you. Will you do that? It's very important. You'll understand when you're bigger.'

'Will you write to me?'

'Of course I'll write to you. Of course I will. And you must write back. But don't just write to me. Write to your daddy. Write to him at his hospital. He'd love that.'

'All right.'

The mother looks at her son, the son at his mother.

'Germany's not that bad. You remember how I told you I was there with Granny, just before the war.'

'You were getting better.'

'I was getting better. I was recovering. I'd been ill.'

'With pleurisy.'

'With pleurisy. That's right. And lots of people had it. It was rampant.'

'What's rampant?'

'Everywhere. All over. An epidemic. Many people died from it.'

'But you got better.'

'I got better. I got better in Germany. Or at least I finished getting better there. And I met some lovely people.'

'Who?'

'I met a woman. A girl, I mean. She owned her own café, a coffee-house. You could order the most beautiful cakes. And a cellist played there in the afternoons. She was a sweet person, but she wore too much make-up. She looked a little like a cake herself.'

'Did you ever meet a man you liked?'

'Yes, I did. He was very like Daddy, except smaller.'

'Was he a Nazi?'

'He was in the army. But his real ambition in life was to become a bee-keeper.'

'Did he?'

His mother gets off her knees, and brushes the wrinkles on her kneecaps.

'I don't know. Perhaps he died. Perhaps he died in the war. His name was Nikki.'

Timmy burrows down in the bed. He shifts his weight to one side, leaving enough room on the other, as he has always done and will always continue to do, for Bernard, his guardian angel.

Claus and Timmy have hit it off. Frau Sterm is certain of it. There may be a little diffidence on either side, but that sort of shyness is only to be expected. Dublin is not quite Dusseldorf, nor Krefeld Killarney. Frau Sterm rather likes the alliterative parallelism. She'll try it on her husband later.

Out in the garden, the two boys are smiling, circling each other. Claus opens his English phrase-book, picks sentences at random, reads them.

'This is not the room I asked for at reception.'

Timmy laughs, more loudly than he needs to.

'Is the museum open on Sundays as well?'

'*Jawohl,*' says Timmy, and salutes in the old style favoured by fascists. Claus looks at him closely. His face frowns. Timmy's unsettled, uneasy. He brings his arm down.

'I had a phrase-book too,' he tells him. 'Only I lost it. I don't know where. On the plane perhaps, or in the airport. But I'll get another. Then we can talk all the time. Can't we?'

Claus hasn't understood. He starts leafing through the Berlitz guidebook again. Thumbing the sections, looking up and over at his new acquaintance every so often. Eventually he finds what he's searching for.

'Can we reserve accommodation on this train?'

Timmy thinks of the train track under the rosebed, of the train-set scattered on the bright carpet upstairs. Is it remotely possible that Frau Sterm would collect the pieces into their box, counting them as she went along? Or that Claus would remember the exact number, the precise tally? Certainly the missing strip would never be found, but what if the whole Sterm family were to realise that, since the arrival of the stranger in their midst, things had been thieved? The word itself they might forgo, they might speak instead of disappearance, but thieving would be what they meant. He would be sent straight home, he might meet the same hostess on the Dublin flight. She might have to serve him breakfast, but she wouldn't look into his eyes. Instead she would look away.

'Is there a couchette available on this train?'

No one could have seen him do what he had done. The window in the bathroom was frosted, the door had been locked or at least he had tried to lock it. Frau Sterm had been nowhere to be found. The neighbouring house with the rosebed didn't overlook the garden. In fact, now that he saw it for the second time, he realised it was a bungalow. He could breathe easy.

'Or even standing room?'

Claus smiles at him. He's been saving the one bad English word he knows, learned from a mischievous scatterbrain in his *Mittelschule*.

'Shit,' he says.

Before Timmy can answer him, Claus bounds across the garden, and bends down at a forsythia tree. Moments later, he's back with a tortoise in his hands. Timmy steps forward a foot or two, and makes to touch the shell; but Claus throws the unfortunate creature high into the air, then catches it again. Timmy can't believe what he's seen, so Claus repeats the trick, then chucks the tortoise deftly to his new-found friend and pen-pal. Timmy returns it; it's tossed back. The tortoise has edged out of his shell. The boys can see its face and feet emerge. They go on throwing it, back and forth, one to the other, as if it were a rugby ball. But soon the inevitable happens. Claus fumbles a catch, drops the tortoise on the concrete walk, steps back, and stares in horror. Neither boy is sure whether the tortoise is still alive or, if alive, whether it's harmed. Neither speaks. A slight breeze darkens the lawn; sunflowers bob in their beds.

'Claus.'

But Claus doesn't answer. He walks the two steps to the tortoise, and nudges it with the toe of his sandal, nudges it in under the cover of a bush. No one will see it there. He'll come out later, after dinner, to examine it again. Timmy wonders if a

tortoise has a spine. Perhaps a chip or even a hairline fracture in
the shell won't matter.

'Shit,' says Claus again. 'Very shit.'

Father Eddy lines up his shot, and putts the ball briskly into the
hole. Timmy claps.

'When I was a lad,' Father Eddy says as he moves to the next
Latin numeral on the clockwork golf course at the bottom of
Timmy's garden, 'Luther was another word for Lucifer. He was
the Devil himself, every bit as bad as Hitler, and worse.'

'Really?'

'I kid you not. He divided Christendom against itself. He made
war on the Church. You couldn't reason with him. And terrible
things happened. Famine, assassinations, sacrilege. So, of course,
when I was in the seminary, everybody looked on Luther as an
utter blackguard. A bandit.'

The priest putts again, more cautiously this time.

'But now, with the Council and everything that Pope John
tried to show us, we know different. We can see with the eyes of
charity, the eyes of compassion. We can see that Luther wasn't all
bad. He was just bonkers. Stark, raving mad.'

The ball wobbles on the edge of the hole, but it doesn't go in.
Father Eddy's vexed.

'Even so, if the Sterms do ask you along to one of their
services, say no. Say you're only allowed to attend the Catholic
church. And if there isn't one in the area, don't fret. The obligation
doesn't bind you when you're abroad. I was in Greece one time, a
couple of years before I was ordained, and I went a month
without mass. I was a spiritual skin-and-bones case by the time I
got home.'

Timmy toes the golfball in, then takes it out again, and hands it
back to Father Eddy. The priest crouches over his putter,
practising.

'If anybody asks you, tell them you're Irish but that you
learned English at school.'

'Yes.'

'Mind you, when you're away out of the country, your real
nationality is Catholicism. The Faith. Think of the Irish monks

who went out to convert Germany. Columbanus, Cillian. Holy men, whole men, men with a mission. You're following in their footsteps. You see what I'm saying?'

'Yes.'

Father Eddy looks around him at the twelve Latin numerals embedded in the lawn.

'Which is that?' he asks, pointing with his putter to the large metal 'V' under the plum-tree.

'Five,' Timmy says.

'And that?'

'Nine. I know them up to a hundred. A hundred is C.'

'Good man yourself.'

It's getting late. Only the upper windows of the glasshouse catch the sunlight. The priest and the boy walk back towards the house.

'Isn't it a strange thing all the same,' Father Eddy says. 'Those Latin numerals were used by Julius Caesar. Augustus used them. Housewives in Pompeii were counting them on their fingers the day Vesuvius burst. And that's not today, nor the day before it either. That's a long time ago.'

'How many popes ago?'

'Many, many, many. And yet, two thousand years later, you can come upon them laid out in a circle at the end of a private garden. Do you know who made that possible?'

'No.'

'Well, you should know. It was the Church. The Church preserved Latin, the language of the very soldiers who crucified Our Lord. That's called an irony.'

'What's that?'

'A wound that gives pleasure.'

The priest stoops to pick a bird's feather from the lawn.

'You could talk to Claus in the Latin you have,' he tells Timmy. 'I imagine he learns it in his school. You know the verb "to love" backwards. And that's enough to start with. It's enough for anyone. Or it should be. You're not nervous? There's no reason to be nervous. Sure, the two of you will be thick as thieves before the plane's refuelled.'

Behind them, out of the cypress-trees, magpies circle the

clockwork golf course, land, and begin to pick at the glinting metal letters.

Herr Sterm leans back from the dining table, and tilts his chin towards the ceiling. Almost from the moment that he entered the house, his nose has been bleeding. Already the front of his shirt is stained, the green tie that he wore to honour Timmy is flecked with red. Yet Frau Sterm continues to tell the boy that this is no unusual occurrence. It happens all the time, it's a sign of health, not illness. It passes after a while, as all things pass. And she ladles more vegetables on to Timmy's plate, and sets the plate before him.

The food is unintelligible. There are strange, anonymous entities Timmy's never seen before. Shape, size, flavour and taste, are all new. He rummages with his knife and fork, sorts and separates the mess, but he can't bring himself to swallow the stuff. He can see fragments of his own reflection on the broad blade of the knife; his lower lip with the scrap of dead skin, his teeth in a white wobble, his eyebrows, eyelashes, eyes. His eyes stare back at him, confessing, concealing.

'Would you like to see a film tomorrow?'

He looks up at Frau Sterm. She seems distant, diminished.

'Yes. Thank you.'

'Would you like to see *The Sound of Music*?'

'Yes.'

Herr Sterm settles his chair back on its four legs again. He holds a large handkerchief to his nose as he speaks in a muffled way to his wife. He speaks first in German, then in English.

'*The Sound of Music* is not a good film. It is anti–German. The music is pretty, but the message, the message is propaganda. But there are other films. There are others; and these we will see.'

They eat in silence. Timmy forces a few mouthfuls of the green and purple rubbish into his mouth. Claus is in another world, playing soccer with the peas on his plate. Perhaps he's thinking about the tortoise; perhaps he's frightened. Herr Sterm begins to bleed again, over the napkin and the napkin ring. He swears in an undertone. His wife shushes him. Silence again for a spell . . . and then the bell rings.

The hall doorbell, its two tones, a little phrase.

The whole table tenses. Mother and father glance at each other. The husband rises, goes out. Frau Sterm peers out the window at the louvre doors into the kitchen.

'I think it is a neighbour,' she says.

And Timmy knows, knows in the pit of his stomach; deep in the boy's belly, there is certain knowledge. Why did the elderly passenger complain about the airhostess? Why had he said he wanted to be a Jew? What made him refuse to visit the cockpit? And how did Hardiman make his penis stand up straight? What was he thinking of when he did that? What was in his mind?

The door swings open. Herr Sterm walks back in. He says nothing. He's holding the train track. Why had he thrown his identification label into the toilet on the train? There must have been a reason. His father is always telling him there is a reason for everything. If so, why were the women sneering on the magazine covers? Herr Sterm begins to beat Claus around the shoulders and neck with the dirty train track. His wife screams. But Claus, Claus doesn't cry, doesn't cry out. He doesn't even try to cover his head. What did Mr McDonagh feel about Jews? What did he really feel? What did '*grossen Frauen*' mean? Why was it funny?

Frau Sterm punches her husband in the side. She pleads with him; he doesn't answer. His nose has begun to bleed again. It drips on to Claus's T-shirt, runs down the back. The boy sobs and shudders. Herr Sterm raises the train track one last time, a soiled stretch, still filthy from the toilet and the garden; raises it, looks at it, lowers it. He runs his hand through his hair.

'I bought this . . . machinery for Claus yesterday. It is a new present. For him, but also for you. To play together.'

Why had he not touched his father's hand? And why had the Allied bombers not bombed the train tracks leading to Auschwitz? Why? And when would he know the answers? All the answers to everything, everything that made him feel scared and strange and examined. He looks at Herr Sterm, at Frau Sterm, at Claus. He feels sick in his stomach, sick and sore. The lenses of his glasses have begun to mist from the heat of his sweat. They start to slip forward down the bridge of his nose until the half of his field of vision is a blur, the other half is sharper than italics.

He says nothing. He says nothing at all.

ELEPHANT BREAD AND
THE LAST BATTLE

We were in the dining-room, the three of us, my mother and my father and my own self, but we weren't having dinner. We were having lunch. It was not like at home, you see, where you would go and have your dinner in the dining-room, and then you would go and sit down in the sitting-room, and after that you would go to bed in your bedroom while maybe your father would go to study in his study. And if everybody that was in the world would have done that, then Jesus would never have sweated blood when he did.

The Prince de Galles hotel is not pronounced the way that you would think. Hotel is the same word and the same way, but Prince is more like the prance of what a horse does; and Galles is really what you would call a girl. That is where we were staying, my mother and my father and my own self, in a town that was called Menton, except, of course, that they do not say it in the way it's written. Instead of which, they say it a bit through their nose and under their breath; and Italy is on the other side of the bus-stop down the street. In the morning, the shadow of the bus-stop is French; in the afternoon, it is Italian. Its name darkens, so it does. It is the same name then, as what the Pope would call it, if it got dark in his study and he went to turn on a light.

The Riviera is where the Prince de Galles hotel has its dining-room. Of course, the Riviera isn't a river, but the people who lived in Menton thousands of years ago thought it was, because maybe they had no pedalos then to go out into it and see for themselves what it truly and truly was. They thought it was a river only, and that they had enemies on the other side of the bus-stop who were putting salt in the water to get on their nerves. Then they invented charts, and when they looked at

27

them, they had the surprise of their lives. The Riviera had no end and no beginning; and they thought, My God. So they stopped calling it the River immediately after that, and called it by its proper name. Ever since that was the day, people have saved up their money for over years until they were able to come to the Riviera and take off their clothes and go down into the water and wash themselves; and that is a good fact for Demandez, my friend on the beach who sells raisins and nutty things, and is an African who has never seen a Zulu in his whole life, but I have. Then, when his parrot died, he had to start to do the cries of the parrot without anybody helping, and he could do the cries of the bird in the black cage in the bar of the Prince de Galles as well, only the bird in the cage went demented, and I made Demandez stop. But the man on the bar-stool bought him a big long drink with an umbrella on the ice, because they had had a bet on the bird.

And that was the last thing that happened on the day before Donal.

My father went down, down, down into the book he was reading, which was a book that was called *The Last Battle*, except, of course, that it was not, because there were still wars in all the countries that could grow bananas, which was why, when I would eat a banana, then I would offer it up to Jesus who would not sweat so much. But the book that my father was reading was about the battle over Berlin at the end of the war. Because of which, he had to take the train to his honeymoon: there was no petrol in the country on the day that they went and got married. It was all needed for the battle.

'Don't,' said my father.

But he did not say it to me. It was what he was saying to my mother.

'Don't what?' she said.

'Look up. Look back. Look around. Look anything.'

She began to stare at her soup as if it were alphabet soup, although it was not, really.

'Who?' she said.

'You won't believe it,' my father said. 'Unless there are two of them. Then they'd be twins.'

There was a question that I had about the train and no petrol because of Berlin, and my mother in the carriage who would have been dressed in all white, of course. Because everybody else in the train would have known that this was her marriage, unless, of course, she would have been a nun on the day that she had become one. But then they would have examined my father with his tall top hat, and known truly.

'Did everybody get up in the carriage and clap?' I said.

'Donal,' said my father, who was getting up out of his seat and standing up. 'Donal, it isn't yourself. It isn't.'

'Did they?' I said, but I think my mother was still trying to remember if they had or, on the other hand, if they had not. Because everybody has to practise the right order of things, even in submarines. First there is the truth, then there is the whole truth, and after them there is nothing-but-the-truth, amen.

'It is Donal,' said my father. 'How are you, Donal? My God, it's been – '

'Don't,' said the man who my father had called Donal, but was he? 'Don't. Enough that it's been. Better a pinch of salt and look forward than a pillar of salt and look back. *Tutto va bene*, as the man said. And this is herself.'

'My wife,' said my father. 'Emily. You remember Emily.'

'Of course I do,' said the man. 'Of course. "Her voice gentle and low, an excellent thing in a woman," as the Bard says. I think. Delighted, ma'am. Emily. Emilia.'

And he reached right over across the table to where my mother was sitting down, and his tie that had palm-trees on it knocked the spoon out of the salt-cellar.

'One of my boys,' said my father. 'The last.'

'But not the least,' said the man. 'By a long chalk.'

He went down on his hunkers, so he did, and he gave me a pretend punch. And I liked his moustache because it was the same colour as his hair, and it was truly soft, which is right and proper for a moustache, really; and I liked the scar that was on his throat because there would be a story about that, which would be most excellent; and I liked his smell. I would have liked to have had a good smell of him if he would have let me and if he did not think that he was breaking a secret by it.

'What do they call you then?' he said.

'Mild,' I said.

'They call him Martin,' said my mother; although, if I was speaking strictly, it was more of a shout than a say, really. I knew it was a shout because nobody at the table that was beside us looked up.

'Martin is a great name,' he said to me. 'Martin of Tours and Martin Luther; and there was Martin somebody who invented grenades that pigeons could drop on the enemy when you blew a special pigeon-whistle.'

'Imagine,' I said, 'if the enemy had the exact same pigeon-whistle as the other pigeon-whistle.'

'Then,' he said, 'the feathers would be flying, and no mistake.'

He held out his hand to me as if I was my own father. And our hands shook.

'My name is Donal,' he said; and he was. 'My mother called me Doe, like in deer; but she never called me deer, like in doe. Sometimes, she called me love.'

'What did she eat?' I said. 'Did she eat soup?'

'No,' said Donal. 'She drank it. She made a noise like the last bit of a bath going down.'

'You've made your point,' my father said. 'You've made it abundantly.'

He was cross because what Donal had said about the pigeon-whistles was not in the book he was reading, and it should have been, really.

'Donal,' said a woman and she came right up to him. She was a fine, fat woman of a lady who would have fallen out of a top bunk if the person below her had not given her the bottom one to sleep in.

'I'm the only one,' she said. 'The only one in the whole coach who doesn't have a room with a view of the Riviera. I come a thousand miles to look at the Riviera, and I'm looking at crates and cartons and the back of a service area. I can look at a service area without renewing my passport. Redwood City has lots of service areas to look at. I want to look at the Riviera, for God's sake.'

'Say no more,' said Donal. '*Pas de problème*. If it's for God's sake, then it shall be did, and it shall be did promptly.'

He got up off his hunkers, and he was a much taller man when he stood up. He was taller even than my father, and my father was at the height of his powers always.

'And a balcony with a bit of sun, Donal,' said the woman who had talked about God. 'I'm not asking for ultra-violet round the clock, but a bit of sun would brighten things up.'

'Mind yourself,' he said to me, and he went away then to examine the truth, the whole truth, and nothing but the truth about the view of the woman who had come a thousand miles to sit and stare at the Riviera and maybe buy some raisins from poor Demandez. And I was trying to make up my mind about whether I should tell her that the parrot was dead, but what I decided was not to. She was upset enough about too much in her life.

'What can I say?' said the woman to my mother, as she walked off. 'Donal is Donal.'

My father had gone back into *The Last Battle* to find out more and more of the things that had happened while he had been on his honeymoon; and my mother had not finished her soup. That was because maybe she had had some soup on the train, and the train went too fast, and her dress was disgraced with a splash, my God.

'Sit straight,' she said to me, 'and eat your soup.'

Wheels was what reminded me of the laundry basket and the delightment of the maid when I fixed the wheel the right way on it for her. I would tell Donal a bit about that.

'Blast him,' said my father who was turning the pages the wrong way back to the beginning. 'Blast him, anyway. I've lost where I was.'

So I lay down in the bath with my snorkel on, and I floated in the water. And this is what I found: I found a sponge; I found the top of the toothpaste; I found the stone from the beach that I had brought up from there in my dressing-gown through the hotel; and I found as well as that, this – a bit of nail from my mother, with blue on it, which was how I knew truly.

That was enough for the time. I took off the snorkel and gulped the good air that I would never get the better of; then I laid out what it was I had found on the cotton-wool that my mother had organised excellently.

'A guide.'

'I know.'

'A guide, for God's sake. I helped him with his first frog. Christ.'

'It doesn't bear thinking about.'

'He was never, you know, officer material. He failed Physics twice. But in the dissecting room, in there, he was no better, no worse. He might have been all right. Some sort of general practice somewhere. Somewhere remote. More rods than clubs. Where he could look at tonsils once in a while, or make a pass at the next pair of ski-pants.'

'It takes more than brains, though,' said my mother. 'It takes breeding.'

But my father was laughing. It was good to hear him.

'He held the cadaver's hand while I was sawing off her foot. God's truth,' he said.

I came in then from the bathroom because it was a noble time to do that, while he was happy. But when he saw me, then he began to talk in the mystery, which is what a mother and a father do if they need to talk to their own selves instead of just to each other. It cannot be done outside of a marriage at all. It is too excellent.

'A charlatan,' said my father. 'A perambulating parody par excellence.'

'And the creams in the capillary region,' my mother said, 'remind me of a portrait in oils.'

'Prognosis?' he said.

'Poor.'

'Diagnosis?'

'Destitute,' my mother said.

'Course of treatment?'

'A radical Donalectomy.'

'God help him,' said my father who was laughing the most that I had ever seen him since the morning I had brought him to meet Demandez my friend.

'God help God,' said my mother. She was not laughing, but that was because she had said God, or because the skin was peeling on her legs where she had not wanted it to happen and where she had hoped to Christ.

'What I saw with my snorkel,' I said, 'was more than the last time.'

She looked at me as if I was not there at all. Then she saw me. She tore a long peel off her arm and dropped it in the bucket. And it was like cling-film, so it was, as if you would have thought that my mother would have to eat her leg before it was a certain date.

'Wash your teeth,' she said. 'You can use my brush.'

'What about what I saw?' I said.

'Tomorrow,' she said to me. 'Tomorrow you can tell me what you saw.'

So that was why I washed my teeth, and then, of course, I couldn't talk. Because if you talked after cleaning your mouth, it would be like eating. Your teeth would be yellow again if you spoke, and they would go black in the night; except, on the other hand, that a snore or a cough did not count, or if there was a fire or somebody touched you who was not your parents. And you could say Goodnight, and you didn't even have to gargle.

'Goodnight,' I said.

My father was looking out the window where the sun was setting truly.

'What are all those gulls doing?' he said to the sun. 'They were there this morning, and now they're still there. In the very same place. Half a mile, maybe more. Straight from where I'm standing.'

Then he sat down and opened his book at the exact place which was what he wanted. He had found his page again.

'Hello, old man.'

'Hello, Donal,' I said.

'No, no,' he said, and he went and lifted me onto the bar-stool beside his one. 'I say "Hello, old man," and you say "Hello, dear boy." They're the rules.'

It was nice on the bar-stool. You could make it go round, too.

'That bird talks,' said Donal, because he was pointing to the bird in the black cage. He can say "Shut Up" in French, and he can say the S word in English.'

'What's that?' I said.

'Shit,' said Donal, and he finished his drink which was a drink without an umbrella.

'Demandez makes him go bananas absolutely,' I said. 'When he can do that, then he wins drinks for himself. If, of course, he didn't have so much children, then the bird would be fine.'

'Right,' said Donal.

'He has so many children of his that what happened is this, dear boy; they have two mothers.'

'Good thinking,' Donal said.

'You could say that again.'

'Good thinking,' said Donal.

'What Demandez needs to do is to go and find a painting that nobody knows is worth what it is really worth; then, sell it. Afterwards, he could have his raisins for the love of what it is that he does, but he would not have to worry all the time. And, what would be excellent, he would have a parrot like always.'

'You should talk to him, old man,' said Donal. 'Lay it on the line.'

'I have had it on my conscience for a long time, dear boy,' I said.

He was dabbing at his lips and his moustache with a handkerchief, because he had maybe messed them with his drink, which was what my mother did about her lipstick, and all of her kisses on the tissues would be collected on Mondays.

'Ask your mum and dad,' he said, 'to motor up to a spot called Rocquebrune. Rocquebrune is out of this world, and it's only thirty miles away.'

'Could you go from the bus-stop?' I said.

'The bus-stop would be ideal, old man,' said Donal. 'The bus-stop would take you right there. Right to Rocquebrune.'

'What is it?' I said.

'It's a castle,' he said.

'Is there a torture chamber?' I said.

'Is there a torture chamber?' he said. 'There's a torture chamber that is more tortuous and more chambered than any other torture chamber I have ever seen in this world or the next world or the last world.'

'Would it make you sick?' I said.

34

'Sick,' he said, 'is not the word.'

'Are there skeletons?'

'There were skeletons,' he said, 'but they were buried. A dachshund went to ground with one of the hip-bones; what they call a femur. After that, they decided to inter them. But it's still a ghastly place. Visitors stagger out of that torture chamber and make straight for the toilets.'

'To get sick?' I said.

'To slash their wrists,' he said. 'To slash their wrists and be surprised at how small the pain is. It's not even as bad as a steam-burn from an iron.'

And I made the bar-stool go right the way round in one go only.

'Well,' he said, 'what the two of us need is a drink'; and he lifted his hand up, and that was that. The barman came to him exactly.

'Same again?' he said.

'*Encore,*' Donal said, '*et deux Cokes.*'

'*Bonjour,*' I said to the barman, and the barman said it to me. I was happy then, truly and truly, because I had said it the right way, which was out through my nose and in under my breath, and Donal had been there when I did it.

'I always have to say *deux Cokes,*' he said, 'because I never know whether it's masculine or feminine, *un* or *une.*'

'Dear boy,' I said, 'that is something for you and your conscience.'

'If we had come to here before this summer, well, there would be the parrot also, and the skeletons; but would there be Donal?'

My father was shaving the foam on his face, because the shadow came in the evening. He was very good at what he did. Where it was the most difficult of all, really, was at the corner of the mouth, when you could not speak for a moment but still your lips were apart as if you were saying My God.

'Martin, Martin,' he said, 'would you sit down for a moment and let me talk to you.'

'He is sitting down,' said my mother, and she dropped another long piece of her peel into the bucket, so she did.

'Martin,' said my father, 'Martin.' Then he turned to where my mother was. 'There's no point. I might as well sell stethoscopes to the seagulls.'

My mother rolled a big peel down her leg as if she was rolling a nylon.

'Martin,' she said. 'Your father was at university with Donal. That was twenty years ago. It was more. It was nearly thirty years ago. It was long before what your father is reading about in his book.'

'We were practising to be doctors,' said my father. 'Donal and I were medical students. I became a doctor. Donal became a bus conductor. He'd walk up and down the bus, and he'd say: Leeson Street, Stephen's Green, Grafton Street, College Green, and the Zoo. When he got to the Zoo, he'd change to another bus. Then he'd say: College Green, Grafton Street, Stephen's Green, Leeson Street, and the obelisk at Donnybrook.'

But the thought that I was minding to my own self was about the elephant bread. Because the elephant bread which is what I fed to the elephant was a bit of it only. The loaf was so huge absolutely that it had no end and no beginning; and therefore Donal might have bought elephant bread from the same loaf on the day that I did the same, and we might have fed the elephant in turns. I would have seen the ticket-machine and how shiny it was, but would I have turned around towards him, and said: Dear boy.

'Because of Donal, I had to walk to lectures for three years,' said my father. 'What could I do? He was on my route. I was too embarrassed to have to hand him my money, and then watch him count out the change. So I walked. I got up early, in the dark, and I walked. Day in, day out, for three years, just to spare his feelings.'

'He didn't have what it takes,' my mother said. 'He didn't make it. He didn't make the grade. He was no good.'

There was another side to the elephant bread, and that was the snake-house. When I made my First Holy Communion, there is a picture of me in everything white with a big snake on my shoulders. And what I think is that Donal was there, because the snake-house is on the way that you would be coming from the elephant bread to the bus-stop. Unless, of course, there was a bus-strike on my First Holy Communion.

'Did the buses go on going when I made my First Holy Communion?' I said.

'Forget about your First Holy Communion,' my father said. 'Your First Holy Communion is neither here nor there. The point is, no. *Nyet, nein, non.* The point is, Donal isn't Winnie the Pooh because he stands you a Coke.'

'*Deux,*' I said. 'Not one.'

'Whatever,' said my father. 'Whatever.'

'Your father buys you Cokes all the time,' said my mother. 'He even sent the Pepsi back, because he knows you don't like Pepsi. He's always thinking about you.'

'And the bit about Rocquebrune,' my father said. 'Rocquebrune is dangerous.'

'I wouldn't slash my wrists,' I said.

'What are you talking about?' he said. 'Who said anything about wrists? Rocquebrune is on a mountain. Mountains go up and up into the sky. People who fall off mountains go down and down and down into the valleys. This is not good for people. It looks bad when you get up close.'

'Your father has seen what happens to people who fall off mountains,' my mother said. 'That's why he needs a holiday.'

'That's why I need a drink,' my father said, 'and I can't even go to the bloody bar, in case our man in Menton is ensconced in it, playing Chopsticks on the piano to some Boston blue-rinse who's getting over a hysterectomy.'

My mother licked her hand and wetted the part of my hair that would not sit still since the haircut I had had myself.

'Donal's a nice poor man,' she said to me. 'He's been through a lot. He's been through the wars, God help him; but he'll be gone in a few days, and we'll still be here. In a couple of weeks, you won't remember what he looked like, but we'll still be here. And when it's Christmas and we put the tree up, then you won't remember what Menton looked like. But the two of us, your father and your mother, we'll still be here.'

She kissed the insides of my hands and then the outsides of them; and I did the same to hers.

★

'How are you, old man?'

I looked up at him from inside my snorkel, because he had known it was me; and down he got onto his hunkers which was his favourite way to be, really. What I was doing was this: I was lying down on my front at the end of the stony, where the Riviera started to go to Africa from. Then, with my face in my mask in the water, I could see with my eyes open.

'I am excellent, dear boy. I am as excellent as elephant bread.'

He said nothing while he knew this to himself; so I studied in the snorkel.

'That's great,' he said. 'More power to you.'

That, of course, was the exact answer for him. It was the time.

'Donal,' I said, 'you have been in the wars, poor man.'

He put his hand in the water at the edge of the beach where I was lying down, because he was not afraid of his jacket.

'How did you know?' he said.

'My mother went and put her finger on it.'

'She's a wise woman, your mum.'

'Donal,' I said, 'she is so wise she cannot find a book that she would go and read. She has read a book twice that the man who wrote it only wrote once. But I wish she had not read the snorkel book all together.'

'Why is that?' said Donal.

'Because,' I said, 'the snorkel book speaks for itself.'

'I suppose it does,' he said.

'Donal,' I said, 'tell me about the wars you have been in, poor man, dear boy.'

He had a go of my snorkel while he went and remembered them. There were lots, truly. But I had time because the sun was enjoying itself.

'Were you in a submarine?'

'No, never.'

'When they ping is lovely. You would never want them to stop. You would wake in the night and you would think that you were at home; but then, on the other hand, you would hear the pings, and you'd be happy, and say: Thank you.'

'There are pings on planes,' said Donal.

'Donal,' I said, 'that's truly true, but there is this to think about. Would you say thank you to them? You would not.'

'My brother was in the RAF,' he said.

'Were you?'

'I had the wrong moustache,' he said. 'Leo was in Bomber Command. He was a ball-turret gunner. And he survived. God knows how. Most of them died. Leo was spared. My father had his photo on the mantelpiece, in among the golf trophies. It was a snapshot in battle-dress: sheepskin at the collar, goggles, the works. Like a Craven A advertisement in the Underground. When people came to the house, Dad used to tell them he was a Spitfire pilot. And then Leo'd walk in, and they wouldn't know what to make of the Roman collar.'

'Donal,' I said, 'when Leo would have found out about the last battle, then did he give his goggles back?'

'I don't know,' he said. 'It's a good question. He may still have them, somewhere or other. Everything that's ever happened in our lives is still lying around, somewhere or other, gathering dust, gathering evidence. Bottom drawers have a greater cubic capacity than the British Museum.'

'Does he have a snorkel?' I said. 'If he has a snorkel, the goggles are gone the way of all flesh.'

'What I know he has,' said Donal, 'is an aquarium. A huge, huge, huge glass tank, with hundreds of the most beautiful fish you can imagine.'

'But you have to examine it first in the book,' I said. 'What is truly necessary is for the fish to be exact friends. On the other hand, you see, there might be one who would think away to himself, and say: I am going to eat you, by God.'

'Quite so,' said Donal. 'Quite so, indeed.'

'Has he got the book?'

'I'm not sure. It's not his aquarium, you see. It belongs to the seminary where he teaches. The students look after it; they have a roster. And when Leo is tired or tense, or both, he strips down to his underpants late at night, after everyone's gone to bed, and he climbs up on the back of a couch and lets himself down, quietly, quietly, into the water; and he swims there in the warmth of it. The little fish glide in and out between his legs; and once, when he got out and stood dripping on this imitation tiger-skin in front of a closed fireplace, he found a tiny, almost transparent fish in the hair under his arm.'

I did not say anything for a while after that, because it was too noble; and the whole world said *Dominus vobiscum*, and because I was in the world, I did too, amen.

'Donal,' I said, 'I would appreciate it if you got married.'

He laughed and laughed, so he did, because he was afraid it was a joke.

'How many children?' he said.

'You are much too old to have children,' I said. 'But you can have grandchildren up to when you are dead.'

'And who should I marry, do you think?' he said.

I thought about this, because it was a question that would be important, really.

'Here is the truth,' I said, 'the whole truth, and nothing but the truth. You should marry the woman who eats the exact same things as you do. Because of which, you would be all the time cooking together. Then what that means is this: you would have your meals together as well. But what is more noble would be the talking. You wouldn't have to write to each other or be on the telephone. You would be so close that there wouldn't be any need to go and shout. You could say everything the way that you and me are after doing, dear boy.'

He had put on my snorkel, and he did not have to make the strap shorter, so he didn't.

'Fair enough, old man,' he said, 'but what if the woman eats me out of house and home? Wouldn't it be better to find a wife who liked different food?'

'No, Donal,' I said. 'It is too important for that. Because if you liked different things to go and eat, you would not do all the cooking together. But if your wife is eating the food that is your favourite, nothing would be thrown away; and if she went and ate more than her fair share of it, you could put a mouse in the fridge. After the mouse, that would be that.'

Of course, we went back across the stony with the snorkel, and then Donal carried me up in his arms because I had no shoes. But I stopped to show him what Demandez had shown me: where the droppings of the parrot were on the big boulder that nobody had picked at. Then Donal set me down and he raced into the rocks, and for a while I couldn't see him. So I put my snorkel on me, to be even.

'Over here.'

There was his head to his tie as it bobbed up and it bounced down.

'Try to hit me,' he said.

'Where?'

'Where do you think?' he said. 'On my head. But you won't be able. I bet you anything.'

His face came up like a diver; and I threw a stone at it.

'Missed,' he said. 'That was nowhere near.'

So then what I did was this. I went and picked up two stones. First I threw one, and then, when I saw him surface, I threw the other. But he ducked down.

'The oldest trick in the book,' he said. 'Pin, one, two, throw; wait; pin, one, two, throw.'

His voice was coming from behind another boulder, really. He had moved in the meantime. That was where I lobbed the long stone. My snorkel had misted, so I was listening; but what I could hear was only the clackety-clack of the palm-trees and the boom of the white breakwater that was like the sound of two oars thrown down inside a rowboat, all thuddy and wooden. Where the stone had landed was not breathing.

'Donal,' I said.

I took my snorkel off and then I put it on again, to give him time. Because maybe he was doing something by himself, and he could not go into the water, on the other hand, in clothes, to do it there.

'Dear boy,' I said.

The noisy trees were worse than before, and I raced then to behind the rock. There, there he was, there he was lying, by God, and I lay down on him, saying one after the other his name. Until his eyes opened at the same time.

He roared laughing.

'Better a moving target than a sitting duck,' he said. 'Can you say that for me three times?'

When I did, he hugged me. And the noisy trees had been cut down; there was no clatter.

'I want to teach you everything I know,' he said.

'Do you know a lot, dear boy?'

'I know this and that,' he said. 'I know the best barber in Avignon and the best florist in Aachen; I know the difference between *Lederhosen* and a *Büstenhalter*; and I know how to say in Italian, "There has been blood in my stools for three days, Doctor". But I don't know, for the life of me, why all those seagulls should be massing out there, the way they are. It is very funny-peculiar.'

'Funny-peculiar,' I said, 'is the truth, the whole truth, and nothing but the truth.'

'So help me, God,' he said.

My father put the book down on the bed beside him.

'It's very heavy,' he said.

My mother was stripping another peel from her suntan. The strips had gone very deep with her all together. She was crucified with them.

'Why didn't you buy a James Bond?' she said. 'A James Bond is more right for the Riviera. Or you could have bought a Hemingway. I mean, you are on holiday. You don't have to be a Renaissance man all the time.'

The last bit of the peel drooped on the lip of the bucket and almost went in, but then it didn't. Instead of which, it dangled there, so it did, because I was watching.

'It's not heavy in the sense of heavy,' my father said. 'It's heavy in the sense of weight. Your hands get tired.'

'Try whipping cream,' said my mother. 'Then you'd know.'

'Look,' said my father, 'let's not have an altercation in front of Clever Hans.'

What I wanted, on the other hand, was to ask them about the money. Because then I could take my hands out of my pockets and let it jingle, and nobody would mind a bit if it did do. What was funny-peculiar was this about it: when Donal was not there on his own bar-stool, neither was Demandez and the dear bird was quiet, really. So I put the money that was on the counter into my pocket, to examine it truly. Instead of which, the coins were not as noble as the money that I have at home, with animals of excellence. What they had was faces only, and not a horse or a salmon or, by God, a turkey too. But the question of my own self was this one: had I gone and made Jesus sweat blood?

'I've worked it out,' said my father, 'that the day Hitler shot himself in the bunker was the same day Father Basil did the eighteen holes with me, and he was reading his Office out of the breviary as he went around in this glorious, glorious sunshine.'

'He was a nutter,' said my mother.

'He was a character,' my father said. 'And he was bright. He had a licence from the Vatican to hear confessions in Spanish.'

'He was a nutter,' said my mother. 'He put his hand on my stomach, half-way through our honeymoon, in broad daylight on the sun-terrace, and he said to me: There may already be a tiny eternal life unfolding inside you. I told him the only thing in my stomach was Dover sole and a pink gin. Then he informed me I shouldn't be flippant, that I wasn't a spring chicken.'

'You were twenty-three,' said my father.

'I was twenty-two until the day we left,' said my mother.

'Did people go and leave money on the counter, really?' I said.

They looked at me in the way they would have done if I had been about to take their photograph of them, but which was the button and I did not know.

'What money?' my mother said.

'What people?' said my father.

'If,' I said. 'I was thinking about an if, really.'

'Think about your teeth,' my father said. 'It's way past teeth-time.'

But then if I washed my teeth, I would have to say it with my hands; and what was the hand for being a bit afraid about it? The money was not as noble now.

'Brush your teeth, Martin,' said my mother. 'Otherwise you'll wind up with cavities; and that means Dentist Dreadful and the motorbike drills.'

My father slammed his book together. It shut with a shock. Then he parted the pages like curtains and he peeped out.

'Sweet Jesus,' my mother said. 'What are you on about?'

'This,' he said, and he held up his fingers. 'A mosquito. I was waiting for him. I knew he'd land sooner or later. I'd have sat here all night, if need be. So now there's one less in the world. That's my good deed for the day.'

'Donal smokes in the bed,' I said. 'He goes and finds out cigarettes in the coach that he does not like for himself, and he smokes them in the same ashtray for the mosquitoes, because they hate it, truly.'

'Teeth,' said my father. And my mother followed me in there, where it was colder.

'I don't like it,' my father said. 'I don't like this frequent fraternising with the loquacious lush. Are we *ad idem*?'

'Later,' she said. 'Later.'

'Why?' he said. 'It's not as if he's onto quadratic equations.'

I watched her in the mirror as she stood at the door and spoke to my father in the room that was not at all reflected in front of me, but the waterfall on her blouse was on the other side of it now, and it was nicer, really.

'He knows roster.'

'Terrific,' said my father.

'He knows *Büstenhalter*.'

'What's *Büstenhalter*?'

And she laughed about that. I could see the gold in her cavities which she was saving up for my wedding ring when I would be married, because when she came home and lay down from the dentist, then she would show me her burst gums and the new excellence in her mouth. But would Donal have to go and dig his mother up after he had found a woman who ate the exact same? I would ask the dear boy, absolutely.

'*Büstenhalter*?' my father said. 'Are you sure it's not just one of his grunts and groans?'

The money would not be quiet. It tittered in my socks so I took them off and poured out the bright lots, because it was like I had been walking on the stony all of the time; but I was in my bedroom only, going and going around it, with the light not on. What I did not know, you see, was the right order of whether the barman would have seen me when I took the money from where it was; and I did not know truly if, on the other hand, a sad policeman would take out a pencil and ask me what my name was and what my religion would have been. Then my father would be too examined by everything to go and read his book, and my mother would walk to the shops for the cutlets in case she would meet me and know from my ticket-machine that I was a bus conductor.

And Jesus would be the bloodiest he had been, ever. He would sweat like a pig, so he would; and I would be saying Leeson Street, Stephen's Green, Grafton Street, and I wouldn't know for a minute that I was the diagnosis of it all.

I took my mother's pearls from out of in underneath my pillow, because it had to be that. And when I had undressed my pyjamas, I swung with the pearls at my own self, and I hit my bottom where my mother would not see the mark because of my togs. So I went on hitting and hitting the hardest that I was able to, until I had done it a hundred and seven times, which was the amount of the ages of my father plus my mother plus me. Then I added another exact ten, in case I had gone and done the sum wrong.

The back of my two legs was not right afterwards, really, but I thought that this was an idea for it: that if my mother came down onto the stony in the morning, and she would call me, then I could stand in the water up to my waist when she said Martin. And I would wave, and she could wave, and she would leave down the bottle of Coke on the right towel.

I put on my pyjamas, so I did, and the pain where I hit behind my body was worse there than the pain of the sunburn in my shoulders; but when I looked down at the floor, the money was still where it was. And I cried in my eyes and my hands to not wake the world.

What I couldn't do was to wake up my mother from the dream she had been having since the first night of the hotel, when she had sniffed the lacquer of someone else on the pillow from her side of the bed, and then the owner had sent her a basket of fruit without raisins because he was so embarrassed. But even if I tried to wake her, she had said her prayers and put the tablet on her tongue to gargle it down, by God, with the red lemonade that she had made go flat by leaving the cap off the bottle. So then I would be walking my fingers over her eyelids, and still she would be down, down, down in a dream she would be dreaming in black-and-white, and my father would go and put on the light, and put on his glasses from where he had left them to be inside his book at the page. And he would look at me and say: Blast you. I've lost where I was.

There was no sound, except if you listened too much. Then you could hear what were the palm-trees, and a toilet that maybe a person had cut his toenails into, because he had torn the sheet with them. So I opened the door while the noise of that was a big distraction, and I went with my snorkel down into the corridor and down the stairs that had no carpet because it was the Riviera, and my heart was as demented as the bird which bought the beers for Demandez: it was bashing its beak on the other side of my skin to get out of inside me. And then I was down in the hall by the postcard stand where the lovely couch could not be sat on by anyone, because of which a queen had sat there once and sewed mittens for a priest who sweated blood in all the right places as Jesus; but when the Japanese had gone and sat there, then the hotel asked him to write a sign out in his language which said: Do not sit here. And he did.

'*Dominus vobiscum,*' I said.

But the darkness did not say '*Et cum spiritu tuo*'; so I knew there was nobody in it, and I was safe to go down more. That was where the corridor had a slope, really, and a trolley would just have taken off by itself if you had forgotten the handbrake because you were blowing your nose. But they had not sprayed the smell of flowers here, and everybody had not taken off their shoes before they went into their bedrooms to have a row.

His light was on. Then I knocked. Inside the bedroom, he was guessing, in a voice that had not lain down. And the door opened.

'Dear boy,' I said. 'Dear boy.' My eyes wobbled. It was the way that my snorkel went, when the water came in into it.

'Jesus,' he said. 'Come in out of the storm.'

A woman was sitting on his bed, who was about maybe to take a bath. She had nice glasses. On the other hand, of course, there was no rule that said: you cannot wear your glasses in a shower.

And then she looked at the snorkel I had brought; but she would have to let out the strap. Her hair was huge and the black of it gleamed in the little light from the bedside lamp where Donal had gone and put her cardigan over it.

'Donal,' I said, 'are we talking about the same thing?'

'What do you mean?' he said.

'You know,' I said.

'No, love. I'm not quite with you,' he said. And then he said, 'Old man.' Because he was so sleepy he had almost forgotten.

'When you eat the same things, and then,' I said.

'No, no, no, no,' he said. 'It's not that. It's not that at all. This is a friend of mine. A great friend. Gosh, no.'

'Has she come to wash in the Riviera?' I said.

The woman was holding her drink on the bow of her *Büstenhalter*. When she smiled, it was excellent.

'Absolutely,' said Donal. 'She's come to take the plunge.'

'Then,' I said, 'she should wear a bathing cap. Because otherwise she would be in knots afterwards, unless she keeps her head above water.'

The woman said something to Donal in French, and then Donal said something back to her which was the exact same. That was their mystery. So I knew they had met on a secret night to examine if they ate the same food, and get married when that was that.

The woman reached forward and stroked my hair with her hand, but the bit at the back from the haircut still stuck up, and she smiled about it to herself. Because that was her problem everywhere.

'Martin,' she said in the properly.

'And this,' said Donal, 'this is Madame Agatha. Agatha Christie.'

'*Bonjour*,' I said; and she was deeply pleased. '*Bonjour*, Martin,' she said to me, and she kissed in between my eyes like a sniper. '*Bonjour; buongiorno*. Have a nice day.'

'Now,' said Donal. 'Tell me. Tell me everything from the middle or the end, but not the beginning. The beginning is always a false start. Tell me from where they ate the fruit and found they were naked. Forget the nature trails and the days when they were only nude. Begin where you thought for the first time that it would never end.'

So I told him the whole, wide world of it, and nothing else at all. He listened with his head in the hearing position, and the woman ate the ice in her drink with the sound of a pencil sharpener. But I did not tell him about maybe being a bus conductor afterwards, because I didn't want to break his heart in front of Agatha.

'It's extraordinary,' he said. 'It is quite extraordinary. You see, that was my money. Ergo, *pas de problème*. I was going to ask you to bring it round to me, because . . .'

'Because then?' I said.

'Because I had to stay in my room.'

'Why?' I said.

'Ah,' he said. 'Because, you see, I was expecting a friend.'

'Agatha?'

'No, no,' he said. 'I wasn't expecting Agatha. But before I wasn't expecting her, I was expecting Fyodor. Fyodor Dostoevski. Fidi is a courier, and he was passing through Menton. He's an old friend from hospital. I was in hospital after the war, and I read a lot. And Fidi was in the next bed. We were bedfellows. I taught him the Irish for sputum and he taught me the Russian for tumour.'

'Was he shot in the same place as well?'

'We weren't shot, old man. It was a sanatorium for people with tuberculosis. We could only smoke two cigarettes a day for a year and a half, and they had to have filters.'

The woman in the *Büstenhalter* was smelling under her arm in the excellent hairs, but my mother would say that the Black Forest belonged in Bavaria. What I thought, though, to my own self was this: that Agatha's name could have been more noble, because she was.

'So I was waiting for Fidi, and then I rang across to the bar just to say it was mine, the money, and, yes, I'd send Martin. And here you are, so there you are. That's called the marriage of true minds; and you must keep whatever it was, for going to such trouble.'

Then they talked in French, and they mysteried for a while; and

I was tired a bit and happy more, though behind me was sorer still.

'Listen, old man,' said Donal. 'Always beware of people who tell you to listen. Got that?'

'Got that,' I said.

'Donal to Martin One,' said Donal. 'Are you receiving me?'

'Martin One to Donal Two. Affirmative, yes.'

'Don't be afraid of your father,' he said. 'Your father is afraid of himself. Don't be afraid of your life because he's afraid of his death. Over.'

'Yes,' I said. Agatha was smiling away at me as if I was truly a photograph she had been remembering for years to go and look for, and where was it, only down behind the back of the fridge when it was carried out like a coffin for the bin-men who had none.

'My brother became a priest because he was afraid of his father. He wasn't afraid of being a ball-turret gunner over the Ruhr. He wasn't afraid of flak from the Germans; he was afraid of flak from a man with catarrh who liked to smell the insides of his slippers. Then, after his ordination, he wasn't afraid any longer. He came out of the cathedral and he gave my father his first blessing. My father kneeled down in front of his son, and called him Father; and his son blessed him in the name of the Father and the Son. My father died ten days later, and they put down myocardiac infarction on his death certificate; but they should have put rage. And my brother arranged everything. He arranged the plot, and he arranged the grave as well. He managed, by some immense fortitude, to appear to be in great form. And why not? This, after all, was his first confirmed kill.'

'Did you serve his mass, then?' I said.

'I did not,' he said. 'I was in Rome. I was in the Eternal City, keeping an eye on the clock, shepherding a party of veterinary surgeons around the mummies in the Vatican Museum. But my brother back home was singing a requiem mass, and he'd left his wristwatch in the sacristy. He was taking his time, you see.'

He got up off his hunkers and took a straw then, which he put in my ear and he looked down it.

'Very still,' he said. 'Still as you can.'

He sucked on the straw, but he did not blow. Then he took it out and looped it into a knot. Agatha was filling herself a good old drink, and she licked the outside of the glass where it had spilled. My ear felt by itself instead of the same as the other one, so Donal turned me round and round, and then I didn't remember which was the different. He went into the toilet and flushed the straw all the way to Africa. And the fear went with it: such was my delightment that I was not sorry for it.

'All gone,' he said. And he came back into the room where Agatha was having her drink to celebrate me.

'Remember,' he said. 'No fathers. When you take away the wrong moustaches and the *Büstenhalters*, there are only small people. Some of them grow up to become children, and we call them names like Papa or Mammy. The rest leave no footprints; only shoe-horns.'

He brought me to the door with his hand in my hand instead of my hand in his.

'I need to spend time with Agatha now,' he said. 'Otherwise she'd be jealous.'

'*Bonjour*, Agatha,' I said.

'*Bonjour, mon brave*,' she said, and she changed her mouth into a kiss as if she was blowing smoke against the mosquitoes, really. '*Vous vous couchez de bonne heure*.'

'*Bonjour*, dear boy,' I said.

'Please don't think I'm cynical,' he said. 'I'm just bitter.'

But when I went into the mirror in my bathroom on the other side of the Prince de Galles, the wind was turning and turning in its sleep, and the palm-trees were cranky. But the rain was coming in out of the Riviera; and when it reached the garden that was underneath my window, it rained on the water-sprinklers and the water-sprinklers started. So I opened my mouth wide, and wider then.

My teeth were not black.

'Crrackle, crrackle. Come in, old man. Crrackle.'

It was he himself, so I did. But it can be hard to run through water, when the water is as high as your heart. Because I had gone out to nine steps from the edge of the stony, where my mother had said was enough, and after that would be beyond the beyond.

'Coming, dear boy. Crackly, crackly, zizz bong.'

'What is a zizz bong?' he said, when I had reached the stony. He was a bit upset about it.

'It's when the crackly scrunches,' I said.

'I was afraid of that,' he said.

'What,' I said, 'is your prognosis about?'

'Oxidation of the ferrous sulphate particles in the third ventricle of the medium wavelength, old man.'

'These were my gravest suspicions, dear boy,' I said. 'But I was hoping to Christ.'

'And he was hoping to God. But God is ex-directory. That leaves you and me, and I have a plan.'

So I put on my snorkel and he spoke his plan down the air-tube in case that anyone would see us whispering, and go and wonder what our secret was on earth.

'I'm going to smuggle you into Italy,' he said. 'And the police will take off their hats and scratch their heads when we tell them how we did it. Over and out.'

'Is Agatha coming?'

'Agatha,' he said. 'Agatha.' He could not make up his mind to let her or not to. Then he decided for the good of his plan.

'No, no, no,' he said. 'I couldn't smuggle Agatha. They watch for her at all the borders. Especially Thierry. Thierry keeps her photograph at the Ventimiglia check-point. He wants her very badly.'

'Why don't we tell him she's gone and died?' I said.

'He'd dig her up,' said Donal. 'Thierry is like that. It's in the nature of people called Thierry. Never call anyone Thierry, even a gerbil.'

We had reached by now where the coach-bus was in the front of the hotel, and it was empty of the men and the women from Redwood City, because they had gone off all together with their shooting sticks onto the stony where the ultra-violet was; but Donal only opened up the side of the coach that you would use for the baggages or maybe your shoes.

'Hop in,' he said. 'In less time than it takes to say the names of all the countries in the world, I'll have you in the oldest one of all. Then you can tell your great-grandchildren you were smuggled into the land of Giotto, Garibaldi, the Emperor Claudius and the Empress Claudia Cardinale. And Hannibal can eat his heart out. *Andiamo.*'

'*Habemus papam*,' I shouted, because that was the most important Italian I knew; and he shouted back to me, '*Viva il Papa.*' Because I had made my own self comfortable by then in what was around me; and he closed the side of the coach, truly, so then it was dark. But I was excellent enough to not mind one blind bit.

The coach went grumbledy-grumble, by God, and that was that. I was a smuggler. But I would not boss anybody about it. What I would do was I would just tell them the truth, the whole truth, and nothing but the truth, down my nose and under my breath, if in case they would have got on my nerves. Then they would not call me Martin, but Mr Martin instead, because Donal only could say old man. That was the rule of it.

Aden, I thought. Africa, and Australia. And South Africa could be Africa, South. Then that was four.

If the Italian soldiers opened the side of the coach, and they had a bayonet, then what I would decide was this: I would tell them that I was a Catholic, but on the other hand I would explain that I could not speak. So they would have to send me to the Pope, because what else could they do? He would give me a nun to bring me back to the Prince de Galles, and the nun would be staying with Agatha before my father had stopped sweating blood. Then, when no one was embarrassed about their consciences, back would go the nun, but she would be happy all together because my mother would have given her Pond's, and my father would have given her *The Last Battle* by this time.

Germany, Greece, Great Britain and Gaul.

You couldn't count the countries in this whole world, but could you count the socks that would have been driven in the coach's boot? Or if the baggages got given the wrong order by Donal, then they would be opened up in the bedrooms by a person examining for a lovely wig, but she would find under everything else that was in it only a tie; and a boy, poor man, would not want a *Büstenhalter*, but his snorkel by itself. That would be a crucifixion for Donal.

I could not remember all of the banana republics, so I said the Association of Banana Republics, which would have been maybe twenty; and I said their name twenty times because that was more fair, really.

The coach was stopping; then it stopped. The racket around me turned into tick-ticking. So I waited. Already, the side was being banged out brightly. And the blue sky sprang back at the sight of me; but the dear boy bent down.

'*Tutto va bene*,' he said to me. 'Listen to that.'

It was birds he was on about.

'Yes,' he said, 'yes. But they're not French. They're Italian. They don't live in any old sky, you know. They room in the *cielo*.'

He bent down more until his trousers were in it, and he scooped up dust in his hand.

'Smell that,' he said; and that is what I did.

'That's Italy,' he said. 'And over there, look, see over there, where the petrol pump has leaked all the long way along to the place that you can put air in your tyres: that's the Rubicon. And behind it, up, up more, up more, there, stop: the telephone wires. Where the dirty pigeon is, that's right, someone is talking to her boyfriend in Bari, to the only person in the world who calls her Jellybean. Her cheeks are smudged.'

'Is she crying a bit or maybe a bit more than a bit?' I said.

'No, no, no, she's not crying. She works in a shop that sells typewriters. That's it. She's been putting ribbons on typewriters for customers who don't know how, and for women who don't want to spoil their nails. But the dirty pigeon doesn't know that.'

'But we do,' I said.

'We do,' said Donal. 'That's the difference between a dirty pigeon and a dirty person. We have the dirt on the whole world, and all of the dirt is Italian. *Adesso andiamo*, though if you change your shirt every single day and have a brother a priest, you're supposed to say it the other way round, which is more refined. *Andiamo adesso*.'

'I like it about the same when it is either way, really, dear boy.'

'Stop,' he said. 'We have to step over this one. Be very careful.'

He lifted his leg up at the highest it could be and stepped over a crack in the road. Which is why I gave him my snorkel before I went and jumped, because it was one thing at a time. That was the right order.

'What was it?' I said.

He looked a bit frightened, but then he got over it.

'It was the thirty-eighth parallel, old man.' And he blessed himself, beginning from his sunglasses.

'Don't be sad,' I said.

'I have to be a teeny-weeny bit sad,' he said. 'We're going to visit a grave.'

'Where?'

'In the last place you would ever think of looking,' he said.

If I had counted as well the one that I was sitting at, then there were about twenty-six graves exactly. Seven were in under the shadow of the wall that was around everything, and one had a lizard. Four more were too tangled up in what was a bush, really. And one had a plastic rose with a drop of plastic water, which was in a tin for corn on the cob. The others were the rest. Everybody in the graves was only given a birthday, but not the time of their Jesus, except for the one who had the day of her death up on it, where Donal was tugging.

'Shit,' he said. 'That wasn't a weed. That was a flower.' And he dug it back down into its home, which it would have been delighted to do.

'Donal,' I said. 'Do you mind me saying?'

'Say away, old man. Say away. Say what you like and like what you say. The Oxford English Dictionary was made for man, not man for the Oxford English Dictionary. Speak the speech trippingly, I prithee, forsooth, alack-a-day, gadzooks, my golly-gosh, indeed.'

'*Mater Dei, ora pro nobis peccatoribus, nunc et in hora mortis,* amen,' I said.

'Amen,' he said.

'Donal,' I said, 'I think I would have thought about this place before it was the last place I would have thought about. Because if

you had to have a grave, then you would have to have a
graveyard; unless you would have drowned at sea before you had
reached a graveyard. Then it would be on the other hand, of
course.'

'Of course,' he said. 'But you wouldn't think of looking for a
very old woman's grave in a monks' cemetery, would you?
Monks are sometimes likened unto old women by pejorative
cads, but they are all of them male to a man. And the funny thing
is that this lady, God be good to her, was married to a Jew. He
was so ashamed of something that had not happened to him, he
had his wrist tattooed with a camp-number by a Senegalese; and,
after that, he got ashamed about something else, and he burnt the
tattoo off with an oxy-acetylene blowtorch. But the wife was
pure gold. Eighteen-carat. Treasure. Buried treasure.'

'Did she call you dear boy?'

'No, no, no,' he said. 'Only Martin of Menton ever called me
that.'

'Did you go and meet her when you were through the wars?'

'I did,' he said. 'I met her after the war.'

'After the last battle?'

'After the last battle of that war and before the first battle of the
next one.'

'After Berlin fell?'

'After Berlin fell. After the fall of Berlin and the fall of
Germany and the fall of Europe and the fall of night. Everything
had fallen down by then. Even the suicide rate. People couldn't
find anything to hang themselves from. The trees beside the
tram-lines were cut down with axe-heads fitted to piano legs, and
when they dragged the trees along the streets, the leaves would
fill like fishing-nets with glass and bricks and bullet-casings the
size of lipstick compacts with no lipstick in them. And the
women would sit on their suitcases, with beetroot juice on their
lips; and between their legs, on the side of the suitcases, you could
see stickers of hotels on the Riviera. The George V, the Victory,
the Supreme.'

'The Prince de Galles would not have been built so long ago as
those ones would have,' I said. 'It has TV.'

He threw the weeds that he had tugged out from her grave

onto the grave beside it, because a monk wouldn't mind one blind bit about some brother weeds in on top of him.

'She's taken the wheat with her,' he said, brushing away at his hands, 'and left the tares behind. I always thought her husband would go first. He smoked so much they took his leg off. Three years later, they gave him a metal one, but he never wore it. He was used to his crutch. Besides, the metal one was so discreet that he got into trouble on the buses when he sat in the seats for the *mutilés de guerre*. So he went back to the wooden one, and he kept the other as an umbrella stand.'

'He could have smuggled with it,' I said.

'Thanks be to Jesus,' said Donal, 'you weren't on duty at the Brenner Pass in October of 1957.'

'Why?'

'Because it wouldn't have been the Brenner Pass; it would have been the Brenner Fail.'

We were out of the graves and through the rickety turnstile that was like a cinema at the gate, except that there was no queue to go in. The coach had not budged from where it was, but the shadow of it had shrieked right across the road in a skid.

'Donal,' I said, 'you can tell me. You can tell me the truth, the whole truth and even nothing but the truth, if that is on your conscience.'

'I don't know where to end,' he said.

'Jesus would not sweat so much if you did, dear boy.'

'I can tell you the truth, old man, or I can tell you the whole truth. Each is always the opposite of the other, of course, and nothing-but-the-truth is a holy terror. Beware of nothing-but-the-truth. Its beginning is truth, its middle is but, and its end is nothing; and nothing is no place to send postcards from.'

'Donal,' I said, 'how many people have you gone and killed?'

We had reached beside the coach, but he did not open up its side. Instead of which, we got on, the both of us.

'I killed a German,' he said. 'But he took the good out of it by being so old. If I'd known he was old enough to be my father, I'd have killed somebody younger. I was furious with him. So I went through his pockets, and he had a nasal decongestant which I kept and used up. Then I found his name and address, and I wrote

56

them down on the inside of *William the Cannibal,* where it said: "When you have finished this book, please leave it at a post office so that someone in the Forces can enjoy it too". A long, long, long time afterwards, I wrote to his family in Oberstdorf; and then I wrote again the next Christmas, and the Christmas after that, too. Eventually, they wrote back to say that, if I didn't stop, they'd get a court order to make me. If you held the envelope up to the light, you could see where they'd rubbed out Herr and written Mister.'

I took off his sunglasses and I wiped them on the palm-trees of his tie, until they were smashing.

'Let's go, dear boy,' I said. 'Let's go home.'

'All right,' he said, and he started the coach till it shook. 'Let's go back.'

My father and my mother were standing beside the postcards and the couch you could not sit on in any language except maybe Latin. The two of them were examining the poor manager's assistant who had started a beard with some red.

'Look,' said my father. He was conducting a bit with his hands, really. 'It's very simple. *Très facile. Très, très.* Either there is sewage or there isn't. One or the other. Black or white. Either the pipe is broken, *comprenez,* or the gulls are having a tupperware party. *Le pipe est frappé, n'est-ce-pas? Le pipe kaput?'*

The poor manager's assistant was slashing his wrists with the shirtcuffs of his shirt, and if he had gone and died on the carpet, then they would have put on his death certificate: sick unto death.

'How do you say sewage?' said my father to my mother.

'Why would I know the word for sewage?' she said. 'That really says something about what you think of me. That just about sums it up, doesn't it? Just because I know what *Büstenhalter* means, I'm suddenly supposed to know the French for processed faeces. Well, thanks but no thanks.'

'*Des fèces,*' my father said to the poor manager's assistant. '*Pourquoi des fèces processés? Pourquoi, je demande?'*

'*Merde,*' said my mother.

'*Malheureusement,*' the assistant said.

'What am I going to tell him?' said my mother.

'He can go to the swimming pool,' my father said. 'It's on the same side of the road, for starters. I won't have to watch him crossing over to the beach. I mean, as it is, I'm on the balcony forty times a day, giving him hand signals. Why they can't build an underpass is beyond me. They can build an underpass for the natterjack toad, but they won't build an underpass for a kid who wears a snorkel in the supermarket.'

'He can't go to the swimming pool,' my mother said. 'The shallow end isn't shallow enough. I measured it with one of the metal chairs. It sank about another three feet when I let the whole of it down, and it was already under water when I let go. Do you want me to tell him he can play with his snorkel in the foot-bath? Maybe he's a bit mystified by the world, but he's not back in the Bronze Age either.'

'All you have to do,' said my father, 'is tell him that some hobgoblin did stinky bu–bus in the Riviera. And I'll buy him fifty bottles of Coke and a hundred straws in case he decides to share them with Jesus.'

But my mother sat down exactly on the seat where you could not, and she knocked over the sign with the Japanese that was up and down it, and she looked at her hands as if she had never noticed before that everything about them was not in the right order.

Then I came down the stairs from where I had been hiding with my gift for the dear boy, and I put it into the inside of my shorts, which was excellent for that. My father was still making himself more understood than before to the poor manager's assistant, and my mother was having a prayer on the couch, so I was out into the front of the hotel in the time it would take to say: My God.

Donal was sitting on a suitcase beside his coach. I saw my own self come up in his sunglasses.

'I'm getting out before the shit hits the beaches,' he said. 'But first I have something for you.'

From the pocket of the jacket he had on him, he pulled forth a great, green waterbottle.

'It's not the canteen that I had during the war,' he said. 'But it's the next best thing, and a half of something is better than two thirds of nothing, as the woman said. It must have been a woman. Only a woman could be that wise.'

'The smell of it is lovely,' I said, having a good sniff of the inside to myself.

'Surgical spirits,' he said. 'And that's not all, as the man said; because that's men's talk, old man. Men love all and nothing. A man's favourite words are all and nothing. But women love the word: and.'

But I wasn't listening one blind bit, really. Because what he had in his hand was goggles.

'They're my brother's. The ball-turret gunner that is, was, and ever shall be. They came yesterday.'

I did not say Thank You. Thank You was for a door that would be opened or maybe a person who examined his watch and said that it was four o'clock. It was not noble enough for what this was.

'I rang him, you see,' Donal said. 'And he wasn't going to give it over. So I said: You're a priest. You have to. It's in your contract. And if you don't give it to me, then I'll rat on you at the Last Judgement. I'll say to one or other of the Blessed Trinity: Listen here, old boy. Before you make up your mind about my brother, let me tell you a little story about a pair of goggles. That shook him up, I can tell you. So he said he'd send them, and I said: May the peace of Christ continue to disturb you. And he said: Fuck you too.'

'*Dominus vobiscum*, dear boy,' I said.

'You too, old man. You too.'

He went and lit another cigarette while I put the goggles on me. They would fit in under the snorkel absolutely.

'You know,' he said, 'years and years and years ago, when car-doors opened the wrong way and men wore hats and the streets of Dublin still smelled of horse-droppings, I took your mum to a film. I, me and myself, the three of us. "Little Nelly Kelly" it was called. Judy Garland was in it, God forgive her. And there we were, your mum and I, by appointment, in the second-best seats. I opened a box of chocolates very, very quietly, not to annoy the people around us; and then I reached over, at a moment of high drama in the life and times of Little Nelly Kelly, and I popped – no, I put – a chocolate in your mother's mouth. In those days, that was roughly equivalent to buying a packet of condoms in plain view of a first date. Your mother didn't spit it out, and I thought a few, furtive un-parliamentary thoughts. A minute passed; another; three minutes went by. I was about to slip my arm around the back of her chair when she took it out of her mouth, wrapped it in the two torn halves of the theatre tickets, and dropped it under the seat of the person in front of her.'

'If I had done that,' I said, 'then she would have scraped an X with her nail on the back of my hand.'

'I had an image in my head,' said Donal, 'of the man who was sitting in front, walking home through College Green and up Grafton Street to Stephen's Green, with a piece of crushed nougat on the sole of his shoe, and his girlfriend saying "dirty", and making him take it off with a stick.'

I thought about this from behind the goggles that were a great help, really; and I thought that I was seeing the Prince de Galles but the first goggler had seen the booms of the burst yellow from below and below him, and maybe the man in the Messerschmitt had not gone and fired at him because he said: My God, it is my pen-pal who collects Hitler stamps. But the goggler blew him up, because how could he know? And when he did, then his wife would say to him that she understood, she understood, and the music would rise up, up, up, like a church.

'Was it nougat you said?'

'Nougat,' said Donal.

'If you would have said Turkish Delight only,' I said, 'then everything would truly have been in the exact right order.'

'Why?'

The water came into my goggles but it was not the excellent Riviera. It was not.

'What do you mean, old man?'

'Why did you not think about Turkish Delight?' I said. 'But you were too busy with your film to think about the truth, the whole truth, and nothing but the truth.'

The dear boy, the poor man, wobbled in the wet of the goggles.

'I love Turkish Delight,' he said. 'Even the name Turkish Delight is delightful. A delightment, truly.'

'Donal,' I said, 'my mother adores Turkish Delight. She knows it is sinful, but she cannot stop herself.'

Then he sat on the suitcase still, and there was not a word out of him while he smoked down over his moustache.

'Agatha is rather fond of Turkish Delight,' he said, when it was the right time.

'Is that the prognosis about it?' I said.

'It is, old man,' he said. 'I am prognosticating.'

'Well,' I said, 'this is the diagnosis part. Dear boy, you are not to look at tonsils or ski-pants too much because Agatha is what should be the matter for your conscience. On the other hand, take her to a nice film and put a chocolate in her mouth. But look at the chocolate during a bright scene, and make sure of yourself it is not a nougat. Because once upon a time, you will live happily ever after, amen.'

'Agatha the good,' he said. 'And why not? She rather crops up, you know, here and there, all over the place, a bit like the Blessed Virgin, really. But I suppose I could become more of a Marian than I've been in the past. I'd need to eat plenty of oysters, mind you. More to the point, I'd need to buy plenty of pearls. They're a much more reliable aphrodisiac.'

He was rehearsing the mysteries he would be saying backwards and forwards with her when both of them would be Donal and Agatha. And he had not even gone and bought himself the box of Turkish Delight.

'I shall arise and go now and go to Agatha,' he said, and up he arose off the suitcase. 'But first I've a plugs and points check at the garage.'

Our hands shook by themselves.

'*Ciao, figlio mio,*' he said.

'Dear boy,' I said. 'Over.'

'Over and out, old man.'

But it was only when the coach had whacked the poor palm-tree at the front of the hotel and turned towards the customs of Italy that I thought then of the gift I had got for Donal from the shop that sold motorbikes and pencils too. It was still in the front of my shorts where I had put it, the pencil for him that was the colour of his jacket, and the sticky pieces of my mother's peel from her arms and her legs that I had been truly collecting from the bucket in her bedroom, which I had wrapped around the pencil from the rubber to the point.

'Good Jesus,' my father said. 'Will you ever learn? Will you never learn? Look, come here. Come over here.'

'Will you not shout at him?' said my mother. 'They'll hear us half-way down the corridor.'

Outside the window, I could see the Riviera on its way to Africa, and a little plane that was trailing a sign, by God, but the sign was snarled; and that would be an excellent way for Demandez to make people sit up and say: Gosh, I would love some raisins and nuts, really. Let's have a search-party for Demandez.

'Number one,' said my father. 'The closest Donal ever came to a threatening situation was when he doused a chimney-fire with a soda syphon. He did not acquire his scar in hand-to-hand combat with General Rommel. He had a mole which was ugly. The mole was removed surgically. The scar did not heal. It formed what we call a chiloid scar. Say chiloid.'

'Chiloid,' I said.

'Terrific,' he said. 'Ten out of ten. Now. Point Number Two. The waterbottle and the goggles. They are called Army Surplus. Say Army Surplus.'

'Army surplus,' I said.

'Ten out of ten. We'll have to change your school. Army Surplus can be bought anywhere. You can buy boots, blunted bayonets, medals, things. There are at least two Army Surplus shops, stores, whatever, here in Menton. Now I'm not trying to detract one whit from what Donal did. What he did was very kind. I'm only trying to help you to live as well as you can in the world that you have to live in. The innocence of doves is not enough for the world we live in. For the world we live in, you also need the wisdom of serpents. That's in the book Jesus wrote, or, more precisely, the book the Holy Spirit wrote about Jesus. The Gospel. What Our Lord says isn't that we shouldn't think loving thoughts, but that we should think them through first; if we don't, we should think them through a second time.

In other words, when we do something loving, we should always do it thoughtfully. Otherwise, it would be thoughtless, wouldn't it?'

'I think it would,' I said. 'But I don't know.'

'Don't worry about knowing,' he said. 'Concentrate on thinking. Once we were hunters and gatherers. Now we're not. Because, in the meantime, we thought about things; we thought about everything. Once, we lived half our lives in darkness; now, if I want to read a few pages in *The Last Battle*, all I have to do is flick a switch.'

And he turned on the light that was beside him, but I couldn't see it hardly because the day was too bright everywhere.

'I don't have to read a few pages from *The Last Battle*,' said my father. 'I've finished it. I've finished all of it, except for one thing.'

'The photographs,' I said.

But that was because my father did not like books that had pictures in parts of them. They were for the bus conductors, really; so even his books that were about art did not have the pictures, and he thought that was officer-material, so he did.

'The Index,' he said. 'The Index is at the back of the book; and the Index lists everyone who fought and died in the last battle. Say Index.'

'Index,' I said.

'Good man,' he said. 'Right. D is for Donal. Affirmative?'

'Yes.'

'D. Here we are. Dieppe. Danzig. Dunkirk. Dresden. D-day, Doenitz, Doppler; and lots more. But no Donal.'

'Stop it,' my mother said. 'Please.'

'He's my son,' said my father. 'How do you think I feel when he makes eyes at a minor-league lounge lizard who goes around patting bottoms belonging to women old enough to be my mother?'

'But Donal didn't fight and die in the last battle,' I said. 'He fought and lived. That's why he isn't in the back of the book.'

'Jesus Christ,' said my father. 'Is it any wonder he sweated blood?'

My mother was running her cold, clean fingers up into the leg of my shorts. Then she pulled them right down to my knees, really. Because I had forgotten about the pearls from under my pillow, and the pain of it was hardly at all now.

'Jesus,' she said, and her hand touched my bottom. 'Jesus. What has he done to you?'

Demandez was dancing with his tray on the stony. He was the most happy of all the Demandez I had seen there, because God maybe had gone and given him a brand-new parrot for his shoulder. The nut-bags and the raisin-bags jigged during his skips. That was the height of his delightment, which he sang.

'I shit, you shit, he shits, she shits; we shits, you shits, they shits too.'

He sprang his way to where I was with everything in the world: my snorkel and my waterbottle plus the goggles of Donal.

'Look at that, man. Look at that, Martin. That is shit, man. Shit on the left of me, shit on the right of me.'

His laughter went a bit down the wrong way, and poor Demandez choked on the peace of his mind. So I thumped him on his back but he laughed until he hurt and had to cuddle himself.

'Oh, man,' he said, 'the light of the day is looking at the shit, Martin. The light is looking at the shit of Demandez and the shit of mad Martin, and everybody's shit is looking at the light. Oh, Martin, look. Look there, man.'

He was pointing on his tiptoes out to the sea.

'There's the shit of Alphonse,' he said. 'In any place I know the shit of the shit Alphonse. And look. Look by it. The shit of the priest of the church of the Rue Bernardin. What a shit. What a splendid shit. It has the odour of the sanctity. And out there, out there somewhere, is the shit of the Oslo woman who said that I, Demandez, is a shit.'

He got down onto his hands and his knees and bashed his head off the stony with his dear, dribbly chuckles. His joy was a hundred parrots.

'The shit of the bishop,' he said. 'The shit of the clerk at the bureau for Algerians. The shit of the concierge who makes the pages of my *Playboy* stick together. The shit of you. The shit of Marcel, the shit of Martine, the shit of the most beautiful

Benjamine the Breton. The shit of the student of the Sorbonne who reads the anthropology with a pen on the beach of Demandez. Maybe the shit of the General Charles de Gaulle. It elevates, man. I have never seen such enormity. Our shit has gone to sea to join the French Foreign Legion. We are all coming up, smelling of roses. Oh, man, oh, Martin, this would be a good day for Demandez to die.'

But he was loving the laughing so much that his tray tipped over, and the nuts and raisins bounced onto the stony everywhere.

'Shit,' he said.

That was excellent for my plan. Because Demandez would be blowing the tiny sand off the raisins until his tray would be ready in the right order again. So I walked along the way of the stony and when I came to where the pedalos were, what I did was I pushed it out, and then I pushed it out more, the pedalo nearest to the Riviera.

'Martin. Martin.'

My father's voice was a shout from the balcony of his bedroom. But I didn't look around behind me. Instead of which, I took a pinch of salt and not a pillar of it. And I pushed down harder.

'Martin. Martin.'

In the water was no weight at all. I put on my snorkel over the goggles and I started to pedal.

'Martin. Martin.'

That was my mother's Martin instead of my father's. She had gone and run down through the hotel, and then run across the road to the beach where the stony began. That was what she would have done, really. I knew from how near her voice was to me. And I could see what she would be doing to her hair while she called Martin between her hands.

'Martin.'

There was shit everywhere. That is the truth, the whole truth, and nothing but the truth. And what I wondered was: is any of it Donal's? But you would never get a right order into that. Because it had no beginning and no middle and no end, really. Everywhere that I looked, it was wherever more.

I leaned down to the water with my waterbottle, and I filled it up to the top with the Riviera. And the Riviera went into it with the excellent sound of blubs, by God. What I would do was, I would keep it until I thirsted; or, when I thought of the dear boy, I would sip maybe two small glugs, one for him and one for the old man of my own self.

The sun was nicer there and Menton was quiet as the night would be without a wind to clackety the palm-trees. It was the most quiet of ever, so it was; because, by now, everybody would have found out about the shit and they would be too embarrassed to go out and buy stamps or cut down trees for firewood. And if anybody went and went to the toilet, then everybody else would just look at them in a funny-peculiar way as if they were alphabet soup.

I stood up in the pedalo and I saw the shit and I saw the seagulls in the middle of the world, and I felt that my heart was breaking but I did not know why. Because I was happy in my delightment and sad in my sweating blood. I wondered if it was the case that my happiness and sadness were meant to be together all the time because they would be eating the same food always. And they would take it in turns to lay the table and say the grace.

A gull rested on the far front of the pedalo. Shit bobbed and dunked beside me. The sea broke evenly as far as Africa. I held my arms out to show that I was a friendly, and to let the world know, really, that I was not mad with anything inside it.

'*Dominus vobiscum,*' I said.

MOONLIGHT THE CHAMBERMAID

The other priests hated it when he smelled his slippers. He was not in Africa now.

'Basil.' Luke had leaned over. 'Basil, do you mind?' But he came too close to the hearing aid, and it howled.

'For God's sake,' said the young priest who had started to grow his beard again. 'We're missing the best bit.'

The scene kept shifting from Michael Corleone at the baptism to another murder. A man was shot through his spectacles; then the priest spattered the baby's forehead. The baby made more noise than the man.

'You make the bones in your hands crack,' Basil said. 'You do it all the time.'

'It doesn't annoy anyone,' said Luke.

'I wish I had a portable in my bedroom,' said the young priest. The baptism was over, and so were the murders, almost.

'You even make them crack at the Consecration,' Basil said.

'That's static,' said Luke. 'Static in your hearing aid.'

'Fellows,' said the young priest, 'can we have some peace and quiet?'

'There's no use shouting,' Basil said. 'Can't you see I'm deaf?'

'How many are left?'

She stood in the builder's rubble where the patio would go, and stared through the dead trees at the seminary. The whole of it was in darkness. Once it had been Sir somebody's house, with boot-scrapers and a ballroom. That was where the students had done their exams, filling up their answer-books like dance-cards.

'Not many,' he said. He was still on his hands and knees. He had made a dyke with his paperbacks to stop the water from the

69

washing machine as it seeped across the linoleum in the kitchen to the carpet in the dining area.

'But enough?' she said. She tapped her stomach a bit to make the baby kick, but it didn't. Would it be a difficult child? Or would it be as easy as Aoife?

'Enough what?' he said, and he put a Somerset Maugham behind an Ernest Hemingway, which helped to stem the floodwater.

'Enough for while we're here,' she said. 'So they won't knock it down and build houses, when we went and paid extra for having a wood.'

She steadied the washing-line in the tea-chest in the middle of the builder's rubble, and she hung her underwear on the inside, and draped the duvet cover and two maternity dresses and a shirt of his on the outside, in case she might upset a priest who was elderly.

Basil sat on the side of his bed and used his ventilator. Then he used it again. Apart from his breathing, it was better than a sleeping pill. When he held it in for as long as he was able to, his feet felt lovely. They felt lovely now.

He would finish the painting tomorrow. He would do all the number forties, and some of the number nineteens. If the good weather continued, he could leave it on the window-ledge at night, and it should be dry for the garden fête. It would fetch five pounds, at least; it might even fetch more. You had to have two people bidding against each other to bring the price up. That was why Luke had offered to act as a plant.

Was that his static, or could it be the mouse? He turned off his hearing aid, and closed his eyes to hear better. If they got into the pipes, the sound was enlarged; if they stayed in the skirting, you might miss them. You might think it was your own mattress.

How could there be light in the room, when there was no moon and no stars, and nobody was playing handball under the arc-lights in the handball court? Yet there was light. There was definitely light. It wasn't coming from the construction site, from the new estate. The whole of that was in darkness. None of the houses had been connected. The young couples were lighting candles. He had seen a man and his pregnant wife drive their car right up to their sitting-room window, and paint it late at night by the glare of their headlights. He had seen that happen only the other day. He was sure of it.

He sat on the bed, in front of the painting of the boat at anchor, though he had not done the anchor or the anchor-chain or the bottom half of the lighthouse, and he waited for the mouse. His fingers picked the strings of the tennis racquet.

'Don't do that,' she said.

'What's wrong?' he said.

'What you're doing,' she said. 'You're not supposed to blow into me.'

His head came up from underneath the duvet. His mouth smelled of the sea, and the Toblerone that had made his teeth sting.

'I wasn't blowing,' he said. 'I was breathing.'

'Anyway,' she said, 'it could give me an embolism.'

'Sorry,' the woman said. 'Sorry, Father.'

Basil was examining the plant. He was certain it had moved during the night. But how could he prove it? He would have to carry out a test. Even without a test, he was almost positive; and, at seventy-eight years of age, almost was more than enough; or nearly.

'Mini-maids,' said the woman. 'First Monday of every month.'

He remembered her now. She was the one who said Sorry when she meant Hello. At Christmas, she had used his ventilator, because she was allergic to wax-polish. When he had used it himself later, the queer taste of her lip-gloss was on it, metallic, tart, like the rim of a chalice against a cold-sore.

'Come in,' he said, and he made a revolver out of his hand, and fired it into his ear, to let her know that he was still hard of hearing.

'Lovely day,' she said.

'A lovely day, thank God,' he said. That was important. It cost you nothing to put in the extra 'Thank God'. One of their own

Order had served ten years in a Soviet labour camp for saying 'Thank God' in a private letter. But nobody wanted to hear about that, these days.

'Maybe it'll be nice for the garden fête,' said the woman.

'Please God,' he said.

She had piled her dusters and her spray-cans on the desk. The letter from the hospital was lying against the base of the anglepoise. He wished he had left it open, bent back at the crease where it kept folding, so she could read it as she wiped the typing keys and the hearing aid. She might feel sorry for him. She might let him talk about Africa for a while, without telling him the whole of her own life-story in return.

'Father,' she said. She was inspecting behind the typewriter. 'Do you eat grapes at all?'

'I do,' he said.

'What do you do with the seeds?'

'I eat them,' he said.

The mini-maid dabbed at the back of his desk with a duster. She was trying to flick something off.

'Mouse-droppings,' she said.

Where the poplars petered out, at the end of the gravel pathway, Aoife tripped.

'No bones broken?' Basil said.

'I told her not to run,' said her mother. 'She's only allowed to run if she's wearing trousers and gloves.'

'And a crash-helmet,' her father said. 'She should really wear a crash-helmet, getting out of the bath.'

Basil kneeled down beside the three-year-old, and showed her the inside of his hat.

'See where I keep my bus-pass,' he said; and she reached in, and took it out, and scrutinised it. After that, she was more interested in the hat. Her mother brushed her tights while she put it on.

'I hope we didn't disturb you,' she said. 'I hope you weren't trying to pray.'

She was about to have a baby. It could only be weeks now. He blessed her quietly, moving the fingers of his hand inside the shelter of his pocket.

'Your little girl is the image of you,' he said.

'Everybody says that,' the father said.

'She's a-d-o-p-t-e-d,' said the woman, spelling it out.

'Then they get totally embarrassed,' said the father.

'She's still the image of you,' Basil said, 'so she's very lucky.'

'Aoife,' said her mother, 'give Father his hat.' There could be anything growing in it; now she'd have to wash her hair twice in one day, and that was awful for hair.

'God bless you,' he said.

'Thank you,' she said. 'Thank you very much.'

The whole family watched the old priest walk away, into the dust-cloud of the site machinery, where someone had tied the dead stalks of the daffodils. He seemed to be sucking on something. He was motionless for a moment. Then he moved on.

'Look at his feet,' said the father. 'He's like Charlie Chaplin. Feet at a quarter to three.'

'Did you see his hands?' she said. 'I've never seen such hairy hands.'

'I know,' he said. 'You could comb them.'

'And his nose,' she said. 'I would just love to sit him down, and squeeze all those blackheads.'

'You have a thing about blackheads,' he said to her. 'You're so happy when you see a blackhead.'

'I don't have a thing about blackheads,' she said. 'I just have a thing about squeezing them.'

'God help Aoife when she hits the blackhead stage,' he said.

'I know,' her mother said. 'I know.'

It was a cold night for that time of year. Basil drew his chair closer to the television set.

'What am I watching?' he said to the young priest who was growing his beard again.

'It's a sort of Western,' the young priest said. 'It's more on the side of the Indians, though, except they're not Indians. They're whites, speaking more slowly than usual. But I'm not watching, really. I'm having a think.'

Basil looked at him. He was nicer without the beard. They all were.

'What on earth could you possibly have to think about?' he said.

'The estate,' the young priest said. 'The new houses. You see the strangest things.'

'It's true,' said Luke, who was writing the new names of Third World countries in an old atlas. 'Right across from my window, there's a bedroom where they haven't put curtains up. They have twins, this couple, and the twins sleep in the chest of drawers. I mean, they pull the drawers out, of course. I thought it was great.'

'A woman was putting creosote on her fence,' the young priest said, 'and I was passing, and I thought, well, I'll stop, and shout across, and tell her that the creosote will kill the sweetpea.'

'I wasn't sitting there with, you know, binoculars and a glass of milk,' said Luke. 'I just happened to see them tucking the babies in.'

'Then I noticed,' said the young priest. 'There was this brilliant sunshine, but she was wearing a big, big coat, right; she was wearing gloves; she was wearing a head-scarf, down over her forehead, up over her chin; and huge sunglasses. You could see nothing.'

'I mean,' said Luke, 'I'm not going to put shoe-polish on my windows because they haven't hung their curtains.'

'Perhaps she's a Muslim,' said the middle-aged albino who was playing chess with himself at the other end of the room. 'There are three thousand of them in the country. They all bow towards Wexford, five times a day; except, of course, for the ones who live in Wexford. They bow towards the American submarines in the Irish sea.'

'Somebody is beating her up,' said the young priest.

'Nobody is beating her up,' said Basil.

'You think that was smart,' the albino said, as he made his move, 'but it's going to cost you. It's going to cost you a bishop, boy.'

'The assault and battery is coming from inside,' Basil said. 'She's on Largactil for depression. It makes you blacken in the light.'

'Since when are you a doctor?' said the young priest.

He had to stand up on his feet before he could answer that; and, as he levered himself out of the armchair, his ventilator rolled down his legs onto the carpet.

'Is it Burkina Faso or Furkina Baso?' said Luke. 'Or does it matter?'

Bending was easy. Bending was always so easy. He picked it up; then he picked himself up.

'Well?' said the young priest.

'He saved his bishop,' the albino said. 'I don't know how, but he did.'

'Well what?' Basil said.

'Well, how come you have her whole medical history?'

He could grow a beard like a boyar, this cub with a five-o'clock shadow, but he knew nothing. When he did, God help him; because even God would not be able to, then. You can only experience another person's suffering by suffering another person's experience; before that happens, you can't so much as tell between a sunset and a sunrise, without first looking at your watch.

'Once upon a time,' said Basil, 'I walked ahead of her into the waterfall.'

Whatever attracted butterflies was what they would plant. There would be butterflies everywhere, over the right flowers. She would explain to Aoife's friends that they were not to hold them; their hands were too small. They would have to play in their pop-socks, because of the stuff she would be putting down to kill the slugs and the caperpillars. When it had rained enough, they could go barefoot.

'Do you know what he said?' she said to her husband.

'Who?' he said.

Joseph Conrad and Charles Dickens were hanging on the washing-line. The moonlight made the covers shine like the way they laminate library books.

'The priest,' she said, and shut the window, and closed the locks, and turned on the personal attack button.

'What about him?'

'It was a farm,' she said, 'when he was a novice, or something.

They had cows, and goats for the priests with asthma, because goat's milk is great for asthma. And he killed pigs.'

'Who?'

'The priest,' she said. 'The priest with the blackheads.'

'What about him?'

She sat on the bed and held her enormous stomach like a hot water bottle.

'When the pigs cried,' she said, 'their cries were higher than a boy soprano's.'

'What boy soprano?' he said.

'If it's a boy,' she said, 'I don't ever want him to be a priest. It's a terrible life. There's something about it that isn't Christian.'

'This is all hormonal,' he said.

'Nobody loves that man,' she said. 'They'll find him in the flower-beds, and that'll be that. Somebody else will use his car until they sell it.'

He had had about as much as he could take.

'Georgina,' he said.

'Georgina?' she said.

'Georgina,' he said.

'Like the woman in the Western?' she said. 'You want to call my child Georgina, because you fancied somebody's bum?'

'It wasn't a bum,' he said. 'Bum doesn't do it justice.'

He threw the duvet off him to show her his erection.

'Is that because of Georgina?' she said.

'It was the scene at the river,' he said. 'Now, what am I going to do with him?'

'No,' she said. 'I want you to hold me. I have this horrible, sort of religious feeling about everything. I want you to tell me all the bills we have to pay. I want you to talk me down.'

He lay on his bed with the tennis racquet in his arms, like a Plantagenet prince on top of his tomb, and he watched the moonlight cross the carpet and reach out to the plant, so that it lit up as if it were the shade of a lamp. Before he decided to sleep, he made a mark on the wall behind the middle leaf, with a powdery antacid tablet.

The mouse had not yet come. He had left a folded slice of processed cheese in an open Bible, with his ventilator propping up the Old Testament.

The garden fête went well. The people from the new estate threw sacking over the barbed-wire fence between their clothes-lines and the college grounds, and got in without paying; but the rifle range and the swing-boats made a killing. The mini-maid who always said Sorry bought Basil's picture. He was embarrassed about that, because it wasn't finished.

'You could do the number threes yourself,' he said. 'Number three is cadmium yellow, but don't worry about the cadmium bit. Yellow is yellow, as far as I can see.'

'I like it just the way it is,' she said. 'Anyway, number three is all the sails, isn't it? There's a three on every sail, see. But that could be the number of the sails, instead of the number of the paint for the colours that the sails should be. So I wouldn't regard it as a failure. I think it was well worth two pounds fifty.'

'Do you mean to say you're going to hang it?' Basil said.

'I'm going to hang it in the winter,' she told him. 'For the summer, I'm going to put it in front of the fireplace, to take away the bare look.'

Eight of his other pictures had been sold. Five were Irish landscapes, painted in Africa; and three were African landscapes, painted in Ireland. Then there was one he'd saved, on impulse, at the last minute, before the raffle started. He had painted it in Ibadan; it showed Dun Laoghaire harbour, with a brass band in the bandstand.

'I'd have bought that,' said the mini-maid. 'It has a message in it.'

'A message?' he said.

'Because of the snow falling,' she said, 'and everybody in togs, even the ice-cream man.'

'There was a curfew,' he said. 'I had nothing to do. The radio wasn't transmitting. The generator was out. I found the painting under the bed, when I went after a cockroach. It was a summer scene, from memory. Then I added the snow. I had a toothbrush and two tubes of English toothpaste. I painted by moonlight.

You could hear the gunfire from the Institute. The smell of it was like hot tyres.'

'It's not that simple, Father,' she said. 'There's more to it than meets the eye.'

'It is,' said the pregnant woman. 'It is Father Basil.'

And they shook hands, he with his right, she with her left, because she was holding a cone wrapped in toilet paper.

'I'm Jane,' she said. 'God forgive my parents for calling me that. I am up to my tonsils in Tarzan jokes. Speaking of which, you were in Africa for ages.'

'I was,' he said. 'I was in Africa for an eternity.'

'Thirty years,' she said. 'I wasn't even born. Actually, I was, but that's between you and me and the seal of the confessional.'

'What is?' he said. 'Your age or your lie?'

'Both.' She seemed a bit put out.

'I thought you were twenty,' he said; and she brightened.

'What is Africa like?' she said.

'Big,' he said. 'It goes on and on and on, as if it were looking for something.'

'Were you in the bush?' she asked.

'No,' he said. 'I was in a city. But there were bushes outside my window.'

She decided to laugh, and he decided to laugh with her. Ice-cream was dropping out of the toilet paper.

'I taught,' he told her, 'in a junior seminary. For thirty-eight years. It's gone now. They blew it up. At least, they blew it in. It was an implosion. The whole place disappeared in a flash, classrooms and dormitories. The roar didn't even shake the cocktail sticks in the drinks on the plastic tables under the awning of the café at the corner. Then the children ducked under the barriers, and rushed with open arms into the dust-clouds.'

'That's so sad,' she said, 'when you think about it.' He looked away for an instant, and she chucked her ice-cream cone behind the holly bush. 'I mean, it's your entire life going up in smoke, really, isn't it?'

'Well,' he said, 'there's no smoke without fire, and fire is what matters. I'd sooner end as ashes than as dust.'

'You sound as if you taught English at the seminary,' she said. 'You would never guess where my husband's books are, at the moment.'

'I suppose I did teach English,' Basil said. 'But they called it Metaphysics.'

'Metaphysics,' she said. 'I love the sound of that word. There's one thing, though, that I'm never sure of, and you'll have to forgive my ignorance.'

'Ignorance is always forgiven,' he said. 'If not, the Last Judgement will be like the slaughter of the baby seals.'

'Well,' she said, 'if you teach Metaphysics, does that make you a metaphysicist or a metaphysician?'

'It makes you wonder,' he said. 'That's what it makes you.'

'I'll kill you,' she said. 'I'll kill you, if it's the last thing I do.'

But she was talking to her husband. He had come up out of earshot, on the lee-side of Basil's batteries. The child was on his shoulders. Her face had been painted a bright voodoo.

'Peepo,' said the little one.

'Peepo,' said the priest.

'If you'd seen the face-painter's bum, you'd understand,' the man said. 'I feel I should go home and lie down for a while, preferably with her.'

'You'll go home and drill holes in the patio,' she said, 'or it'll flood the next time it rains.'

'Peepo,' the child said.

'Father Basil, this is my husband,' she said. 'When you've finished pinching yourself, you can call him Albert. If you call him Bert or Bertie, he'll go off and sulk somewhere. But you can call him Al, if you like. It's short for allowances, as in making.'

They were very much in love. He could see that. Unhappy couples always made an effort. If they held hands, you knew they were separating.

'I apologise for his crudities,' she said. 'He's into bums in a big way.'

Basil was foosthering with his hearing aid. The static was like brushfire. Their voices reached him through a burning bush.

'Our Lord was the same way,' he said. 'Skid Row was where he held his clinics.'

'Peepo,' said the child. 'Peepo. Peepo.'

When the fête was ending, Basil walked with his ventilator down the avenue as far as the bricked-up gate lodge, picking up goldfish that had been thrown out of the car windows. Two in their plastic sachets were still alive; the dead one at the speed ramp he put in his pocket, to entice the mouse out. Then he cut across the lawn towards the pond behind the red-hot pokers in the garden of St Joseph the Worker.

The child was already there, without her parents. Did they want her to drown? He held her by the hem of her dress as she leaned out, over the scum and the ice-pop sticks, to drop two dead fish she had found, by their tail-fins, into the winking water.

'I have a tortoise,' she said.

'And he has you.'

'He's a girl,' she told him. 'But he's only a baby girl.'

He gave her the two asphyxiating fish in their sachets, and she threw the knotted bags straight in, before he could stop her. They sank slowly. She kissed them goodbye.

'Home again, home again, jiggedy jig,' she said.

A bluebottle settled on a drifting styrofoam cup. He stared at it.

'The pond freezes in the winter,' he said. 'When you walk on it, the ice makes the very same sound as sticks in a fire. Then it creaks, and it cracks, and the water comes in over your wellingtons. Bless us and save us, you say.'

'If my tortoise could swim,' she said, 'he would be a tortoise turtle.'

She gave him her hand; he led her by it. They turned, and walked away.

'Of course,' he said, 'it should freeze upwards, instead of downwards; but it doesn't. God doesn't mind about the rules, you see. He was thinking about the fishes.'

'Would you look at Basil?' said Luke. 'Would you just look at him?'

The three of them were standing on the steps of Mount Tabor, looking at the booths being dismantled. Behind them, in the hall of the Retreat Centre, the bearded lady was taking newspapers out of his brassière.

'Where is he?' the albino said.

'Do you see a big blur?' said Luke. 'That's the copper beech. He's behind it, with a wee one.'

'Suffer the little children,' said the young priest who was growing a beard.

'Let the little children suffer, you mean,' said Luke. 'She'll be telling her analyst all about it in twenty years' time.'

'What's he telling her?' the albino said. 'The moving plant?'

'The swimming pool,' said the young priest. 'It has to be the swimming pool.'

'No way,' Luke said. 'I know Basil like the back of my hand. It's the boy in his national school.'

'I don't know that one,' the albino said. 'I must have been in Ecuador.'

'The boy who came to class in his father's trenchcoat,' Luke said.

'A rubber trenchcoat,' said the young priest. 'Basil is always particular about the rubber.'

'What about it?' the albino said.

'He had nothing on, underneath,' the young priest said. 'He was naked, except for the trenchcoat.'

'Why?' the albino said. 'Or was it rag-week?'

'His parents were poor,' said the young priest. 'They were stony broke.'

'I wish I could lip-read,' Luke said, and he stood on his tiptoes to watch them, the priest and the child among the thistles and the popcorn. 'I bet you a tenner it's the trenchcoat.'

'I wonder,' the albino said. 'I wonder a lot about those African exploits.'

'I'm not talking about Africa,' said the young priest. 'I'm talking about Ireland, when Basil was a boy.'

'Basil was never a boy,' said Luke. 'He was born with a set of false teeth, and a list of discount laundries for senior citizens.'

'On the other hand,' the young priest said, 'have you tried counting his Christmas cards? It takes you into three figures. Well into three figures.'

'And he sends none out,' said the albino.

The priest and the child were out of sight now.

'He's been good about the slippers,' Luke said. 'Ever since I read him the Riot Act.'

They were silent for a moment. It was almost a moment's silence.

'*Deliverance* is on tonight,' said the young priest. 'What do you say to takeaways?'

'*D'accord*,' said Luke, who loved France, because he had never been there.

'*D'accordo*,' the albino said. He had been to Rome, and they had not.

'Were you in Africa?'

They were searching for fresh goldfish in the field beside the drive, where he had milked cows and thought about Isaiah in a perfect summer when only the water was rationed, and boys of his own age baled out of burning cockpits in parachutes that did not always open.

'I was,' he said.

Even a parent with a strong service couldn't have hurled a fish this far; yet he let her wander on, and ruin her shoes with candyfloss that stuck to the straps.

'What happened?' she said.

'Africa happened,' he told her, 'and I happened in it.'

She thought about this, while he wiped her feet, and the thin strings of candyfloss clung to the hairs of his hands.

'Then what happened?' she said.

'Well,' he said, 'once I buried a child in a violin case. That was during a war. Then I was caught, and I was put in a swimming pool.'

'Can you swim?' she said.

'There was no water in the swimming pool,' he said. 'They let the water out, and then they put us in. The soldiers guarded us. One of them sat on the diving-board, petting his machine-gun, the barrel and the stock, as if he were stroking the ears of a golden retriever. On the Sunday, they let me say mass in the deep end. My altar boy was an ambassador. One of the guards came half-way down the ladder, and I went half-way up, and I gave him Holy Communion.'

'What did he give you?' said the child.

He was still trying to pick the sticky threads off the winder of his watch. The feel of them made him flinch. They nuzzled his palps like a small, soft sac of spider-eggs under a window-ledge. His fingers remembered, remembered everything, everything he had washed his hands of, in a life without gloves. Wherever he had been, his hands had been there before him.

'What?' said the child.

'What's that?' the priest said.

'What the guard gave you.'

'I gave him the host,' Basil said, 'because he had given me the wine.'

'My mummy drinks wine,' she said. 'My daddy drinks Guinness.'

'When the mass was over,' he told her, 'I was taken out of the swimming pool, to hear the charge. The soldier who read it out had to borrow my glasses, because his were broken. He cleaned them on his arm before he gave them back to me. I told him he could keep them. I told him I had two pairs, but I didn't. I had only the one pair. I don't know why I told him that. It is a mystery to me. It is a mystery in me, somewhere. He thanked me, and I was led away. They brought me into the changing-room, and beat me everywhere, except around my appendix scar, because the stitches hadn't been taken out yet.'

'And after that, what happened then?' she said.

'Not much,' he said. 'As you get older, less and less happens more and more often.'

She was looking around her, slowly and sadly.

'There is no more goldfish,' she said.

So he took the dead one from his pocket, and threw it behind him, without turning. He could leave an Oxo cube for the mouse.

'We'll go back and find your mummy,' he said. 'They'll be wondering.'

When she saw the goldfish in among young nettles, he had to cover his hand with his coat-sleeve to free it. She ran ahead of him, making sounds like an ambulance.

'Where is Africa?'

'Over there,' he said, pointing to the trespass sign and the pine-tree that was so gigantic they had cut a cavity the size of a car-port in its lower branches.

'Maybe,' she said, 'I will go there on Sunday.'

She stood at a drain on the side of the drive, and pitched the goldfish in.

'Go straight to the pond,' she said. 'I don't want any messing. Do you hear me?'

He had caught up with her, and was rummaging for his ventilator. He could see her parents strolling down from Mount Tabor, and Luke kick-starting his Kawasaki.

'My tortoise comes from Africa,' the child said. 'He ate a bus-ticket. Then he went into his house for two days.'

'He was dreaming,' Basil said. 'In the dream that he dreamed, he was making a journey. When he woke up, he was back where he started. Then he knew it hadn't been a dream. It had actually happened. Everything was the same, only more so.'

She was tired. She leaned against the window. The moon was as beautiful as an ad she had seen. It made grottoes of the site machinery. Her love-bites paled into insignificance.

'Tomorrow,' she said. 'We'll go to the hospital tomorrow.'

He was reading the novel of *Deliverance*, because he had just watched the film. How could a poet have written it? It was wonderful.

'They haven't given him his clothes yet,' he said.

'I'm not a trendy,' she said. 'I want the baby baptised before he goes on bottles.'

'You're only going to breastfeed for a fortnight,' he reminded her.

She plucked her eyebrows for a bit. Her mouth was bloodshot, like an exit wound. If he had not been married to her, he might have said something he meant. He wanted to leave the light on, and play with her vagina, while her eyes were so detached.

'Every so often, life is always so sad,' she said.

She held her face in her hands, as if it were a mask, and the twine had snapped. His finger traced a chalk-line of pressure from her shoulder to her waist, and then bisected the line. He watched the pink until it faded to a flesh-tone.

'I'll bring him the dressing-gown you don't wear,' she said.

'He doesn't need a dressing-gown,' he said. 'He has his own dressing-gown.'

'Priests don't have dressing-gowns,' she said. 'They're like the army, or prisons.'

'He's not a priest,' said her husband. 'At least, he's not a priest yet.'

'But he will be,' she said. 'He'll end up like Father Blackhead. Unless he falls for one of the nurses.'

'Christ,' he said, 'the man is so mixed-up inside, they give him plastic cutlery. He's been spending forty pounds a week on sprays and stuff. Even now, he's borrowing atomisers from the other patients, whenever the staff aren't looking. And you want him to say "I do" to the first student who takes his blood-pressure?'

'I wish he would,' she said. 'I wish he'd fall in love, and be unhappy forever. I wish he could realise that a third of something is better than the whole of nothing at all.'

Basil could still smell the candyfloss on his hands. Then he reached for his slippers. The streets of the city filled with bicycles and sunlight as he breathed in and breathed out. Children stripped the metal wiring from the matchwood fruit-crates.

Moonlight cleaned the room, and left it tidy as the bleached rectangle of a two-star motel. He breathed again. Outside, in the garden of St Joseph the Worker, the wind had strengthened. The trees clattered and chortled, like lobsters.

He tried to cut his toenails, but he couldn't. His feet were beyond him. Perhaps he had wrenched something, some part of him that had no English equivalent, a nerve-end with a name like a Roman massacre, when he threw the goldfish backwards, behind him. So he gave up, and left his socks on, in case he slit the bedsheet two nights running.

The Oxo cube was in the middle of the floor. He had crushed it with the top of a fountain pen. He lay on the bed, with the racquet between his legs.

If I had to end as catgut, he thought, I would rather go out on a high note, as a violin and not as a volley.

'Father Basil,' said Jane. 'I hand it to you. You do the mass beautifully here.'

They had come out of the church in the college grounds, and were standing in the light of an overcast day.

'Could you hear me?' he said.

'No problem,' she said. 'Loud and clear.'

'The public address system interferes with my hearing aid,' he said. 'And the racket from the machinery on your estate was making the candles tremble. Have they never heard of the sabbath?'

'The builder's name ends in Owski,' she said, 'if you know what I mean.'

'I don't,' he said. 'What do you mean?'

The little girl had emerged, as if from nowhere, out of the silence of his left-hand side. She held her tortoise up to him. One of its legs was half-way out; the rest of it was in hiding.

'Hello, priest,' she said, in a voice like Donald Duck's.

'Hello, tortoise,' said Basil.

'Today,' said the tortoise, 'I had a noodle doodle.'

'I had sardines,' Basil said. 'But I scraped off the tomato sauce, for a friend.'

'What friend?' the tortoise said.

'A mouse. A teeny-weeny mouse.'

'What is his name?' said the little girl. She was quite interested.

'Public Enemy Number One,' said Basil.

The child got down on her knees with the tortoise, and tried to feed it a cigarette butt. They watched her, while they thought of what to say to each other, until somebody came.

'The church is so beautiful,' she said. 'It's so soothing.'

'It's not meant to be,' he said. 'It's meant to be a place of prayer.'

She felt sorry for him. It must be dreadful to be deaf, and get everything arse-ways.

'Has it changed much?' she said, raising her voice and standing closer.

'When I was a student,' he told her, 'there'd be sixty priests saying mass, each at his own altar, up and down the sides of the church. You'd see them in their cloth of gold and hobnailed boots, kneeling, bowing, elevating. In we'd rush from the piggery, us students, with our missals smelling of silage, and we'd serve them. Cowshit and cruets.'

'The good old days,' she said.

'The good young days,' he said. 'We were curious about the world, and curiosity about the world keeps the world at bay.'

What on earth was he talking about?

'You are so, so right,' she said. 'Al is always saying that.'

'Winter or summer,' Basil said, 'the altar smelled like a woman. That was the rosewater. The nuns put rosewater in the steam irons.'

'I think you're very olfactory, Father Basil,' she said. 'Al is very olfactory, too.'

'Mummy,' said the child, 'the tortoise is doing a tut-tut.'

The three of them watched the last of the dinosaurs excrete a slow and stately motion on the footpath. The child petted his shell.

'That is his first tut-tut in his new home,' she said. 'He is pretty happy about it.'

Luke and Al were in conclave.

'I didn't want to talk to Father Basil,' Al said, 'because I always end up on the wrong side of him, away from his Sony. Then I have to shout, and I hate shouting.'

'He's the wrong man to ask about a baptism,' said Luke. 'He's never done one.'

'You're not serious.'

'It's a fact. Moreover, it's true. Marriages, yes. He's done more weddings than a great many couples care to remember. Every fourth sermon, he goes on about the crippled couple, and the crippled twins they had, afterwards. The last time it was triplets, but he is pushing eighty. Of course, he does confessions, lots and lots of confessions, what with being deaf. Mind you, the only people who come to confession these days are pensioners, and they're all deaf as a post, themselves. It ends up sounding like an exorcism.'

87

'But no christenings?'

Luke was wrapping his stole around his wrist like a bandage.

'He did do a christening,' he said. 'He christened a boat on the Niger. He christened it Port of Call.'

'How did that go down?'

'It didn't,' Luke said. 'It was sold as scrap.'

'Don't mind Aoife,' said her mother. 'She's in another world.'

'I know,' said Basil. 'We call it the college grounds and the new estate. She thinks it's earth, air, fire, and water. You should send her to school before it's too late.'

'I don't know,' she said. 'I really and truly don't know.'

She was on his deafer side, so she looked at him freely. He was something of a headbanger, but harmless. Besides, he smelled like her grandfather, and she had liked her grandfather, until he went blue in the face and died in front of her, which was awful for a seventeen-year-old.

'We have to go to a hospital,' she said. 'Not a medical hospital, either. We have to visit a friend; a cousin, in fact. He was in before. He made two stools for us, and he couldn't eat cheese until he stopped taking the pills. Now he's back in. He's the world's worst worrier. Do you know that he's crying in each and every one of his baby photographs? It had nothing to do with teething, either. It had to do with his genes. I just hope and pray it doesn't come out in the baby. Genes can go sideways as well as down, you know.'

She made him bless her bump, and he did, but discreetly. There were people around.

'I don't know what to bring him,' she said.

'Bring him two hundred cigarettes,' said Basil.

'He doesn't smoke,' she said.

'With filters,' he told her. 'Otherwise the poor man will get his fingers burnt.'

Aoife had discovered that the tortoise would come out, if she turned him upside down. She set him on his back on the ground, and spun him with her hand. He went in again, fast. There was no end to what you could find out about tortoises.

'Aoife,' she said. 'Aoife. Stop the messing. We've to go now.'

'To the dreams?' the child said.

'Yes,' said her mother. 'To the dreamers. Each of them dreams a bit of the world, and, if they didn't, the world would be undreamt of. Now hurry up.'

'What about my tortoise?' she said.

'He can mind the boot,' she said. 'And afterwards I'll bring you to the café where the piano plays by itself.'

Actually, it was a lovely place. They had put in wind–chimes, and a little waterfall. You could eat off the carpets, if you wanted to. In fact, one of the patients was, until a nurse had a word with her. The nurses had nicer accents than the doctors.

'Declan,' she said, 'do you have Plan B, or does the Order have a group policy?'

He had been making an elaborate child's jigsaw of the world, with animals on every piece, and all of the penguins missing from Antarctica, so there was a hole at the bottom.

'Do you know what you should do?' said Al, and he lit two cigarettes at the same time, one for himself and one for the man with the eyes like two scooped-out oyster shells. 'You should make some pieces to finish the jigsaw, or maybe get somebody to cut the cardboard, and then draw, you know, draw the penguins in. You're great at drawing. Aoife still has, you know, the Meesther Mouse one, with the sombrero.'

'Don't be silly, Aoife,' said her mother. 'Don't put that there. There aren't any camels in Australia.'

But it fitted exactly, in between the koala and the kangaroo.

'It's not meant to be there,' she said. 'You'll break it.'

'It is meant to be there,' her husband said. 'Look at the cover. There. That's a camel.'

'Well,' she said, 'whoever made this jigsaw needs his head examined.'

The man in the dressing-gown was tipping the ash from his cigarette into the palm of his other hand. The nurse had forgotten to trim his thumbnails. Their moons were half-way up.

'Look,' said the child, 'there's tortoise.'

It was sitting on its bottom, reading a comic, beside Lake Uganda. Tortoise-shell spectacles perched on its button nose.

'So it is,' said her father. 'They must have made the jigsaw before he left Africa.'

His beard, she thought, was the colour of builder's rubble. You could not hope to get better with a beard like that. A beard like that would get anybody down.

'No,' said the child. 'Do you know what? This is not tortoise. Tortoise is not like that, Daddy.'

'She's growing up, at last,' her mother said. 'Did I tell you about the dwarf, Declan? The dwarf on our estate. It's so embarrassing.'

'This,' said Aoife, 'is tortoise's mummy. Because, look.'

'Bring it home,' said the man in the dressing-gown. 'Bring it home to show tortoise, and he can look at it at night, before he goes to sleep. Then he'll dream about her.'

'No,' she told him. 'Tortoise is not one of the dreamers. He is a bit of the world.'

'I dreamed about you,' he said. 'It was lovely.'

The two adults got up to go.

'When they let you get dressed,' she said, 'you won't know yourself. The nurses will be queuing to give you your pills.'

He wanted to say something, but he found it hard.

'What is it?' she said. 'What is it, love?'

'You wouldn't have change,' he said, 'for the cigarette machine?'

They sat in the café, and he stirred his cappuccino until it was cold. He hated the taste of them, but he loved placing the order.

'Well?' he said.

The piano that played by itself was absorbed in the slow movement of a Beethoven concerto. The child sat on the stool in front of it, and turned the pages slowly, pausing and parting as the music paused, until she had worked her way right through the album of traditional Irish airs, and the last phrase slid toward silence at the very same moment.

'No fucking way is he going to christen a child of mine,' she said. 'He'd probably go to pieces at the font, and start telling us all to love one another.'

★

The plant had moved.

He chalked behind it with the antacid, rubbing the grubby tablet up and down, until it broke in half. The space between the two chalk-marks, the new one and the one he had made before, was the width of a coin, of a lucky penny you might lose in the lining of a coat. No mouse could have moved a plant-pot. It would take a rat to do that, or a house-pet, and there were neither in this place. There were men, and there were mini-maids: that was the sum total.

He was reasonable; and it was reasonable to be rational. The mini-maids might have shifted it. Yet they came only once a month, with their J Cloths and their canisters of Pledge, their diamond cluster rings on string around their necks; and he had always, always been there to receive them. They would talk about black ice and anti-cyclones. He would feel sorry for them; they would feel sorry for him. The room would begin to smell like a hedgerow. Then the supervisor would look in, and the mini-maid would ask him to hold her cigarette, and the hedgerow would be bulldozed.

Not one of them had ever disturbed it.

He had told the albino. He may have told Luke; he couldn't remember. It was possible they were playing a prank. They might have stolen into his room, while he was out, or in the church, or watching the 'Antiques' Road Show.' They knew he never missed it. Moving it around would make a great story. The whole community would be laughing behind the Sunday supplements. The Provincial would permit himself a February flicker.

Yet it had moved before he mentioned anything. It had turned in a slow astonishment towards the moonlight, as if the moonlight were the dry rain of the sun. He had been there. He had seen it take place. He was a witness, and an eye-witness. Therefore, it might have happened.

He would lock the room, in future, and take the key with him. He would ask the rector for the master-key, if necessary. Then there were things you could do with tape and bubble-gum, along the inside of the door, to show if anyone had broken in. That would put a stop to all monkey-business.

He rolled his shirtsleeves up to the elbows, and dipped them in the moonlight, rinsing his wrists.

'Serenese,' she said. 'He's on Serenese.'

She held his cheeks apart as he moved inside her. Then he was about to come, so he thought of his father putting on five pairs of underpants when his rectal cancer reached the bleeding stage, and his heart hardened, and his penis softened, and he started again.

'It doesn't sound like medicine,' she said. 'It sounds like lingerie.'

'What does?' he said.

'Serenese,' she said.

'Serenese what?' he said.

They were quiet for a while. The moonlight ghosted their silence. It whitened his eyes, and blackened her eye-shadow.

'Who are you thinking about?' she said.

'The woman,' he said, moving up and down; but slowly now, more slowly. 'In the café.'

'She was so common,' she said. She scratched at his anus with her finger. 'She was as common as dirt.'

'It was the way the seat sighed when she stood up,' he said. 'It sighed, and kept her shape for ten minutes.'

'She was common,' she said, and she moved her finger farther in. 'She had hair up to her belly-button. Her boobs had two different tan-marks. She was a tart.'

He tensed from his toes, and came.

'Good boy,' she said. 'Good boy.'

They lay, and listened to the tumble-dryer in the kitchen. His nose nuzzled her.

'That's how the baby hears my heart,' she said. 'It's like a tumble-dryer.'

He drooped his face in her hair, and breathed through his mouth the taste of diesel and the bubbles she had made for Aoife from the washing-up liquid. Her free hand found a fresh scab on the nape of his neck, but it was not quite ready to be picked. She made a mental note.

'That must be why people buy tumble-dryers,' she said.

They were tender, and disappointed. They hugged, to put off looking at each other.

'I hope you cleaned yourself,' she said, wiping her finger on his bottom. 'I hate it when you don't clean yourself.'

'I hate it when you do,' he said.

'Get out, Al,' she said. 'I'm itching.'

He went downstairs, and smoked a cigarette, and watched three minutes of a documentary about dowries in the Punjab; and then he went upstairs, into the child's room, and tickled her hand until she turned in her sleep.

'I love you,' he said. 'I love you more than I love anyone. I love you more than I love Mummy. I love you more than I love God. I love you more than God loves you.'

He slipped back to his room, naked except for his wife's flip-flops and the nicotine stains on his fingers. She was kneeling on the bed, drying the stain on the sheet with the hair-dryer.

'I'm going to ask Father Basil,' she said. 'I'm going to ask him to do the christening.'

'He's never done one,' he said. 'I told you.'

'That's the point,' she said. 'It'll mean much more. He won't be rushing through it. He won't be looking at his watch. It'll be special.'

'Suit yourself,' he said. 'You know me.'

'Besides,' she said, switching off the hair-dryer, 'when you say it, there are all those Bs. It's a good omen.'

'What's a good omen?' he said.

'Basil,' she told him, 'will be baptising the baby, but not belatedly.'

The surgeon showed Basil to the door.

'What a beautiful day it is,' he said.

'Thank God,' Basil said.

They shook hands. The warm wind from the street carried a fragrance of buses and sun-oil into the hall, like an Interflora delivery. A woman who was almost as pregnant as the chatter-box on the new estate, struggled up the stone steps and squeezed between them.

'I'm very sorry,' she said, and went upstairs, holding the banister, like a polio case.

'Don't tell me that poor woman's got cancer,' Basil said. 'Not on a day like this.'

'No,' said the surgeon. 'She's for my friend across the landing, the honourable member for the stroke of midnight. He's a psychiatrist. You can always tell his patients. They look like passengers walking past a Customs officer in the Green Zone.'

They shook hands again, because Basil had forgotten that they had already been through that part of it.

'Are you sailing much?' he said to the surgeon. 'You must be sailing a lot, in weather like this.'

'I have the stuff in the boot,' said the surgeon. 'I'll be out in the Bay by six-thirty, if I'm lucky. I've three more cases.'

'Are they the same as myself?' Basil said.

'One is,' the surgeon said. 'Two will be grand, please God. The third is very problematical.'

'Poor man,' said Basil. 'On a day like this.'

'Actually, he's very happy,' said the surgeon. 'I inherited him from the honourable member. We do the odd bit of horse-trading.'

'Tell me this,' Basil said.

'Surely,' said the surgeon, and he guided Basil toward the steps at the same time. He had heard the phone ringing in the surgery. That would be his daughter, calling from a pub, to give him the low-down on the second Physiology paper. If she dropped it again, he'd buttonhole the examiner at the club regatta, and tell him a few home truths, in no uncertain terms.

'I had conjunctivitis a fair few times in Africa,' said Basil. 'Apart from that, though, and wearing glasses, my eyes have always been, you know, up to the mark.'

'And you're wondering?' said the surgeon, who was beginning to wonder himself. His receptionist had finally answered the ringing.

'Are my eyes any use?' said Basil.

'What's happening to you,' said the surgeon, 'won't in any way affect the vision you have at present.'

'I don't know how to do it,' Basil said, 'but I would like to leave my corneas.'

94

The receptionist was tapping at the window, and pointing to the phone in her hand.

'No problem,' said the surgeon, as he started up the steps. 'Don't worry your head about it. It's the easiest thing in the world.'

The receptionist was smiling, giving the thumbs-up sign.

'Here we go, here we go, here we go.'

He had not known it was the last day of the steam-train service, out along the coastline to the dormitory towns. Half of the passengers were in fancy-dress. It was like Gilbert and Sullivan without the chorus or the choreography. He had never seen so many frock-coats, malacca canes, hooped petticoats and Plymouth Brethren bonnets. The boy beside him was dressed for the Boer War; his girlfriend decked herself as a Whitechapel tart, and drank white wine from a tartan thermos: it dribbled down her chin and throat, and into her private parts. She wiped her mouth, and the subaltern's moustache fell from the bounder in the boater and the big striped blazer, who was leaning above her, holding the hand-strap. It lay in her lap like a shaped pubis, a pucker of lipstick, and everyone laughed, everyone died laughing; everyone sang again.

'Here we go, here we go, here we go.'

Could they not sing something nice from Gilbert and Sullivan? The one that he could not remember from 'Pinafore' would be beautiful, on such a beautiful day. On such a beautiful day, they would sing it as beautifully as the boys had, in Africa. They had belted it out, no bother to them; and the child who could not climb the rigging, because of his stumps, had soaped the decks instead, had sung, sung, sung his heart out, and his little leper's ribs a birdcage full of larks and linnets, soaring and stopped, under the footlights that went on fire, sometime in the second week, the same week that the community fridge was stolen.

That was the year, whenever it was, that Princess Grace Kelly had married your man. But it did not matter about the date. Yesterday evening was as much buried in dust and ashes as the pricelists in the storefronts of Pompeii. It was past. That was the

95

point. It was past, and it was past understanding. He understood that much.

'Here we go, here we go, here we go.'

They were passing the bird sanctuary, where two children had been drowned and there were no birds at all. Four boys, five of them, were walking into the water, lifting their arms above it, letting it lap the tops of their legs, the strings of their togs. One of them cupped a cigarette he was smoking, and ducked down under. When he surfaced, it was still alight. He blew a cloud: the others cheered. Even the boy on the wall, the boy minding the clothes, clapped.

'Tickets. Tickets, please.'

He had been about to bless them. He had moved the fingers of his hidden hand, the hand in his pocket. But the train was moving too quickly, and the ticket inspector was saying 'Sorry, Father', and already he could hardly tell them from the seagulls.

'A quid for a quickie,' said a Coldstream Guard to the Whitechapel whore. His chin-strap was under his nose. That was the wrong way, surely.

'A tenner to watch me, and twenty to match me,' she said. 'Plus you have to quote something in Victorian.'

'I can only quote Access,' he said, but he found a twenty-pound note in his cuirass.

'I meant, in today's money,' she told him. 'Can your pound of flesh stretch that far?'

She laughed, and the others around her laughed, and he laughed too, eventually.

'In today's money?' he said. 'I'm afraid I don't know what you're worth in today's terms. Anyway, I don't have change of a fiver.'

An ordinary passenger had squeezed through the nineteenth century, and had taken the window seat, opposite Basil. His hands kneaded his knee-caps. Perhaps he'd been praying.

'Beautiful day,' said Basil. 'Thanks be to God.'

The man nodded. His lips made a shape, but no sound. When he breathed, bubbles shone for a second at the sides of his mouth. Then the gleam was gone until he breathed again. The noise of his breathing was like feet moving through undergrowth. It was stricken, obstructed; twigs and the slick whiplash of dry stalks. Basil was glad when the youngsters sang again.

'I'm sitting at a railway station,
Got a ticket for my destination.'

Could he be an asthmatic? Could that be it? Why didn't he use his ventilator, then? Of course, he might have forgotten it. Basil had forgotten his a thousand times. Once, they had had to give him cortisone in the back of beyond, when he was upriver, inspecting schools. He had filled a plastic petrol container with boiling water, and lain in bed, holding it against his chest to ease the breathing; and he had drunk, drunk half a bottle of whiskey, into the bargain. Afterwards, he had prayed for the inventor of cortisone each day for three months, until he forgot about it. Ever after, he carried a ventilator with him, day and night. When he said mass, he brought it to the altar. That was the way he was. He was a belt-and-braces man.

A Frankenstein lookalike was taking pictures of his peers. The pictures came out in a matter of minutes, and everybody passed them around to everybody else.

'I'm not Frankenstein,' the photographer was saying. 'I'm Frankenstein's monster. Frankenstein looked like a lab technician.'

Should he offer him his ventilator? Come to that, should he give it to him, outright? He was not going to need it, himself. The dampness of this year's autumn need not disconcert him unduly.

'I'm sorry,' he said. 'Excuse me.'

But the man did not hear him, over the wheels and the laughter. He was rubbing foreheads with his own reflection, while the small bags of spittle frothed and failed between his lips. The tiny veins on his cheeks were the tributaries of two parched river-beds running down his face on either side. They were like those rivers in Africa, that try to cross the desert, and make it almost half-way, perhaps, and disappear, like the print of a lizard's tail on the sand, when the wind begins to blow.

Basil leaned back in his chair.

The man was emphysemic. He might have lung cancer, even. That must be the worst of all, because you would have the remorse to cope with, and you would want to stop at, say, a cinema queue, and tell the smokers not to, not to, on such a beautiful day.

'Why not "Imagine"?' said a Hussar with handlebar moustaches.

'That's shit,' said the Whitechapel whore. 'That's for a folk-mass.'

'What about "Me and Bobby McGee"?' said Frankenstein's monster. He was still taking photographs.

'Nobody knows the words,' said the tart. 'They say they do, but then they break down. Or everybody starts humming at about line three.'

It came over him like the tiredness a man feels, when he sits down for the first time after a day's work, and his wrists tremble on the arm-rests, from ten hours with a saw and a spirit level. Suddenly he felt grief, or what he thought might be grief, because he had nothing to compare it with, apart from Africa, and leaving Africa. He had always assumed that leaving Africa had been a clear case of grief, but perhaps it was wrong to speak in those terms about a place and a posting. The man who was sitting opposite might be leaving a wife and children. It was true that he wasn't wearing a ring, but he might have taken it off years ago, because his finger had grown too stocky, and put it for safe-keeping in his sock drawer.

'Silent night, holy night,
All is calm, all is bright.'

They had found the one song they could agree on. They sang it with oomph, quick-time, like a Waffen SS march. The emphysemic pumped the sole of his sandal on the floor, and stared out the window at the moored boats turning in the wind from Africa.

When they had sold the seminary, he had been touring the secondary schools, two hundred miles to the north. On the day of the sale of contents, he was holding a heavy blackboard, with the answers written on it, at the slanted skylight windows of the gym where the boys were sitting with their left-handed fountain pens that you could buy in bulk for half the price. The invigilator had noticed nothing, of course. He was content with the brand-new Winston Churchill five-shilling piece Basil had given him, tucked in a satin cufflinks' case.

'That's not "Silent Night",' said the bounder in the boater. 'That's "Away in a Manger". "Little Lord Jesus" is "Away in a Manger", for Christ's sake.'

'What about something Country and Western?' said another prostitute, who was blowing down into her dress to cool herself.

' "Me and Bobby McGee" is sort of Country and Western,' said Frankenstein's monster, and he lifted the pleats of the prostitute's crinoline, and took a photograph of her thighs, before she could say Boo.

'Easy on, lads, easy on,' said one of the regular passengers.

The auction was over, and the building had been emptied, when he came back to the city. He had walked about the house, from room to room, listening to the clean carpentry, the altered sounds, filling the blond rectangles on the walls where the watercolours of his Irish mountains and his Irish mountain ash had hung. A few fouled antimacassars were all that were left. Someone had used them to protect his hands while he wrenched the fans out of the ceiling.

'This isn't lacy sea-spray stuff,' said the monster, as the picture cleared. 'This is Marks and Spencer's.'

Basil had got down on his hands and knees, and collected the maroon paper-slips with the longhand lot numbers written on them, and stuffed them into his pockets, moving on all fours through the folding doors that had been stripped of their knobs and their locks and their oblong finger panels. Dozens of the slips petalled the community living-room, because the chandelier had been sold in a hundred sections. He gathered them in fistfuls, and the pins nipped him, and one of them slipped under a nail, and he could see it sliding in; and it made him whimper. He sat on his bottom, and listened to the wind fidget under the roof like the indecision of mice.

Those lop-sided pops from the man's mouth had done it. His breathing had made Basil breathless. The priest loosened his coat, and squeezed his fingers in under his collar to open his top button. But there was none; it was missing. He got up then. He could not stand it any longer; he could not sit it out. He pressed past the degenerates, along the carriage, and out of it.

' "Eleanor Rigby",' one of them said. 'I vote "Eleanor Rigby".'

'Eleanor Rigby' it was. They begin to sing it, softly at first, and then more aggressively, because the train was drowning it out. Some of them shut their eyes, and one of them tidied her hair as she intoned the words, and then she remembered the holes under the arm-sleeves of the dress she had rented, and her brown bun tumbled.

'I forgot I had holes,' she said, and they hooted; and a Degas dancer rested her head on Mr Gladstone's shoulder.

He was in the corridor, with his collar in his hand. He reached up, and pulled the cord. No one would notice. There were too many people around. He waited for something to happen, for whistles and pistons, for the train to dry-retch to a stop. But nothing did happen, so he pulled it again. Then he was afraid, and ashamed. He hid in the toilet, sitting on the bowl that had no seat, sucking on his ventilator.

They were stationary. The hissing of the train had faded into the humming of bees in the good-for-nothing hedges. His feet widened and warmed as he exhaled. When the dizziness hit him, he ducked his head.

There was a knocking, which was not his heart.

'Who's in there?' said a voice.

Basil looked at his face in the mirror. The two halves of his head were broken by a long crack in the glass, a map of the Nile that ran right down, and found its source in the cold-water tap-drip.

'I am,' he said. 'Me.'

'Open up,' said the voice. 'Come on. Open up.'

He had put his collar on. He blinked at the guard.

'Sorry, Father,' the man said. 'Some cunt pulled the cord.'

'How do you know it was a woman?' said one of the Victorian ladies.

'I'm not saying it was a woman,' the guard said. 'I'm sure it wasn't a woman.'

'Then why don't you say that?' said the girl. 'Why don't you say that some hairy bollocks pulled the cord?'

'Can you settle an argument, my good man?' said Franken-stein's monster. 'Is it the emergency cord or is it the communica-tion cord?'

'Look, Miss,' said the guard.

'I'm not a Miss,' she said. 'I'm a Mrs; I'm Mrs Langtry. I'm one of Edward the Seventh's mistresses.'

'Let's have a show of hands,' the monster said. 'Emergency or communication?'

Basil went back to his seat, and sat down. It was still warm. It had all been a matter of minutes, a moment of time. The emphysemic was asleep, his lips swollen and soft like a monkey's anus.

'Father,' said the Whitechapel tart, 'you can have this. You're in it.'

It was one of the Polaroids. Behind the epaulettes of the soldier who had moved at the wrong second, and the laughing teeth of a gaslight prostitute, he could see himself and the man who made bubbles.

'No, thank you,' he said. 'I'm not photogenic.'

He handed it back to her.

'Are you sure?' she said. 'Dead sure?'

'Cross my heart, and hope to die,' he said.

'Going once,' she said, 'going twice, going three times.' And she crumpled it between her gloved hands.

From the way they had been sitting in the snapshot, the two of them, the way they were looking at each other, the man who was dying and the priest without his collar, anyone would have thought that the picture showed two people who had boarded the train together, who had chosen to sit together, and were having a conversation about coastal erosion or the benefits of the free pass. They might have been taken, even, for two friends.

You could not believe your eyes in this world, he thought to himself. You could only believe your blindness. With a calm, compulsive liar, you knew where you stood.

The train braced itself, and began again.

'Here we go,' they chanted. 'Here we go. Here we go.'

'Father,' said the brother who was washing the floorboards in the hall of the house. 'I have messages.'

'I see,' Basil said.

'Don't stand there,' said the brother. 'Go that way. Your doctor rang.'

'What did he want?'

'He wanted,' the brother said, wringing a chamois, 'to know how you are.'

'What did you say?'

'I said I didn't know. Then a lady rang.'

'A lady?'

'A lady,' the brother said. 'When they call me Father, I call them ladies.'

'Who was she?'

'No idea. I didn't ask her. She said you know her. She said you know her daughter. She said her daughter has a tortoise.'

'I know the child,' Basil said. 'I know the tortoise.'

'She wants you to christen her baby. She wants you to ring her. Of course, she said "call". "Have him call," she said.'

'What did you say?'

'I said I didn't know.'

He drew his hand out of the galvanised bucket, as if it were a police exhibit, and blew the suds off. The number on the inside of his wrist had begun to run.

'Is that a zero?' Basil said.

'No,' said the brother, 'that's the way I do my sixes. That's a zero beside it.'

'That's an eight,' said Basil.

'No,' said the brother. 'That's a hair.'

'You'll be the death of me,' Basil said. 'Do you know that?'

'That's right,' the brother said. 'That's right. Kill the messenger.'

He let it ring for a long time, but there was no answer. It must be a larger house than he'd realised. He rang again and waited, adjusting his aid almost to maximum.

'Hello,' said a voice, and the voice cleared his throat, or tried to.

'Good afternoon,' Basil said. 'Could I trouble you to speak a little more loudly?'

There was the slightest pause, as if the voice were speaking from the other side of the world.

'Hello,' the voice said. 'I'm sorry to say I'm not quite in at the moment, but I should be fully in, in just a little while. If you'd like to leave your name, rank, and telephone number, I'll get back to you just as soon as the de-briefing is over. Please wait for the pips, and then deposit.'

He could hear somebody laughing in the background. It was distant and drowned-out, but it was still there. He must have a crossed line, or a crossed wire, or whatever the technical expression was. He pressed his hearing aid to the hand-set.

'Pip,' the voice said. 'Pip, pip, pip, pippity pip.'

Now the laughter was louder. Perhaps the boy with the beard was ringing from the same extension, at the wall-phone on the upstairs landing, outside the oratory of St Stephen the Martyr.

'Is there anybody there?' said Basil.

'Pip,' the voice said. 'That is the final pip out of me.'

'This is Father Basil,' he said. 'Father Basil from the college. I am trying to get through, but I don't understand what I've done. I think I've done something wrong.'

There was a different tone, now, at the other end. He moved the hand-set from one ear to the other, but he could hear nothing. The line had gone dead.

He took a walking-stick from the upturned shell-case that some serving officer had salvaged from the birch-woods of Ypres, and turned by a trick of decoration into an umbrella stand, and he set off out. Otherwise, they might think he was a boor, or doddery. They might think twice about him; they might not think at all. They might look elsewhere.

'Oy yoy,' said the brother, down on the maplewood parquet. 'Not there, for Pete's sake. Go around the wet, will you? You're leaving your bloody great footprints all over the place.'

He draped his coat along a low stretch of the barbed-wire barricade, and swung his left leg over. The right was more difficult, because of the pin. He held it under the knee, and hoisted it. Then he was down in the trench, among the foxgloves and the stacked, synthetic gutters, where the cats came to bat the shrews when they were bored with the dirty soup-bowls of low-fat milk.

The lenses of his glasses were already yellow with pollen and the dust of the construction site. He leaned against the belt-drive slate conveyor, and inhaled two cold puffs from his ventilator. It was either Heatherview Drive or Heatherview Crescent, he thought; or perhaps it was Heatherview Grove. Whoever had named the site had worked from picture postcards and a springtime setting, when he christened it. No one had told him that the farmers would ignite the fields on the feast of St John the Evangelist as the newlyweds were hanging out their washing.

Yet he blessed them, blessed them with his hidden hand, as he picked his way along the flints of a future path, wishing the thin walls well, and the washed company cars; blessing in brief Latin courtesies the pulverised muck where the broken bamboo sticks bore brief Latin inscriptions, and tripping twice, three times, on the severed arteries of grey ground-cables. Shelters with even numbers stared across a mud-flat at shelters with numbers that were even odder; and metal milk-containers with moveable clock-hands sunned themselves on the doorsteps. Fresh varnish on the doors was furred with tiny insects; the spy-holes glinted.

'Amen,' he said. He was out of breath again, sucking through his teeth the good flavour of putty and hosepipe and hot zinc. They were the smells of Africa. He could be there; he could be there now. The blackbird, even, calling from somewhere behind the cement-mixer, could be the mina that they kept at the college, and trained in total darkness to imitate the thrush and the curlew, the cries of home, by playing and re-playing hour-long quarter-inch tapes that had been sent out from Dublin in the diplomatic pouch.

He opened his eyes and saw a white man in cricket trousers, measuring a strip of mud with a long retractable ruler; and behind him he saw the tortoise, tethered to the stake of a rose-tree by a yard of thread which was sellotaped to the centre of his shell.

Their car was in; but the upstairs curtains were drawn. He peered in the living-room window, and saw the child, asleep in front of the television, with her head on a large toy tiger. She had been watching a cartoon. He could just make out a little boy, or girl, talking to a giant and to Queen Elizabeth of England, or, at any rate, to someone who resembled her. Perhaps it was 'Jack and the Beanstalk'. There was a giant in that.

He didn't want to ring at the door. He didn't want to disturb them. The mother must be resting; it was almost her time. So he wrote his name in the dust on the outside of the window; he wrote 'Father Basil'. Then he wrote it in reverse, which took more time, beginning with 'l' and ending with a small 'f', in order that they could read it easily and at once, from indoors.

'A single blow like that would kill a man.'

They were watching a barroom brawl in a Western called 'Paint Your Wagon'. The albino had the best chair, because he had got the picture to stay still.

'It's only a comedy, Basil,' said Luke, and he made the bones in his hands crack as he stretched them over the edges of the arm-rests.

'I know it's a comedy,' Basil said. 'But they do it in the tragedies, too. Nobody seems to realise that a single blow can kill a man. I hit a boy when I was small, and his nose bled for a whole morning. His copybook stuck together.'

'The Pope likes boxing,' said the young priest whose beard had matured to the point where it looked like a small attachment for a vacuum cleaner. 'When the day's work is done, he blows out all the candles and he watches satellite sports stations.'

'He may like boxing,' the albino said, 'but he knows fanny adams about the Marquis of Queensberry rules. He's a bareknuckle boyo. He'd poleaxe you between press-ups.'

'Poleaxe is a bit below the belt,' said Luke. 'When he was over, you had his picture on your key-ring. You kneeled through the mass in the Phoenix Park, and you weren't even there. You were watching it on television.'

'It was Basil made me kneel,' the albino said. 'He kept on at me the whole time, with his Praise the Lord this and his Praise the Lord that.'

'I never said Praise the Lord,' Basil told him. 'What I said was *Laudate Dominum*. You may all be social workers without so much as a razorblade between you, but I know my genealogy.'

'Blast and damn it,' said the small attachment. 'There it goes again.'

Legs and lingerie stormed across the top of the screen, and heads in stetsons bounced in the lower part of the picture.

'It's Basil,' he said. 'He's making it go wonky. He has the power.'

At least they had stopped hitting each other with broken bottles. He couldn't bear to see a skull being struck, its sub-atomic libraries going up, archive after archive, in great big bonfires, a burning of books. For it wasn't the body that was the temple of the Holy Spirit. It was the other way round. The temples were where the Comforter made his home. She would find that out a hard, hard way, the chatterbox who was due any day now. She would ask for gas or a gag. She would learn that labour is the deliverance of a brain and not the delivery of a body. The head fights and the rest follows. He had seen it in Africa, and gone away and been confused, so that he consecrated the wine before the bread, and wondered for years if it had been a valid mass.

'Come on now, Basil,' the albino said. 'Concentrate. This is important. Make it go back to the way it was. Heads up and tails down.'

'There's no more fighting in it,' Luke said. 'There's just a few songs. I've seen it before. I saw it with a woman I had to visit, because her husband had gone off the road into the reservoir, only it was winter and all of his windows were down. But she wouldn't talk about it. She gave me fairy cakes and we watched "Paint Your Wagon". This is as true as I'm sitting here.'

'Nobody move,' the albino said. 'Nobody blink. Nobody breathe.'

He had got the picture back, and the colour too. The colour was almost right. The whiskey would not have alarmed a whiskey drinker. It might have been twenty-year-old. It was on the counter, too, where it should be, about to be drunk down.

'Easy does it,' the albino said. 'Everybody stay where he or she is. It has to do with the distribution of weight in the room; and it has to do with waves.'

'Waves?' said the boy with the beard. 'What waves?'

'I don't know what waves,' the albino said. 'Waves that are everywhere. They go in and out of you, and you don't know it. In an age of superstition, we called them spirit-voices; in an age of science, we call them soundwaves. So stay where you are.'

But Basil had had enough. If it had been 'Zulu' or 'The Caine Mutiny', he might have stayed. What he liked in a film was dialogue, that and the marvellous moment when a man sees clearly through himself for the first time, the sand of his life turned into crystal by the moved, unmoving glassblower. That was usually at the end of the film, unless it was modern and European, in which case it would be at the start. In either event, he would always have to busy himself, lace his boots or pull his socks up, to ensure that nobody in the community had noticed the bright slime on his lens.

The picture rose and stuck like a dumb waiter.

'For Christ's sake, Basil,' they said.

He walked on his tiptoes past them, and past the albino kneeling at the television.

'Remember,' he said. 'A single blow is all it takes. Right through a double-period of Geography, while the teacher was explaining glaciers, the poor boy kept his legs as far apart as possible so the blood wouldn't ruin his trousers. In the afternoon, when school was over, I filled my shoes with thumb-tacks, and I walked home in them.'

'You're a saint,' Luke said. 'Harry Secombe will sing at your grave.'

'I did it because I was terrified,' said Basil. 'I was terrified of my parents. I was terrified of having to take off my clothes and lie over the nest of tables.'

She waited for the port to cool, and swallowed it then in one go. He had put in too much sugar. Even the lemon was sweet when she nibbled it.

'Well?' he said.

'Can't you wait a moment?' she said. 'It has to cross the placenta.'

'I meant the phone call,' he said, and he took off his shorts, and folded them to hide the stain. He would have to wear his togs tomorrow. The washing machine was up to its old tricks.

'He knew it was you,' she said.

'Of course he knew it was me. I told him it was me. But then I told him it was a recording. "This is a recording," I said.'

'He's not stupid,' she said. 'He may be simple, but he's not stupid. He's as old as electricity; you're not even as old as the transistor radio. So it has to be dinner; and I mean dinner. I mean a tie and a top button. I mean no smoking between courses.'

He felt it at his feet, and looked down. The tortoise was climbing his flip-flop. He threw it in the air like a baby.

'Get it out,' she said. 'Get it out.'

'What's the matter?' he said.

'It follows me,' she said. 'It follows me the whole time, as if it knew.'

He brought it out onto the landing, and put it in the empty wickerwork laundry basket beside the bathroom door; and he picked up bits and pieces of apple-peel from the carpet, that the child Aoife had been feeding to the Hoover, and he dropped them in, too. Then he went back to bed.

'It's only a tortoise,' he said.

'I tried to get rid of it,' she told him. 'In the supermarket. The lobster tank had no lobsters in it, and Aoife was filling the dwarf's trolley with seven of everything, but he didn't mind. I slipped him into the tank while her back was turned.'

'Was there water in it?'

'That was the problem. He didn't seem to be able to relate to water. Maybe he's too domesticated. Maybe he can only be normal in Africa. He began to drown on me.'

'Who got him out?'

'I did. I had to put my arms right down into it. Thanks be to God I was wearing a sleeveless top.'

'What about Aoife?'

'What about her? Aoife was Aoife. When is she not?'

That was the third time she had been off-hand about the child since the test proved positive. The truth was, pregnant women got away with murder.

'What do you mean?' he said. He left a pause of anger between the first word and the second word. It was just long enough.

'I mean that she was thrilled,' she said. 'She thought I was giving him a bath. Then she introduced him to the dwarf. "Hello, tortoise," he said, "I'm Bashful," and the tortoise put his foot out, or his paw, or whatever, and the dwarf shook it with his thumb and his index finger, and there was just no way I could rescue the situation. "Morgan," I said, "I am so, so sorry about this." '

But he was thinking of the girl he had seen at the photocopier that morning. He was thinking of how her short skirt clung to her behind like a bat's wings. He had let her go ahead of him, although he had more to do.

'We'll go the Pine Forest,' she said, 'some fine day when it isn't raining too heavily, and we'll lose him. We can tell Aoife that he found a hole which led to his mother. We can tell her that God wanted him to tell all the tortoises in Africa about Ireland, because otherwise they would never have heard of it, and that would be terrible. If she gets upset, I'll bring her into town, and she can help me choose the bottles for the baby.'

He had turned away from her in the bed, as he always did when he was imagining other women, and he had begun to fantasise about the girl at the photocopier, even though he could not remember what she looked like. He assembled her from the dead bits and pieces of a hundred bodies, until her eyes opened and she sat up slowly, a Frankenstein in fishnets.

'Al,' she said, 'he's going bananas now.' Her face shone with more than face-cream.

'You know what that is?' he said. 'That's alcohol poisoning.'

'It was only a small drink,' she said. 'There'd be more in a fruit salad. He hadn't moved a muscle since twenty past one. Here, have a feel.'

The skin of her stomach rippled like the membrane of a motorway during a tremor, when the phones rock on their cradles in the perspex roadside booths, and drop, and dangle by a plastic flex, bobbing above the heaving border flowers.

'Where?' he said. 'Where?'

She pressed his smoker's finger, the one that Aoife sucked,

against the east of her belly. He could feel the bulge broaden and gulf. But he was still angry.

'I don't know,' he said. 'I don't feel anything.'

There was another way he had not thought of before. He could try it tonight; he could try it now. If it worked, they could write what they liked on his death certificate. It would be all Greek to him.

He had nothing to water it with. He bent at the tap, while it was still lukewarm, and let it fill his mouth. There was plenty, and to spare: he had taken out his dentures. They sat on the wash-hand basin like a prim police exhibit. The dentist who had made them twenty-five years ago drank his own chloroform, cured dysentery, piles, and poor sexual performance, and had even driven out demons in exchange for American dollars. Back issues of the *National Geographic* flapped in his pick-up clinic, because he had hosted two lady zoologists who were writing a feature article on monogamy among the rhinoceros, and who were waiting for the war to end and the border to open, so that they could travel another thousand miles of nitroglycerine heat with their rehydration pills and their crateloads of courtesy biros.

They were probably dead by now. They were no spring chickens then, those two tough birds with their Presbyterian practicality. And the dentist, ditto: he was long gone, surely. Yet the teeth were still sound. He could cut a raw carrot, no bother; it was toffee he had to be careful with. He would shine them up, and leave them to someone. He might leave them to the little girl with the tortoise. To the rest of the world, he would leave his very best wishes.

The fluoride in the water had seeped into the root-work of his wisdom teeth. He waded through the moonlight to where the plant was, and dribbled over the leaves a sleek trickle of last week's downpour. There was laughter from below, from the brethren downstairs; but he could hear the tiny, rainforest tickerings like a clockmaker's workshop, the tinkle of drinking. It was not his hearing aid this time. It was not his hearing, either. It had nothing at all to do with him. Therefore it might be real.

He turned the pot around, away from the moonlight, so that

now it was straining toward the typewriter that had no ribbon. He would keep the shutters closed throughout the hours of daylight. He would look up the times of sunrise and sunset in the newspaper, and he would lock them accordingly. Only at night would he open them, and let the moon melt on his floorboards. If, after that, the light leaves swung through the small hours, a slow, soundless swerve toward the sky outside his window, then he could close the book on the *Encyclopaedia Britannica*. Its each and every volume would be a delicatessen for the moths of the world.

That was not laughter from underneath him. That was dirty laughter. These were the men who had to get up and go out, daily, six and seven days and nights a week, to resurrect the living, to give their people comfort and courage and the strength of character to take the bus to work instead of throwing themselves in front of the traffic. Baptisms and burials were their meat and potatoes; yet they spent the evenings watching celebrities doing charades, when they could have been looking at 'Dial M For Murder' or having a good discussion about where exactly the Jesuits went off the rails.

Baptisms. Basil sat himself down, and wrote the word in bold block letters on a loose sheet of graph paper. He would have to say something, of course. It needn't be a homily or, God forbid, a heart-to-heart; but he would have to make the professional pitch at some point, whether or not it caused embarrassment among the faint-hearted guests at the portable font, the ones who would be talking in raised tones and sitting with their legs crossed, in order to prove that they had not been harmed irretrievably by the church of their childhood. The woman who was having the baby would invite them in droves, that sort, and what could he tell them? Those mortgaged youngsters with their All-Bran breakfasts, their Australian wines, who thought they were secular because they had credit cards and bikini scars from their tied tubes. No one had ever told them that the God of all that is, was, or ever shall be, the God of Southern Comfort and the Northern Lights, howled on his hunkers over his own diarrhoea, pressing the prolapsed haemorrhoid back into his bottom before he wiped himself with the palm of his left hand, and walked with difficulty towards the synagogue in Nazareth. No one had ever told them that their fitted kitchens were made from the wood of the Cross, that Christ was alive, at large, dangerous and armed, a panther far too cunning for any Neighbourhood Watch.

On second thoughts, he could tell them a few yarns about Africa. Luke had said it was always best to stick with stories, provided that you kept to three anecdotes per abstraction, and wound the whole thing up at five minutes, no more, no less.

'Never,' he had said, 'ever, ever, underestimate the stupidity of your audience. Jesus never did. Look at the parables. Basically, they're idiot-boards.'

He would settle for Africa, so. It had slipped in the ratings somewhat, since Latin America barged out of the background; but it was still good for a pep-talk at a christening. He would tell them about the river, and about river-blindness. He would tell them about his friend, a man he had been ordained with, a man who wore tablecloths and a snorkel when he went to the hive for honey. When the river-blindness began, six months into his first posting, he had started to measure little distances: the bed to the light-switch, the bed to the toilet-bowl, the sacristy to the centre of the altar, the altar-rail to the tabernacle. Then his eyes had frosted over; they became two boiled sweets. He sealed his eyelids with sellotape. It was the first sound Basil heard each morning, the fellow's fingers searching for where the sellotape started.

Stories. He wrote the word in longhand under Baptism, and thought about it. Why had he doodled cobwebs inside the capital B? He was not a Celtic monk, tracing an Alpha or an Omega in the juice of a pulverised beetroot. He petalled the marks he had made until they were posies.

At first, he thought it was himself, the sputum shifting in his chest; but no, it was another noise. When he looked down, the mouse looked up at him.

'Stay,' Basil said. 'Good mouse.'

His hand roamed quietly over two encyclicals and a pair of perfumed insoles for his slippers.

'You're a pretty mouse,' he said. 'Did anybody ever tell you that? You are, you know. A very, very pretty mouse.'

Where in the name of the good Jesus was the racquet? Had the weirdy-beardy down the corridor borrowed it? Certainly, the mini-maids hadn't been in. Luke had told him they'd be back in a fortnight, and to take down the notice which read: Clean by all means, but touch nothing. His fingers crept around the *Confessions* of Saint Augustine and the *Dublin Bus Timetable*.

'Did you ever read Beatrix Potter?' he said to the mouse. 'I did. I read Beatrix Potter when she was still alive. I could have written to her, if I'd known she was still alive. But I didn't. I always thought that people who wrote books were dead.'

He hadn't talked so much since one of the houseboys threatened to jump from the bell-tower. He had talked to him for hours, talked about the tape from Ireland with the birds' cries on it, and how they had thrown it out when the record-player arrived, and how a real bird had rescued it from the bin beside the boiler, and used it to insulate his own nest behind where the tomatoes never grew properly, weaving the magnetised strips among the twigs; and he was half-way through Mr Churchill's insomnia and the five beds that he slept in, and the ice-cream traders in the street below were selling tubs at twice the price, when the boy jumped. He had fallen fifty feet, and walked away from it with nothing more than tendonitis; but the woman who cushioned his fall had a shattered collarbone and a broken sternum.

The mouse was enchanted. He sat up and flossed his whiskers.

'Attaboy,' Basil said. He was feeling leather. He gripped the handle, hoisted his arm up; high, then higher. That was as far as he could get it. His armpit would be at him in the morning.

'I love you,' he said. 'I love you, too.'

But when he opened his eyes and stared down at the edge of the racquet on the floor in front of him, the mouse had gone. The backlash of the blow had reached his wrist already, and his shoulder was in spasm by the time he had picked part of a paw and the pink stump of a tail from the glossy wood of the frame.

He lay on the bed in his clothes, and he used his ventilator. Then he used it again. From deep within him he could hear his heartbeat beating like a tom-tom. He remembered the sound from a Hollywood movie, how the bwanas looked up briefly from their gins and tonics, and the alcoholic heroine played 'See How My Saviour Stands Besides Me' on the Steinway in the corner.

'Basil, can you hear me?' It was Luke at the door, rapping.

'What is it?'

'Did you fall? We thought we heard a fall.'

'How can you hear a fall?' Basil said. 'Do you mean an impact?'

'Basil, I'll break down the door, if I have to.'

'Don't do it,' he said. 'The man from the hardware shop would charge you thirty pounds to hang it on its hinges. Anyway, all that you'd see would be a very old man on a very new bed; and that sight, my dear Luke, is not one of the Seven Wonders of the World.'

There was a short silence on the other side of the wood-wormed panels.

'There is still half of the table-tennis table in the coal-shed, Luke,' he said. 'You could smash that, first thing tomorrow morning, if it would make you happy.'

'Goodnight, Basil,' he said. 'For now.'

The old priest listened for the footsteps fading. All he could hear was the mucus breaking inside him, the pops of a thaw. He lay with his eyes wide open, trying to sleep.

The tail was neither here nor there. The paw, however, was another matter. If he tried to cross the tennis-court, to make it to the culvert, the owl with the plastic tag would breakfast on him. It would end up in a nature programme on the children's channel; or had they taken them down, their tripods and their telephoto lenses, those teachers from the technical college? Then he'd collect the beer-cans that they left, fill them with sand, paint them white, and use them to strengthen the chinks in the roof of the district dispensary.

But that was somewhere elsewhere. That was not here.

The shudder down his spine was no figure of speech. Yet it baffled him. He had walked past noisy trenches that were overflowing with corpses, like an ash-tray after a party; he had seen a man's face slip from his skull as if it were a fried egg flopping out of a pan. But his fingernails and his hair had gone on growing, and the bats had gone on pollinating the orchids outside his window, and he had looked forward to the *Irish Press* on each third Monday of the month. Now he was sleepy and unsleeping with a new nervousness.

His finger was still sooty from writing on that window; he could smell the consultant's hand-cream on the elbow of his jacket. He could smell his own mouth, for that matter, the gumboils, the mercury of it. But he wanted only to sleep. He had had enough in his life of the sleep of the just. What he wanted instead was the sleep of the unjust. The unjust slept like babies.

He was sorrier about the mouse. He had not meant to injure it, or cause it pain. He had intended only to kill it.

'Aren't you going to wear your belt?' Al said.

'At my age?' said Basil. 'Is it worth the effort?'

'Not really,' Al said. 'If we did crash at high speed, you'd probably be dead of a heart attack before you went through the windscreen.'

'We won't crash at high speed,' Basil said. 'You're a very slow driver.'

'If you drive at forty, you get all the lights,' Al told him. 'That's my philosophy.'

'You're an Aristotelian,' Basil said.

'Am I?' said Al. 'What are you?'

'I don't know,' Basil said. 'The truth is, I am dying to find out. But when I do die, I shall certainly spend my initial forty thousand years chatting up Aristotle. You see, even a priest never forgets his first night of love.'

They laughed at the same moment, for the same length of time. Then they said nothing for a while, in an intimate way. Basil was feeling glad and giddy. It hadn't happened for years. Of course, he had a knack for talking to young men, or a certain sort of young man, the mongrels rather than the thoroughbreds. They should have made him Master of Novices in the year that the Communists sent a dog into space, but the opposition had put it about that he talked to himself in the glasshouse; and that was that.

'Would you mind it if I called you Basil? Father is not really me.'

He thought about it from five different points of view, as they crossed the canal and bore left.

'Why not?' he said. 'My mother did. But not Baz. Baz is out of the question. There's a species of bubble-gum in Singapore, called Baz. It bursts at the size of a beachball; then the face looks like a chemical burn, with bits and pieces where there shouldn't be.'

'Basil is nice,' Al said.

'And I shall call you Albert,' said Basil. 'Al is not a trustworthy name.'

'We were thinking of Basil for the baby.'

'Don't,' said Basil.

They were silent again. Al lowered the window and held his cigarette against the outside mirror.

'I think I knew your father,' Basil said. 'He was a great man for the knife.'

'He was,' said Al. 'It broke his heart when they brought in lasers. There was a time, you know, when a woman hid her breasts when she saw him coming.'

'How many now would he have cut off, all told?' said Basil.

Al blew the bright, blue smoke from his lips and nose.

'Enough for two continental holidays a year,' he said. 'Plus our college fees, when the time came.'

Basil was quiet for a moment, working it out.

'Tell me,' he said, 'which of the cancers would you specialise in, if you wanted to make a killing?'

'Breast is best,' Al said. 'Or the lung, the lung maybe; the rectum; I don't know.'

'The colon?'

'You'd want to ask a doctor. You could ask my brother, if he was around. He's another great man for the knife. Lives in Perth. Cuts the transverse fold of the eyelid out of Oriental women to take the slitty look away. A single session, he can do half-a-dozen. Then he spends evenings on the motorway, in a car full of speakers, driving up and down, up and down, fifty miles, sixty miles, under stars he doesn't recognise, because the air-conditioning in his house never works. Whiskey on the rocks, marriage on the rocks, rock around the clock.'

'It sounds,' said Basil, 'very like the early life of a saint.'

'You think so?' Al said. 'It reminds me more of "Alfred Hitchcock Presents".'

He was looking at Basil's hands. They were really, really hairy. They were almost gross. It had to be said. It had been said. Jane had said it. The child would probably try to comb them; and he might even let her. He was that sort, his near-at-hand, unnecessary body a winter wardrobe of scarves and gloves in a stable summer of light to the world. That was the way with the priests. No wonder they lived till kingdom come. No wonder every second centenarian was called Alphonsus.

'You never thought of it, yourself?' said Basil.

'Thought of what?'

'Surgery.'

'Father, all I ever thought about was becoming an international contract killer. I thought about it for years. I'd have a place in Paris; I'd have a penthouse. I'd overlook accordions, cobblestones, that kind of thing.'

'The Irish College would suit you down to the ground,' Basil said. 'And you'd have a marvellous alias: you'd be a priest. No one would ever dare to open your violin case, if you were a member of the Order of Melchizedek.'

'I'd sit in the Louvre, and sketch. I'd sketch whatever you're supposed to sketch. It would be nice. I'd learn something. Then, twice a year, three times a year maximum, I'd get a phone-call.'

'That's about my average,' Basil said.

'Twenty-four hours later, I'd be in Bogotá; I'd be in Mombasa.'

'Stay out of Mombasa,' said Basil. 'I had the runs in Mombasa. It was the watermelons.'

'No finesse. No monkey business with telescopic sights. I'd just walk up with a Magnum and blow him away.'

'I was right,' Basil said. 'You do want to be the very spit of your father, but in a slightly different way. Otherwise, you'd lose face.'

'It's only a dream,' said Al, 'but it keeps me going. In the office where I work, the walls are grey. My few first grey hairs drift down onto a grey carpet. The soap in the toilet is grey, and I go there often. The noise of the plumbing in the place makes me want to pee every twenty minutes. It's more hustle than bustle in my section so you hear the plumbing clearly: plop, skitter, plop. It's nice to close your eyes, blot out the colour of wolf, maybe strip a styrofoam cup like a daisy. He is going mad, he is not going mad, he is definitely going mad. One phone call, and I'm packed for Budapest. Just point him out to me, and it's dead on arrival, cash on delivery.'

He had driven past his own house, at the top of the keyhole cul-de-sac. Now it was a question of reversing without letting on. The priest was no fool, and no knave either. He might think him strange.

'You need a few fantasies to keep your two feet on the ground,' he said to Basil. 'There's nothing like two feet on the ground to give you altitude sickness.'

'But they're not fantasies,' Basil said. 'They're dreams. Where would we be without them? When I was on sleeping pills, I had no dreams for five years. No wonder I wasn't myself. But in Africa I always took my holidays six thousand feet above sea-level, and I had dreams so strange I used to count my rib-cage when I got my six o'clock call.'

Al stopped the car and stepped out of it. All he had in his inside breast-pocket was a folded invoice for two mortice locks and the man's labour. It would have to do. He dropped it in the letterbox at the side of the road, studied the hours of collection, and got back in.

'Sorry,' he said. 'It had to go out tonight.'

Now he could turn in the nearest drive; no one would be any the wiser. The old man must be ninety, and counting. His eyes had almost gone out.

'I never asked,' Basil said. 'How is your father?'

'He's much the same as he always was,' said Al. Actually, he couldn't remember whether it was twelve or fourteen years since he had read the wrong lesson at the requiem mass, because the pages of the lectionary had blown backwards in a breeze from the sacristy door.

'He enjoys poor health,' he said.

The not remembering was, in its own small way, a little victory.

'I'm sorry,' Basil said.

'No need,' said Al. 'The verb was enjoy.'

Basil studied the eyes of his driver in the overhead mirror. Perhaps he had been serious about contacting killers. Perhaps he was a nutter. God help his poor family with a child coming.

'He always kept his hands like so, at ten to two exactly, on the steering wheel,' Al said. 'He was that kind of a creature. His greatest ambition for the whole Western world was two soft bowel motions a day, though he never achieved it himself. When he did, he told us.'

They had been inseparable. Basil could see that.

'What I'm trying to say, Father,' said Al, 'is that you don't have to go to Africa to go to Africa. Look around you. We've arrived. Can't you hear the extractor fans? The women of the village are preparing food for their menfolk. The hunters will be home soon with the day's kill. It may look like takeaways in asbestos, but it's antelope with froth on its gums. They'll eat in silence in their cooking space. It's not yet time to talk about the dangers of the day, the flesh-wounds, the fresh wounds, how the desk at the window with the double-adaptor and the outside line was given to our enemy, and what does that mean, Nkosi? Are the spirits with us still, and, if not, what happened in the name of Christ to the two-litre bottle of vodka from Belfast?'

'This is where you live,' said the priest, pointing.

'The women are frightened of their warriors' silence, and the warriors like it that way. They've frightened no one else since the great sun rose, and it makes them feel better. They climb the ladder to their sleeping quarters, and their wives lie down with a pillowcase over their heads while the warriors empty the talcum powder out of their socks. Five minutes pass, five minutes of feeling, of feeling time pass, of feelings passing. Then there's the sound of someone walking to the bathroom, someone walking unnaturally, as if the sand had turned to pebbles, the pebbles to stones, and the sandals are too far behind to go back for. But the man, he's already asleep. He's sleeping on the skulls of his ancestors. He won't hear the toilet flushing; he won't see the toilet-water clearing like a Disprin. That's her moment, the moment she loves most, when the water turns simple again, and she can see right to the bottom.'

'Africa is not like that,' said Basil. 'It is just a place where I happened to find myself.'

Al was sniffing the air. He came round the front of the car, and opened the door for the priest.

'There's a smell,' he said. 'Do you get it?'

'There's a fragrance,' Basil said. 'Is it rubber? I rather like that smell. It comes of mending punctures, till I was so tired of doing it that I bought solid tyres.'

They walked over levelled earth the colour of Milk of Magnesia, towards the house.

'Don't tell her we were on the lawn,' Al said. 'She has a thing about the lawn. She's put a lot of work into it.'

The windows were open everywhere. The two men peered in at London fog.

'Shit,' said Al. 'You can't cook a roast and watch a soap at the same time.'

He searched among his keys for the right one. There were so many of them. There were more than Basil had had, when he deputised at the orphanage. The boys had loved it when he let the key-ring slide through the hole in his pocket, and come out at his foot.

'It's my fault,' Al said. 'I put the TV where she could see it from the kitchen through the folding doors. But it goes back tonight.'

The clock went *hic, haec, hoc*.

'Amazing,' the pregnant woman said. 'Really amazing. I always thought that leprosy was a sort of metaphor.'

Her eyes were wet with tears. The husband's were a bit runny, too. It was the glasses, then, that had saved Basil, because the room was still foggy from the roast pork that was sitting in tinfoil on the crazypave behind the house.

'They weren't all lepers,' Basil said. 'Some of them had been mutilated.'

'It doesn't bear thinking about,' she said. 'Why would anyone do that?' And she flapped her arms as if she were following aerobics on breakfast television; but the smoky stuff was there to stay. It would break your heart, so it would.

'It made them better beggars at the airport,' he told her.

'They had an airport?' she said.

'Yes,' he said. 'They had an airport. They had air traffic controllers. They even had an air traffic controllers' strike.'

'My God,' she said, 'I had no idea they were that advanced.'

Al was probing the soup. What was the need for the floating green stuff? Even when he covered it, the green stuff bobbed up again. There was no call for that. Besides, he was miffed about the conversation. Of course, it was the same whenever they entertained the priesthood. Her cousin in lock-up was no different. Instead of talking about the price-war between supermarkets, they went all moody and Passover. You couldn't even glug a glass of rotgut, and let it skelter down your gullet: you had to brush it like Holy Communion.

'This is goodish plonk,' he said. 'I might try it in the soup.'

'Father, forgive him,' she said. 'What can I say? The man's an animal, except at weekends. At weekends, he's a vegetable. Twice a year, he might be a mineral, and then that's only because he's desperate for a drink, and all he can find is rum and Coke.'

Al poured himself a pleasing, ploppity glass of wine, and got in between the old man's fingers before the priest could close them over the cut crystal.

'I don't know,' he said. 'I just don't know.'

'That's Albert's way of introducing an assertion, Father,' she said. 'You just ignore him, and enjoy your soup.'

'The factory,' Al said.

'The factory?' said Basil.

'Where the lepers, you know, decorated the bells for the Christmas trees, instead of begging at the airport. That's painstaking work. Let's not beat around the bush. That is very painstaking work. For anyone. For you, for me, for her. Especially if, you know, you're down a couple of digits. In addition to which, it's work which might not give you a massive adrenalin boost indefinitely.'

'They stuck at it,' Basil said. 'They always wanted to buy the bells they were proudest of, to keep and show people. The best of the Nativity scenes were done by a young Muslim who used to hold the brushes under his armpit; he worked the airport at night.'

'You gave them back their dignity, Father Basil,' said Jane.

'No one can give a man back his dignity,' the priest said. 'Because no one can take it from him in the first place. It's a virus for which there are no known antibodies.'

'Well,' she said, 'you gave them love.'

'No,' he said. 'I just gave them more money than they were earning on the streets.'

She liked him so much. He would be such at a hit at the baptism. All right, he didn't look like Teilhard de Chardin, but you would not notice his blackheads, really, until after the church, at the party. What you would notice instead would be the sorrowfulness and the stillness, like the day the horse-fly went all suddenly hushed on the window in the kitchen, after hours spent buffeting the glass; and she had known it was dying, and that it was looking at the world of the green garden, without under-standing itself, or the garden, or the look that was exchanged between them; and she had picked it up and carried it outside, feeling silly and right, and left it on the grass. And afterwards she'd rung her cousin the doctor, to ask him was it a symptom, and was she sick, and should she be taking a tonic; and he had said What, listen, listen to me, the test, the test is positive, and her heart kicked inside her like a baby.

'You gave them life,' she said. 'You had children of your own, and you a priest.'

He was awkward about it. Compliments he could cope with, but this was an obituary. So he studied the endless cutlery on either side of his soup-dish. Everything was the same size. That was unfair. He would have to wait for the wife to pick hers, before he could be sure.

'I met a man,' Al said. 'He was American, right. Black as my boots.'

Basil bent down and looked under the table.

'Your boots aren't black,' he said. 'They're grey. And they're not boots. They're shoes.'

'You know what I mean,' Al said.

'I do,' said Basil. 'Do you?'

Jane was stacking the soup-bowls on her bump.

'Are you ever going to grow up?' she said to her husband. 'You're old enough to be having a mid-life crisis. Could you not act your age?'

And she went off out to the kitchen, where she made less noise than was strictly necessary. That was to worry him, of course, so that he'd wonder if she was crying, or trying not to cry, which was worse, scraping at her eye-shadow with her fingernail in front of the iron that doubled as a mirror. But he wasn't worried, and he wasn't going to be. It was she who had brought up Africa, Almighty God, and the Afrikaner mentality; it was she who wanted to talk about the pitfalls on the road to Damascus instead of the potholes on the road into Dublin. She should have known better than to start the dance with a slow set. That was a surefire way to make your partner sweat; and, if he sweated, he'd have an anxiety attack about his deodorant. Then you could kiss goodbye to the first meeting of mouths.

'Don't take a blind bit of notice, Basil,' he said. 'It's all hormones. I could write a book about hormones.'

'We could all write a book,' Basil said; 'but we don't. It's one of life's larger mercies.'

'She'll be fine in five minutes. She's just putting some clingfilm round a tender moment. When she serves it up in six weeks' time, it'll still be rare. The whole house will be like *Night on the Bare Mountain* for twenty minutes. Then we'll make up, and watch Phil Donahue. That's her way. That's the way it is.'

Basil was fumbling in his pocket for his ventilator. He could feel tablets, or the lost beads of a rosary, but the inhaler was not there. How could he have forgotten it? Where could he have forgotten it? And why? There was always a Why mixed up in it somewhere.

'What?' he said.

'When the baby comes, bingo. You know what I mean? That's it, that's the bright lights. A little boy who'll lie on his back and smile at her and pee in the air, and she'll want a photo of the peeing, the precise moment of it, and I'll be doing a Pony Express to the local pharmacy for more flash-cubes.'

'I never played bingo,' said the priest, who was still searching for his ventilator. Because this hadn't happened for ages. In point of fact, it hadn't happened for years, and that was much longer.

'I knew when I met her,' Al said, and he topped his glass from the new bottle. 'It was sometime in the spring. My nose was all bunged up. We talked for an hour. Then she had an appointment. I waited with her at the bus-stop until her bus came. But it didn't, so she thumbed. She asked me to go away, because no one would stop for a woman who was with a man. I didn't know her surname, but I knew I was going to marry her, or at least sleep with her a few times. "What's your second name?" I said. She said, "Elizabeth," and got into the car that had pulled up. "I'm going to marry you," I said. I left out about the sleeping bit. "All right," she said. I said, "I mean it. I'm going to treat you like an objective." "Why?" she said. I said, "Because you're the first person who has ever really misunderstood me." She didn't say a word, but she bent over more than she had to, getting into the car. When they drove off, I walked down into Dame Street, and I opened an account with a building society.'

He had talked about the spring, and his nose being blocked. That could only mean hay-fever; and where there was hay-fever, there was antihistamines. He would ask him for one, or two, or even three. Three would keep him going until he got back to the college.

'What do you do when you can't breathe?' he said. 'What do you do when you suddenly seize up?'

Al looked him straight in the eye.

'I'll look you straight in the eye on this one, Basil,' he said. 'When you find that you're seizing up, what you need is a person who completely and utterly misunderstands you.'

He leaned across the table and put his hand on the priest's hairy fist.

'Has anyone ever completely and utterly misunderstood you, Father?' he said. 'You can tell me. I won't remember tomorrow morning.'

'Perhaps,' Basil said. 'Perhaps, yes; perhaps, no. Perhaps yes and no.'

'Isn't it wonderful?' Al said. 'Isn't it such a complete and utter relief?'

He was unbuttoning his fly when he heard a voice from the next room; so he flushed the toilet as he urinated, because he wanted to drown out the skittish noise of the spatter. The rest of the house was too silent for its own good. The both of them, husband and wife, must be scribbling their insults on kitchen paper at separate work-tops.

The landing light was on, but the room where the voice was coming from, that was in darkness. He peeped in, and saw the child, asleep among lions and lambs, her head on a ruined pillow and her bare bottom in the air, mooning serenely at the carbon of the universe.

'There were no two ways about it. She must marry the mole. The roots of the chestnut tree would soon become the banisters of her new home, and the slippery wet of the earth would be her only drying cupboard.'

From beneath the discarded bottom half of the child's pyjamas on the carpet, a woman's whispering voice was telling the darkness a story; and the darkness was all ears. Even the streetlight peeled like a poster over the built-in wardrobe, and lay in a scroll on the sticks of the xylophone.

'Thumbelina stood at the stale and slimy hole she had to go into, and she looked around her for the very last time. Then she looked around her for the very first time. The brand-new leaves were landing on the tips of trees, like a sudden decision of butterflies, and even the ants were breaking ranks to do zigzags on the last of the mushy slush. How could she ever say goodbye to so many welcomes?'

He was afraid to turn the cassette off. She might wake up, and let a roar out. What would her parents think? They would think what they liked, and what they liked to think did not bear thinking about. He slipped the leaking bottle of milk from beneath her cheek, and eased her onto her side, and covered her. She smelled of deep-down in the bed. Actually, it was nice.

'Goodbye, friendly sun. Goodbye, clever colours. Goodbye to everything that made my eyes water, whether the heaviness of the light or the light of heavy things, or only the dust from sweeping.'

He could see now; his eyes had grown accustomed to the grey drizzle. He leaned forward and counted the crayon pictures on the wall behind her. There were seven, nine, ten of them, each of a child who was holding a balloon, a pumpkin-head on a pink triangle over two matchstick legs. The arm was a drip-stand, the balloon a watery oblong like a saline sachet, and the stretching trees around her surged to the height of the four prongs of her feet.

The other marks were mysteries. They were birds in flight, or else her hand had slipped. Ws drifted everywhere; Ws and Ms, like a choir-practice of carrion crows. But the saw-blade smile on the pumpkin-head continued evenly from the bedboard to the window-ledge.

'The mole was watching and waiting. He could hardly see her, though he thought that the melting yellow was the slow fall of her hair; and the blur inside the yellow must be her face, the snout and whiskers he could sniff at leisure when she stepped down daintily into the darkness which he had prepared for her.'

A happy childhood was a poor preparation for life in this world; and she was a happy child, at the height of her powers. So he moved his hand above her, making the sign of the Cross, and he blessed her. He was not sure if he had blessed her before; he was blessed if he could remember. The day before yesterday was as remote as his ordination. His ordination was as recent as the day after tomorrow. The here-and-now was neither here nor there, imaginary as mathematics or the moment when the passengers in the deckchairs cheer and order drinks and set their watches forward a full twenty-four hours, and the children rush to the rails to see for themselves the international date-line that all the tannoys are trumpeting; and there is nothing, there is nothing to see. There is only the ship's shadow over the deep, and one hand cutting another hand's nails out of an open port-hole.

She was turning in her sleep, rolling away from him into the wall. The streetlight gloved one grubby hand. She was a tap left running in the winter, a thread of brightness; in the great ground-frost, in the clamp-down of the ice-up, in the frozen sex of zero and minus, she would see them safely through. She would speak for them all, the boilers out the back, tanks hiding in the attic, the camouflaged immersions. She would speak in a flow.

That was not a water-bottle at the bottom of the bed. That was a tortoise-shell. It might be the tortoise-shell of the child's tortoise; it might be the tortoise itself. If it were, it was alive. It was a living thing. Perhaps it was asleep, but that was not the point. The point was, how could the parents permit it? Surely to Heavens it was unhygienic. A tortoise might have been any-where and everywhere in the course of a single day spent being a tortoise. Had they no imagination?

'Father Basil,' the wife called. 'Father Basil.'

She was down at the foot of the stairs. He could tell by turning up his aid almost to the forest fire position. He moved to the door. They would meet at the landing. They would think he'd been constipated.

'Earth calling Father Basil.' What was his name, the husband, he was with her.

'Father Basil calling Earth,' he shouted, and drew the door behind him. The string of a helium balloon that was bobbing like a buoy against the pebbledash paintwork of the child's bedroom, twitched for an instant in the warm current; and rested again.

There was a ping from the cassette.

'Page Seventeen,' said a woman's whispering voice. 'Page Seven, One.'

'Come clean,' Jane said. 'Out with it, Father.'

'It's a hung jury,' her husband said. 'That right, Basil?'

Basil spooned another edge from the strange, indigo mound of his dessert.

'It really is very, very interesting,' he said.

'You should have been a diplomat,' Al said. 'Do you know that? You should have been our man in Baluba Baluba. You should. Or an undertaker. You could have been an undertaker. You're so diplomatic. I'm a spade-for-a-spade sort. I hate this garbage, but it's in. It's so in. If people were honest, they'd ask for ice-cream. Ice-cream and chocolate sauce.'

'I'm not saying it's *cordon bleu*, Father Basil,' said Jane. 'If you wanted *cordon bleu*, you'd have to go to the hospital.'

She had at long last managed to tilt the table-talk in the direction of the baptism. The hospital itself was only a transit-point, of course. What she needed to establish first and foremost was the use of the font. A tin pan on a tripod in front of the altar was not acceptable. It was not acceptable at all. What she wanted was the baptistry. The baptistry had lovely lead-work windows and lots of bearded, bald-headed monks looking up to Heaven surprisedly, as if they'd just felt a drop of rain, but weren't a hundred per cent sure. Then the font itself was a joy, marbly and granity, and steeped in history, and so forth. True enough, that poor unfortunate albino of a priest had told her that the old font was retired, and that nowadays the ceremony was done differently. But what was a baptism without a baptistry? So she had said, 'Ceremony? Don't you mean sacrament?' And he had had the grace to blush.

'Hospital?' said Basil. 'What hospital?'

'Where my cousin is,' she said. 'My cousin the deacon. Declan.'

'The one who was going to do the baptism?' said Basil.

'Exactly,' said Jane.

'The nosh is pretty good up there,' Al said. 'I ate his lunch twice last week. There was even ice-cream and chocolate sauce.'

'We were talking to him about the baptism,' said Jane. 'We talked the whole thing through. He understood perfectly.'

'I'd say their chef is French,' Al said. 'I'd say it's more a case of "*Ça va?*" than "Hi, how's it going?" But it's not just the cooking. They have a paging system. They have carpet-tiles in the service lifts. They have a whole crazy-golf course. And the windows. You should see the windows. On a dark day, they get brighter; on a bright day, they get darker. They're photo-something or other. Plus they're as thick as the village idiot. I kid you not. You can throw a heavy chair against them, right? What happens? The legs of the chair come off. That's what happens.'

'They have a beautiful chapel,' Jane said. 'With a beautiful stained-glass window, and a beautiful smell. Of course, they don't have a baptistry. They don't even have a font, let alone those awful, awful, tripods and bed-pans.'

'How is he?' said Basil.

'How is who?' she said.

'Your cousin,' he said. 'The deacon. Declan.'

'He's alive,' she said, 'which is more than can be said for the dead. But he won't see it that way. He has an attitude problem. Instead of living each day as if it was his last, he mopes around the place as if he was about to die.'

'Tell him about the aftershave he sprinkles in his shoes,' Al said.

'What about the aftershave he sprinkles in his shoes?' she said.

'It cost me thirteen pounds,' he said. 'That's what about the aftershave. And the nurse, she gives him a pen with six colours in it, and she makes him draw his mood. The whole thing stinks.'

'He's eating,' Jane said. 'He's not on hunger strike. He's getting beefy. I thought he'd be skin and bones, but he's put on a stone since this time last month.'

'He's a growing boy,' Al said.

'He's assuming flesh,' said Basil. 'That's the end and the beginning of it.'

There was a thud on the ceiling, the strong stamp of a foot or a big book falling. They all looked up.

'Jesus,' said the husband.

'God Almighty,' said the wife.

'The tortoise,' said the priest. 'It fell off the bed.'

They went back into the living-room for their last drinks. Al spread his legs at the cocktail cabinet and assumed the frisking position.

'Christian Brothers' port it is,' he said. 'Your crowd doesn't mess with the grape or the grain, does it?'

'I'll have a jug of rain,' Basil said.

'You'll have to turn some of my wine into water,' Al said. 'Otherwise, it comes straight from the sink.'

'The sink is fine,' Basil said. 'The holiest water in the world wells in the kitchen sink.'

'I can squeeze a lemon into it,' she said. 'Or a lime. I have lemons and limes. I have both.'

129

'Water,' the priest said. 'Water would be enough. Water would be more than enough.'

She saw her opening. It was her last chance.

'I hope the baby will feel that way, at the baptism.'

Basil shifted one buttock slightly, and the chair made another outlandish, abdominal sound. He hoped she knew it wasn't him. He might have to get up and inspect the Family Bible. Even the arm-rests were passing wind.

'I've always taken the view,' he said, 'that a baby is baptised in the waters of the womb by the mother who carries him. It's her prerogative; it's her priesthood. And why not? After all, she is creating an eternal life.'

'Father Basil,' she said, 'you have the most wonderful insight into women.'

'Down the hatch, Basil,' said the hobbledehoy. 'A port in any storm.' And he handed him a brimful of best Californian. Soggy cork scraps bobbed like life-jackets in the new stem-glass. Truly, this was a safe house for the alcohol molecule.

'Declan wouldn't talk about it,' she said. 'All he wants to talk about is baptism by fire. He sits there in a four-star funny-farm and he talks about how disillusioned he is.'

'Disillusionment,' said Al. 'Disillusionment is a long, Latin word for the sulks. Am I right, Basil?'

'He says he can't respond to anything,' she said. 'Then the paging system tells them it's time for dinner, and off he goes.'

'I'd like to try the dinner,' Al said. 'The lunch was mighty.'

'It used to be different,' Basil told them. 'There'd be scrambled eggs on the walls of the dining-room; mouse-traps in the nurses' station; and china fruit in china fruitbowls on every wet window-ledge.'

'Really?' she said, and she shuddered. 'I don't think I ever want to go to Africa.'

'The families came on Sundays,' said the priest. 'The women shaved their fathers and their grandfathers, and cleaned the razors over the ashtrays. The children scraped the dried food off the walls with cake-knives. They wore brown paper bags over their hands.'

'I'm going to say the whole lot of this back to his nibs,' said

Jane. 'Word for word. Maybe he'll learn to be more grateful for what's on his own doorstep, right here.'

'Now I suppose it's room-service and nice nurses,' Basil said.

'The nurses are a knockout,' Al said. 'It would make you ill.'

'But what makes you well?' said Basil.

'Prayer,' Jane said. 'Prayer and patience.' She looked down at her bump, and was very moved by what she had said. Her eyes prickled. It was not the cigarettes. She raised her face to Basil so he would notice, but he was frowning at the port-glass in the fur of his fist. He had fleckety things of cork on his lower lip.

'Prayer and patience, and the work of the Holy Spirit,' she said. She was not going to be ashamed of her faith. Her faith had come up with the goods; so there.

'The work of the Holy Spirit is a mystery,' Al said. 'I prefer solutions. I prefer to let my fingers do the walking, up and down the entries in the Golden Pages. Something isn't happening; you look up Infertility Clinics. Something is happening; you look up Consultant Psychiatrists. I'm not saying a word against the Good Book, you understand. I'm only saying that the Golden Pages is a terrific sequel.'

'Yes,' Basil said. 'Yes, it is. Everything in the Kingdom of God is royal. The invention of a ventilator is as much the work of the Holy Spirit as the parting of the Red Sea. Perhaps even the paging system has a place in the plot. Your cousin Desmond – '

'Declan,' she said. 'Think of Declan the Deacon.'

'Declan,' he said. 'Declan is terrified. He's hiding in a locked room.'

'He's out of the locked ward now,' said Jane. 'He has the run of the place.'

'Hormones,' Al said. 'Hormones. Father Basil was talking about a metaphor.'

'No,' said Basil. 'I was thinking of Pentecost. Pentecost was not a metaphor. What happened on that day was as real as food-poisoning.'

She glanced at her watch. They were well into injury time. She would give it another two or three minutes. She lay back, her knuckles tapping out the first few phrases of *The Blue Danube* on the tumour of her belly. She was thinking of Basil's blackheads, of her fingernails feasting on them, how some would squiggle and others would spurt. It was more than a nose; it was a proboscis. The backs of her fingers bounded on the drumskin, and the foot of her baby scraped across the pout of her navel.

'I don't know,' she said. 'It's all so complex.'

'No,' said the priest. 'It's just complicated.'

She looked at her watch, as if she had discovered a bruise.

'My God,' she said, 'it's almost midnight.'

'It's not almost midnight,' her husband said. 'It's almost twelve. That's all. It's five to twelve, in fact.'

'I know,' she said. 'It's five minutes to midnight.'

'It is five minutes to twelve,' he said. 'I'm the head of the household. I decide what is a symbol, and I decide what is not a symbol.'

But he got up anyway, and beat the cushions on the sofa into shape.

'What time is it in Africa, Basil?' he said. 'Is it dawn over the Dark Continent?'

'I'd have to think about that,' said Basil, standing up slowly.

'You're mini-series material, Father,' Al said. 'You know that? You minister to lepers, you minister to lunatics, you minister to the likes of us.'

'I never ministered to lunatics,' Basil said.

'But weren't you a chaplain?' Jane said. 'In the place with egg on the walls.'

'I was never a chaplain,' he said. 'I was only a chap.'

She was baffled. She looked at him. What was he saying to her? What was he not saying?

'You mean you were a patient?' she said.

'I always dreamed of being a man of patience and commitment,' he said. 'It never happened. Or, rather, it did happen; which is why we should be wary of dreams. The dream will seek us out, and find us wanting. I ended up as a patient who had been committed.'

Al was counting the gaffes he had made about nuts and other pistachios. Already he was on to the toes of his second foot, in under the leather, jigging them one by one. But his cracks had been standard issue. Actually, they were quite loving. Besides, Baz should have come clean earlier.

'Not to worry,' he said. 'Welcome to the clubbed.'

'But why? Why?' said Jane. 'I mean, it must have been awful for you.'

'I don't know why,' Basil said. 'Once upon a time, I was living happily ever after; then I wasn't.'

'I'm sure it was Africa, Father,' she said. 'Africa gets every-body down.'

'God gave me a drought,' said the priest, 'to put by for a rainy day. I said to him, "Lord, I don't want a drought. I want hot and cold running water." But what could I do? There isn't any ombudsman for two o'clock in the morning.'

She roused herself; she rallied. She would not let it spoil the evening yet. It could spoil it later, but not yet.

'Well,' she said, 'all I can say is that you've shared something special with us, and we feel special because you've shared it with us.'

'Ditto,' said Al. Had he really told that joke about the basket-case in Broadmoor? He couldn't remember. He hoped he hadn't. He had only been trying to lighten and brighten the atmosphere. But that was his sworn duty: he was *mein Host*, for God's sake. He could hardly be criticised for lightening and brightening.

'What's done is done,' she said. 'That's my motto.' She was a bit miserable, though. Was there anybody normal left?

'I'd better go,' said Basil. 'They'll be sending out a search party.'

'Declan,' she said, 'is on Serenese. Does that ring a bell?'

'I was on Lithium,' he told her. 'I was on it for years; but not now.'

'What is Lithium?' she said. He was so matter of fact about it. You would think he was talking about Hedex. It made her a little bitter. His ease was a failure of loyalty to whatever had gone ape inside him, out there, out in Africa.

'Lithium?' he said. 'They use it in the firing pins of the detonators on nuclear warheads.'

'Good Jesus,' she said. 'Excuse me.'

The three of them stood for a second in silence.

'What is that noise?' said Al.

'It's a bluebottle,' she said.

133

'No,' he said. 'It's a mosquito.'

'It's me,' said Basil. 'It's my chest.'

It was a cloudless night, yet there were no stars. There should be a number you could ring at any hour of the day or the darkness, to find out simple things, and be told them. A pleasant voice would ask you to hold for a moment, and then it would tell you there were no stars because.

Basil cut across the construction site to the arc-lamps on the gantry. That was where the boys had hacked away the barbed-wire at the entrance to the college grounds, and made a dirt-track for their bicycles. The hanged cat had been taken down, and the spiders were slicking their webs at the mouths of the pre-stressed pipes that would be lowered into the ground by lunchtime. But he walked past them, feeling his way among the shaggy trees that were shedding already, shedding like camels, and folding in his coat-flaps as the small snags of the undergrowth whisked at his hips.

There was nothing above him. That comet's tail was not a comet's tail: it was a late-night package flight to somewhere in Spain, where the children would bury their fathers in sand. The Russian had been right, the cosmonaut who had seen God nowhere in his travels. They shouldn't have given him a medal; they should have shot him for returning to the world as a theologian. For the Lord of Life was not the God of galaxies; he was the God of garbage, who had gone to ground in the green mess of the present moment.

Basil could feel a prayer coming on. He said it to himself, in case there would be a courting couple on the grassy slope behind the shrubs where he had first read Thomas à Kempis in the year of Stalingrad. Provided the young man's hands didn't cross the equator, it was goodly and gracious work, and they had a right not to be bothered. So he prayed silently, and he used contractions freely. It was too late in the day for the old formalities.

Lord, he thought, I don't ask you for a sign. It would go to my head, anyway. I would be a bore about it. But I'm going to die, and I don't know how to. I do know when and where and why, barring accidents, of course; but I don't really know how to go about it. The most important moments of my life have passed me by, because I was so involved in them; they came home only as an aftermath, and never at the time. But I want to die like a dog, really. Dogs die the way we're supposed to. Do you remember the labrador? I will never forget that labrador. I had to stop myself from closing his eyes. I was reaching out to.

The ground under his feet was packed with dead. That was why it was sprung and bumpy, like an egg-box. He looked around him. The pocks and bulges of the building site were a monkey's bottom, hairless and straining. A half-dozen houses beyond it, his host and hostess would be drying the glasses or putting out their clothes for the morning. They had a good marriage, the man who wanted to kill for money, and the woman whose fear of insanity would eventually drive her mad; but not, he hoped, before the children had grown up and gone away. The children were entitled to search for their own unhappiness. Each of them, both of them, the girl asleep in her gingham nursery and the still unsleeping baby to be born, would find their devious ways into the mystery by routes no other soul had thought of.

But this was mawkish; he would stop it that instant. He had been lulled, as ever, as always, by the inside of a home, a child's whiff on the furniture, and the sad comedy of youngsters playing their parents; and he had been duped in turn, appearing for no extra fee as a Tibetan mystic, frost-bitten, beatific, all barefoot in the blizzard, Heatherview's holy man. He was not at all pleased with himself, and he tinkered with his hearing aid to listen more ably to the facts of darkness, to the woodland creaking like a quayside, the tomcats in the skip beside the hydrant, and the rats leaving the houses, staggering over the hula-hoops, their bellies full of blue pellets, to die of thirst under the drenched hedges.

He would give up the drink. It was alcohol that made his silences mean something, and it was alcohol that turned his journey into a journal, into thumbnail table-talk. He owed it to his failures not to be anecdotal about them; they deserved that much consideration. He would not be personal in future, about his life or his death; and he would not take them personally, either. And he said 'Amen', out loud, regardless of Romeos and

Juliets, because his thoughts seemed like a prayer, and had been difficult to work out.

The community house was in darkness. They were all in, so. The lights were left on everywhere only when the lot of them were given a group ticket, to the Bolshoi or the pantomime on ice, and the boy with the beard would wear his collar in the car, because his tax was out of date.

'How was your breaking of bread?' said Luke. He was sitting in the hall, wearing his crash-helmet.

Basil hung up his hat.

'It was a very Catholic affair,' he said. 'More sacrifice than meal.'

Luke was lifting and dropping the visor on his helmet. It was a very large headpiece for such a small scooter. But that was Luke all over. He was more helmet than horsepower.

'I believe you're doing a baptism, Basil.'

'So I am,' the old man said. 'I'd almost forgotten.'

'They don't do them in Latin any longer,' Luke said. 'Had you forgotten that, too?'

'No,' said Basil. 'I hadn't forgotten. We'll all be buried in English; it's a terrible shame.' He was trying to think of something hurtful to say; it was hard, at the end of a long day. 'Why aren't you watching television?'

It was the best he could do, at short notice.

'They're showing "The Love Boat" on one station,' Luke said, 'and "Fantasy Island" on another. That's not late-night viewing. That's not the fruit of the forbidden tree. It's homemade apple-pie. I don't want to spend the small hours holding hands with Middle America.'

'I would have thought that a film called "Fantasy Island" was right up your alley,' Basil said. He was rather pleased about that one. It was a palpable hit. No doubt about it.

'You think?' Luke said.

'I do,' said Basil. 'You need a rest. You hunger and thirst after hunger and thirst all the time. It must be very tiring.'

He was walking up the stairs and had almost reached the landing, when Luke shouted to him from the barley-screw foot of the banister.

'While you're in your bedroom, having hallucinations about potted plants and your Doctor Livingstone days in the jungle, I'm out helping people,' he called. 'By the time you're snorting sprays over the breakfast table, I'm working through my lunch-hour. I feed the hungry, I clothe the naked, I comfort the orphans, I visit the sick, I tour the prisons. So don't think you have a monopoly on righteousness. Quit the three score years and ten lark.'

'Three score years and ten?' Basil said. 'You flatter me.'

'I don't,' Luke shouted. 'Three score years and ten is a Harvest Festival. Anything over that is hitting Hallowe'en.'

But Basil had closed his door behind him; and there on the floor in front of him was the mouse.

'You,' he said. 'Of course.'

He reached for the racquet and crushed him cleanly against the carpet. It was the simplest thing he had done all day. There was blood, to be sure, and pulverised bits that had the consistency of gristle; and the tucked skull cuddled the splay of the paws like the face of a foetus squashed in a medical jamjar. But the blood could be left for the mini-maids, for the woman who always said 'Sorry' instead of 'Hello'; and the furry squelch he could dispose of, himself. He eased it onto the racquet with his foot, and whooshed it out the window. The racquet glittered with hairy grease; he threw it out, too. It clattered over the corrugations, and hissed through a slithery bush.

He could hear nothing more. He could hear nothing at all; and he could hear it more clearly than ever before. Over the roof-line of the new estate, the light of a single burglar alarm winked like a solitary star; and above it, to the left of centre, a single star flashed like a solitary burglar alarm. Over and above and beyond all that, there was only blackness, split for a second by a hairline lesion in one of his lenses. Then the star went out, and the light of the alarm was switched off, and he sat on his bed, and reached for his slippers.

Veni, vidi, vici. That was the sum of every story, the total of all truth. He had come in, he had seen what was happening, he had reached for the racquet. There was no limit to what you could achieve in this world, if you felt nothing. You could build hospitals, or you could bomb them. You would not be brought to your knees in the sodium space of seconds between the doing and the having done, when the images blinded your retina like a migraine, and you walked with your head thrown back and your arms thrown forward, into the Fahrenheit, into the ton of light.

He sniffed his slipper speculatively. He wanted the brown-bread droppings of cattle, ginger and petrol on the breeze, the censer smoking in the thurible on a stool in his bedroom to ward off mosquitoes as he stapled the hem of the acolyte's alb on the vigil night of Easter Saturday in one or another year of the Lord; and the boy had rested his arm, and then his head, on Basil's shoulder, until the priest had made him eat Dolly Mixtures, and be damned to the regulations. Tractors were pulling the coffins in the street outside, and from the secretarial college at the corner he could hear the elderly Britons on sentry duty, with cricket bats on their shoulders.

He did not want to think about the tractors. They were for a different mood. They were for when he thought about the nature of man's existence. Tonight, he wanted to think about his life.

Al turned 'The Love Boat' off at the ad-break. Then he went upstairs. How could the Americans sell such rubbish to their own allies?

'Are we pals?' he said to her. 'Do we rub noses?'

Her eyelids glistened with Preparation H, and she had taken the eyes out of the teddy bear. That was it, then. Nothing at all was going to go bump in the night, tonight.

'Why did you bring up infertility clinics?' she said.

'I didn't bring up infertility clinics,' he said.

'I was the one who sat on a bus with your jiffy bag,' she said. 'Do you think that gave me a buzz? Do you think I sang "Here Comes the Sun" to the whole upper saloon?'

The commercials would almost be over. He was wondering. There was the odd swimsuit nibbling at a back-passage. But the actors were dorks.

'Why did you say Grace?' he said to her. 'You don't know how to say Grace.'

'I thought he'd say it,' said Jane. 'He's the priest. He should have said it. He shouldn't have made me say it. Now he probably thinks I'm not religious.'

'I'll tell him,' Al said. 'I'll set the record straight. I'll let him know about the parachute jump for Pakistan.'

'Bangladesh,' she said.

'You say tomatoes,' he said, 'I say tomatoes. The point is, you got tendonitis for the Third World. You are one hell of a woman. You deserve another medal. You deserve another shoulder-pad.'

'At least I go to church,' she said.

'You go to churches,' he told her. 'There's a difference. You go to churches to look at fonts. You take Polaroids, and bring them home for a second opinion.'

'At least I go,' she said. 'You haven't been in a church since you played the Backside of the Ox at play-school.'

'What about the power-cut?' he said. 'Where do you think the candles came from?'

But her eyes had left the room. She was patting her bump like a sand-castle.

'Why?' she said. 'Why?'

'I'm listening,' he said. 'When am I not listening?'

'Why does the foetus suck its thumb?' she said. 'It shouldn't, really. It's not cause and effect. It's not stimulus and response. Theoretically, it's not supposed to, but it does. Why?'

'It's waiting for the next cavalry charge of Cossack vodka,' he said. 'It's biting its nails with excitement.'

'And why?' she said. 'Why are we mammals? Why are we not marsupials? Marsupials have it down to a fine art.'

'You're at the Why stage,' he said.

'I'm past the Why stage,' she said. 'I'm at the Wherefore stage.'

'Stick with the way things are,' he said. 'Stick with the surface of things. All the protein in the potato is in the potato-skin; yet we throw the potato-skin out.'

'You throw the potato-skin out,' she said. 'Not me.'

She was obviously determined not to be reasonable; so he slipped in beside her, and drew the Western hemisphere on her belly with a purple marker-pen. She liked that.

'Why is it always the Atlantic?' she said. 'Why is it never the Pacific?'

139

'I can't do South East Asia,' he said. 'It's all udders.'

She lay back, and thought about this and that, and made two mental notes and seven decisions. He had finished South America, and was putting in Trinidad and Tobago.

'All I want,' she said, 'is one priest and one font. I'll bring the baby. But can I find what I'm looking for? No, I cannot. Right, I'll scratch the font. Forget the font; on with the tin pan. All I ask is a priest. Ideally, he should be a male celibate, ordained, and in good standing with the personnel people in Rome. It would be nice if he could speak English, it would be even nicer if he could speak it non-regionally; and it would be nicest of all if he were not a total fucking head-banger.'

But Al was saying nothing. He went on with his work, putting in a lot of little oxygen bubbles for the islands of the Caribbean.

'Algae,' she said. 'There was sort of algae on the nose bits of his glasses.'

He had made the Gulf of Mexico too small. He always did that. He always, always did. Most of the Bermudas disappeared into the sweat-pores of a tiny crinkle.

'Half the time, I couldn't make head nor tail of what he was saying,' she said. 'There should have been sub-titles. I kept looking for them, between the candles.'

'There were,' he said. 'But it was hard to read them, because he was wearing black.'

The child had woken, and was calling from next door.

'A head-banger,' she said. 'I went and did a kiwi soufflé for a head-banger.'

'He's not that bad,' said Al. 'He's bouncy. He goes back as far as gun-boats, but he's still afloat. He's still buoyant.'

Aoife called again. She was not taking silence for an answer. She was not even taking it for a reply.

'Buoyant means nothing,' she said. 'The Dead Sea is buoyant.' She turned away from him, holding the lips of her vagina apart by the hairs and flapping them to cool herself. 'Go in and see,' she said. 'Be firm with her. Make her lie down.'

'Chapter Seven said this would happen,' he said.

'Chapter Eight says it gets worse,' she said. 'Chapter Eight is a chamber of horrors. They push the pram in front of a double-decker.'

'Daddy,' the child called. 'Daddy.'

'I'm going to throw that book out,' he said. 'I'm going to throw them all out.'

She put the matchstick through the light-switch, and turned it off.

'You do,' she said, 'and I'll burn those magazines you read.'

He went into her room. She was sitting up in bed, spotting the carpet with the last of the bottle. He gathered her into his arms, adjusting her against him until their hearts were in the same place. Then he held her like the shopping, the food and drink of her, as if he were afraid the bag might burst, and the messages scatter.

'Look,' he said, pulling the curtain back. 'Look. Moon.'

'What about it?' she said. But she looked up, to where it was stuck in the satellite dish of one of the houses that had two bedrooms and less brick.

'Three men went there,' he said. 'They went in a spaceship. Whoosh for a day; whoosh for another; whoosh for a third. Then they landed. They landed with a bump. Out they got with their spades and their buckets. The first man dug-a-dug; the second man dug-a-dug; but the third man stopped and looked back. "Look," he cried. "Look," he wept, "Look," he broke down. "Earth."'

'What about it?' the child said.

'Earth it was, earth it is, earth it ever shall be,' said Al. 'They sat down on their bottoms, and they looked and looked until their helmets misted over. All they could see was the ends of their noses. Up they got, in they sat, and off they went. Whoosh for a day, whoosh for a second, whoosh for a third. Then they landed. There were their little girls with their buckets and spades, and two new bruises on each of their knees and two new cuts on each of their elbows; and that was not that, because that was this.'

She was smiling at his ear. He kissed her right between the eyes.

'Bum bum,' she said. 'Bum bum, willy, poo, fart.'

Basil vested in the sacristy. He walked out onto the main altar, stood at the lectern, and chatted informally with the empty benches for exactly three minutes. Then he paused the stopwatch. So far, so good. He'd have broken the ice by now, and the people in the pews would be at ease, expectant, even eager. He had been humorous, but not hilarious; jolly, but not jokey. After all, it was a sacred occasion, and there were babies present. The two very funny stories he had thought of, could wait for the bunfight. A party setting would be more appropriate.

Where was the leaflet of the liturgy? He found it, smoothed it on the lectionary, and started the stopwatch. But that was not the right way. He had zeroed it. He would have to remember the first three minutes, and add them on at the end.

'My brothers and sisters,' he said to the dim, deserted church, 'we are happy today to welcome a new baby into the Christian family.'

Of course, he would not have to be so declamatory on the day. Somebody would be able to work out the public address system. Luke had a motorbike. He would know about electrics.

'We will be known by our name in this life and also in eternity, so what name have you plural chosen for your baby?'

He answered for the parents, and carried on. It was not at all as formidable as the old Latin, God be good to it, this mish-mash of an itsy-bitsy catechism, but it meant well, and there was plenty for him to do in it. He worked his way down slowly through the prayers and blessings, da-da-da, the readings, more blessings, da-da-da, to a point at the close of Section Four where a brief homiletic excursus might not come amiss. He marked the passage with a B for Basil, and went on and over the page.

The holy oils, the hallowing of water. These he must mimic, and did, lifting and dropping his hand, while he hummed some suitable musical intermezzo, an air with an age-old atmosphere, Catholic, cultic, free of the spineless shilly-shallyings of the new committee men. Then a pause for reflection, before the profession of faith. The rejection of evil had replaced the rejection of Satan. It was good theology, but poor theatre. They had cut out all the best bits.

'Is it your wish,' he said, 'that this child, or children, be baptised in the faith of the Church? It is. Right.'

He baptised his hands, and waited thirty-five seconds on the stopwatch for the flash-cubes and the clapping. Then he continued, da-da-da, doh-re-mi, through the prayers and blessings that remained. There were so many of them; there were too many of them. And where was the bittersweet psalter gone, the truculent, manly worship of the God of Jacob? These were not invocations; they were after-dinner speeches.

He did the Amen for the congregation, counted to ten, and paused the clock again. He was feeling fine; he was not out of breath. He would not have to use the ventilator once. He could use it for luck in the sacristy, before he came out.

His hands were a problem. He accepted that. They would appear in the pictures looking Transylvanian. He searched in the sacristy presses until he found some strips of bandage that were still sticky. They had a nice smell, too, a smell of secondary schools. He inhaled it happily, peeled the protective film away, and ironed the dressings onto the back of each hand with the palm of the other.

Fabric Plaster For Cushioned Protection, he read. All-Purpose Economy Mouldings. At least it had rhythm; it had a tum-tee-tum to it. That was more than you could say for the blessing of the parents or proxies. It was a damn sight more.

Through the window he saw her, the child, Aoife, rambling over the tarmacadam in a pretty thing, a dress of some sort, the colour of butterflies, or was it ladybirds? At any rate, it was the sort of thing she should be wearing on a nice morning, a morning like this; and you could tell she was a girl. You did not have to work it out in your head beforehand.

He tapped the window with his bandaged knuckle.

'Peek-a-bye,' he called. 'Peek-a-bye.'

She was blowing bubbles, or trying to. The little stick kept dribbling. She was probably breathing too hard. You had to go softly, softly, like soothing a cinder, coaxing it. Where was the paid assassin when his daughter needed him? Where was her mother, for that matter? She was off gallivanting with the girlfriends, that was where.

'Aoife,' he shouted. 'Aoife.'

The scream startled her. She dropped the coloured can, stared for a second as the contents spilled slowly into the shape of a squid, and took off, terrified. He lost her among the cars, the wildfire of the chrome.

'You stupid bloody woman,' he shouted. 'It's only me.'

He would never understand them. Their world was worlds away. He yanked the bandage from his hand, and the pink skin stung like a steam-burn. But it did look better; it looked much better. He would not be modelling gloves or engagement rings, after all. He would be making the sign of the Cross over the bewildered, geriatric scowl of a sleeping infant. So he snatched the bandage off the other hand, and the hairs tore thoroughly. The underside of the adhesive might have been one of those long Vapona strips they hung in the cafés over the tables, with the black intestines of insects bristling as the clarinet player came into his own.

He held them up to the light and turned them slowly, the two, trustworthy hands of his. It had never occurred to him to thank them, fingers and fists, but he did so now. He had always thought that he knew them like the back of his hand, but he had not. His body was beyond him. He was inexpressibly happy. He wondered what was for lunch.

Jane lifted her bottom and edged the seat in closer to the table. That was because the coffee dock was empty. She wasn't afraid of bugs in the begonias; not really. That had been a witticism. It was just that hospitals made you lower your voice. It was out of respect for the suffering, actually; the suffering, and the ninety per cent hopelessness. The check-out looked like Honolulu, but the dentist with the gladioli would be back in twelve months' time, and they'd take his Samsonite suitcase and sign him on for the shuttlecock quarter finals.

'Declan,' she said, 'you need to sit down and write out the questions. You need to have a list with you. Otherwise, you'll forget. The consultant can't be expected to know what's on your mind, unless you ask him.'

'I shall do,' said the deacon. He was cutting the filters off a new packet of cigarettes with a razor. Jane thought the razor was very encouraging. The fact they would let him have a razor was a sure sign that he was getting back to his old self again. Of course, one swallow did not make a summer; but the thousand-mile journey began with the first step.

'Is "shall" the same as "will"?' she said to the nurse. 'He can be so crafty.'

'Speak up, Declan,' said the nurse. 'You have a beautiful speaking voice. Use it.'

The nurse smelled of perfume. She positively reeked of it. Surely only consultants could wear perfume. And she had studs in her ears. The next thing you knew, they'd be wearing eyeshadow. Everything had gone to the dogs.

'I shall, so I will,' said Declan. 'And I will, so I shall.'

'Ask him,' Jane said. 'Ask him about the anti-depressants. Tell him you love cheese. Tell him you'd love to try another anti-depressant, where you could eat cheese. Tell him you'd love that. Then ask him about the baptism. Tell him you'd love that, too. No harm comes of telling.'

'Yep,' said Declan. 'Yep, yep, yap.'

'Watch the old whispering, Declan,' said the nurse. 'The whispering is not humility. The whispering is passive aggression. Watch the passive aggression. We've talked about this before; we're talking about it again; we'll talk about it again and again. Are you hearing me?'

'I am,' he said. 'You have a beautiful speaking voice, too.'

'Fine,' said the nurse, and she stood up, brushing her bottom. There was absolutely no call for that kind of carry-on, either. This was not some sort of Prohibition speakeasy. But now that the majority of nurses were sufficiently middle-class to date the doctors, things had gone lackadaisical. That was the only word for it.

'Bye, Jane,' the nurse said. 'Bye, Dec. Be good, or else.' And she walked off out the door of the coffee-dock, past the matchstick model of the Parthenon that a former doctor had made, and the soles of her shoes made light little smacks on the parquet as she passed away out of sight.

'Is she yours?' said Jane.

'Yes,' he said. He was quite proud. 'We've been together since I came in. But she told me not to get too attached, because she's going to Malta next week for a fortnight. She sent me a card already.'

'A card?' said Jane. 'How do you mean, a card?'

'A postcard,' he said.

'Speak up,' she said. 'You're being very passive.'

'She said she wouldn't have time, when she gets there,' Declan said. 'So she wrote about twenty cards while she was on night duty, and she slipped them in under the door in the morning. Everybody on my floor got one.'

'I see,' said Jane. 'She's a poacher turned gamekeeper. She's a head-banger.'

'They were Maltese postcards,' he said. 'They had Maltese stamps, even. She was there last year.'

'And she's looking after you?' she said.

'She washed my hair this morning,' he said. 'She put the shampoo in twice.'

'Was that nice?' she said. 'Did you like her doing it?'

'Yes,' he said. 'I did.'

She leaned in even closer than she had.

'Did you have an erection?' she said.

He was concentrating on the filters. There was only one to be sliced through. The others lay in a neat pile by the ashtray.

'Well?' she said. 'Did you?'

'No,' he said. 'But I pretended to. It would have been rude, if I hadn't.'

'You might have one, the next time,' she said. 'Try to have one, the next time.'

'She's going to Malta in a week,' he said. 'Why are you whispering?'

'God created the world in a week,' Jane said. 'The important thing is, you're feeling normal in one situation. You can build on that. You can go on to feel normal in another situation. Then, before you know where you are, you'll have normalised the whole shebang. But you have to believe in yourself. If you don't believe in yourself, everybody else will start believing in you. It's a complete pain.'

'Would you please stop whispering?' he said. 'There's nobody here.'

'And you have to believe in the future,' she said. 'You have to believe in the future tense.'

'I do believe in the future tense,' he said. 'I just have problems with the future perfect.'

She got up to go. There was so much static in the chair. Where did it come from? Her hips were crackling. She slapped her bump without thinking about it, and the baby stirred. He knew her knock.

'At least, you know what the problem is now,' she said. 'You've eliminated everything that the problem isn't. What are you doing with those filters, Declan?'

'It's to stop people asking me for cigarettes,' he said. 'Nobody smokes them without the filter.'

She stooped and kissed the top of his head. His hair was ever so glossy. She had green fingers, that nurse.

'Ask her to cut your beard,' she said to him. 'With the smallest scissors you can lay your hands on. But do your toenails yourself. And see the consultant.'

'I'll be seeing the registrar,' he said. 'He can't speak English, really, so we walk around the grounds and pick lavender. He's as black as my boots.'

She ducked down under the table for a good, long look.

'Your boots aren't black,' she said, 'and, besides, you aren't wearing boots. You're barefoot.'

But he was beginning to cry, without making any sound. He put his face down into the ashtray to save the tablecloth.

Basil had thought of a terrific opening line. He would joke about for the first three minutes, and then go serious suddenly. It would be what you might call a sudden, stark contrast. The knowledge of water is not H_2O he wrote. The knowledge of water is thirst.

It had to be said. That was a grand beginning. It was wind, strings and brass from the word Go. He would say it, and then stop; and let a silence settle. The pause would be pregnant. The men in their mobster suits and the women in their pill-box hats would be waiting, and wondering. Beads of sweat would trickle down the insides of their arms like a slow horse-fly. He would allow twenty, twenty-five, even thirty seconds, to elapse, to pass out of eternity into time, before putting the question: What does this mean exactly?

They'd have been jealous of this one, the Three Stooges watching the set downstairs. It wasn't a bad idea to have written it in consonants, to have taken out the vowels, and made it harder to decipher. They were always snooping; they'd have seized it, and made off. He'd have heard it back on Sunday in a sermon from some Johnny-come-lately. Nothing was sacred, not even the copyright on your own omissions, the things you had not said, the things you had not done.

When the plant began to sway in the soft mosquito nets of the moonlight, Basil would have kneeled, but he was too sore. The pain was roaming tightly inside him, as dry and heavy as an anticyclone. Only his head was clear of it, and God was welcome to him from the neck down. Yet he felt tender towards them, those inner organs he had never noticed. They had kept him useful and attentive beyond the average age expectancy, as a donkey calms a thoroughbred when the two are grazed together.

The plant was swaying still. He sat, adoring it. He would say nothing. He would try not to think. He would be a boy again, sitting in a scullery, slipping his mother's dress-gloves down over the barrel of his father's rifle, and crying because he knew he would remember this moment of joy when he was dying of old age at the end of the century.

'What drives you?' said the consultant. 'You have this great drive.'

'It was always a Ford Escort,' Basil said. 'But I don't use it now. I'd be afraid of something happening while I'm at the wheel; I'd be afraid of knocking a child down.'

'You're right,' said the consultant. 'And the insurance would never cover it.'

There was no doubt about it. The old priest was a great man for shaking hands. This was the second, no, the third time. The consultant kept his right hand out of his pocket, to be sure it would be dry. Dampness always connoted shiftiness. Look at poor President Nixon.

'Anyhow,' Basil said.

'Indeed,' said the surgeon, and the two moved another six feet toward the hall-door. If the phone didn't ring soon, or the receptionist come back from feeding the meter, he might be standing here with this tumble-down padre until Doomsday.

'It's a great relief for a man like me,' the surgeon said, 'to be able to deal plainly. I seem to spend so much of my time gift-wrapping the grim news. With a priest, though, you can cut to the main verb, no nonsense. You can sweep aside all the subordinate clauses; and your facial muscles get a rest, too. A priest always refuses the blindfold.'

Basil suddenly felt very proud of being a priest. He studied himself in the mirror, with his hat on; but the mirror was convex.

'I think about the hereinafter a lot,' the consultant said. 'I think about it out in the boat. You feel quite religious. The sea brings it all home to you.'

'The only thing that brings it all home to you,' said Basil, 'is having no home.'

'Do you know what?' the surgeon said. 'I was thinking that very thought the other night, when I was out in the bay, becalmed. I was looking at the house-lights lighting up along the coast, and thinking of all the people who were turning on lights, here, there, and everywhere. It would really make you think. It made me think.'

He had got him to the door. Now it was a simple matter of opening it; and he did. Basil stepped out between the boot-scrapers, and stared up at the sky. The lumpy grey of its rubble reminded him of fresh vomit. He had mopped it up enough to be an expert.

'Dreadful day,' the surgeon said.

'It is,' said Basil. 'Thank God.'

'Thank God, indeed,' said the surgeon. He had spotted the traffic-warden on the other side of the street, but she had almost finished, the receptionist. She gave him a thumbs-up sign from behind the bonnet of his car. She was worth her weight in gold. He must get her an umbrella for the winter.

'You'll like the place, Father,' he said. 'It's personal, it's private, and it's very professional. The staff are A One, absolutely A One. They're immensely motivated, and they're always there. Only a bleep away. One of the bereavement counsellors sailed a Dragon to the Faroe Islands, so they're match-form men, league-table types. And the thanatologist is a delightful human being.'

'Yes,' said Basil. 'I'd like to meet him.'

'Her,' the surgeon said. 'You'll know her to see. She always wears red.'

But Basil was pointing upward to the fresh vomit. Between the vapour-trail of a jet-plane and the smoke-stacks of the biscuit factory, an arrowhead of arctic terns was heading straight for the rugby grounds.

'Look,' he said.

'I know,' the surgeon said. 'It's so bad they've called the races off.'

'No,' said Basil. 'They're heading for the South Pole.'

The surgeon let the tips of his fingers rest on the seam of Basil's shoulder.

'It's better this way,' he said to the strange, excited priest. 'If anything happened to you in your bedroom, your community would never forgive itself. There are monitors in the other place. There are buttons under the pillow. They have thought it through completely.'

'And my eyes?' said Basil. 'What about my corneas?'

The consultant thought about it. He was trying to retrieve a line from the Bible, but he wanted to get it right. The priest was, after all, a priest. He would know the stuff inside out at this stage of the game.

'Because of your consideration for others,' he said to Basil, 'a people that sat in great darkness will suddenly see trees moving.'

The receptionist passed through them on her way in. She was so pleased with herself for having pleased him. She trickled the remaining five-penny pieces into the surgeon's hands.

'Attagirl,' he said.

Aoife and Al were in the bath together. She was combing the hairs on his legs with a plastic slide, while he rolled an ice-pop up and down his chest to cool it.

'Can I pee?' she said.

'No,' he told her. 'The bubbles would go.'

So they sang a song to the dolphin they had seen on the children's channel, the time he spread the dressing-gown in front of the set in case the Pacific splashed out of it.

'Diddle-di-deedle-do,

Where do you do your poo?

In the sea or in the loo?'

He could hear her coming up the stairs. Either she was angry, or the weight of the pregnancy had put lead in her boots. Her steps battered the chipboard, trap-door style.

'Here's Mummy Bear,' he said, and he lifted the child onto his lap, because she had begun to blow the bubbles off his penis. 'Never pee in the bath, and never pee when the train stops.'

'Pee the pee,' she said, joyfully. She was a water baby.

'Will you love me when I'm little, and you're big?' he said. 'Will you marry a man who has the very same smells as me?'

'All right,' she said, and she squirted the leaky alligator on his belly-button.

The landing had gone silent suddenly.

'Is that you?' he called.

'Yes,' said Jane. 'It's me. I'm back.'

He slipped into the green water until it sipped at his nipples.

'Are you in there?' she said.

'I am,' he said.

'I thought you were,' she said.

'You were right,' said Al.

'Pee the pee,' Aoife sang, 'poo the poo.'

'I wrote that letter,' Jane said.

'What letter?' he said.

'You know what letter,' she said. 'That letter. Then I dropped it round.'

'Jesus Christ,' he said.

'Jesus Christ,' said Aoife.

'I gave it to one of the priests,' she said, 'to give to him. He said he'd give it to him. He thought it was a birthday card. It's Basil's birthday. I said it was just a note. He said that was just as nice.'

Al levered himself out of the bath.

'Stay,' he said to Aoife. 'Stay.'

She had gone into the bedroom. He followed her, piling the suds from his thighs onto his privates in case there might be boys playing in the wood at the bottom of the garden. He did not want to look ridiculous.

'Why?' he said to her.

'Because,' she said to him. 'That's why.'

'Thank you,' he said. 'That's all I wanted to know.'

The suds were drifting slowly down his penis. He felt so humiliated. He scooped them back again, shaping them with his hands like a plaster-cast.

'If it has to be a head-banger,' she said, 'let it at least be a family head-banger.'

'You're the head-banger,' he said. 'You're the head head-banger, you are.'

'Am I?' she said. 'Am I? Because if I am, it's only because I'm banging my head against a brick wall every day. That's why I am, if I am.'

'I am sick to death,' he said. 'I am sick to death of pathology. I was the child of pathology. I was the fruit of the union of two pathological parents. My mother made me bring seaweed from Sandymount for her seaweed bath. My father taught me the facts of life by producing a skeleton from a cricket-box that he kept under the bed. He laid it out on my mother's side, and he demonstrated the bones with the aid of a shoe-horn. "This is where you go in," he said, and he tapped the shoe-horn on something that looked like antlers.'

'Would you not cover yourself?' she said. 'You might be seen.'

'I am not going to put up with pathology,' he said. 'I am not waving any olive-branches at bizarre behaviour. I am coming at it with both barrels, so be warned. I am going to blow it away.'

The last of the foam had slopped to his ankles. He picked up the tortoise and held it against him.

'Why do women wear perfume?' he said. 'That's what I asked my mother. I was thirteen. She said to me, "It's because of a bad smell that they let out." But I wanted to ask my father, to be sure, to be certain sure. My father would know. My father knew everything. He knew that the mayfly had no mouth; he knew that the body weighs a fraction less after the moment of death, because the soul has shed it, and gone up, up, up, and away, like the little balloon I lost in the zoo, out over the lion-cages; and he even knew that Christ had been crucified by the wrists and not by the palms.'

'Your father was a lovely man,' Jane said. 'He helped arrange adoptions.'

'I wanted to ask him,' Al said. 'Why do women wear perfume? But it was late, it was twelve o'clock, it was midnight. I was downstairs, in the darkness of the drawing-room, listening to the Beach Boys with a stethoscope; and he was upstairs, prowling round, the ends of his braces in his pockets to stop them jingling, putting slices of white bread down his underpants to soak up the blood from his rectum.'

'He put up with a great deal,' she said.

'He was never happier,' Al said. 'It was almost sexual.'

It had begun to rain. She could hardly see it at first, but the ground was darkening. The farmers would be so pleased.

'Will it last?' she said.

He put the tortoise on the bed, and she let him. The windows were beginning to spot. It made her want to go to the toilet. It always did. She loved the bright drool elongating downwards, the sperm on the pane, and the goat-bell background noises of a little light shower.

'Mummy,' Aoife called from the bathroom. 'The water is getting wet.'

'What do you really want, love?' she said to him. She was drowsy with pleasure.

'I want to be like the family in the Kellogg's Cornflakes ad,' he said. 'Do you know the family in the Kellogg's Cornflakes ad?'

She bent over him on the bed, and kissed his penis. It smelled lovely. She would love to have put a tiny blue bow on it.

'No,' she said, 'I don't think I know that ad.'

'Maybe I'm aiming too high,' he said, 'but that is what I would really like to be.'

He had forgotten that it was his birthday.

'How old are you, Basil?' said the boy with the beard that

looked like a vagina. Actually, he had shaved it off. One of his girlfriends must have got to him.

'I don't remember,' he said, but of course he did. The two things you cannot forget are your youth and your age.

'We're not going to sing "Happy Birthday", Basil,' said Luke, 'because that would only embarrass you. Instead, we're going to sing "We'll Meet Again". I even went and xeroxed the words.'

Basil was counting the candles. Why were there thirteen? Thirteen was not a multiple of anything. Today wasn't the thirteenth. He hadn't been in the house for thirteen years; he hadn't left Africa thirteen years before. He was baffled. He forgot for a while about everything else: the hot pain in his side, the south-facing room that would soon be reserved when the occupant's coma had ended, and the note from the middle-class mother-to-be, the note with the cloudy colours and a hint of the scent of paprika on it. He had taken it out and read it once, twice, three times to himself, and he had had to admit that the handwriting was worthy of the nuns, of a better class of nuns, even. She might have been taught by the Sacred Heart, or the Faithful Companions of Jesus.

'Don't give me any of the sponge,' he said. 'I only eat the icing.'

'You have to blow the candles out, first,' said the albino.

Basil sucked in his cheeks. If he'd known there were only thirteen, he wouldn't have used his ventilator in the toilet under the stairs.

'Not yet, not yet,' Luke said. 'Douse the lights, somebody.'

He extinguished ten in one go, and then another two; but the last, the thirteenth, gave him trouble. The other priests were laughing until you couldn't hear the television. He tried again, and gave up. It had to be a hoax. He wet his thumb to snuff it, but the flame freed itself.

'It's hell-fire,' the albino said. 'We looked for brimstone on the building site, but they only had blasting-powder.'

'Here,' said the boy without the beard. 'You can have my icing.'

Basil was suspicious. This was an overture; and there was no overture without strings.

'You can keep your icing,' he said. 'I've enough icing.'

It was almost nine o'clock. The rest were drifting back towards their favourite chairs. The boy raised his hands and lowered his voice.

'Father,' he said, 'we have to live in the world we haven't been given.'

'I said that,' Basil said.

'I know you did,' said the boy. 'That's why I'm saying it now.'

'Well, don't,' said Basil. 'It's mine.'

'Father,' the boy said. His voice was dropping and dropping.

'Speak up,' said Basil. 'I can't lip-read, you know. I can see them at long last, but I can't make sense of them.'

'Father,' the boy said, 'there is no moon.'

'Fine,' Basil said. 'Am I to pass that on?'

'The plant in the pot,' said the boy. 'Moving about, and things. Doing little jigs in the moonlight. There is no moonlight. There is no moon. Not at the moment; not for days now. I have the whole lunar calendar in my appointments diary. I can show it to you. I can give it to you. I can tear it out, and give it to you.'

'I see,' said Basil. His voice was thick from the icing. He put more in his mouth.

'The light that comes into your room,' said the boy, 'is the light from another light. The light on the building site is what bothers you, not the light of the moon. It's as bright as bedamned. I know. I used to work on a building site. I was on the night-shift; we worked right through. The whole place was lit up like an air-raid. It bewildered the birds. They sang at two in the morning. You could hear them when the tapes in the ghetto-blasters ran out. While you were turning the tapes, you could hear the blackbirds and stuff.'

'You're not going to believe this, Basil,' said the albino. 'As a special birthday tribute to yours truly, ITV is running "Octopussy". How about that, then?'

But Basil was leaving the room, a forgotten fistful of icing in his hand. He would read the note again, and then think about everything; or he would think about everything, and then read the note.

'Some of it's set in Africa,' said Luke. 'You might recognise it.'

'You might recognise yourself,' the albino said. 'You might be in it.'

'Africa,' said the boy, 'has never been in a Bond movie. Africa, or Ireland.'

And they argued about the significance of this, for almost seven and a half minutes, until the film came on.

It was raining hard. The igloo of froth at the corner of the car-park underneath his window must be the bodily resurrection of the little girl's bubbles, where she had dropped her canister and bolted when he waved to her that morning, or the morning before, or the morning before that. But he was not about to get into a state over it. He closed the inside shutters to block out the building site, and sat on the edge of the bed in the healing, alkaline silence. Motes of his own making floated across his field of vision, and he jiggled them about until they assumed the constellation of the Plough. That was fun, and it filled five minutes, almost. He eased his feet into the soft sheepskin of light from the overhead sixty-watt bulb, and ignored the plant's first rapturous jitterings. There was a strong draught crossing the room; that was all. It was no wonder he'd lived on Lemsips through the winter. Let the pot rock and roll, if it wanted to. It was no burning bush, neither bush nor burning, and he was not Moses; and nor, for that matter, was Moses himself.

He broke the tablets in two, and put the halves back in the box. He would take them whole, without water. He was choking on everything else; he might as well choke on them.

The laughter of the bright young things below shot through the slits in the floorboards of his bedroom like the sharpened blades of swords.

'Please,' said the child. 'Please, Father Blackhead.'

'No,' he said. 'And that's the last time I'm going to say it. Now I have to read my Office.'

'Is this your Office?' she said.

'In a manner of speaking,' he said. 'This is where I say mass, and forgive sins. This is a church. Up there is the altar.'

'God is in the plus sign,' she said.

'That is a cross,' he told her. 'It is not a plus sign. And God is everywhere.'

He went back to his breviary, but she would not budge. She was as bad as Joan of Arc in front of the Dauphin.

'You're a holy terror,' he said. 'Do you know that, missus? God help your husband.'

'Please,' she said. 'I put a plus sign on his shell.'

At last, he relented. If anyone spotted them, he could fall back on his senility. After the flower that had done a flamenco, they would believe anything.

'Not there,' he said. 'Not the altar. Come to the baptistry.'

There was less likelihood of a priestly swoop in there. It had hardly been used since that calamity of a Second Vatican Council. Now the unfortunate font was a ballroom for earwigs. They had gone so far as to store aqualung equipment in it. The Protestants must be laughing all the way to Lambeth.

'Right,' he said. 'We'll do it here. This is a baptistry. Can you say baptistry?'

'No,' she said. 'I don't want to.'

'A baptistry,' he told her, 'is a place built specially for showing little girls and boys to God, after their mummies bring them out into the world to live in it.'

'In what?' said the child. 'In here?'

'No,' the priest said. 'In the world.'

'My mummy has a boob to feed the baby,' Aoife said.

'Yes,' said Basil. 'That's right. She'll hold the baby to her heart, and the baby won't be afraid of anything, then. He'll grip your finger, and he'll think: "That is my sister Aoife, and she is just great." And you'll think: "That is my little brother, or sister, about whom I am very pleased. Would you just listen to him, for goodness' sake." '

'When I was born,' the child said, 'I was five-and-a-half months old.'

Basil put the tortoise into the font. His curiosity would get the better of him in due course. Sooner or later, he would peep out.

'When I was born,' Basil said, 'I was twenty-three. A bullet came in through a pane of glass, and the glass flowered. I had a rose-window in my very own bedroom.'

'Just do the baptism,' she said. 'Go on.'

'What name do you have in mind?' he asked her.

'Tortoise,' she said.

'That's not a name,' Basil said. 'He's a tortoise already. "Tortoise" is a police description, not a term of endearment.'

'He wants to be that,' the child said. 'He wants to be the same as his name.'

'Fine,' the priest said. 'We'll call him Tortoise.'

'Not Tortoise,' Aoife said. 'He is Tortoise the Tortoise.'

'Better still,' said Basil. 'There won't be any confusion.'

He was crawling out of his shell now, blinking, his eyes as ancient as Africa. He had been exhausted long before the antelopes mutated in the Great Rift Valley. He had given up for good before Kilimanjaro had ceased to grow an inch an era, and the first hunters had heard in the crackling of the campfire tomorrow morning's ibex step among the skipping twigs. By the time that Jesus slid into the waters of the Jordan, he had counted every star in the sky; and by the time that Queen Victoria presented Lake Uganda to the Kaiser as a wedding present, he had calculated the seed-time of the sand as well, to within the nearest billion or thereabouts.

Basil felt a rush of fellow-feeling.

'Does he want to be baptised?' he said.

The child was feeding him grassblades, breadcrumbs and a destroyed Brussels sprout. The pockets of her pinafore were bottomless.

'Does he?' said Basil.

'Yes, I do,' said the child, in a tortoise voice.

'Does he promise always and everywhere, to the best of his ability, to be a tortoise, a whole tortoise, and nothing but a tortoise?'

'I do,' said the child. It was a squeaky voice, like the Disney chipmunks; or was it Tom and Jerry?

'Does he promise never to want to be anything else, a hippo or an oyster-catcher, but to go on, year in, year out, becoming more and more of a tortoise until he eventually is one?'

'What's an oyster-catcher?' Aoife said.

'Never mind,' Basil said. 'Does he?'

'I do,' said the child.

The tortoise was trying to climb the font, but the law of

gravity was against him. He went in on himself, of course, except for one paw. That was a habit with him, the one paw. He had learned to go on as if everything had already happened.

'Then,' said Basil, 'by the authority vested in me by my state of health, I pronounce you baptised. I name you Tortoise the Tortoise, the Tortoise of Aoife. For your motto, I give you "Totally Tortoise", and I bless you. I bless you in the name of the God who made you. In the name of the Father and of the Son and of the Holy Ghost.'

'Spirit,' said Aoife.

'Spirit,' said Basil.

'Amen,' the child said.

They lifted the tortoise out of the font, and set it on the floor. He would be two ashtrays in six months.

'We have to give him a present,' Aoife said. 'We have to.'

'All I have is money,' the old priest said.

'Tortoise loves money,' said the child. 'He lets me mind it.'

When she saw him passing in his clerical black, Jane pulled in to the opposite side of the road where she lived, and parked there. Then she put on her sunglasses. Old people never remembered cars, but a hearing problem sometimes sharpened their eyesight. So she waited for him to go by, with her head down. How could he wear a heavy coat on a day like this, a beautiful, balmy day, as warm as the skies in the snapshots of their honeymoon, when she'd taken off her top on the third day, and the sun had been rough with her, rubbing the skin the wrong way, so that her breasts stung in the shower? Even the men on the building site had stripped to the first hairs of their hip-bones, and the ice-cream man was out. She could hear it, in among the clothes-lines, 'Greensleeves' on a glockenspiel.

Why was he walking so slowly? He must have all the time in the world. He was not like her at all. Her time was nearing at the speed of deserts. She opened the sun-roof rowdily, and the baby beneath her flinched in the phosphor fire-storm. She could feel it. He was so busy, so brimful. He would be walking at eight months.

Basil had stopped outside their house. Surely to Heavens he wouldn't walk across the new grass; he could not be that thoughtless. But he moved on after a moment, and she picked at the black grease of her sweat on the steering wheel, scraping it with her fingernail and flicking it down among the pedals, between her feet, until he had reached the corner, rounded it, and disappeared. Then she went in.

Al had put on his answerphone. He was not supposed to do that in the last three weeks; he was on call. But it was typical. She would check his petrol later on that evening, and she would find he was driving on reserve. She was sure of it. They were all the same, the sons of Adam. They were Cains posing as Abels.

'Al,' she said, 'It's about Declan. You know he isn't supposed to eat cheese, because of the m-e-d-i-c-a-t-i-o-n. Well, he did. He went off to a delicatessen, and bought everything: Brie, Stilton, Camembert, you name it. He ate the whole lot in the park. Nothing happened, except they took his clothes away.'

She waited for the sound of the end, like the sound of a lift arriving. But there was still time.

'Should I ring the Adoption Agency?' she said. 'I have this terrible feeling they're going to send flowers. I don't mind the flowers, but I don't want their letterhead all over it. That would be awful for Aoife. Please ring me. I'm in the directory under your name.'

She sat in front of the open fridge to cool herself, and she ate a tin of baby-food. She must check with the police about road-works between the house and the hospital.

'Seventeen,' she wrote down. 'Call the police.'

Al and Basil could not avoid meeting. The shouting was only because of the din on the building site.

'How now, brown cow?' said Basil. 'What news?'

'God is dead,' said Al, 'and women are still having babies. Also, I forgot to put my aerial down in the car-wash. It's a shame, too. I always loved coming up out of the underground car-park and driving into all this light and music at the same moment. It made me feel like Lazarus, looking at women's throats again, through the eye-slits in my shroud.'

'And how is the woman of the house?' yelled Basil. Periphrasis was a godsend when you couldn't retrieve a personal name.

'Hormonal,' Al said. 'Very hormonal. Still filled with the Holy Spirit, of course, but inclined to be bolshy. Wears her high-heeled shoes from time to time, just to make me feel an inch or so below the national average; and stormed out of the place two nights ago, when I asked for cheese sauce. Mind you, she put her dinner in the oven first. I'm a bit of a beaten husband, really, but I can't complain. She never hits me in the face; it's always the small of my back.'

'Will you be there,' Basil screamed, 'for the birth itself?'

'They'll call me when the head comes out,' Al said. 'I'll be there for the cord being cut.'

'The cord is never cut,' Basil shouted.

'You're right,' Al bellowed. 'We're born with strings attached.'

'No, no,' Basil blared through his cupped hands. 'What I meant was, when the cord is cut, it's not just a knot. It's a tie. Do you see what I'm saying?'

'I do,' Al shrieked. 'I do, of course.'

They looked around them. The first of the fallen leaves were twitching feebly in the soft cement of the new footpath. Birds sorted themselves on the telegraph wires in a sheet-music of their own making. Middle C was the key to it.

'She had a scan,' Al called to him. 'But the baby covered his genitals. She gave him a right lecture. I think he's ashamed of sex, already.'

'And Aoife?' Basil said. He was not about to shout her name among the rooftops. 'How is Aoife?'

Al led him by the elbow away from the earth-movers.

'I can't hear you,' he said. 'What did you say?'

The man must be wearing his wife's perfume. He smelled like a fly-spray.

'Aoife,' Basil said. 'How is she?'

'Terrific,' Al said. 'I've promised her a sheep that pisses into his nappy if you tilt him one way, and does sheep-droppings if you tilt him another way. I swear she's going to be a genito-urinary specialist.'

'She's her grandfather's grandchild,' Basil said. 'How is your father? Is he still enjoying poor health?'

'Very much so,' Al said. 'Never better.'

'And your mother?' Basil said. 'How is she?'

'Alive, I think,' said Al. 'At least, nobody's stopped me in the street to shake my hand.'

Basil pretended to be thinking about this. In fact, it was all a matter of timing. He had learned it from a Jesuit.

'What's your name again?' he said.

'Al,' said the man, the man who would go bald in ten years' time, and grow a beard. Aoife would be out buying brassières by then, filling them with facial cleansers for the girlfriends at McDonald's, or squatting at night over a doll's mirror to watch how the inside of her lips darkened with blood on the second day of her period. The sun would breed in her, the moon bleed in her. She would do metalwork and algebra, and eat turtle-soup for a dare at a waterfront restaurant in Lanzarote.

'Al,' said Basil. 'What is that short for?'

'It's short for Al,' the man said.

'Don't be a devil's advocate,' said the old priest. He had remembered now. 'The devil pays his counsel a huge retainer. It amounts to a king's ransom.'

'It does?' said Al.

'It does,' Basil said. 'But you end up missing out.'

'Missing out?' Al said. 'Missing out on what?'

'The missing pieces,' Basil said. 'We have all the bits, but all the pieces are missing.'

Al shifted the shopping to his other hand. He would have to get home fast. The ice-pops were beginning to melt.

'You're a dark horse, Father Basil,' he said.

'I had a dog in Africa,' said Basil. 'I bought him from a Methodist. The dog used to bark at the Consecration. It was excellent propaganda. Actually, one of the altarboys was feeding him arrowroot biscuits at the right moment. Then the Methodist died. Two of us found him hanging in his bedroom. We tried to cut him down with the electric knife, but the power had been switched off. He had even tied his shoelaces together, and put the expensive European vase on the floor, away from the chair.'

'Life can be a bitch,' Al said. 'A real bitch.' She would macerate him if the ice-pops melted. No wonder he needed a permit to own a wife.

'I went to the graveyard,' Basil said. 'The service was out of the question, but I went to the graveyard, Bishop or no Bishop. I was ashamed of myself for not going to the church. I brought the dog with me, too. They weren't allowed in graveyards, but I brought him. I stuffed my pockets with arrowroot biscuits, and in we went.'

'Basil,' said the man with the shopping bag which was starting to weep. 'Is that a true story?'

The priest glanced at his watch. Whatever time it was, it was the same time there. If he got in the truck and drove east, for as long as it took to mend one fan-belt and drink two cans of hot beer, he would have to move it forward by exactly one half-hour; if he didn't, he'd forget again, as sure as God existed, and arrive when the school was locked, and the janitor blotto.

'True?' he said.

'Really true,' Al said.

'Of course not,' Basil said. 'You have to find the truth for yourself. I'm only giving you the facts.'

'Father Basil,' said Al, 'I'm going to have to say goodbye.'

He held out his hand. It was freezing from the ice-pops. Basil shook it.

'Goodbye, sir,' he said.

Aoife was wandering around the construction site, eating her nasal secretions. The priest hailed her.

'Hello, little woman.'

'Hello, Father Blackhead,' she called. Why did she call him that? Where did they get their notions? The last of his hair was as white as the polar ice-cap. He patted her head and took a greenfly out of her fringe.

'What are you eating?' he said.

'My snickers,' she told him, and she pulled another long one out of her nose. 'My daddy says I can. Do you have children?'

'No,' he said. 'I don't.'

'Why not?' she said.

'It's a short story,' Basil said. 'A very short story.'

She took his hand in hers, and led him over to the dead rat.

'Look,' she said. 'Look at Mister Rat.'

He was quite a brute, too. Basil poked him with a bicycle spoke, or perhaps it had come from an umbrella. He turned him over, and back again. His paws begged at the sky. He was as dead as one could hope for.

'Is he in Heaven?' Aoife said.

'He is,' Basil said. 'All good rats go to Heaven.'

'Maybe he was bad,' Aoife said. 'Maybe he was a dirty rat.'

'Everyone goes to Heaven,' Basil said. 'Anne Frank and Hans Frank, and even the man who invented the wheel.'

'Why does everyone go?' the child said.

'There's nowhere else,' said Basil. 'That's why.'

'Will you go?' she asked him.

'I'm afraid so,' he told her.

She leaned down and spread newspaper over the mess. The breeze tweaked the corners of the racing results.

'Will he be happy in Heaven?' she said.

'He will,' Basil said. 'The place is crawling with rats.'

She was very doubtful. She picked her nose again, and examined her finger.

'I think he would be happier here,' she said.

'I think so, too,' said the priest. 'But that's between ourselves.'

She was looking round now, as if someone had called her. He was about to reach for his hearing aid, to turn it up.

'Tortoise,' she said. 'Where's tortoise?'

'He's somewhere,' Basil said. 'Somewhere is never very far away. It's a long word for here.'

'Tortoise,' she called. 'Tortoise.'

She ran ahead of him, and they went back over the same ground, toward the eucalyptus and the yellow oblongs of pulverised grass, where the timber had been stacked under tarpaulin. The child produced a pea-pod, and brandished it. Then she tried a lettuce-leaf.

'Look, tortoise,' she cried.

Basil was not sure that a tortoise liked pea-pods or lettuce-leaves. It was strange to think that he had lived so long, and did not know the dietary requirements of a humble creature.

'He's always going off to Africa,' the child said. 'He is always trying to go home.'

He could feel it beginning inside him, like the start of a landslide. He should not have bothered to have his coat cleaned. It was a waste of good money. The ground was so mucky.

'Aoife,' he said.

It was as if his ears had been syringed. He could hear everything, everything. All of the four-letter words in the world were kissing his ears like the great Amen of a mezzo-soprano. He dropped to his knees. He had forgotten to tell the albino that he could have the car.

'Tortoise,' Aoife called. 'Tortoise.' She was in tears at the thought of herself. Everything ended in tears, because everything was a children's game. He swung from God the Father's beard, like a boy in a plum-tree. His hat slipped from his head. The hairs of his head were numbered. He had numbered them himself. There were a hundred and six, not counting two in the hat-brim. He knocked his glasses off with the dead, disobedient arm. He did not want to fall on his face, and injure his corneas.

'Aoife,' he said. 'Get your mummy. Go and get your mummy.'

He lay on his side, and looked up at her. Where was she? The light moved in on him like an octopus.

'You have to say the rules,' said her voice, the voice of the child with the tortoise. 'You have to say Ready, Steady, Go.'

The mouse had come back to be killed properly. That was why. He had waited all night long in darkness, crouched in his caramel bloodstains, the goo of his stump; waited for him, for Basil, for steps in the corridor, for the doorhandle, for the door, the explosions of light. That was why.

'Ready,' he said.

Al was watching his colleague at the Amstrad. Her end was in sight; her ass was a joy. He wanted to pet it, to sniff it. He tipped his cigarette in the plant-pot, and realised it was genuine. He had always thought it was a fake. He found a styrofoam coffee-cup in the bin, and went off to the toilet to fill it with water. It would not mind the odd bit of coffee.

'Ready,' the child said, laughing.

'Do what I did, Jane,' said her neighbour, twirling the egg on the work-top in the kitchen. 'Have an epidural. Lie on your side, and read a Sidney Sheldon novel. How long did Aoife take, anyway?'

'O, Aoife took ages,' said her mother. 'Aoife took an eternity.' And she stopped the twirling egg, and broke it into the frying-pan.

'Steady,' Basil said. Something was tearing up his ribs, like root-work; the bones sprang back. Even the pain was appalled; it fled to every part of his body, and beat on the bones of his foot.

Luke hugged the alcoholic. 'Listen,' he said, 'I'm not telling you to do the six weeks. Do the first day first, then the second, then the third. Mark off the days of the month, like a bingo card. They're great folk in the Unit. I'll talk to your personnel people. There's always hope. Always. Hope is as much a part of us as nitrogen. Run a razor over that bit of designer stubble, and I'll drive you down to the school. You can see them coming out. But you can't talk to them, Basil. You can't trick with a court order.'

'Steady,' the child sang. She was giggling with joy.

Declan walked up behind the altar, and began to tear at the crucifix that was nailed to the wall. The old woman from St Lucy's ward watched, beaming. Her lap was full of scapulars and commissioned knitting. But he couldn't free the wood. He pulled down the figure, instead. His hands bled backwards down his wrist. He sat down on the carpet, and held the figure to him, like a mandolin. 'I love you, you bastard,' he said.

Basil's face lay in his breakfast; the All Bran, the three sardines.

'Go,' he said.

They all came out of the church together, and stood in the light of the late morning. Actually, it was so overcast that it might have been brighter inside. They had turned everything on for the old priest.

'The best in the world,' said Luke, 'but an awful bore, God rest him. Parts Two, Three, Four and Five came with Part One.'

'And the inappropriate laughter,' said the boy without the beard. 'I'll miss that.'

'He chewed his food like Gladstone,' the albino said. 'It was eighty chews per swallow. Did I tell you I found a pair of trousers in his filing cabinet? They were filed under T.'

But Al was monitoring one of the mini-maids who had come to the requiem mass. She was as slim as a man's first volume of verse, that one. He would love to have a browse.

'I'm worried about Aoife,' Jane said. 'Aoife was there. That wasn't right.'

'There's no such thing as a peaceful death,' Luke said, 'but there is such a thing as a quick death; and Basil got a quick one. It was a blessing. He was timber before he hit the ground.'

'He'd been sick, you know,' the albino said to the pregnant woman beside him. Who she was, he had no idea, but she looked full term. He hoped to Christ she wasn't going to pop there and then. Funerals could send women into labour. They were swarming with chemistry.

'Very sick,' said the boy without the beard. 'We found stains.'

'In his bedroom,' Luke said. 'Right beside the bed.'

'Bloodstains,' the albino said. 'He'd been passing lots of blood.'

'Of course,' said Luke, 'he never breathed a word.'

'It was partly humility,' said the albino, 'and partly bloody-mindedness. In other words, it was all Basil.'

'He'd gone a bit in the head, too,' the boy without the beard said, and he cork-screwed his index finger upwards.

'He thought,' Luke explained to Al, 'that a plant in his room was dancing the dance of the seven veils.'

'Maybe it was,' Jane said. She had decided to be a liberal for at least the next hour.

'It was plastic,' the albino said. 'It was a plastic basil bush. We gave it to him as a joke.'

Al offered cigarettes, and everyone refused. He was miffed by that. He strolled away to smoke on his own, in the general direction of the mini-maid. The others stood on the steps of the church, and watched the child that Basil had terrified, as she wheeled an inflatable turtle in a sailor's cap across the sycamore seeds of the car-park.

'I'll keep an eye out for the tortoise,' said the beardless boy.

'Don't you dare, Father,' said Jane. 'I've had to promise her a budgie.'

'Budgies are nice,' the albino said. He had thought about it for a long time, and had made up his mind on the matter.

'Budgies are grand,' she said. 'I'm going to let this one fly around the kitchen; and then, after a decent interval, when Aoife's begun to lose interest, I'm going to let it fly around the kitchen, with the kitchen window open. I might even open the kitchen-door.'

'I understand,' said Luke, and everybody laughed; and the albino slapped his thigh, because he had been to the theatre so often.

'Domestic life, how are you,' he said.

'Nazareth never won the Tidy Towns competition,' said the beardless boy. 'That's a Basilism for you.'

'That's not a Basilism,' said Luke. 'That's one of mine.'

'Actually,' the albino said, 'I think I came up with that one.'

But Jane was looking out over the dormitory suburb, where two of the couples living on her road had already erected 'For Sale' signs on the grass-seed of their front-garden allotments, which was dreadfully disturbing, when you let it sink in.

'You don't know the half of it,' she said to the priests. 'There's a pair up the road from us, and they're having an affair. They put koala bears in the window, as a sign that the coast is clear, when her husband and his wife are out. And the ex of the woman at the corner was breaking-in at night, and re-arranging the furniture, just to make her a bit uneasy; but the police caught him red-handed last week, when he was repairing the tumble-dryer. It would make you wonder. It really would. There are so many head-bangers.'

'Speaking of which,' said the beardless boy, 'I don't want to raise your hopes unduly, but I have a notion that "One Flew Over The Cuckoo's Nest" is on tonight.'

'It won't be the same without Basil,' the albino said.

'Basil was never there,' Luke said.

'Yes,' said the albino, 'but you were always aware that he wasn't there.'

But Jane was listening to her insides. Something seemed to be happening. It was something small, something slight, yet something strange. What could she do? Her copy of *Everywoman* was on her bedside table in her bedroom. She could send Al, but where was Al? He might have gone home already, to hang a sock on the washing-line because Aoife had watered it the night before. She was on her own, so. She was alone with three priests who were all head-bangers.

'It's a great, great movie,' one of them said.

Was it her first contraction? How could she tell? She had never had a contraction before. It was something, though; a displacement, a tiny little landslip. She would sneak inside the church, and have a peek. Perhaps she was showing; perhaps she was spotting. She could slip into the old baptistry, where no one would notice, and scrutinise her underwear forensically. Then she would get them, one of them, to drive her home. She would sit in the back, of course.

'Big Moose? Big Chief?' they were saying. 'What was the name? Then he throws the faucet through the window, and he runs away into the titles.'

'They left the lights down for ages,' the albino said, 'so people wouldn't be caught crying.'

She could feel it again, the downwardness. It made her light-headed. There was something inside her that was not her at all, but other, another. It was falling, falling into place. God had done this for her, and the doctors, of course. She could not call him Basil. That would be ridiculous. But she might choose Basil as a second name, and then reduce it to a middle initial, or drop it altogether.

Now she must find a toilet. She was bursting to go. Yet she had drunk nothing since the night before; nothing at all. She licked her lips. By the end of the day, they would be in tatters. They would be a sight.

'Is something wrong?' said Luke.

'She was very fond of him,' said the albino.

Her eyes filled up. Their faces slurred. The hairs on her arms stiffened with pleasure.

'Please,' said Luke. 'Is anything the matter?'

'No,' she said, 'no, no, no, no. Nothing's the matter.'

ALL IN A DAY'S
DONKEY-WORK

They had been in the field since early morning, the two donkeys, and now it was almost noon.

'Noon,' said the older donkey. 'When has it ever been noon for the likes of us? Why can't you be ordinary and say midday? I say midday, and I've seen more of the world than you have. I've seen Damascus. Have you seen Damascus?'

'Not yet,' said the younger donkey.

'There you go again,' said the older. 'Not yet, he says. Why can't you say No? Why can't you say Never? I say No and Never. I'm not ashamed to say No or Never, and my father's father grazed in the Bekáa Valley. He carried a wounded legionary, a pure-bred Roman veteran, for forty miles to a field hospital after the battle of . . . the battle of . . . somewhere terribly important. He wrote poetry, that soldier did, all the way to Sidon, with his legs in splints. He didn't just copy it. He made it up himself. The quill that he used was a feather from a kestrel. My father's father had the ink-stains on his right ear and part of his coat for years afterwards. He was proud of them. He wasn't ashamed to be proud. And he wasn't ashamed to say No instead of Not Yet or to say midday instead of noon.'

Whatever you chose to call it, this part of the day was a torment. Even the shadows were crawling on their hands and knees in under the olive-trees to escape from the sun, and the trickle of dirty water near the drystone terrace was as thin as a line of little black ants. Only a few short weeks before, it had gushed its grey-green gallons among the spittle-spiders, and the taste of it had been as sharp as toothache, as sweetly stinging as the cold of night when an owner lifts a heavy harness off a sore shoulder-bone. Now it was almost gone. There would be more wet in an old man's beard. It was nearly time for the cistern and the blindfold.

'Only a few short weeks ago,' said the younger donkey.

'Only a few short weeks ago,' said the older. 'Why can't you say: It doesn't seem long since. It doesn't seem long since, was good enough for my mother; and my mother grew up and grew old in the service of one of the most distinguished, not to say dynastic, families in Jerusalem. The head of the house was a temple-priest. He was so high up that everyone was afraid of him, except his daughter. She got away with murder. At least, she got away with manslaughter. But she was kind to my mother. She used to brush her down, like a racehorse. But my mother never let it go to her head. She wouldn't have been ashamed to say: It doesn't seem long.'

He was cross and he was cranky because he'd been tethered, and the rope didn't reach to the shelter of the olives. The younger donkey had been working it out in his head, and now he was sure. There was only one thing to do. He would leave the shade himself. Then they would both be standing in the terrible sun that knew nothing about them. On the other hand, the possibility existed that the older donkey might look upon such loyalty as a bit too high-handed; yet it was a risk worth taking

So he stepped into the light; and the light hurt him all over.

The older donkey was pretending to snap at a horse-fly, but he saw what had happened. It looked for all the world like an act of great comradeship, of one creature reaching out to another. If that were the case, it was in its own way acceptable. However, it might be the opposite. It might be a hard and haughty gesture of charity. After all, he had his dignity to consider. If he lost that, he would have lost everything. For long years and lean years, a labouring lifetime of grass-blades and hailstones, he had preserved his dignity intact. His private ambition, in fact, was to bring it with him safely to his grave. That would be a noble undertaking.

Yet he softened when he saw the younger donkey tug at a thistle. That was to suggest he had left the shade to forage, and not to flank him in fellowship. It showed breeding.

'It's no fault of yours you were once bought by a rabbi,' said the older. 'But living with a priest has given you airs and graces. You won't put good manners on the universe by using words that go on and on like the sound of a struck gong. My mother's mother wasn't laid to rest. She had her throat cut when she got cataracts. Stick with words like dust, thirst, straw and faster. As my poor great-aunt's sister used to say to me – '

But he broke off and looked away over the drystone terrace. Two men, three men, one the owner, the others strangers, were walking down by the dead orange tree towards the boundary line of the field.

'Not Romans,' said the younger donkey. He was looking too, through the flies at his eyelids.

'Not Romans,' said the older. 'Builders, maybe. A building job.'

'Or lighter,' the younger donkey said. 'The sheep have been sheared. It could be wool. Wool's no problem. I hope it's wool. Even a large load is still light, if it's not too damp. What I hate is timber. Timber and fish.'

'You've been spoiled,' said the older donkey. 'All that silk and stuff, those featherweight fabrics from up North. The Arab at the Needle Gate, he had you spoiled. He was worse than the rabbi. You forgot what you were. You forgot dust, thirst, straw and Faster. But I didn't. I did not. That's why I'm as old as I am today.'

The three men had arrived. They were talking among themselves. The owner, as always, a little dour, a little distant, the hair on his cheeks neither bristle nor beard, a fleck of fruit-peel on his lip from the lemon he had rubbed against his teeth to sweeten his breath; and the other two, the strange two, alert, lively, excited even, their hands a contradiction: one pair smooth as calf-skin, the other burly, a stone-breaker's. So they were neither carpenters nor coppersmiths, plumbers or plasterers. The first must be a farmer or a farmer's hired hand; and his friend, the one with the graceful, groomed fingers, must be a secretary of sorts, a salaried scribe in the Prefect's office.

'Must be,' said the older donkey in an undertone. 'There's no must be about it. At the most, they might be. When you've reached my time of life, you'll have learned that the road from might to must crosses a wasteland without wells in it.'

But the younger donkey was right. They were not the usual sort, the two strangers, who hired them by the hour to porter luggage or laundry. Besides, they seemed to trust the owner. That was a sure sign.

'That one?' said the man with the manicured nails.

'This one,' the owner said, easing the slip-knot on the tether of the older donkey. 'I need the other to draw water.'

The man with the huge hands, the farmer, hitched up his tunic, counting out coins from a cloth money-bag. His lips moved as he added. He was using his ears too, twitching them in a private tally.

'As long as it's not a corpse,' said the older donkey. 'I carried a corpse once at the Feast of Tabernacles, and it behaved badly. I rolled in wet nettles for an hour to sting the stench off my sides.'

They were leading him away, the two men, over the white scree where the tom-cat brought his pigeons, and the caterpillars dropped among the entrails.

'Doctor,' the owner called, 'if there's trouble, leave him at the harness-maker's. Across from the sentry post. He's family.'

But the man with the half-moon on each of his fingernails did not turn back. And when he waved, that was only because a mosquito had sipped for a second at the lobe of his left ear.

'Trouble?' said the older donkey. 'That comes under Faster.'

The afternoon had cooled and chilled, and the shadows had come out from in under the trees and stretched out in exhaustion on the ticking ground. Soon it would be dusk, or, rather, it would be evening and then night. The stars would whitewash the night sky, and the younger donkey would do as he had always done, and give a name to one or two of them, their gleams, their gutterings, the names of beasts of burden he had known and nuzzled in the past of his life. Many of them, most of them even, had died in ways which were not worthy of a donkey; and the names and nicknames by which he had turned glints into glows, lights into lanterns, was one way of obliterating hammer-blows, hooves lurching, leather aprons on a work-bench where the bright blood hardened like glue before the dragonfly could fight free of it.

But that was for later. That was not for now. For now there was the boom and the blindfold; the steady, sightless circling of a deep hole in the ground, the noose and the nose-bag, thud of his heartbeat, hoof-beat, the asthma of the windlass; and, deep within this tiny din of tackle and gland, the blue-black water welling up, willing to, the gloss and slosh of its goodness. That was the best thing, the sole thing. The younger donkey had always loved water, because water had always loved him, without any conditions. There were times in the cramped cistern when he could only continue his circles within circles by thinking of those who would draw from this source, the slobber and stillness of so much wet. A woman way past caring might ease her feet in a clay tub, picking a scab with the stalk of an apple; a boy might douse his hair in a full basin to drown the headlice in it; and a Roman soldier's sweetheart would crumble costly powder in a saucer to dab some shocking colour on her eyelids. Then, when the three of them were sleeping, a white mouse would sit on the tank, and sip, and almost fall in.

The younger donkey thought of these things. When he grew tired, he thought of them again; and again, when he was still tireder. But it was no use today. He was asleep on his feet when the older donkey returned.

'Well,' said the older donkey. 'Well, well, well. What a day. What a day it's been. You should have seen it.'

'I can't see you,' the younger donkey said. 'Is it light or is it dark?'

'It is a day that would open your eyes,' said the older donkey. 'Stop a moment. Smell me.'

The younger donkey stopped, and the windlass and the water stopped as well. He sniffed strongly. But it was difficult with the nose-bag.

'Oil?' he said.

'Perfume,' said the older donkey. 'A child threw it at the man who was on me, but she missed. He laughed. He picked her up. They rode in through the gate together. I was walking on rice, on head-scarves, palms, more palms, coats, capes, cloaks, the skins of otters, badgers, pine-martens, shawls, stoles, bracelets, bangles, more rice, more palms. They decked me with a necklace of wildflowers. A huge collar, colours galore. Hosanna, hosanna. It went on. It went on and on. Rice and palms and the women walloping their bosoms. Hosanna, hosanna. What a hullabaloo. What a crowd. Young and old; more young than old. I can count to a hundred, and I did. I counted. But when I'd reached a round century, there were more to add up. There were ten times more; there were thirty times more. And the man who was sitting astride me, I thought he'd weigh a ton from the look of him; but, no, he was light as a smile in summer. Not that he was smiling. He was crying. From happiness. He broke down under the burden of his joy. You may find that hard to understand. That's because you're young. When you're as old as I am, wise and weather-beaten, everything will be made plain.'

The younger donkey stood stock-still and stared straight ahead into the blackness of the blindfold. Who on earth could such a man have been? He had heard of palms and rice; he had even heard of ointments flung at the feet of men who mattered. But he had never heard of a winter wardrobe thrown on the roadside like a sheep's abortion. That was a puzzle. It was even more difficult than a puzzle. It was a perplexity. It meant that the man on the older donkey's back must have been a great man, and perhaps greater than a great man, a man who had no illusions about either greatness or goodness, a man who lived from day to day by dying from night to night. That was a man who might find water in places where water would be afraid to find itself.

'A boy, a nice boy, from the yeshiva behind the onion fields brought me chickweed,' said the older donkey. 'And he said to me, he said, I had earned a place in the stories. That's what he said. He said I had done well. And he said it with respect. That's the point. For a very young man with more blackheads than bristles, he said it in a tone which respected my dignity.'

But the younger donkey was lost in thought. Lostness was one of the occupational hazards of thinking. He had decided that long ago. It was one of his four insights, two of which had to do with water. The other he had forgotten.

'Yes,' said the older donkey, as he stood at the doorway and examined the night that was blotting out the day. 'It was no chore, what I did today. Chore is not a good enough word. What I did today was a commission. I didn't just carry out a job; I executed a challenge.'

★

It was the dead of night. Owls sank on the feeding shrews.

The older donkey had picked his way down into the field again, and the owner had come to the well with a young boy who carried no light. They freed the younger donkey and led him out. Starlight glittered like ground-frost over the out-house.

'Fast,' said the owner. 'Faster.'

'Where?' said the boy. 'Where are we going?'

'We are going,' said the owner, 'to a lost-property office.'

'What's that?' said the boy.

But the owner was in another world.

'Faster,' he said. 'Faster.'

The boy's nose was running with a head-cold. He wedged his thumb in one nostril and blew hard through the other. Mucus shot to the middle of the road and jellied a small stone the size of a baby's skull. Now it would become a game.

'Hosanna, hosanna,' the owner was saying. 'I've heard it a hundred times. I've heard it a thousand times. I must be older than I thought I was. I heard Hosannas on the Jericho road, back when my brother was buying his way into the salt business, and he's dead so long I can't remember what he looked like. His voice, yes. He had the same voice as the cantor with the goitre. But his face has faded. It went away like a little cut. First the scab and then the skin. That was the way it was. There was no heigh-ho; there was no hosanna.'

He had said as much before, but never so much. Not since the strap split and the basket slipped, and the figs fell in the fresh vomit. Yet that was different. He was frantic when the figs happened; he had tried to wash them in the horse-trough. He had been beside himself. Tonight, he was not beside himself. He was inside, deep down, deeper than a donkey could ever dare to go.

'Faster,' said the owner.

They were nearing the walls of the city. The stones under his hooves were turning into cobbles, the cobbles into flagstones. Ahead of him, the boy was aiming sneezes at the sheep-droppings.

'For a week,' said the owner, 'they'll throw kisses. After that, they'll throw stones. I could have told him. I was there. My throat was hoarse from calling out to him. Hosanna, hosanna. Two crushed knuckle-bones on his left hand. A working man, a blacksmith, a bricklayer. Two crushed knuckle-bones will be the least of it when they start to stone him. And I'll be there. I'll be there with a stone as big as a turnip. I'll stand in the sun so he won't make me out. Because that's the way it is. The folk who turned his head today will take it clean off his shoulders tomorrow. Believe me. The wine of great gladness is always served in a sieve. My mother was right.'

The flagstones had come together. There was no more grass.

'The road,' said the boy. 'Look at the road.'

But you could not see the road. The smooth squares of its surface were buried beneath layer after layer of laundry. It was as if an enormous canopy had collapsed in the middle of a marriage-feast.

'It's weird,' said the boy.

'It's wonderful,' said the owner.

It was like a massacre, the donkey thought. It was as if a whole host had fled naked into the night, leaving behind them their clothing like corpses, a mound of soft deadness. If he stepped in among it, a hand would flop from a sleeve, a mouth belch like a toad.

The man and the boy were at it already, heaping up helpings of white and brown and black tunics.

'No jewellery,' the owner said. 'We're not the first tonight.'

'What do you mean?' said the boy.

The man was loading cloaks on the younger donkey. Their smell was spices and sweat.

'Never mind what I mean,' he said. 'Fetch me whatever you find. And faster.'

The boy picked his way among the tunics that were left, kicking a collar of colours galore, a necklace of wildflowers.

'Two aprons,' he said. 'One plain, one with a pattern of cedars. A few head-scarves. And the rest is rubbish. Palms, more palms. Palms everywhere. They must have stripped the trees from here to Heaven.'

'Hurry,' said the owner. 'Aprons and head-scarves. Hurry.' He might have been baling hay in a high wind.

'There's a veil with gold-leaf on it,' the boy said. 'It's big enough to hide in. But a donkey went and shat all over it.'

'I don't care if the prophets pissed on it,' said the owner. 'Bring it.'

The donkey was nosing pellets of rice on the pavement. In the light of the darkness of the small hours, they were like hailstones. When he trod on them, they made the same sound: the short scrunch of a squashed roach. He would think of rice in the winter when the hail stung him like a fan-tail of sparks; and in the summer, when he carried grooms to their weddings, he would think of hail as the children poured rice into his ears. In that way, he would achieve the dream of every donkey: peace of mind in a field with no flies.

They were heading homewards. The flagstones caved into cobbles. The wind wore a hint of honeysuckle.

'What am I looking at?' said the owner to the boy.

'Clothes,' said the boy. 'The clothes we collected.'

The owner laughed. He might have been the man with the lady's long fingers, the man without the crater of a callus on either of his palms.

'I'm looking at a wife. A young wife, a new wife. A woman with teeth in her mouth, front and back. A woman with breath that doesn't smell like a shoe. That's what I'm looking at. And I'm saying hosanna.'

The cobbles had stopped. It was beaten earth from here on. Dust, thirst, straw and faster. The walls of the city had sunk without trace in the darkness behind them, but the stars stood their ground. They had no glimmering.

'Why do you mind so much about teeth?' said the boy.

'I mind about many things,' the owner said, 'but I was starting from the top.'

He had thought, the young donkey, that the sum of the silks and the cottons would be light as a feather; and he had been wrong. They had started to weigh like a ton.

It was so late when the younger donkey stepped down into the field that it was almost early morning. The sky had gone grey in the face. In a matter of minutes, the rooster would throw a tantrum on the hen-coop, and the sparrows would begin their jittery whisperings like bandits using bird-calls as a signal. Then it would be daylight.

'Dawn,' said the older donkey. 'After all, it's not every day that the sun rises. Usually, it just gets bright.'

He had been tethered again, but he drew the rope behind him with great dignity, like a chain of office.

'The years are falling off me,' he said. 'I thought it was mange, but no. I'm shedding a winter coat. That's what it is. I've phlegm enough for the Negev, if I had to cross it.'

A horse-fly settled on the snout of the younger donkey, and he let it. There might have been a time when he crawled into the sloughed skin of an adder, and drowsed, and dreamed he was a ladybird, luck on the thumbnail of a pigtailed toddler; and then awoken, or awaked, or woken up, to the blinding midday sun that made light of his night-crossing.

'My father's father went down in history for that forty miles to the field hospital,' said the older donkey. 'The soldier in splints, the quill from a kestrel. It's travelled, that one has. Travelled the world. Ephesus, Athens, Rome. Yes, Rome herself.'

'Itself,' said the younger donkey. 'Why don't you say itself?'

But the older donkey wasn't listening.

'The point is,' he said, 'that a man with two sprained ankles writing mush to his mistress, even if the mush was in metres, doesn't amount to a legend. Not now. Not in my lifetime. It isn't even an exploit. Or a deed. Because he didn't deed it; he just did it. When you've reached the time of my life, you'll have learned that the road from doing to deeding crosses a wasteland without wells in it.'

The rooster sat among the droppings of his wives, and started to crow at the world. The greyness had gone out of the sky. It was turning as white as a sheet.

'Bonnets and bearskins,' said the older donkey. 'Rice on my muzzle, rice raining down. At my hooves, at my feet, the scent of squashed flowers like the smell of snuffed candles. Shawls thrown from the turrets hovered above me like hawks. Palm after palm, the palms piled up, as if they were feeding a fire. I came close, I admit it, I came very close to passing out with

dignity; it came over me like a fainting fit. Because I was doing
something my father had never done; and that, you see, is a
working definition of happiness. I, who had been a baggage-
animal, am no longer baggage: I am an animal; I, who had been a
beast of burden, am no longer burdened: in every atom of my
being, I am pure beast.'

The sun blazed a trail towards them, towards the older donkey
who stood, shaking, and the younger donkey who shook,
standing.

'I wish I could hear myself talking,' said the pure beast. 'But
my ears are still ringing from all those hosannas. I don't think
they'll ever be right again.'

He twitched them here and there, searching for silence, the
stillness of small noises in place of the roaring. For it was one
thing to be deaf to the world, and another to be deaf. Then you
might miss the sound of the brown bounce of a twig as a sparrow
shot from its tip, or the sound of a goat as it scratched at an abscess
on its knee in a field four hundred yards away.

'The left one is worse,' he said. 'The man who was sitting
astride me got upset, overcome, if you will. Overcome, I
daresay, by his dignity. And why not? How often does a whole
city empty itself like a full bladder to flood around you? Of
course, he got swept away; of course, he cried. His nose bubbled,
his eyes welled up, and some of the stuff slid over my ear and into
it. I couldn't shake it off. Drool and goo, long strings of it, sticky
as egg-white. I got such a start I very nearly did something
inappropriate. I very nearly spoiled a head-scarf with gold-leaf on
it. Fortunately, my dignity was still in the saddle.'

The older looked hard at the younger donkey.

'Where were you?'

The younger donkey tried to remember back. It was hard to
retrace your steps if you had been walking on flagstones. It was
easier to notice your prints on soft earth or on hard muck. Sand
was still better, the best of all. You had only to look back, and
you could see at a glance the mile after mile of little holes you had
made as you went deeper into the desert, and you could see how
they stretched in a straight wobble all the way behind you to the

line of the horizon where the sky lifted its hem over the world like a rich man stepping over a puddle.

'I was here,' said the younger donkey. 'I was drawing water from the well.'

'Drawing water?' the older donkey said. 'You mean you were in the blindfold. That was yesterday. You were in the blindfold yesterday. What about last night? Where were you then? When the owner came with the boy, and led you away.'

The younger donkey stared into the sun, and let it blind him. Then he closed his eyes and watched a red ball roam in the blackness.

'There was a camel-train from Galilee,' he said. 'There must have been a hundred of them. There may have been a thousand. I was collecting the dung.'

'Louder,' said the older donkey. 'I can't hear you. Louder.'

But the younger donkey was moving away, clopping through the greenflies to the drystone terrace where a line of long-legged black ants balanced on a slide of boulders, their slow, sleek trickle like a leakage of water.

Dust, he thought; thirst, he thought; straw, he thought; and water. The thought of it washed him, washed through him. His tongue cleaved to the roof of his mouth, a wine-skin hanging from a rafter; waiting the day, waiting the wedding.

Ants poured in a stream over the stones.

He gave thanks.

'You'll have to shout,' said the older donkey. 'Either that or make signs.'

The stream flowed between his hooves. He bent his head, and drank.

TWO WINDOWS AND A WATERTANK

The lamb lay on his own hard droppings in the little wooden box, and tried to count men. But he was too tired to sleep.

That was something the ram would have understood. The ram loved a contradiction. If you thought of a good contradiction, he would wait until you were out of earshot and then repeat it to one of his peers. He would never let on that he was not the first to have thought of such a contradiction. Instead, he would stare at the sky as if it were a ewe he had never noticed before. And his fleece would stir in a private breeze that bypassed every branch in the field.

'There is a tiredness beyond tiredness,' he would say, 'and the tiredness of that tiredness will never tire itself out.'

The lambs would shake their tails, the sheep would shake their heads, and the ewes would make sheep's eyes at him as he mounted his boulder.

'You cannot contradict that,' they would say. 'He is always and everywhere one contradiction ahead of you.'

'And not an adjective to be spotted,' said one of the three sheep who were in his tutorial down by the dry bed of a brook that had lost its nerve two years before the lamb was born. 'The master has moved beyond the eroticism of subjectivity, beyond the heat-haze of the adjective. Except, of course, when he is making love to one of you ewes. It does sometimes transpire that, during the contradiction of such congress, he emits involuntary adjectives of a quite colloquial kind.'

'Quite,' the ewes would say. 'But that in itself is another contradiction, and therefore perfectly consistent.'

'Absolutely,' said the trio in the ram's tutorial. 'It is through the contradictions of personal witness that we accomplish the impersonal wisdom of utter contradiction.'

187

'I don't think he would have said "utter",' one of the ewes said. 'Perhaps he said butter, or mutter. Utter is one of those adjectives.'

'Utter is a verb,' a sheep retorted. 'It means that you bleat in a special way, a solemn way; and, if you don't utter, that means you say nothing in a solemn way. When we say nothing, that's because we've nothing to say; but when the ram says nothing, that's because there's nothing to be said. So he utters not a word.'

'Utters not a word,' said an older sheep with a streak of sky-blue dye on his shabby fleece. 'You mean that he keeps his mouth shut. Will he keep it shut on the day that three men wearing aprons drag him behind the watertank? Because there's nothing more to be said beyond the corner of the watertank, but that doesn't stop them. They skid on their own piss behind the watertank. The air-bubbles on their gum-boils babble like frogspawn, but they can't say it, they can't speak it; this is the unspoken become the unspeakable. They know that much. Even the ticks in the tangles of their wool know it. They know that the unspeakable is not a word. It is a sentence.'

'As long as it isn't an adjective,' said one of the ewes. 'Unspeakable sounds very much like an adjective to my ear. It sounds as if there were something coming after, as if something had been left unsaid.'

'Perhaps', said another of the ewes, 'we should agree among ourselves to speak in future not of the unspeakable but of unspeakableness. Unspeakableness is a difficult word for a sheep to say, and therefore enacts its meaning in the act of being meant.'

'Quite,' said the other ewe, who was piqued by this insight. She had been leading up to it in her own good time.

'Shame on the lot of you,' said an ewe who was standing near the nettles where the shepherd had pissed that morning, angling at the highest of them. 'Shame on you all to be talking about such things in front of these little lambs.'

But the others made allowance for her. She had not lambed that year; she had not lambed the year before. The ram had done his best. You could not ask him to do more. She was a ewe who was more mutton than mother. That was her contradiction. The leather-aprons would not be long in coming. Her watertank was filling, filling fast.

'They'll be sheep in a short while,' she said. 'Let them be lambs for now.'

The lamb that lay on his own hard droppings in the small wooden box had been there. He had seen and heard these snatches of smalltalk in a bumpy acre of burnt ground beneath a sky that was as blue as the shepherd's basin of dye; but touch and taste had drawn him from the gossip of the grown-ups to an ulcerating teat and the hot tickle of milk in his throat. For his mother smelled of droppings and lilac, and the smell of lilac and droppings had led him by the nose to the big, pink blisters on her belly long before the last saliva crusted into mucus on his eyelids, and the mucus crumbled, and his eyelids opened, and the light immediately blinded him to everything that was not this world.

'Let them be lambs for now?' said the older sheep with the streak of sky-blue dye. 'Let them be lambs for ever, is more like it. Born in the spring, slaughtered in the spring, served as spring lamb in the officer's mess; their kidneys nibbled by some Sanhedrin lickspittle, their brains dipped in a wine sauce by a featherbrain on overtime from the local cat-house, and their bones – the masterwork of their mothers' wombs – tied in a sailor's knot with a greasy string for the dogs on sentry duty at the ordnance depot.'

Some were silent; the others said nothing. The sheep with the streak studied the skyline intently, as if he had scented a fox or were listening among the crickets for the shepherd's emphysema. But that was the way he arranged himself, always, in the aftermath of his insights. He would stare at the skyline, just as the ram examined the clouds. It allowed the others time to feel, to feel deeply, to feel deeply inadequate. That threefold use of spring, for example, was a masterstroke of style, syntax and sentiment. When he went the way of all flocks, when he walked to the watertank, he would be calmed and comforted by the knowledge that a number of his own agnostic outbursts, raised to the status of strong phrases out of the sex and dysentery of his days, would be bleated back and forth through the small hours in the sheep-fold and the upland pastures. Brooks, bridges and bazaars would be the venue for their setting forth, their staying put. They would become as much a part of the herd's inheritance as clover or gangrene. They would be spoken – even spoken of – way beyond Palestine, in places there were no words for, because there were no words for sticks or secateurs in them.

Something else was possible, too. Of course, the sheep with the streak of sky-blue dye had been standing a long time in the sun. But it was still possible.

His words might even make it as far as the goats. It had been his life's dream, that. If it became a life's-work, why then, the watertank held only water.

'Prayer,' said one of the ewes, 'is your only answer.'

'Prayer is not an answer,' the sheep with the fifth leg said to her. He stopped and counted.

'Five,' said the ewe.

'Thank you,' the sheep with the fifth leg said.

'Seven.'

But *thank you* did not count. When the sheep with the fifth leg totalled his words each evening, he omitted expressions of gratitude. For the rest, he subtracted grassblades, one for a word and two for the use of the passive voice, from his next day's grazing. The time that the ewe had been interfered with by two pig-tailed boys, he had fasted for a full week.

'Prayer,' he said, 'is not an answer. After all, we speak of a favour as an answer *to* prayer. In that case, prayer can only be a question. If so, the question remains: to what is prayer a question? Or to whom? For a what implies a thing, but a whom implies a something. We do not question stones or shepherds. We question a sheep. Now I'm not prepared to get into an argument about this. The sheep with the streak of sky-blue dye would like nothing better than a row. He would like to remind you yet again that he has never seen the sheep in question; therefore, the sheep in question does not exist. On that basis, of course, his own father does not exist. He has certainly never seen him.'

'I've lost count,' said the ewe. 'You went over a hundred, and I began to feel queer. It always reminds me of the way my mother counted down to the watertank. From the time the shepherd put on the leather apron to the time the woman poured water over it on the washing-line.'

'Go on about the sheep in question,' said another ewe. She preferred to talk about things that were not close to home. The leather apron was neither here nor there; instead, it was everywhere; but everywhere was a hard place to look at in particular.

'A sheep that is born of a ewe is of few days, and full of trouble. He cometh forth like a flower, and is cut down. You all know it. You all know it by heart. But you must know it *in* your heart as well. You must know it through and through your heart. You must know it in every possible prepositional way. You must pray it; otherwise it will prey upon you.'

'But it doesn't sound like a prayer,' said one of the three sheep in the ram's tutorial. 'It sounds more like the opposite. It sounds like you haven't got a prayer.'

'Don't go and get all upset about it,' said the ewe who had made the case for the use of the noun Unspeakableness. 'It's only another contradiction. Anyone would think it's a life-and-death struggle you're talking about. We're just chatting.'

'A sheep-that-is-born-of-a-ewe is not a prayer,' the barren ewe decided. 'If it were a prayer, it would rejoice more. It would sing and dance. But it doesn't sing and dance. It just grumbles.'

'It would be a prayer if it had a Lo or an O at the start,' another said. 'If it said, Lo, a sheep that is born of a ewe, it would hit the high note. It really needs the Lo. If it's a question, there should be a Lo in front of it; if it's an answer, an O.'

'It's like in the legions,' said the sheep with the streak of sky-blue dye on his fleece. 'When the Romans marched against the radicals, the officer commanding would say to his centurions: Lo, we shall attack by moonlight and be massacred. Then the centurions would say to their decurions: O, we shall attack by moonlight and be massacred. And they in their turn would tell the ten men under them: Ho, ho, we shall attack by moonlight and be massacred. And the troops would say it back, straight out, so that nobody was in any doubt about the details of their next shift: O no, we shall attack by moonlight and be massacred. Then they could all sit down and skewer some cabbage-leaves and lizard for their last supper together; piss, pass wind, parcel mementoes for a pal in a luckier cohort, or watch the shadows lengthen as the sun went down, flossing their fine Italian teeth with a hair they'd cut from their girlfriend's nipple as a keepsake.'

'Sometimes,' said one of the ewes, 'you talk about human beings in a way that almost makes me think you could be talking about sheep.'

'They do give birth in much the same manner,' said another ewe. 'They suckle their young attentively; and, as a recent trauma to one of our own suggests, they copulate according to our customs. Those youngsters from the yeshiva – '

'Are not the same as us,' said a sheep from the tutorial. 'Water and wool is what they know. Cramps and colic. They sit and strew adjectives around the place, as if they were shelling peas that were bad. But they know nothing of us, nothing of our pain, the pain of contradiction, the prolapse we carry. They do not even know about the watertank.'

'They know they shall attack by moonlight and be massacred,' said the sheep with the sky-blue streak. 'Each and every rank repeats it in turn. Like the ewe and the cometh and the flowers, it is their prayer. It orders and ordains them. They know where they stand; they know where they'll fall. The bewilderment has gone away. They hum and hug each other, though it's hard to hear now. The silence is like deafness, a dead-of-night quiet, more mute than muffled. One man hands his needle and thread to the cook; another lifts a dying starfish out of a dried rock-pool and wades with it up to his waist into the ocean.'

'Tommyrot,' said the sheep with the fifth leg. 'You're talking about the men who laid the cobblestones behind the watertank.'

'Not that we're sure about the cobblestones,' said an ewe.

'Slates,' said another. 'Lots of loose slates. I have a hunch about it.'

The tutorial group had their mind made up. They bleated together.

'The ram says sand,' they said. 'Sand makes more sense. The Roman arenas are sanded; so is a delicatessen. None of us was born yesterday. Let's not pull the wool over our eyes.'

But the ewe who had not lambed for two years shook her head from side to side.

'The place behind the watertank is just a patch of grass,' she said. 'We'll probably graze while they sharpen the knives.'

'You've been there, I imagine?' said the sheep with the fifth leg.

'I imagine I have,' she said.

'So have the Romans,' said the sheep with the sky-blue daub. 'So have the mackerel. The god of this world is the god behind the watertank. His priests are carrion crows. And his scriptures are the casualty lists that a butcher calls a bill of sale.'

The ewe who was keeping count of the words used by the sheep with the fifth leg was in a bad way. In fact, she had gone to pieces.

'It's all that talk about the you-know-what,' she said. 'About the rectangular aquatic receptacle. It makes it impossible for me to add things up properly.'

'Why can't we have a good old sing-song instead of all this mumbo-jumbo?' said another of the ewes. 'Look at the day that's in it, big and becalmed, and a load of us with long faces as if it were winter and our fleece was tinkling with the icicles. Well, I tell you this: we're a long way from hypothermia half-way up a glacier. We're in a green garden where the grass is only waiting to be eaten; so what I'd like to see is a little more commitment to the present place and time, and cut the sheep-droppings. I don't know who started this conversation, but, if I did, I'd give him – or her – a bloody good butt, so I would.'

'I'll tell you who started it,' said the sheep with the fifth leg. 'Him with the streak, that's who. Then he went on about the Romans. There was no end of adjectives about them. They came fast and furious. And that wasn't the last of it. He compared them to us. Now I know they say simplicity's a saintly attribute, but I draw the line at simplification. Everybody who's anybody knows that a sheep is not only complicated but complex. A sheep thinks; a sheep knows that he thinks; he may even think that he knows, though, of course, when he thinks about it, he knows that he doesn't. In sum and in short, there is nothing in the whole, wide world that is remotely like us, apart from the aboriginal *lumpen* of the goat-class, the poison ivy on our family tree; and they will never, needless to say, be admitted into the fold.'

'If you don't shut up soon,' said the ewe who was counting, 'you'll have nothing to eat tomorrow except your own words.'

The lamb that lay on his own hard droppings in the little wooden box had finished feeding at about that moment. He had lolled on the sheltered side of his mother, sticky and blinking, breathing in and breathing out urine and buttercups.

'Look,' she had said.

Two mosquitoes were mating in a man's footprint twelve feet away; pigeons pestered their chests in the dying sycamore; and above them, the ewe and the lamb, swifts soared and spun in their tart detours.

'Listen,' she had said.

To the tiny infiltration of the wind among the grass; to the slick whiplash of a gecko's tongue under the juniper; to the strangulated grunts of a man with kidney-stones between the bush in flower and the bush in leaf.

'Touch,' she had said. 'Taste. Smell. This is the whole, wide world. It is neither all that whole or all that wide. It may be the other way round. It may be broken and narrow; but it is the world. It does not have an opposite. The opposite of the world is nothing at all.'

The clouds had lifted over the city of Jerusalem, and the moon whitened the roof-tops like a fungus in a fruitbowl. Mould settled and softened. The colours of daylight drained like a downpour into the clever sewers. Where the green laughter of children had grassed the side-streets, men moved through a grey area, staring at the blotches on the backs of their hands as if they were ringworm. Toddlers on a balcony could find no snail where the sick glints petered out; disgruntled mothers threw fresh tablecloths in a corner for a second wash; a jittery lover drew his leg away from the dry poultice that the moonlight left; and the dead mackerel in the market near the library stared open-eyed at the justice of fish-scales silvering the scrubbed deal tables.

But the lamb could at last see something. There was that to be said for it.

Through the air-holes of the pigeon box, he could make out walls, windows with shutters, a cobbled yard; in the corner, fireflies sparking over an ox-cart. There were lights too, lights in the lower and the upper window, lights that made shadows, shadows that blackened the walls like a fire. Yet he heard nothing, neither laughter nor dishes, the wine-skin farting as it emptied or a finger flicking gristle on a candle-wick. All he could hear was his heart, its jumpy knucklebone beat. He must always and everywhere listen to that, for his mother had told him so, had told him often. But how could you listen to your heart if you only heard it when the vixen padded through the olive grove or a sheep was taken through the pining crickets to the watertank?

The upper window was all shadow now, walls and ceiling. The whole room had been gutted. It was as black as the hen-house after the chickens died, the time the farmer started the fire with dripping and sandalwood to kill the infection; the time he tested a drumstick on the simpleton to see if the dead poultry could be eaten. There must be many people behind that upper window; and their shadows were enormous because they were sitting so close to the light.

But the lower window, opening onto the yard, was clear. There was one slim shadow of a man and he was making shadow-shapes with his hands and fists: a bird, a bird with a broken wing, two birds. And now the shadow stood sideways to the light, and the shadow of a penis stood out against the shadow of the stomach and the thighs. The man who had made the shape of a wounded bird was working the handle of a jug over his penis, until it fitted and he took his hands away, and the weight of the pitcher hung from him without help. Clapping, the clapping of another man and at least one woman, fetched faintly to the air-holes in the pigeon-box.

The sheep shook his head. The ringing in his ears did not ring true. He did not want to be hard of hearing. He did not want to be deaf like the poor conscript soldiers who were massacred by moonlight, the dirty infantry whose world would die away like whispers as they hummed and hugged each other; for they had picked their ears and found no wax on any of their fingernails, and wondered why the screech-owl and the nightingale were silent as the darkness wore on and wore in. But the shrew had heard the screech-owl and had ducked among the barley; and the surgeon in his bivouac had heard the nightingale and had gone on twisting gags for the amputations.

'Shit.'

He heard it clearly. It had come from the lower window, from well within the room. His heart steadied; the sound of it softened. When he could not hear it any longer, he would be himself again.

'Shit.'

There it was again: a man's voice, perhaps the man with the pitcher and the penis; the ram. The ram saying 'Shit' about something or other, just as the shepherd had said it about almost everything, from drizzle to grass-snakes. He had heard it as clear as a dragonfly stepping into a lily. 'Shit.' He pressed his eye to an air-hole.

A man had appeared at the upper window; a broad-shouldered man with a beard, carrying breadloaves. He seemed to be listening too, his head tilted, his hair fallen forward over his eyes so that he held it back with the fingers of one hand. Then he turned, turned away, and his shadow shrank and soared and shrank again as he moved around the room, stooping and standing. He was serving whoever else was with him. It was a party, then. They were celebrating. They might be masons who'd won a franchise for all the milestones between Rome and the ram's boulder; or lads who wore leather aprons during business hours, toasting the millionth lamb to lie among the garlic on their trestles. They had probably closed a deal or closed a sale. Something, at any rate, had closed or was closing profitably for them. Now they could close their eyes and make-believe they drew their water from the well and not the watertank.

'Listen. Listen to me,' said the same voice that had said 'Shit'; and the lamb's eye moved to an air-hole lower down. Now he had the ground-floor frames in focus, a small softness of lamplight through a moth's wing dangling in a failed web.

'I'm not asking you to imagine that I'm God Almighty. I'm only asking you to pretend. If you can just pretend for five minutes that I'm God Almighty, then we can both of us get down to some grass-roots theology.'

The shadow with the pitcher was a Roman. Clean-shaven; crew-cut; a conscript. The weals of the knapsack on his shoulders still had the shine of jelly on them; they had not yet hardened into scar tissue. He was young, he was drunk on strong wine and weak women. He was seeing the world for the first time, and no one had told him how he might see it for the last time. No one had told him about the massacre by moonlight, or how he would sit among his mates at the shoreline, staring straight into the sun as it went down and down, the whole horizon heaving with the heat of it like a horseshoe hissing in the ice-cold downpour of a pump. No one had told him any of this. Instead, they had told him where to come for cock-fights and where to go for girls.

'The Senate ought to name a day for the erection,' he was saying. 'Set a day aside in the calendar. The Feast of the Erection. Then we'd sit at home, right. We'd sit there in our dressing-gowns at a nice little table, with these big beautiful hard-ons sticking out of us, right, and all the women, all the women, you see, they'd file through, and they'd leave gifts.'

'Gifts?' said a drier, darker voice, the voice of the one who had been clapping, the one who was hidden, the one whose shadow kept scrambling up and down the wall like a boy climbing a sand-dune.

'Gifts,' said the conscript, and he made his penis bob a little. 'Perfume. Little bottles of perfume, the sort that dries up overnight if you don't put the top into the thing. But no touching. If they wanted to pat or if they wanted to pet, well, they'd have to put foxgloves on their fingertips.'

'I hate foxgloves,' said the darker voice.

A woman was arranging herself over the window. She had rolled up layers of thin, transparent stuff the lamb had never seen before, rolled them up over her body from her waist like a piece of parchment, and was holding them under her chin to leave her breasts bare. Now she bent over the window-ledge, gripping it with her fists.

'Liquorice,' said the conscript. 'Little you-know-whats of liquorice.'

'I hate liquorice,' said the darker voice.

Her breasts were very large. They were too large for such small shoulders to bear. What a terrible burden they must be in the heat of a hard day. But perhaps she was feeding. Perhaps she would go from here to her own home to lift a child, and nurse it, and not mind, or mind too much, if it were cranky with colic or got sick on the thin, transparent stuff she was wearing. She might even roll it up in the same way again. Then it would not matter.

'You hate everything,' said the conscript. 'But I love life.'

He stood behind the woman, and started to ease himself in. But he stopped after seconds, and withdrew.

'That bush needs some pruning,' he said. 'And I've a very sensitive glans.'

'Of course you have,' said the darker voice. 'You're a very sensitive fellow.'

'You do it,' said the conscript to the woman who was leaning over the window-ledge; and she turned and looked at him, and he made signs with his fingers and hands, and she understood. She reached in under herself, with the flimsy silks still bunched beneath her chin to let her breasts swing free, and she opened herself and helped him into her.

'It's just that I can't stand hairs on my glans,' he was saying to the shadow that rose and fell from somewhere in the middle of the room.

The man with the breadloaves was standing silhouetted in the upper window. Perhaps he had been there for a while; perhaps he was passing. But the breadloaves, at any rate, had been handed round. Now he was carrying wine. There must be twelve or fifteen of his friends in the room: the jug was as large as the earthenware flasks the shepherds used for the foot-wash after work. How strange it was to be squinting through an air-hole at all this gaiety and gladness, the wine-skins and women of two-legged folk who knew nothing. Yet the lamb too had chased a yellow spider through the charcoal of a campfire on the evening of the day that two hobbled sheep had hopped in silence and without once looking back, to the place of places in behind the watertank.

'Listen, listen.'

It was the conscript. His voice was slurred now. He had reached the point when he would have drunk the sediment. Beyond that again, he would drink a second time whatever he threw up.

'Listen,' he said. 'I'm sort of paying you the middle rate, you know; so, really, I think you could raise some dimples in those cheeks of yours. I mean, it is your holiday, after all.'

'Passover,' said the darker voice.

'Right. It is your Passover, so let's not pass over it in silence. You know. Let's have a holiday atmosphere.'

'I like that,' said the darker voice. 'I like what you punned on.'

The man with the breadloaves and the wine-jug had gone from the upper window; and the lamb was glad of it. He had made him feel heavy somehow, heavy and then heavier, as if he were a dry sponge slowly soaking up water, a weight creeping through lightness. He had enough to be getting on with, without that.

'I don't believe it.'

The conscript had reached around the girl, and was flapping her nipples with the palms of his hands.

'I mean, I'm not Publius fucking Ovidius fucking Naso, I know that. And I'm not Marcus fucking Crassus either, and I know that too. But there's a girl with tits like turnips in a brothel in Pompeii, and she went down on me for no extra charge. I mean, these aren't nipples. These are navels, you know. I'm not asking you to grow grapes for me. I'm not asking for nipples like grapes. No. But these aren't even . . . raisins. I mean, you're supposed to be enjoying it too.'

He pulled out of her; and even the lamb in the pigeon-box could hear the slickness of his leaving. But the girl stayed where she was at the window, with her dresses under her chin, looking at something in the darkness of the yard – twine or a watering can – that the break of day would prove had never been there.

'Fuck it. Fuck it.'

The conscript's arm was swiping at something as he reached to unhook the shutters.

'Fucking mosquitoes.'

'It's the smell of sex,' said the darker voice. 'The old man always waited for an on-shore wind; the mother prayed for heat and a dead calm.'

'Fucking mosquitoes,' said the conscript. 'Where I come from, there aren't any mosquitoes. If you kill a mosquito, people bring their children to see it. And that is what I call civilisation.'

And he closed the shuters and latched them. The lamb could see him punching the weaker, wobbly slats with the flat of his hand, punching them one after the other, until the last chink of light had been blotted out. The voices of the soldiers furred and were far away.

But the upstairs shutters were still open. The slightest of breezes made them creak tinily, as if, in a puzzled, painstaking way, they had the sense at moments of a time before timber, when their gallons of greenness were matchmakers to the starlings. But they could not bear the memory; it would kill them in labour. Better to listen to the rust and the dry-rot, to the dormitories of woodworm.

The lamb stood still; or, rather, he stood stiller. He had imagined it. He had imagined what he thought he had heard. He was tired and he was terrified. Tiredness and terror make wolf-cubs out of shrubs, watertanks out of wicker-bins. His mother had said so. There were no droppings in her milk.

He listened with his ear against the air-hole. This time, it was even clearer. There was no denying it. Someone in the room behind the upper window was talking about sheep. Perhaps it was the host, the bearded man with the broad shoulders who had stood against the light and left the lamb with a slightly sinking feeling. Indeed, it must be he, because he was speaking slowly, as if to elderly, enfeebled individuals or perhaps to scatterbrained children of six or seven. He was in command as well: he was not afraid that his pauses would be ambushed by some upstart with his own ideas. And he was still talking about sheep.

Perhaps he was a shepherd. He was talking about shepherds. He was talking about them in rather glowing terms. It was unlikely that he had ever been a sheep. His sense of the whole business was profoundly human. If he were a lamb for a day, if he inhaled pigeon-shit and pigeon-feathers in a cramped crate, if he were brought by the scruff of his fleece to the great clearing behind the watertank, then he would soon change his bleat. As it was, he was only talking about sheep as a simile. He probably meant people. That was the way with human beings. Sooner or later, every damn thing in the world, from weeds to waterfalls and back again, was supposed to speak volumes about their inner life. The whole universe lined up in a queue stretching to infinity, centipedes, watermelons, meteors, antelopes, icicles, cloud formations and the very stars in the sky. Nothing was sacrosanct. Everybody had to sign the register of available contrasts and comparisons. So a man with a grim face becomes a man with a granite countenance, though even a brain-damaged guinea-pig could tell you that granite is the quietest and most cultured stone you could ever scratch your ticks against.

Yet he listened again, the lamb did, because he was curious. He pressed the soft inside of his ear against the splinters of the air-hole, and held his breath back for as long as he could.

The man was still at it, full flight: sheep and shepherds, missing sheep, black sheep, and then the sheep-fold. It always came back to the sheep-fold, to the sheep counted and accounted for. There was talk of wolves and wolf-packs, but it held no water. It held no water because it held no watertank. Truly the sheep with the streak had been right: the last word is always with the unspoken.

The lamb lay down on his droppings. He had lost interest in the man. It was only a matter of metaphors after a meal, the sheep this and sheep that. There was more harm in a horse-fly. If you had watched a ewe chewing her bubbly purple afterbirth while the jackdaws flipped spatters of eyeball from her strangled lamb, then you could talk; but you would not want to. And if you had watched the ram being dragged from his boulder by the men who used to worship under the poplars, then you could talk; you could even utter. But you would not say a word; you would say nothing. Only the ewes had started a countdown, and the lamb had mouthed it through the milk-stain of his lips. There was the sound of the ram's horn snapping like a stick of chalk, and a trail of blond obscenities marking the way to the watertank, as if the father of the flock were leaving twists of wool on a wilderness of thorns so that others might step safely.

'And his last words,' said the ewe who had invented

Unspeakableness as a noun and not as an adjective, 'were the very words he used when he was filling and fulfilling us in quiet places, away from the children. The last words that he spoke – Shit, Fuck, and Fuck You – were expressions of abiding love. So long as that message is remembered, the ram will never be forgotten. We ladies felt him in us for a brief while. Our posterity will feel him deep within them forever.'

But the ewe who had not lambed for two years was staring into the sun. The corpse of a caterpillar swung from a branch above her; and a mayfly fretted about winter forage. She was the next, then. She would be taken in ten minutes. The lamb had learned that much with his first mother's milk. Yet she ate a little grass, from time to time, and she still shivered her fleece when a tick quickened the tempo of its sips. Because your living went on into your dying until even your dying was done. That was when the only thing you could hear from behind the watertank was the voices of men talking about women's holes.

When the ewe had asked him, in those last few minutes, to do it for her, the lamb was puzzled. Wasn't she barren? And, besides, he wasn't thirsty. He had drunk his way into drowsiness; his mouth squelched when he spoke. But she had said that he might be thirsty someday, with a thirst beyond the power of any teat, because water could put out fire but it could not put out ashes.

He had known then that her mind was wandering. He lay down beside her and sucked at the hard warts that were as dry as droppings; sucked until he had wind-pains from the air he was drinking. Then she had got up and gone away, and they had come for her. She had left without looking back, which the ewes considered bad form and a poor example to the juveniles.

Already the grass where she had lain down while the lamb sucked was bending back again.

'Feed my lambs. Feed my sheep.'

But for what? And for whom? For potluck at Passover, that was for what. And didn't he know that a lamb is nursed by its mother, and needs no hired help? He had better wise up, or he wouldn't be long for this world. Plainly he knew little of sheep, and less about shepherds. He was obsessed, or deluded, or both; he was living in a pastoral idyll, in a wet-dream of pan-pipes and watercress. He should leave the town for a time, this fellow with his breadloaves and his wine-jars, and go live in the country. He would find out fast that to live in the country is to survive off the land.

'Feed my lambs. Feed my sheep.'

First the fattening, then the thinning. From the fields to the fold, from the fold to the pen. Convoys driving through the dust-clouds, lambs losing their mothers, the ewes shrieking, boys beating them back with blackthorns, lewd whistles, orders barked in Aramaic, and the oldest sheep in the flock carried five miles beyond a massive coronary in the heaving heart of the press. To be fleeced, then. Sorted and sheared, stripped naked, running naked through the lines of laughing men, stumbling into the sheep-dip, blinking, blinded, your bleats vibrating differently in the ricochet and report of a new space, a sanded surface, walls and, somewhere, somewhere near, somewhere nearer, an overhanging immensity of water.

'Feed my lambs. Feed my sheep.'

It would not cause so much as a ripple. It would have been done. There would be stock to nourish the infant born with rubella, and the teeth would be mixed with mortar to block the ants' nest under a verandah.

The lamb closed his eyes, but it was just as dark without them.

The smack of a footstep mixed itself up with the noise of the ram slithering down through the jittery scree; and the lamb awoke to find he had been sucking at a nail-head. Rust peppered the tip of his tongue. It was worse than the pus from a pimpled teat; and he had thought at the time that a pimpled teat was the outermost edge of the world. He had told the other lambs about it, and they had acknowledged his seniority. In time, he might have his own tutorial.

There were footsteps. He had been right to imagine them. He moved to the air-hole.

It was the woman that the Roman loved, the one who had held her bits and pieces up under her chin. She had come out into the yard and was standing now beside the ox-cart where there were no more fireflies. Pleat by pleat she was hauling up her skirts like nets with nothing in them, bundling them at her waist. Then she stood with her legs apart, wide apart, as wide apart as possible, and crouched slightly, as if she were a Bedouin about to give birth.

The Romans had begun to sing, but they were quarrelling over who should sing first and who should sing in harmony. The shadows in the upper room were as solid and as still as the shadows of pines.

It seemed to go on forever, the woman's diarrhoea, the soaked flap and fish-slap of its falling down on the tart, tiny cobbles. Because it would stop, and then start again. But she sang while it lasted, sang in a strong voice some frisky, fair-weather love-song, all kisses and distance, as if she were sitting cross-legged at the campfire and the men and women round her had stopped humming the air to listen to the words. She was trying to cover the sound of her own pattering slops; and only when they had stopped, and she could step back from the mess, still with her skirts held high, her cheekbones shiny with sweat, did the campfire die and the hand-claps drift away.

Back in the lower room, the two Romans were tossing a coin to determine the order of the middle verses in a marching song about the cunts of Cappadocia. But it was quiet upstairs. You could almost hear the wine soaking into the bread as the men at their meal jabbed the shells of their scones into their mugs.

She had been listening too. No one in the world had taken a blind bit of notice. She could be sure of that. She waited another moment, then unpinned one of the little linen pieces she was wearing, a strip of coloured cloth, and used it to wipe herself along the insides of her thighs, between her cheeks, behind her knees. Where she had spattered her espadrilles, she rubbed roughly, first with the cloth and then with straw. The lamb could hear her breathing. He could see her breath. It must be colder than he thought.

> You may like the tarts of Carthage,
> You may love the stews of Greece
> But the cunts of Cappadocia light my candle.

'Well,' said the Roman with the sensitive glans. 'At least we're in fucking agreement about that much. Now, the fourth line. The wick is not in the fourth line. The wick comes in the fifth.'

Where had she hidden it, that little capsule of perfume she was carefully opening? In the folds of her skirts, in the canvas of her shoe? The lamb had not seen her take it out. He had been distracted by the singing of her boyfriend. But there it was, in broad moonlight, and the smell of it was like a massacre of pink blossoms, heaped petals after a hailstorm. His nostrils opened at the air-hole.

She dabbed at her temples and her throat, and in behind her, over her bottom and down the back of her legs where there were hives. Then she threw the cloth she had cleaned herself with, down by the wheel of the ox-cart, and rummaged at her blouses until her breasts fell free. The flats of her hands worked frantically over them.

> Now the cunts of Gaul are smaller, it is true, it is true,
> And there's room for two or more in the whores of Isidore
> But the cunts of Cappadocia measure up to much, much more.

She was still trying to make her nipples stand up, but it was not going to happen. They had shrunk into themselves. She could not even sting them into life by wetting them with perfume. The lamb thought of the barren ewe and the dry tit he had tugged at. Perhaps nothing would come of this woman, either. Then all of her dressing-up would be in vain, and she would never find a man who would want to be close to her.

'It's not Isidore,' said one of the Romans in the lower room. 'Isidore is in the song they sing in the Fifth. There's room for two or more, yes. But the whores of Isidore is fuckology.'

'Fuckology, is it? Do you think you're some sort of fuckologist all of a sudden?'

'I know what you are, anyway. You're just a fucker, that's what you are, fuckface.'

She was gone. She had clumped away in the two extra inches of her espadrilles, with the reek of wild-flowers and colitis on their bright, tight laces. Before the Romans had made up their minds about the whores of Isidore, she was back in the room and at the window, opening the shutters, letting in the night.

The lamb was sorry about her. He was even sorry for her, which was silly, really. But the ram was not around to remind him that the star knows nothing of the starfish, or the seahorse of the stallion; and that the likeness of names or the naming of likenesses does not alter the reality; which is, if the lamb remembered it rightly, that reality cannot be altered. Or perhaps it was the other way round. It might even have been the first part of the second half, and the second part of the first.

He could hear the soldiers leaving as he thought it through again. Whatever the ram had said on a mild morning of low cloud-cover, had lifted and dispersed. He was still sorry for the woman. He did not know why, and might never know why. Indeed, it might have nothing at all to do with knowing. It might have more to do with the way she had dragged her feet as she went back in. There was a stagger in the step, and that was the espadrille; and there was a refusal to stagger, and that was not the espadrille.

The sheep with the fifth leg would have understood about the stagger. From the lamb's first week in the world, he had coached him to record the chick taken by the lizard, the lizard by the adder, the adder by the ferret, the ferret by the wolf, and the priest in his leather sandals stroking the newborn calf, praising a presence which had made all this possible.

'Amen,' said the lamb. Because it was so wonderful, the way the sheep said it. And his eyes roamed and rested and roamed again, over the sparrows and the shepherd's ragout, and the wasps freighting pollen to the green eye of a tree.

'Listen to me,' said the sheep with the fifth leg. 'That's not it at all. What I'm saying is that we live in a hierarchy of the fang, an empire of the dentist.'

'Two hundred exactly,' said the ewe who was counting.

'Did you make hierarchy one or two?' said the sheep with five legs. 'It's not higher archy, you know; and neither-here-nor-there is one word too, because I use hyphens.'

'Will we say one hundred and fifty?' said the ewe.

'Say a hundred,' said the sheep. He was hungry, and the grass was good.

'The world,' he said, 'is a sad, sick shambles. Once it was a place of relationships; but now, through some terrible fault of the flock, it is a place of relations only. The ship is missing. Yet there is a tomorrow. It may not come tomorrow. It is not that sort of tomorrow. It has a capital T, for one thing. But it will come. And when it does, the lion will lie down with the lamb.'

'And that's not just something people say,' said the counting ewe. 'It is written.'

'It is written down,' said the sheep with the fifth leg. 'The down is what matters.'

But the sheep with the streak of sky-blue dye in his wool had not been impressed. He had stalked away and sat in the dry bed of the brook where the ram's tutorial had met before the master was purged by the pastors of the flock; and, even though the lamb had gone to him and gentled a spike of thistle from his tail, he had kept himself to himself that day. It wasn't until the morning that the shepherds came for the lamb, and the ewes had brought his mother to the far side of the field to discuss the buggery by the boys, that the streaked sheep spoke.

'Listen,' he had said. 'Listen to me. You're too young to be told these things, but you'll never be any older, so here goes. You're going to die. You're going to die soon. It's not the end of the world, but it is the end of your life. That's the bad news. The good news is that I'm going to die as well. Your mother's going to die. We're all going to die. That's the way it is. When we're born, it's all shit and piss and blood; and, when we die, it's the same old story: shit and piss and blood. Between times, we're between stools. The grass grows under our feet, and everything's green in the garden. But there comes a time when the time comes. It comes towards you, it comes to you, it comes for you. And that's that.'

The sheep seemed to be crying. Something or other glistened among the cataracts.

'I don't know,' he said. 'If there is some great alliance forged between the sheep and the goats, our discipline, their cunning; then, maybe. There are centuries of suspicion to be overcome.'

There was mustard in the wind, and body odour. So the lamb smelled them before he saw them, the two brown blurs in the heart of the heat-haze, shapes of the shepherds elongating like the long droop of a drop of mucus from a muzzle.

'Don't listen to that moron with his talk of tomorrow,' said the sheep with the dye in his wool. 'Faraway hills may be greener, but they're not as green as he is. The lion lies down beside the lamb for one reason, and only one reason; and our friend may try to fool you, but he can't kid me. If it weren't for the fifth leg, he'd have found out long since that there's no beyond the beyond; there's only behind the watertank. But the shepherd thinks the fifth leg is lucky, and he's not about to throw away his talisman.'

They were closer. He could see them.

'When do you know?' the lamb said. 'When do they tell you about the massacre by moonlight?'

One of them had something in his eye. The other was helping. He could hear their voices.

'You don't,' the sheep said. 'They don't say "Next"; they don't say "Now". As far as our intelligence can say, it might be any sort of password. They might be talking about the price of vinegar, or a boy who charges you more because he's lost his milk-teeth and so goes down on a man without biting. They keep you guessing, you see. They keep you hoping.'

They had reached the field, and stepped down into it.

'Don't do any goodbyes,' said the sheep. 'It's worse that way.'

The two men were talking about women. He might have known they would be.

'I still think it would have happened,' said the smaller shepherd. 'If you'd brought the two women together, you'd have seen something.'

The sheep with the dye had moved off and was grazing.

'I don't know,' said the other shepherd. 'I just don't know.'

'Pharoah's daughter and the mother of Moses,' said the first one. 'They would have held hands. They would have hugged each other. They would have said Shalom.'

The heat of the sun had gone. He was in shadow. They were behind him.

'This?' said one.

'That,' said the other.

His mother was running towards him from the far end of the field.

*

There was the sound of a latch being lifted and a latch being dropped. The lamb was at the air-hole in an instant. But it was not the shepherd, and there were no leather aprons on the ox-cart. He was safe still.

The man with the breadloaves and the wine-jar had walked into the yard, and was sitting down. He was as big and broad-shouldered as the lamb had thought, but he looked tired now. From time to time, he reached up with his hand to draw the long strands of his hair back behind his ears; and, when another man joined him on the work-bench, he said nothing. The two of them sat there, back to back, leaning against each other, and the lamb stirred on his droppings in the pigeon-box, and wondered at the sight of two humans who were not talking. Here was the host who had been thinking aloud through the course of a long supper; and here was one of the wined and dined, one who had listened and learned. Yet there wasn't a bleat out of either of them now, or any of that cranky, punctual gobbledygook about God or garlic or girls' backsides.

They just leaned against each other, and were silent; and the man with the breadloaves let his head fall back, and farther back, until it was resting on his friend's shoulder.

If they had known that he was there, the lamb, there the whole time, there in the yard, how strange that would have been. But the sheep-trails and the goat-paths of their table-talk could never lead them to the stone's throw of a crate beside an ox-cart. And, even if they did, the most he might expect would be some straw squeezed through the air-hole. The man with the breadloaves was not about to knock the pegs out of their apertures, and set him free. He was no different, really, to the shepherd's mother, the one with the terrible thrombosis in her ankles, the one who told the children stories about wolves and lambs while she knitted winter bedspreads from the wool of a frost-bitten flock. The whole thing was a hoax, from start to finish; and, if he were free again, he would travel the length and breadth of Palestine to tell everyone, even the goats, God help them, that they had all been hoodwinked.

The man with the breadloaves bowed his head as his friend picked lice from his hair. The lamb could hear their crusts crack between his thumb and his finger; a bright, brittle splitting. But the man still said nothing. Only, he hummed as his friend groomed him; at first, an air without words; and then the words within the air, their shadow, like the fingertips of wind on water; and, always, the friend's hands hovering, pause and pinch.

> *Thy teeth are like a flock of ewes,*
> *Which are come up from the washing.*

The lamb was certain. He was certain sure. It was the love-song that the woman had been singing during her diarrhoea. He remembered the bit about the washing, and then there was lots of wanting to be with someone. In fact, it went on and on, and it was quite nice in its own way, even if it did exploit his unfortunate species from line to line; but that, it seemed, was in the nature of human nature. They were not natural at all.

> *I went down into the garden of nuts,*
> *To see the green plants of the valley,*
> *To see whether the vine budded,*
> *And the pomegranates were in flower.*

He sang it differently, the man with the breadloaves. You could not clap your hands at a campfire, listening to that. Instead, you would be still; you would not look at the singer, and you would not throw the pine-branch with the needles on it into the blaze. Even the greenfly on your knuckle would be safe for the span of that singing. And when it was ended, you would be almost relieved. You would bow your head until the tear had dried on the inside of your nose; and then you would kill the greenfly and look down the breasts of the girl sitting beside you.

> *I am my beloved's,*
> *And his desire is toward me.*
> *Come, my beloved, let us go forth into the field.*

It must be a popular song for the two of them to know it, the man and the woman. It was certainly an improvement on the cunts of Cappadocia. The woman had sung it gladly, and the man had sung it sadly; but at least they had sung it. The Romans had shouted. They were deaf to the world. They had not even heard her during her diarrhoea.

But perhaps the man with the breadloaves had. Perhaps that was why he had started to hum while his friend was delousing him; or perhaps there was even more to it: perhaps he knew the woman. His being there on the very same night might have something to do with her. In that case, the song might be a code between them. The meal behind the upper window might be a ruse on his part or her part. If they couldn't be together, then they wanted to be close, or close by. It had to be so. Any other explanation made complete sense. They were lovers. They were bound up together. You could only understand one in terms of the other. Because, at the end of the day, you would find them under the same roof. It might even happen that, at the end of all roofs, you would find them under the same sky. They would sing a different song then.

It was all too quiet by half. The lamb peeped out.

The man with the breadloaves was by himself. But it was more than that; he was on his own. There was no sight nor sound of the friend who had been helping himself to the lice. He was quite alone. Now he knew how it felt. There would be no more talk of missing sheep and lost lambs. Loneliness is the thought of the flock and the fold, and your eyelids closing on the rising breath of the beast beside you. What could any search-party know about that? A search-party is not lost.

The man leaned down under the wheel of the ox-cart and picked up the cloth the woman had used. He mashed it in his fists, wiping his palms clean; shook it out, and ran it slowly over his face: forehead, cheeks and throat. The little phial of perfume still stood on a cobble near a melon-seed that had been punctured for a child's bracelet. He took it up, opened it, and sprinkled some on his feet; wet his wrists then, letting the dribble run to his elbow, and rubbed them against each other. He was like a woman whose father has said yes to the man of her choice, and now she is about to meet him, for the first time, without a chaperone. She moves slowly with the slowness of light curtains filling; and the world makes no more noise than the sound of needlework.

He must love her a lot. That was all that the lamb could think.

Perhaps he had mounted her, and been demented ever since. But he would have to reckon with the Roman. The Roman was something of a ram in readiness; and there was no doubting his degree of attachment to the girl. You had only to remember how he dangled the pitcher from his penis, to realise how strong his feelings were. He was hardly likely to hand her over as if she were no better than the tarts of Carthage. On the other hand, of course, if he discovered she was sterile, beyond the help and handiwork of any apothecary, he might think twice about his serenading. He might blow her away like a clipped toenail. Then she would starve. Her stomach would swell with hunger until it was bloated; and the people who passed her on the road would bless her with the blessing for all women whose time had almost come.

Either that, or she would become like the woman who visited the shepherds, and brought them behind the tree for an apricot or a cheese wrapped in bay-leaves.

There was the sound of a startled owl, and the lamb shot to the air-hole. But there was nothing. The man had stood up suddenly. That was all.

The lamb settled among the pigeon-feathers. They were real. He laid his muzzle on them, and they stirred away from his breath.

But now there was another sound, and he knew it, knew what it was. It was the trickle from the culvert in the dry-stone wall of the field, and the plash of the slow, single pills of water onto the lichen.

He leaned against the box and listened. The feathers sprang back.

Now the trickle was stronger. It was his mother pissing in the sandstone by the dry bed of the brook. Her pee poured down, and a terrified spider turned in his flight to face it.

It had stopped. There was nothing at the air-hole except the man who was shaking the last drops from the perfume-bottle onto a drenched cobble. He had been emptying it while the lamb daydreamed.

The feathers lay in their old places on the bed of the box.

He closed his eyes among them. He would imagine nothing else; he would imagine nothing at all.

Yet an olive-branch was creaking in a warm breeze from the south, and it brought the scent of cinnamon from a kitchen; that, and the smell of fine mosquito netting made from fish-line. So it was the olive-tree at the end of the field, where the pruning hook had broken from a handle made of olive-wood.

The feathers were dancing. He could not help himself.

The man's weight rested on the shaft of the ox-cart, and the chafed joint of the shaft winced with a dry whine under the load. There was no olive-branch, no olive-tree, no olive-wood; and the feathers dangled from a dead web at the lid of the pigeon-box.

But the man was listening to something, and listening almost as a sheep might; so the lamb also listened. Perhaps he could hear his friend returning, the one who had cleaned his scalp when his flesh was crawling. Or it might be the woman, come back to search on her hands and knees for her precious bottle of perfume. It might even be the Roman. He had found out the full truth, and the story made sense now, perfect sense. He would slaughter everybody, sell up, and retire to Cappadocia.

But there was no sound of anyone approaching: no casual footfall, no cantering sandal, and no espadrilles. There was only a tiny, rhythmic ticking, and that was mere metal, a sheet of something or other cooling and contracting into the small hours, long after the sun had brought it to the point of pain. The sheep could even say where the ticks came from, those infinitesimal rips like a dry mouth peeling open. From above and behind him, from the very place the man was looking at now, some bin or basin was closing in on itself.

It couldn't be. The lamb lay down, and stood up again; turned in the box, hunkered, heard nothing, and crouched on his droppings. Of course it couldn't be. There wasn't an apron in sight. No one had mentioned anything about the price of vinegar. No one had said a word about boys of six or seven who hadn't any milk-teeth. The greasy moonlight found no stain on the character of those cobbles. This was a good place, a place where men blessed bread and talked about sheep who were missing, a place lovers could come to and be lovable in. Nothing bad could happen in this decent dwelling, apart from the diarrhoea, and that could happen to an emperor. It had happened to the ram several times.

There was no doubt, no doubt at all. You wouldn't have a sing-song behind the watertank. The shepherds had never taken their wives behind the watertank, and nobody had ever been deloused there, in a kind way by a good friend. The shepherds did that under the olives when the sun drove them out of the field. Sometimes they would play with themselves before they had a sleep; and the one who couldn't breathe through his nose, because it had been broken and badly set, would put the wicker strainer for the milk-pail over his face so that the flies wouldn't shit on his tongue.

The lamb had thought his way through, and now he had thought his way out. It could not happen here.

Someone was pulling out the wooden pegs at the side of the pigeon-box. Someone had worked the first of them free. Now the second. The lamb heard it fall, heard the quick clunk through the drumming of his eardrums.

The lid lifted and lay open.

Starlight sprang down; a feather rose and rocked itself. There was a smell of perfume, and a man's hand with a vein in it, twisting a hank of hair behind his ear; and then it was gone, the hand and the hank, and there was only the stink of the stuff the woman had used to cover up her diarrhoea. The lamb spied through the air-holes at the yard, at the windows and the walls, and there wasn't a sinner to be seen. The ox-cart and the cobbles had it to themselves.

The lamb didn't know what to think, and he didn't want to think what he knew. Instead, he waited to see what would happen next; and nothing did. Somewhere in the middle distance, he could hear a tomcat mousing over barrels, and a club-foot climbed an outside staircase, one step at a time. But the stars had not blinked and the windows had not yellowed with the chink of candles; and the ox-cart was still rooted to the same spot. Even the terrible ticking of the watertank had stopped; if, for that matter, it had ever started at all. He might have mistaken the sound of rope straining a pulley, or the call of some small insect he had never encountered before. It might have been the love-cry of the cockroach, which the ram had always said was the oxygen of the universe. It might have been all of these, and more; but it was not what he had thought. Yet he didn't look up to see. If he did, he might be seen in turn. Better to brainstorm, and lie low.

No one had come. No one was likely to. Where had the man with the breadloaves gone? He had lifted the lid, and disappeared. That was practical of him. That was far-sighted. He had time to have his hair groomed, and to smell sweet, and to lecture at length on pastoral responsibilities; but he failed the test when he forced a lock, and skedaddled. If he had any sense of pastoral responsibility, he would have brought the lamb to somewhere safe, a shelter of meadowsweet where an apron was for young girls baking sweetbread and the water came in satchels from a hole in the ground. But no. He had walked away slowly, without turning round to look back. He had gone straight ahead of him.

It was a trap, then. It might even be a plot, or a conspiracy. It would be madness to step out of the pigeon-box, to walk in the yard, to spy around the gate into the street where the conspirators might even now be moving towards him with their shoes in their hands, over the grape-seeds and the horse-hair from an officer's helmet. It would be worse than madness: it would be lunacy.

There was nothing wrong with the pigeon-box. They had even put in air-holes for him. They had forgotten to give him water, it was true, but they might not understand the needs of a sheep. If they had, there would be something, a bowl of sorts. As it was, they had left the pigeon-feathers to soften the bottom of the box. They had thought of that. They had been thoughtful.

Green pastures, still waters. The sheep with the fifth leg had spoken of these to the lamb, and he was a wise sheep. The lamb liked him. He had only once made a joke at his expense, a joke about the fifth leg, and that was because the other lambs had dared him to. But he wouldn't have joked to his face, and he would never have joked about the green pastures and the still waters.

'Still does not mean stagnant,' said the sheep with five legs. 'Never mind the ram. Still means, you know, not just still, but still. You have to say it slowly. The same goes for green. You have to draw out the greenness in it. Because these are not just holy words; they're the terms of a legal agreement. They're binding on both sides. On the party of the first part, and on the party of the second part. You and I are the party of the second part. It has nothing at all to do with humans. It is about sheep, and only about sheep. Goats are a part of some other plan. Never mind what the sheep who's dyed in the wool might tell you. I know.'

He did. He did know. He knew about the still pastures and the green waters; he knew about the staff and the rod, which are not things but somethings, the somethings of something else altogether: the whole flock's future in a faraway field. No ticks, no tooth decay, no septicaemia; and the fox-cub would be feeding from the barren ewe while her twins kerfuffled.

It was nice to think about that; and the lamb did.

The sheep with five legs would not have been taken in by the man with the breadloaves. He would have seen him, and seen through him, in the same instant, without once batting his eyelids. The man was nothing. He was no kind of shepherd, let alone the party of the first part. The party of the first part did not have headlice or a cloth used by a girl who had botulism. If the lamb had been blinded by him, so that he couldn't see or make anything out at all, then he might have believed his eyes. But he was no fool.

It would be daybreak before he knew where he was. Then they'd load him in the ox-cart and bring him to a farm. There'd be chickens on the big stone slab where the women washed the laundry, and the clean, clear smell of matzo over the midden. Children would tickle him like a puppy, and the baby would be eased onto his back until it blubbered.

'But the best will come later,' his mother had said. 'When your wool becomes a bib for a teething infant, or a jacket for a fisherman in a boat so far from shore you can't even see it. Can you imagine that?'

He had thought that he could.

'Can you imagine your own wool travelling through the world? Nablus and Hebron and down to the Dead Sea?'

'Through the whole, wide world,' he had said.

She was so happy for him then that she wasn't able to speak.

'The whole, wide world,' she had said. 'And it is.'

The lamb decided he would lie still, and think about that until the first yellow-hammer. After that, he would think about the new farm and the sheep he would meet there. First, though, there was one thing left to do. Otherwise, there might be trouble; he might be blamed.

The lid of the box did not budge when he tapped it with the side of his head. He tapped it again, and it moved slightly. So he hit it with the hard part of his skull, and it tipped a bit. He walloped it again; and this time it tilted.

The lid came down with a bang.

LIPSTICK ON THE HOST

Thursday 11 January

My breath went up in smoke. I could see it. I stood there and I
swore. But the one who started the swearing was the handyman.
Back before Christmas he swore blue the heating would be on by
today. So I tried the other classrooms in C building, and what
happens: same story. You could deep-freeze fish in them.

'An air-lock, ma'am,' he said. The ma'am is his revenge. It's
been ma'am since he heard me saying factotum to a parent. He
went and looked it up, of course; and the irony is that I bought the
dictionaries for the library.

The principal was all Happy New Year, Meggie; so I said it
will be if I get the A post on the seventh try. All smiles he was,
and not wearing his wedding ring so that everyone could see the
tan he got at that tropical place in Monaghan with the glass dome
over the pitch-and-putt.

'Do you top it up every night?' I said. God forgive me for it,
but I hate the first day back, and I don't want to take it out on the
kids, ever, ever, ever. Besides, a principal is paid to take abuse, so
let him earn his thirty pieces.

What else?

The other Meggie was playing piano concertos on her
Walkman over by the timetable, but she had the earphones
pressed against her stomach. She's only five and a bit months
gone. The thing is ridiculous. But you know the other Meggie. It
has to be Paganini in a baby-gro; otherwise the world will self-
destruct. And she wants a girl, but she doesn't feel the baby's high
up enough, and this is a bigger problem than the plight of the
Palestinians.

And I would be the same. God forgive me.

I told the other Meggie I'd almost finished the cardigans, but that was a downrighter, because I messed the armhole borders on the sleeveless top when I was watching *The Sons of Katie Elder* on Boxing Day, and I haven't had the heart since.

'I don't know how you do it,' said the other Meggie. 'You're a great old trooper.'

The woman is thirty-four. There's six years between us. She was an elderly primagravida when she had her first. One of her own sixth years was in the public ward down the corridor. She kept the baby with her in the room in case she met the sweet sixteen-year-old in the nursery.

'You'd know how I did it,' I said, 'if you came to the knitting classes in the night-school.'

'With two small children?' she said. 'And three if you count their father, which I do.'

I got out of it before she had time to tell me it was all ahead of me, and then I'd soon find out. But I thought of a good retort to the line about counting in the father. What I should have said was that, yes, the poor man was as innocent as the unborn babe. Of course, I only thought of it when I was getting into the car, but I can save it for some other time, soon.

Then, just when I was pulling out, the principal came galloping over the grass towards me. The man is more than capable of making great strides when he wants to, and today he wanted to. Would I double-check two of the papers filed by a girl in fifth year? I told him that I'd double-checked at the time, and slept badly, though I think that may have had more to do with the fact that I wasn't drinking decaffeinated during the corrections.

'I don't understand,' he said, which is the closest he's ever come to an insight. 'The girl's been in the A stream since she started.'

'What I don't understand,' I said, 'is the whole, wretched examination system. Don't you see that one in every four women has to lose out because of it? Fiona was the casualty of her own basic biology.'

He looked at me as if I was a complete mystery.

'Blood,' I said. 'Bloatedness. Cramps. The disappointed tears of the endometrium. How would you fancy writing half an answer-book on *Paradise Lost* if you were passing kidney stones? I'll tell you this for nothing. The girls in my group are going on the pill a month before they walk inside any exam centre.'

That left him standing. At least, it left him standing there.

Tuesday 16 January

I didn't sleep again. I didn't sleep on my side until three; and then I didn't sleep on the other until whatever time it was that the curtains started to lose their colour. Perhaps I should get a clock without a tick; or perhaps there's caffeine even in the de-caffeinated.

I am forty-one since ten past ten this morning. If I'd been machine-gunned by the Baader Meinhof on the way to work, the headlines of the evening papers would have read: Forty-Year-Old School Teacher Machine-Gunned by Baader Meinhof; and if they'd mowed me down at lunch-time, in between *Great Expectations* and *Ode to a Nightingale*, the World Service would have announced that a forty-one-year-old woman had been left to bleed to death at a Bank of Ireland pass-link. The Archbishop of Dublin would arrive in his Fiesta at the house with Maltesers for the children, and the neighbours would have to explain that the only egg I ever hatched belonged to a budgie called Samson, though I called him Samsona, with an accent on the O, when he hid behind the fuse-box and laid it.

The Maltesers would end up being eaten by that little shit next door, the one who charged me a fiver for mangling the grass with his father's Flymo. And his mother would tell him there'd be children in the house for the summer holidays. They might build a tree-house in my eucalyptus.

Anyhow, I would rather be forty-one than forty-two. I would rather be forty-one than forty. If you say you're forty, everyone thinks you're lying. Forty-one sounds more sincere. It sounds more lucky. Religion has made a disaster of forty. Forty years in the desert; forty days with the Devil plaguing you like a life-insurance salesman. Maybe now the angels will come and minister to me. My answerphone is always on.

I lay in my bed this morning, and I thought. Silly of me, really, to mix the two of them, the shut-eye and the open me, the queen-size queries in the king-size quilt, the grape and grain of it. And a waste of time, too. Like searching for your contacts in a power-cut.

It was so quiet. Only the milkmen and the priests were up, and the night-nurses feeling tired for the first time, because now they could, and putting away their jigsaws of a harbour or a P. D. James paperback. But the priests would be sitting on the side of their beds, waiting for their erections to go down before they said their prayers at the prie-dieux; and the nuns would be putting on fresh sanitary towels under their skirts, and then hoovering the altars, I suppose. And I was lying in my bed in a shrinking nightdress, with a cooled hot-water bottle between my legs, and a soft toy elephant called Xerxes whose only terror in life is the spin-cycle of a Zanussi; and my hands were still forty then.

Where is the soul? It is somewhere between the mouth and the anus, but where?

These are my resolutions for the first period of being forty-one: think about Esperanto. Why not? Read *The Mediterranean in the Age of Philip the something* by Fernand Braudel. Abort the trip to Stratford. Talk to the principal about a week in Paris for the fifth years. Yes, they won't learn a word of French, but that's not the point. They can go to a typical French café and eat chips; they can go to a typical French bar and watch the videos. They can smoke, get drunk, make merry, and the boys can go to the peep-shows in Pigalle. I'll bring the girls down the Seine, up the Eiffel Tower, and throughout the best of the bargain boutiques. The main thing is, they'll be away from their parents for a week. They deserve that much.

Also: paint the bathroom. I am having second thoughts about the Matisse prints on the wall behind the bath. The other Meggie saw them after Christmas, and she put two and two together like a flash.

'Do you miss not having a shower?' she said. 'I need to shower twice a day. I was really afraid at one stage that I was becoming neurotic. But then I discovered it's the norm in Europe and the States.'

If I'd had the attachment for the sink right there, I would have strangled her. But my mother stopped examining her breasts, and said: 'When I was small, we used to go to the toilet at the end of the garden; now we go to the toilet in the heart of the house. That's called civilisation.'

For once, she was almost mum again.

Friday 19 January

If the heating does not work by this time next week, I swear that I am going to organise a sit-in. I said so to the principal. I said, 'I am blue with the cold.' And he laughed at me. 'You're blue in the face, anyhow,' he said. Oh, he thought this was great altogether. It was all round the staff by the break. The other Meggie was in stitches. 'My husband will love that,' she said. My husband. Always my husband. Never his name. When he makes her pregnant, he gets promoted to my husband. Mind you, George is a pretty shitty name for any man, God forgive me. I bet my bottom dollar he has an alias at the office.

In the afternoon, I showed my weak sixth years the cartoon of *Animal Farm*. Apart from the line across the middle of the picture from something in the video machine, they seemed to love it. I would have asked the mechanical drawing teacher for some help with the line, but the man has such a chip on his shoulder since the day he changed my puncture, and it rained. 'Actually,' he said, 'that's sleet, and, while we're talking about nomenclature, I'd just remind you that I'm a mechanical drawing teacher; I'm not a mechanic. You're an English teacher, but that doesn't mean you know your way around the London Underground.'

So we put up with the line, and the kids were great about it. Then we had a discussion about the different endings, and about how the cartoon drives the pigs out at the end, and the book doesn't; and that is because Orwell (whose real name was Eric and not George) was writing a novel and not a work of fiction. So, by slow stages, we brought the whole thing from Hannah and Barbera to Marx and Engels, and I let them chew gum and we ended up talking about sex.

I love those children. They are still alive. They may not die for another three or four years yet. They are so excited about packing groceries in the supermarket and passing out at concerts and feeling each other's faces in the roller disco. None of them has the cop or the can-do to get through any of the state examinations, so they won't have the qualifications to emigrate. Their Leaving Certificate will certify only that they cannot leave. They'll sit in their council houses and watch American sit-coms on a Japanese TV, and wash down an Italian takeaway with Bulgarian rot-gut; when they wake up out of their stupor at four in the morning, the only light in the room will be black and white, a re-run of *Bonanza*.

They know nothing of this. What they know is gel and demo tapes and the hourly rate for serving glasses of Heineken to the sort of men who like to dangle their children's pictures on their key-rings but who take great care to be home again, home again, long after the bedtime story has fallen onto the floor as the child turns in his sleep. So I say nothing to them, and we read *The Rape of the Lock* instead of finding out how little the enormous Latin words in the small print of the supplementary assistance forms can mean when they're translated into English as spoken in Ireland. And Morgan discovers that, no, there's no rape in this poem by Alexander Pope, and he goes back to building the spaceship Challenger out of matchsticks; and I let him. His moonshine is a wiser thing than my daylight. I want to touch him, to stroke his dirty hair with my fingers, but I can't; not with the new nonsense in the Board of Management regulations.

Did the shopping. Of course, I did the shopping. I always do the shopping, but this was different. I was turning into the middle aisle, where they demonstrate the sausages, when I saw Leslie. Leslie with an M, Leslie from my own time, my own school, the Dominicans; the nice Leslie, not the one who used to put things from her nose under the seat of her desk and no one could say anything about it because her father had hanged

himself, God forgive me; but the nice one, the one who used to
eat my beetroot and give me her bread. So I looked for the
sausages, and they were demonstrating sherry, and I took two
without thinking, because that was what I was trying to do:
think. You should have seen the demonstrator looking at me.

'I've a streptococcal throat,' I told her. 'It's very comforting.'

Then I went off round the other way, by the face-creams and
the Immac, and, lo and behold, who was coming down with
her trolley but Leslie with the M. But she hadn't seen me. You
can always tell in a supermarket when someone has seen you
and is pretending they haven't. You just cannot conceal guilt.
Perhaps if you're Dutch or Finnish, but not if you're us. And I
started piling Pampers into my trolley, and wipes for a baby,
too. I don't know why, I don't know what it was, it was such a
downrighter.

'Peggy,' she said.

'Leslie. Leslie, I do not believe it.'

Our trolleys touched. Hers was sky-high with stuff. There
were mountains of cat-food galore.

'The last au-pair would only eat seafood, if you don't mind,'
she said. 'And I mean smoked trout, not tuna out of a tin. So she
had a shelf-life of exactly two and a half weeks before I packed her
back to Luxembourg. But it taught me a lesson. The new one's
from the south of Spain, and I think there's some African in her.
In fact, I wouldn't be at all surprised if the cat-food's an
improvement on what she gets at home. Of course, I don't show
her the tins.'

Then she got down to brass tacks. I told her three, from eight
to ten months, and my husband's a petro-chemical engineer in
Abu Dhabi.

'What exactly is a petro-chemical engineer?' she said.

'Well,' I said, 'it has to do with the chemicals in petrol, and the
engineering of the whole business.'

She threw her husband out seven years ago, when the children
were old enough to feel the same way. He comes back each
Christmas for the Christmas dinner, but last Christmas he kept
crying inappropriately and then he cut himself quite deliberately
when he was carving the turkey. He is, in fact, an attention-

seeking alcoholic, but he goes to Occupational Therapy twice a week and plays miniature snooker with the schizophrenics.

I asked her about the Dominicans.

'Beetroot?' she said. 'I don't remember beetroot. Maybe that was the other Leslie, the girl with no breasts whose father strung himself up.'

Suddenly she had to go.

'By the way,' she said, 'those nappies would be much too small for a ten-month old.'

'He's so small,' I said, 'I can still hold him in my hands.'

And I was so this way and that in myself after she went, that I put the wrong year on my cheque at the check-out.

My mother rang. She has found another lump on her breast. That makes twelve since the Christmas lights went on in Grafton Street.

'But you won't look,' she said. 'You won't feel. You're not a feeling person. I wish I had a son to feel for me.'

She needs a new cylinder of gas. She needs a new light in the coal-shed. She needs someone to do something with her television, because she can only get two stations with the rabbit ears. She needs Centrax.

'You had hundreds of Centrax last Saturday,' I said.

'I gave a few to the policeman at the corner,' she told me. 'He's been very upset about his little daughter. All of her hair fell out with the radiation, but he's still expected to be Batman by anyone who's lost their banker's card.'

'I will get you more Centrax tomorrow,' I said. 'I'll bring them with the cylinder, and we'll see about the set.'

'*Gone with the Wind* is on tomorrow,' she said. 'But not on the rabbit ears.'

I will not look at my mother's breasts. I will not feel them for lumps. I don't care if she breast-fed me for two weeks. Milk does not stay fresh for forty years. For forty-one years. Her breasts are a flop. They hang down like gloves left to dry on a radiator. I will have no hand, act or part in them.

God forgive me.

I made myself a decaffeinated coffee; then I poured it down the sink. I want to sleep. I want to hibernate until ten past seven. At ten past seven it dawns on me again. It dawns on me that I need a clean bra and an antacid and a change of tyres on the black ice of the back roads. If I didn't have a car, I could fall on the footpath and break my hip, maybe. Then I could stay in bed for three months, and sleep, and read biographies, and watch every video with Donald Sutherland in it.

What I watched tonight was *The New Avengers*. Steed is great, and so is the other man. Purdy is pretty dreadful, God forgive me. Why the woodwork teacher swears she's the living image of the other Meggie is a mystery to me; but then, of course, he's gay, so he'd see things differently.

There was a time when the boys in the senior cycle used to call me Emma Peel. When the last American helicopter took off from the Embassy compound in Saigon, we sat in the classroom, listening to the radio. I was standing in my Emma Peel outfit behind a boy who turned the collar of his jacket up so I wouldn't see the boils on his neck, and I loved him for a moment. Then the broadcast ended, and we all went back to the uses of the adjective. But I gave that boy an A in his next two essays.

Hobbes was right. Life is nasty, brutish and short.

Tuesday 23 January

I met a man tonight at the night-school. He's in the Furniture Restoration class that the woman who was a Wren is giving, but he's not a homosexual at all. I always know a homosexual or an ex-priest or someone who's been in and out of hospital with breakdowns. This man had nothing wrong with him, in the sense that he wasn't walking round with a drip-stand. Obviously, he has his own scar tissue, but he didn't have a bull's eye on his breast pocket, the way the professionals do; and, in fact, he told me afterwards that he just wants to repair some nineteenth-century veranda furniture that he's had in the attic since Noah. But everyone else at the table during coffee went straight ahead and assumed he was gay, because they all brought the conversation round to how Michelangelo and da Vinci and Botticelli were queer, but there was nothing queer about the Birth of Venus or the Last Supper. I stayed well out of it, I can tell you. Besides, he was looking very puzzled.

'Is there a Renaissance course?' he said to me. 'I didn't see a Renaissance course listed in the brochure.'

'No,' I said. 'There's a Gay Studies.'

And he laughed. His name is Antony. I'm pretty sure he's not Antony because he got tired of being called Tony; I'm pretty sure he's been Antony since Day One. And he's Antony like in Antony and Cleopatra, not the patron saint of swineherds. He is beautifully co-ordinated, except for the socks, and his voice is as deep as bedamned. It's probably a thousand feet below sea-level.

'Was it in the family?' I asked him.

'What?' he said.

'The nineteenth-century furniture for the veranda,' I said.

'No,' he said. 'I bought it from a company that went bust in the middle of a tour. I think they were doing a Wilde play.'

Muggins, of course, thought he meant the other sort. Daring, audacious, saucy, sex.

'They weren't closed down?' I said.

He laughed. I could have killed myself. But I smartened up my act in a second.

'Garden furniture would be needed,' I said, 'for the disclosure scene in *Importance*. And you could use it in *Salomé*, if you were doing a nineteenth-century version of the whole Herod *mise-en-scène*. Salomé could dance her way in and out of the nineteenth-century stuff while the king could sit in his bathchair and be pushed around by the butler.'

'What would you think,' he said, 'of serving John the Baptist's head on a nineteenth-century hostess trolley? I have a nineteenth-century mahogany hostess trolley to restore.'

'That,' I said, 'would be a stroke of genius. It would be the *pièce de résistance*.'

Then we could laugh together, while the others were disagreeing about the Arabs and whether they went to men for pleasure and women for breeding, God forgive them.

Antony and I would be contemporaries, except that he's a

much older contemporary. I'd say he's fiftyish, late-forties; but if he wasn't balding, he'd pass for five years younger. His cufflinks had his own initials on them, and the collar of his shirt was detachable, so he might be a barrister, maybe, because they wear wingy things in court. Or he might be a professor of something, Sanskrit or Middle English. If he's only a lecturer at his age, then he has a drink problem, and they can't get rid of him because he's permanent and pensionable.

The other Meggie barged in at this point. Volunteers from the staff are going to read the *Collected Works* of William Shakespeare as part of an Alzheimer's benefit on the Open Day in February, and will I play a few of the roles?

'Well,' I said. Because what could I say? He was listening.

'Oh, come on, Meggie,' she said. 'You're the longest-serving English teacher on the staff, and you're naturally very theatrical.'

'I only wish,' I said, 'that I had your talent for drama.' But I think hers was better. Of course, she had time to think it up. I was put on the spot.

'She must be due in May,' Antony said, when she'd clumped off.

'She's always due in May,' I said. 'That way, she's off until Christmas. She lets her husband out on the August bank holiday, and gives him a seven-day pass.'

And he laughed. He has great teeth, except for one at the edge of his mouth which is a bit fangy. On the other hand, I wouldn't be mad about a man going to an orthodontist. It sounds sort of insecure, really. It's all right for women, of course, because a woman's body is money in the bank, although the rate of interest never keeps up with the rate of inflation. Besides, women aren't expected to keep their mouths shut anymore; they're expected to open them in a wide smile so that everyone can see how much their husband earns.

He drove off in a Morris Minor. I just happened to see him. Either he's broke or he collects vintage cars. I imagine he collects vintage cars, because he says 'idea' with an R, like Angela Rippon, and he has lovely Protestant skin and Protestant cheekbones. Then again, he could be a Catholic. There was a lot of interbreeding among the Anglo-Irish to keep the stock going.

A stupid policeman stopped me at the roundabout. First, he checked my motor-tax; then he was rude about my seatbelt. Then he called me ma'am.

'I'm pregnant,' I said. 'My nipples are very sensitive. I never wear the seatbelt when I'm pregnant.'

I had to sit there for a whole half an hour with my hazard lights on, until someone came on a motorbike with a breathalyser.

'Go on home now,' he said to me, 'and try to be good.'

When I brought in the washing, that brat from next door had tied a knot in the legs of my tights. If the father weren't unemployed since Hallowe'en, I'd break his arms.

What else?

I would not describe Antony as balding, actually. It's more that he has very fine hair on a high forehead. You could be easily deceived. The other Meggie talks about my hair being red; but, of course, it isn't. It's Titian. The woman is colour-blind. No wonder she didn't make it to the second interview for the job in TV.

Tuesday 6 February

Here I am in my dressing-gown at the space-heater, and I do not know for the life of me what has got into me today. Do you know that I just told my mother I would look at her new lump? She was dumbfounded. Then she said it wasn't necessary, that she'd go to a doctor. But I had said I would; and I meant it. Am I going mad or going sane? This is what I ask myself.

My mother has heard of his family. They were huge in Tipperary. One of them was a nun who kneeled for a fortnight on her bare knees, with holes in her habit where her knees would have been, stitching back together a cloak that belonged to St Thomas More when he was alive, but then it turned out to belong to Cardinal Wolsey, and she died of a brain haemorrhage. And one of them died from mercury poisoning during treatment for syphilis, God forgive him, but before he died, he wrote the definitive book on steam-flies.

Of course, Antony never said a word about any of this. He is too classy, basically. But my mother had it all off pat. If she had only written it down, she would not be a snooper. She would be a genealogist.

I want to go back to this morning, to when I was sitting in my dressing-gown beside the space-heater, but it was bright then instead of dark now.

It had started to snow. I was searching for something to wear, and wishing that the union were run by women and not by men, because then we could commission a staff uniform from a top couturier, which would save the hassle and the havoc of putting tops and bottoms together at the last minute, and having to eat your yoghurt at the steering-wheel. But men won't reason that way; they just rationalise.

The snow made it worse. It wasn't even Walt Disney snow; it was muck. I thought that, if only it had done this on a normal working day, I could have climbed back into bed with *Pride and Prejudice* and a strong Lemsip. And then I remembered being a single digit in a pom-pom balaclava with a pair of whiskery mouse-mittens, running round and round a tiny garden beside an enormous garden shed, catching the snowflakes on my tongue and letting them melt there, not touching them with my teeth; but my mother would say that the garden was enormous and the garden shed was small, and that you learn about dimensions in Mrs Fogarty's Geography class when you grow up and start bleeding.

I took off my bra because it was chafing a tiny pimple under my breast, and, as I put another on, I just happened to see myself in the inside mirror of the wardrobe. They were still beautiful, my breasts; or, at least, they weren't poignant. They were perfectly womanly and matter-of-fact. The brown was not too much, and there were no veins at all. They weren't old enough or ugly enough to be photographed in a newspaper; they were still young. If there were a picture of them in the *Irish Times*, lots of people would write letters to the editor about decency and degradation. They would, actually.

Yet I'd woken up and seen the snow and cursed it, God forgive me; I was too far north in myself to taste it on my tongue, and to scamper round in wellingtons that my mother had stuffed with kitchen paper and the parish letter. Because man had his five ages and woman had her three stages: tricycles, bicycles, and cycles. And the cycles were spin, fast, and irregular.

I ate three bananas in a traffic jam, and arrived at the Open Day when they were half-way through *The Tempest*. The other Meggie was reading in for me, and serve her right too. She had me down for Caliban.

The principal met me on the way in. He was colder than ever. Really, you would need a snowplough to get through to that man.

'Meggie,' he said. 'I knew you wouldn't let us down. I told them all you had to pay a price for being a primadonna; and that price was punctuality.'

He was wearing cream trousers to impress the parents, but he'd sprinkled his inside leg rather a lot in the loo.

'Look,' I said, 'I know you're pretty pissed at me, but this is ridiculous.'

'You're overshooting the mark, Meggie,' he said.

I thought about my A post. Life is too long to worry about the future.

'That makes two of us,' I said.

And off he went with his glad little goose-step, and his big accordion file in front of his fly.

I have to hand it to her. The other Meggie had done her homework. She must have borrowed the Bard from the local library, because I know for a fact that the only Shakespeare she has at home is the record of *West Side Story* and a school's copy of *Hamlet* with the titanically pregnant pencil-notes in the margins, such as 'Hamlet is fed up' beside the 'too too solid flesh' soliloquy and 'The End' underneath the last line. But, by God, she went through the plays with a fine comb this time. *Inter alia*, I ended up playing the nurse in *Romeo and Juliet*, the mad mother of Coriolanus, Goneril, Bottom, Iago, Falstaff, Toby Belch, Cinna the Poet, and Patience, an attendant to Queen Katharine in *Henry the Eighth*. The last one must have given her an orgasm, God forgive me. Not that I begrudge it to her. George is in dry dock these days.

Notwithstanding this, that, and the other provocation, I did get one good part. I played Lady Macbeth. My accessory was that nice young Physics teacher who went all born-again during his elation and started celebrating the mass with croissants and Piat d'Or until they took him away. He was terrific today. He really got into the king's disintegration, except for the Billy Connolly carry-on. Not that Macbeth has to be from Balliol, but you have to draw the line somewhere. Me, I did Lady Macbeth in much my own voice, and afterwards, a few of the parents clapped, which they didn't have to. It would be lovely if you could turn your fiddle into a violin just by wearing an evening dress.

We were in the middle of *Antony and Cleopatra* at about five, five fifteen, and I was playing Proculeius and Domitius Enobarbus and Canidius and the Clown, and three or four other hats in the cloakroom, when, lo and behold, at the very back of the Assembly area, right beside the project on desalination in the Third World, in walked a beautifully co-ordinated man, except for his socks, with fine hair on a high forehead and beautiful teeth, except for one at the edge that was a bit fangy.

The woman beside me was weak at the knees with hunger, and she hadn't had a cigarette for at least two hours, so I offered to take over from her. Thrilled, she was, and she disappeared towards the Prayer Room with a styrofoam cup for an ashtray.

Antony had taken off his coat and was folding it properly, inside out, on a table at the wall. Then he lifted himself up onto the table, and sat there, under one of the large space-age posters from the fifth-year exhibit on damaged sperm. Of course, I was wondering why he'd come. Of course, of course, I was. What occurred to me was the obvious explanation. He had a son or a daughter who was moving into secondary, and he was vetting the place to get a feel of it. That would account for the furniture story, too. But I was sure he wasn't married. I had that hunch about him. I can always tell when somebody's married or separated. I can even tell a man who's divorced from a man who's bereaved. Apart from anything else, a divorced man will never keep his wife's photo on the mantelpiece; and a silver frame is a sure sign of earth to earth and ashes to ashes. In fact, there was a time when I guessed about an adoption, and I was bang on. It had nothing to do with the parents being redheads and the child being dark. It was more subtle than that. Plus, needless to say, you always know when a woman's having her period. For starters, she tells you.

He was looking straight at me.

'It is my birthday.

I had thought t'have held it poor; but since my lord

Is Antony again, I will be Cleopatra.'

That threw a right spanner in the works. I'd come in at the wrong place. I was supposed to pick up with 'That's my brave lord!' But, after a moment, we went straight on. To be perfectly honest, I think we should have been skipping from the start. *The Two Gentlemen of Verona* is nothing to write home about. If Shakespeare hadn't written it, nobody would have. And the same goes for everything after *Antony and Cleopatra*. They are miles too long.

'You were great,' he said.

'What brings you here?' I said. I wasn't being nosy. It was a salutation.

'I'm involved a bit with Alzheimer's,' he said.

'Are you a doctor?' I said.

'I'm a gynaecologist,' he said.

I had the feeling I was missing something. It was very disconcerting.

'You don't mean that babies are born with Alzheimer's, do you?'

He laughed. He's a great man for the old laugh, Antony is. It's more than a personal trait; it's a personal talent. And there's no meanness in it, because it welcomes in the world, bar nothing. My father was a genius at laughing: always a hand on your shoulder, never a hand at your throat. He even laughed on the day before he died, when he said to me: You will always be unhappy, Meggie, so try to make as much money as possible.

'No,' Antony said. 'Babies are not born with Alzheimer's, though I did once have a dream that I delivered a ninety-year-old child.'

'What happened?' I said.

'He asked me to show him the world. So I carried him over to

236

the window and showed him the street below. It was six o'clock in the morning, and the pigeons were following the bread-vans. There were some people. There were some trees. A man in a vest opened his window and broke a sausage into bits and pieces on the window-ledge. Then the ninety-year-old baby began to cry. He was very quiet about it, though. He made no sound at all. One little tear found its way down his face, but slowly, like a nudge of white medicine down the side of a green bottle.'

I was beginning to wish I hadn't asked him. It was just that we were in the middle of the Assembly area, and people were being roped in to stack chairs. Besides, the other Meggie had noticed us.

'The trees were filling with light,' he said, 'like a fishing net filling with salmon. Their leaves threshed with flashes. And the ninety-year-old baby said that, if he lived to be a hundred, he would never see anything more beautiful than the street below the window where he had been delivered. Nothing, he said, had prepared him for such loveliness; and nothing now remained to be seen. He asked me to strangle him with his cord. I offered to baptise him first, but he told me that his tear-duct had stood in for the priest. So I tied his cord around his neck like a shoelace, and I knotted it.'

'What about his mother?' I said.

'She wouldn't look at him. He was too much flesh and blood to be real.'

On the one hand, it made a change from talk about the county council salting the roads before it snowed again; on the other, the principal was loudly lamenting the damage done to a library copy of Shakespeare's plays by the hooligan who'd coloured the parts of Bottom, Goneril, Falstaff, Lady Macbeth and Patience, an attendant to Queen Katharine, with an orange highlighter from the Art room.

'What gives you those dreams,' I said, 'is port and cheese.'

'We won't have either, so,' Antony said. 'We'll have Cointreau and Turkish coffee.'

He smiled a lovely smile at me, and his pointy tooth was quite nice, really. That would be the way he'd smile at some unfortunate woman who'd been infertile for twenty years, and then, lo and behold, she suddenly finds she's pregnant with twin girls. And she'd want to be taken, there and then, on his great green billiard table of a desk, but he wouldn't let her. No, he would walk out in the rain to shake hands with her husband, who'd be sitting in the car, watching the meter run out.

'Are you in a car?' he asked me.

I was half-expecting the midget out of *Fantasy Island* to walk through the Assembly area. But there was only the other Meggie, having her stomach patted by the little albino in first year. So I told a complete downrighter about the car being broken down because of no antifreeze. And the next thing I didn't really know, I was in the staffroom borrowing the ocelot coat from the German teacher with the very deep voice because she's taking hormones for something. I did leave a note, of course, that I'd been in a rush and took it without realising, and only realised when it was too late, and that I'd do her lunch-break supervision if she wanted to get to the clearance sale at 'The Stork's Nest' next week. Because I've heard her talking about a Balkan pinny for the four-year-old who thinks that the local wino is God the Father on account of the fact that he looks like the Lord in her cartoon of the Flood.

But that is not the point.

The point is the restaurant. I had not even heard of the restaurant: it is that chic. Obviously, I knew he was taking me out to dinner, but I wasn't going to be naive and ask him where. I am not exactly from Oklahoma. I mean, I've read *Ulysses*. In fact, I've read *Finnegans Wake*. Admittedly, that was for charity. But, still. So I didn't say a word. I just expected a steak-house or a wine-bar. After all, he could see I wasn't dressed to the nines. To the sevens, maybe, but that was it.

There were no prices on the menus, not even his. There was no James Last in the background. It was all nouvelle cuisine. The waiters were either French or homosexual, or both. And the one waiter who definitely wasn't homosexual, because he wore a wedding ring, was camping it up like nobody's business. Perhaps he was trying to ingratiate himself with the ethos. The decor was very sort of Austro-Hungarian; if I'd heard somebody ruminating in Czechoslovakian at the next table, I'd hardly have noticed.

As it was, though, there were only two other people in the place when we sat down: a very tall woman with masses of hair and a very short man with hardly any hair at all. Later, a rather arty quartet came in, and lit their cigarettes off the candles on their table.

The candles were gorgeous. They went with the wallpaper and the chandelier. The chandelier tinkled like wind-chimes because of the way they'd positioned the fans. Only the cutlery was a problem. There was no difference between any of it, so you didn't know which to choose for your starter. I can never remember if you begin from the outside or the inside. It must be who knows how long since I made one of my great entrances into a posh place, feeling the raw skin smart under my arms, keeping the audible smalltalk up, watching the women glance at me for a single, splitting second and then skip ahead, like someone leafing through a programme note for the *Matthew Passion*, not even skimming the list of sponsors. Even before my father ambled in, candid and dandified, flicking the cigarette cellophane wrapper from his fingers as he squinted around the room for a sight of our table, they'd have sized me up as too tall with a bad bone structure and a lot of white gold on a goose-flesh throat.

These are the bitches, God forgive me, that I'm supposed to look upon as sisters in the struggle. So I'd sit there, realising that nobody else was wearing drop-earrings apart from me and an elderly woman who looked like the Dalai Lama. And my father would be telling me how much I was like my mother, and my mother would be feeling her breasts; and my father would pour sherry into his consommé while I searched my handbag for my studs.

'Monkfish?' said Antony.

'Did I say monkfish?' I said.

'You did,' he said.

'I'm sorry,' I said. 'I was thinking of a special occasion with my parents. It was a long time ago. At any rate, it was some time ago, sometime. What I'd like is the chicken à la this and that.'

He thought that was hilarious, and he ordered his the same way.

'What are you having?' I asked him, when the two waiters had gone.

'I'm not quite sure,' he told me. 'It's either smoked reindeer or octopus in a wok.'

Actually, it boiled down to a shoulder of lamb with rice and kidney stuffing, which I've seen in Delia Smith, but it did look nice. So did the print on the plate, a sort of Toulouse-Lautrecy thing of a girl in next-to-nothing, with one of the kidneys doubling as a g-string. The same girl featured on my chicken, or underneath it, except that she gave every impression of more-or-less interfering with herself in a drowsy manner. At least she wasn't feeling her breasts. That would be the Ides of March.

We talked about everything.

What did we talk about?

We talked about the polar ice-caps and who was Elizabeth Taylor's first husband. We talked about Pope John XXIII and how nice he was, and we talked about the signs in Canada which read: Please walk on the grass. We touched on just about everything, and just about everything touched us. He had never known the Arabic for Jerusalem, so I told him: El Kods. I had never known that a rhinoceros is monogamous, which you would not think, really, to look at them. We took a lot of wine for our stomach's sake, but why not? I love that pins and needles feeling. The Muslims haven't a notion what they're missing. Thanks be to God Our Lord consecrated wine and not fruit-juice. It means that the Church can wag the finger at beer and spirits, but the Loire valley has a theological failsafe.

'Finish what you have before I pour this,' he said. 'It'd be a shame to mix them.'

He is a gynaecologist. I should have guessed from his hands. His hands are thoughtful and cared-for. No woman would be afraid of them. They are too fatherly for that. Instead of being afraid, you would be the opposite. You would buy new underwear and a new outfit for each visit, and spray the inside of your thigh with an atomiser when the nurse called you. He would stroke your bump, and beam. Then, as his fingers slipped ever so quietly inside you, you'd read the Latin diplomas and degrees that hung from the picture railing on the opposite wall, and wonder why his name didn't have a H in it.

'Are you a Roman Catholic?' he said. That was because we had been talking about the chaplain and what a clot he is.

'No,' I said, 'I'm a Dublin Catholic.'

He laughed when I said that. To be honest, I almost wish he didn't laugh quite so much. It's usually a sign of profound personal unhappiness. Cheerfulness is a quiet condition; glee, on the other hand, is only desperation on a good day.

'I'm a Dublin Protestant,' he said. 'Very low church. When I was little, the select members of the vestry evicted the rector because he dressed the altar with cloth and candlesticks.'

'Do you still go to church?' I asked him. I didn't know if I should say 'attend' or 'practice' or 'receive'. The only Protestants I know are so high church that two of them served as stewards at the Papal mass in the Phoenix Park.

'I don't have a very strong supernatural sense,' he said. 'Nature is super enough for me. The world is pretty phenomenal, when you think about it; and even more phenomenal, when you don't.'

'But the supernatural and the spiritual aren't the same,' I said. 'An atheist can be much, much more spiritual than, take for example, someone who goes to mass each morning. Or, for that matter, to morning prayer.'

Wasn't it just as well I did that Catechetics course five years ago? And the funny thing is, I only did it because it meant I got off early on Tuesdays and Thursdays for the whole term, God forgive me.

He looked straight at me. Honestly, he can look straight at a person with as much confidence as if he was wearing photochromic glasses. No wonder the secret police people in South America always wear them. But in Antony's case, I suppose it is the gynaecology. He would be looking into your eyes as he turned the baby.

'Of course I'm spiritual,' he said. 'It's in the nature of human nature to be spiritual. We can't do anything about it, unfortunately. But spirituality doesn't have an enormous amount to do with my brother, say, belting out motets at a sung Eucharist. It has more to do with my brother scampering round the house when he was four, shouting "Easter eggs. Christ has risen. Easter eggs." It's very down to earth, you know. It's got its feet on the ground. It's soiled. The odour of sanctity is the stink of the laundry bin.'

I was absolutely fascinated.

'You never told me you had a brother,' I said. 'I always wanted a brother.'

Strictly speaking, this was not true. I always wanted a sister; but my mother wanted a son for herself, which would have been a brother for me, so it wasn't a total downrighter.

'My brother,' he said, 'works in Brussels. Notwithstanding his birth certificate, he is a bastard. I can't deny he has a heart, because he recently furnished irrefutable proof of the fact by having a heart attack. Belgium, alas, has an excellent health-care service, and he continues to exhale toxic quantities of carbon dioxide daily. He is, in fact, plenary proof of an old thesis of my father's, which I debated for the Government at the semi-final of a schools' competition in the year that poor Princess Margaret was not allowed to marry Group Captain Peter Townsend.'

'What was that?' I said. Well, I had to. The ball was in my court.

'That the tragedy of modern medicine is that it saves too many lives,' he said. 'We lost. I stood up and said I was glad we had. The boys wouldn't speak to me on the bus afterwards.'

'What had your brother done to you to make you call him a bastard?'

'I called him a bastard,' he said, 'because he was the very opposite. Primogeniture was his middle initial.'

Here are the details I found out over the third bottle. Or perhaps it was the second, and the waiters had moved it to another part of the table. I'm not quite sure, because the pins and needles were so delicious up and down me.

The family home was not in Tipperary at all. It was in Kildare. But it might as easily have been in New Caledonia, wherever that is, because it was only a family home. It wasn't a home and it wasn't fit for any family, let alone the two indoor staff who got the chop when it suited the parents. Antony says you would have to be Thucydides to understand what went on. The mother was a misfit who bought tupperware so she could throw stuff round the kitchen without breaking the Queen Anne serving dishes, and she was boorish to every black she met, on the basis that a first cousin she never cared a hoot about had been whipped with barbed wire by a mad Mau Mau. When Antony told her he wanted to become a gynaecologist, she said it didn't surprise her. She had been expecting the worst since the time he went to the upstairs toilet for an hour and a half and came out of it again without flushing it. That same evening, his father walked him round the garden and talked to him about Oscar Wilde. The first line of the first scene of the first act of his awful, awful tragedy had probably been written down on the day he decided to sleep without pyjamas. It was a lesson to all fourteen-year-olds. And Antony had said he was thirteen, not fourteen, thirteen, and the father floundered and said he was sorry and was Antony quite sure?

Antony was quite sure. It was about the only thing he was sure of.

'Look,' said his father. 'I don't care if you're thirteen months. Your mother says that you're obsessed with the idea of other people's private parts. You want to touch them, she says. You want to rummage in the wrong places. Well, let me tell you this: that's a one-way ticket to pus and prison and Paris. Believe me. So look before you leap. Think twice. Think about Oscar; think about Wilde.'

In fact, he hadn't time to think about either. To keep his hands out of mischief, the father decided that Antony should knock down the orchard wall during the summer holidays. When he'd finished, the old man changed his mind: he was adamant the orchard looked better the way it was before. By the time the bricks were back, his mother had his trunk packed for the start of school.

'Let me top you up,' he said; but the business about the bricks had made me so giddy I spilled some. That was how relaxed I was. The pins and needles were in my nose at that stage.

Maybe I was too much off my guard. I told him about my mother feeling her breasts, and then I was sorry. The truth can be more of a lie than any downrighter. But I tried to make up for it by telling him how she used to laugh at the love-bites on my throat, and how she used to write Dear Johns for me when I was upset; and perhaps she would have done, if I hadn't worn polo necks and scarves, and hidden my letters in the one place she'd never have thought of ransacking, which was under her mattress.

'She sounds a marvellous lady,' he said. 'I'd love to meet her.'

Is that good or bad? Or both? I don't know about the lady bit. Men who call women ladies generally treat them as maids. That, at any rate, is my vast experience of the sons of Adam. The principal ladies everyone, but his wife has to wait for the children's allowance to get her highlights put in. Then he reads her the Riot Act for inviting in the Jehovah's Witnesses who called at the door, and giving them some Neapolitan ice-cream with a cup of tea. He doesn't call her lady then. He calls her woman, and not the way Our Lord used to say it.

On the other hand, 'I'd love to meet her' is tantamount, isn't it? Or is it?

I got him off my mother by talking about my father, and how he used to read for the monks around the corner. Not one of them turned up at his funeral, let alone a proper procession.

'How do you mean?' he said. Of course, being an Anglican, he wouldn't know about silence in the refectory; so I told him how my father read to them during meals.

'From scripture?' he said.

'No,' I said. 'From novels. *The Guns of Navarone* and *Murder on the Orient Express*. They'd eat their noodle soup and try to work it out before Poirot did. Of course, they couldn't talk, so they had to pass slips of paper up and down the table, with the name of who they thought was the murderer written on them. Then the novice master opened a kind of bookies, so the abbot called a halt. After that, my father could only read things like Wilbur Smith. Still, it was a break from all the printing and praying.'

'From matins to vespers,' he said. He really is very *au fait* for a Protestant.

I went to the toilet then. Actually, I would have gone if I hadn't needed to, because you can't guzzle all night, and not go. It would make you look like a hardened drinker, and I'm anything but; so much so, that whatever liqueur they put in the fresh fruit salad was beginning to go to my head.

The loo was at the other end of the restaurant, near the place where you pay. There wasn't sight nor sound of a register anywhere, and I had to ask myself: Is that classy or is that contrived? I can't help being a bit intellectual, even when I'm slightly pissed, God forgive me. But I did spy with my little eye something beginning with M, so I filched the *à la carte* with the prices on it, and brought it in to the toilet with me.

When I think of the poor people starving, my God. The avocado mousse with the prawns and the vinaigrette would have paid for three bottles of moisturising cream, and the chocolate and hazelnut choux buns would have bought a box set of Beethoven piano concertos. I was so amazed I had to sit down. I would never have believed that so many women were having babies. And you have to subtract the working-class mothers, because they have them on hire purchase: free at the point of delivery, and pay for the rest of your life. By the time they're thirty-five, they look like Golda Meir.

Maybe the money is in the hysterectomies. Hysterectomies are *haute couture* these days.

There was a bit of a crisis over the toilet paper. There was no toilet paper. I searched in my handbag until I remembered mopping up the wine. So I had to wipe myself with a five-pound note. Can you imagine? Whoever abolished the one-pound note was not thinking imaginatively. He was a man who just shook himself when he'd finished. But I wasn't going to flush it out into the North Atlantic. A five-pound note is eight pounds and six-pence before tax.

I dried it under the warm-air hand-dryer, and it was fine. I'll put it in the collection box on Sunday, and I just hope somebody sees me.

When Antony went to settle, dear God, I thought of the menu in the loo; but they had another. In the worst-case scenario, I would have told him that I'd taken it to work out my half. There are some downrighters that are downright necessary.

I made him drop me off at the corner where the all-night shop is. It wasn't so much that I didn't want him to see the state of the house; it was more that I couldn't exactly remember what the state of the house was. I told him I wanted to do some all-night shopping.

'You're a tonic,' he said, but he was laughing.

And he was laughing.

He said, laughing.

I think I would go for Number Three.

The all-night shop was closed. 'We never close', it says; and then, beneath that, it says 'Closed'. That's not a sign; that's graffiti. I took out my orange highlighter and I wrote, 'You cannot have it both ways' on the glass.

The people next door had piled all of the eucalyptus leaves from my eucalyptus tree back on my front lawn and off theirs. Do they think I'm in a plot with the prevailing winds, or what? Ever since he lost his job and I helped him fill out forms for his entitlements, the man hasn't once acknowledged me. Even at mass, when there were no more hosts in the ciborium and the priest with the Parkinson's had to go back to the tabernacle for more, while the two of us stood there like a pair of fools at the altar-rail, he didn't turn round and say anything, which you can do nowadays. It isn't exactly a breach of canon law to say 'How are you?' And when the priest came back, I knew he'd receive whichever way I didn't. Sure enough, I received in the hand, like always, and he received in the mouth.

I think he hates me more than a liquidator. And his wife is worse. She is so angry. It should be in the dictionary, this anger of wives. 'Anger. Noun, intransigent. The characteristic emotion of wives.'

I was naked to the world when my mother rang.

'Where were you?' she said. She was quite annoyed about it.

'I was at the pantomime,' I said. 'I was at *Babes in the Wood*, but there was a bit of *Jack and the Beanstalk* in it, too.'

'What were you doing at a pantomime?' she said.

'I like pantomime,' I said.

'You're a bit long in the tooth for the tooth-fairy,' she said.

I felt awful about being naked. I kept trying to hold the phone with my jaw while I covered myself.

'I had to use the rabbit-ears tonight,' she said.

I got a hold of last week's *Sunday Times*, and wrapped it round my middle. Poor Bertrand Russell was having a good old gawk at my ways in and ways out.

'Listen,' I said. 'I am not a television-ologist. Ring the cable people.'

'Are you a bit drunk?' she said.

'I am crashingly sober, as always,' I said. 'I am the patron saint of the dehydrated.'

'You are drunk,' she said. 'We're onto the next chapter.'

'How are those lumps?' I said. 'I've been thinking about them.'

'Mrs Cassidy's Alice had twins,' she said. 'Two boys.'

'Well,' I said, 'she should take them to see *Babes in the Wood*.'

'Tie your hair back,' she said, 'in case you get sick.'

Then we were cut off, which is just as well, really, although I did want to ask her one thing. I wanted to ask her what year it was that Princess Margaret couldn't marry Group Captain Townsend. If I knew that, I would know more about Antony.

There is one thing that I think I should do before I lay me down in the tender, temperamental arms of Mister Morpheus. I think I should put on my coat and my boots and pitter-patter down to the all-night shop with a J Cloth. There are things that should be left unsaid. The world goes without saying, and the silence speaks for itself.

Besides, I think I might have signed it at the bottom.

Wednesday 7 February

It was snowing real snow while I slept. The garden looks like the forty Christmas cards of the garden under snow that the thalidomide artist painted, and which I never got round to sending anyone. I don't even know where I put them now.

I was so happy to see the snow. I could bask in the bed for another couple of hours, and blame the car. But then I remembered the car was parked outside the school, from last night, from Antony; and my headache went to my head again, and this time it was a real gnasher.

If I'd known what a strange, familiar day it was going to be, I wouldn't have turned off 'Morning Thought', God forgive me; especially since it was a rabbi, and they're always at pains not to be too transcendental at twenty to eight, when the mirror will just not look the other way. I think I have too many mirrors in this house, anyway. No wonder the principal shaves in the car.

Xerxes was in the tumble-dryer when I left for work. Poor little African elephant with his ears like a map of India. He did nothing to deserve it. I hope he won't be too scrunched up and scraggy when I take him out. I haven't had the courage yet. If he's gone lumpy, it'll be a rotten omen; but I had to do more than dab at him. He was stinking.

Of course, it could have been worse. At least I got to the toilet before the bulk of it. If I drank more regularly, this would never happen.

The bus-fares are twice as dear as the last time I was on one. The mood is worse than the money, though. People who use buses all the time should be entitled to free counselling on the Health Service.

I was Mrs to the conductor and I was Ma'am to the student beside me. He was dug into a crossword. I helped him with 'atrium' and he was delighted. Then I helped him with 'follicle' and he was polite. So it was mum's the word when he couldn't work out the word 'mammary'. Then I heard a still, small voice.

'Miss.'

It was Elton from first year. The poor child was wearing socks over his hands. I'd have given him mine, but the parents would be up in arms; it'd probably go before the Board. So I bought him some Batman transfers for his sneakers in the shop beside the school. Then he ran off to shake the snow out of the baby poplars. He is still young enough to be the Word made flesh. In twenty years, he'll be the Word made fish, flesh and fowl.

I had a great session with the fifth years and Milton. We talked about the paradox of him being a Puritan who adored the city of Rome; we talked about the paradox of a Christian scripting mighty fine speeches for Satan, and then we talked for a time about *The Exorcist*, because they wanted to. Mind you, I always thought *The Exorcist* was an over-eighteen. They all agreed the best scene was where the head turns round and she vomits everywhere. That was when I tried to get them back to Milton and how his use of lovely, long Latin words is a compensation for no sex. It is, actually, a kind of cunnilingus.

Should I have said that? Perhaps I shouldn't have said that. You can show them pictures of the electric chair or a baby eating blue-bottles in a back-street in Bangladesh, but you can't tell them that people receive each other like Holy Communion.

'Antony,' I said.

Tony at the back must have thought I was cross with him; so he made a special effort to contribute something.

'I think he feels a bit sorry for Satan,' he said.

'Why do you think that, Antony?'

'Well,' he said, 'you wouldn't want to be Satan, if you ended up like him. Hell is hell, even if you own it, lock, stock, and barrel. I know he tries to make the other devils look on the bright side, but that's like shaking hands in the supermarkets if you want to get elected.'

This is the boy the other Meggie wanted to put in the remedial class.

'Miss,' he said.

He had his Ghostbusters T-shirt on, over two pullovers, and he smelled of wet runners and the Clearasil stuff he keeps in his satchel for his blackheads. I wanted to bring him home with me, and give him Seven Up and carrot soup for his cough, and rub him down with a big bath-towel.

'Uh huh?' I said.

'Why is the sterilising fluid called Milton? Mothers are always asking me to carry the baby stuff to the car for them because they think the bags will burst. And I noticed it was Milton.'

I had a better idea, instead of the nonsense about carrot soup. Some afternoon, I'll let him into the principal's office, and he can phone his father in Australia.

'That,' I said, 'is because Milton kills ninety-nine per cent of all known germs.'

But I did warn them not to say anything about the sexual side to Milton's language. An examiner would only deduct marks.

What they want on the third floor is a thousand words on 'Beauty is Truth, Truth Beauty', and not a thousand and one words on 'A Day in the Life of a Dole Queue'.

The chaplain strolled in at the coffee-break. The rumpus over whether he should pay for his coffee or not pay for his coffee has been smoothed over. He pays. One of the gym teachers told him he shouldn't be drinking coffee at all, because of the conditions of the coffee-pickers. I felt like telling him he shouldn't do cartwheels, out of a spirit of solidarity with folk who have rheumatoid arthritis. But, of course, he was gone by that stage, so I had to settle for second-best and say it to the chaplain.

'Ho, ho, ho,' he said.

I asked him straight out. I had been turning it over and over.

'Tell me,' I said, 'can I receive Holy Communion in an Anglican church?'

'You can receive Holy Communion in a swimming pool,' he said. 'Though it would help if the swimming pool was empty.'

I bet you anything he knows how I voted over whether he should pay or not. I bet you anything.

'You know what I mean,' I said.

'Do I?' he said. 'Are you quite sure? You're an optimist, so. You believe that it's possible for two people to understand each other.'

'Look,' I said. 'I have four more classes on the trot.'

'I have to see a woman who's dying,' he said. 'I have to tell her she's dying.'

'Give me her phone number,' I said. 'I'll pass on the message.'

He looked at me as if I were the one who should be on tablets. The church, the church. My church. What are they doing to it? What are they doing to me? The man hasn't a clue. He wouldn't even think of warming the water before a christening. And it's the same with a First Holy Communion. Only a man would think of bringing children to the altar when they're seven and not before, when their front teeth are full of gaps and they can't smile properly for the camera. Only a man would not notice the little things that make the big things bearable.

'Can you receive Holy Communion at an Anglican eucharist?' he said. 'That's what you mean.'

'What you have done,' I said, 'is indeed awesome: you have put it in a nutshell.'

'Well,' he said, 'there are two possible answers. Both are questions. The first is Why? The second is Why Not? Now the Why is your own affair. As to the other, as to the Why Not, I think one could say, in all fairness, why not Why Not, so to speak. That would be my feeling, at any rate.'

'Are they the same?' I said. 'Are they one and the same, or are they more or less the same?'

'Look,' he said, 'Pius XII is dead. There is a death certificate to that effect. This is a brave, new world. Personally, I wouldn't be inclined to take an Anglican eucharist quite as seriously as I would take a Roman Catholic eucharist. I would take it about two thirds as seriously. If I received at an Anglican eucharist, well, I suppose I'd bow my head two-thirds as much as I would at mass; and I'd pray for, say, six minutes instead of nine. The collection would also be *pro rata*.'

'You make it seem like Coke and Pepsi,' I said.

But he cut right across me.

'What did you eat for dinner last night?' he said.

'Chicken,' I said. 'Chicken with a sort of grape stuffing and a coat of fried mustard and herbs.'

'Well,' he said, 'instead of getting into a left-brain, right-brain wrangle over the sub-atomic particles of a consecrated wafer, why don't you go away and think about battery farms? If there's providence in the fall of a sparrow, what do we say about the Final Solution to the poultry problem?'

I could think of nothing to say that wouldn't have seriously infringed his constitutional rights.

'You'll have to excuse me,' I said.

'Why?' he said. 'Why should any of us be excused?'

He's been reading another of those bizarre books that he writes his name in Greek on the cover of. It's only a matter of time before he throws in the towel, marries a woman my age who wears pigtails, and starts cultivating a hundred-and-forty-five varieties of snowdrop. The other Meggie gives him three years, and makes him feel her stomach when the child moves.

'Well,' I said, 'if I don't get a move on, the third years aren't

going to discover why we shouldn't over-use the verb, "to get".
And that would spoil their day.'

I got up then.

'You might warn them about the double negative while you're
at it,' he said.

'Take care of yourself,' I said right back to him.

'I love you too, Meggie,' he said.

The man is a mystery. I will never see inside him. It would be
easier to find out what's inside the Queen's handbag.

It's half-past one, heigh ho, heigh ho, and home from work I
go, when . . . what?

There is a man. There is a man I know. There is a man I know
who is standing on the slush in the middle of the parking area.
This man is beautifully co-ordinated; I cannot see his socks. He
looks like an ad for pipe tobacco. He smells like the duty-free at
Zurich airport. His face does not light up. It lights up and down
and across. Even the ears that his mother taped back for his prep-
school picture are smiling.

He remembered that the car was at the garage. He thought I
might like a lift. Buses are a bore when the roads are bad. Aren't
they? Aren't they? Meggie?

My nails are maggoty with chalk. The skin has gone soft. I will
never use the blackboard again. I will use the overhead projector
always. For now, for today, I hide them under *Paradise Lost*.

We sit into the car. Well, of course, we sit into the car. We
hardly kneel, do we? Boys stand on the pedals of their bikes, and
look in. Two girls are putting on black nail-polish. I think about
each part of my body, from my hair to my toes, of what I washed
and what I failed to wash, of the scents and the sprays that I chose
or failed to choose. My mouth, thanks be to God, is clean and
cold from a cold, clean yoghurt. My breath smells of pineapple.
The snow has begun to fall again, the large, lazy flakes, like slow
confetti at a wedding when you pause the video. The wipers
flump across the windscreen, three times each minute. The flump
of them is lovely, lovely, lovely; and the world is as quiet as a
classroom in the summer, no rustle in the warm woodland of the
desks.

I can smell the forest five minutes, ten minutes, fifteen minutes before we reach it. That is because I gave up smoking when I did. I can smell the trunks of the pines of the new plantation as sharply as the sticky resin on my hands when I dragged the tree from the boot of my car on the night two months ago that my mother found a lump under her armpit. But I wouldn't be lost if I didn't know where we were; I would only be lost if I didn't know why we were going there.

The chaplain is holding her hand, and telling her. She frowns at the apricot ceiling, as the student nurses lead her prancing three-year-old down the long corridor into the kitchen to find him a carrot for his snowman. She asks the chaplain to empty the cold water from the cold hot-water bottle into the hyacinths on the window-ledge, and she turns away from him as he does so, turns away from him into the wall.

The sky is very far away. Its whiteness has the thin transparency of hand-cream. The doors of the car shut with the smack of gunfire. Then it is still again; it is a silent picture. I take a few steps forward. The sound of my shoes on the snow is a kindness almost, like a pencilled tick in a book full of uncut pages. I stop, and the silence steps in again. Flakes of the falling snow are already at work on the brand-name in my footprints. There is so much of it up there that I begin to wonder. Were snowflakes cherry-blossoms in a previous life? Should we have risked it, coming here at all? I think about being stranded, and how dreadful that would be. I would have to sleep in my underwear; I would have to sleep naked to save my underwear for tomorrow.

I put out my tongue and a snowflake landed there; landed and melted; landed and melted and melted into me. I did not touch it with my teeth.

A snowball hit me in the bum. Actually, it was quite hard. In the Bernese Oberland, of course, if you were staying in the Hotel Rainer Maria Rilke, the snow would be all powdery and delicious, and snowballs would be great gas on your way to the samba at the après ski; but this was Irish snow.

'Antony,' I said; but I didn't say it in that way.

That only made him throw another. All in all, he threw four, not only at you-know-who, but also at you-know-where. I don't think my bottom's quite that big. At least, I hope it isn't. I gave her a good, objective look-at in the bathroom an hour ago, and I've seen a lot worse in the magazine I confiscated before Christmas. Of course, some men are more that way than others; and he is a gynaecologist. Perhaps familiarity can breed contempt. It can certainly breed.

'Just look at the snow,' I said. It didn't seem fatuous at the time. Anyway, I meant the snow falling rather than the snow fallen. 'Can you imagine what it must have been like when they opened their windows in Normandy, and saw thousands of parachutes parachuting down when the Allies landed?'

I said this for three reasons, obviously. In the first place, it might give a clue to his age. Nobody in the staffroom had the remotest idea when Princess Margaret didn't get married; and two of the male teachers were positively rude about royalty. In the second place, men like to talk about war. So I read in *Cosmo*, which I wouldn't necessarily have believed in, say, *Bella*, or *She*, but *Cosmo* can sometimes be almost insightful. The piece on a first baby in your forties was spot-on.

I have forgotten the third reason, but it was just as good as the other two.

'Are they parachuting in, or are they baling out?' he said. He is terribly clever when he wants to be. I was still trying to work out some line about gravity or free-fall while he told me about an uncle who died at Normandy. Apparently, it was a load off the family's mind, because the man was a compulsive liar, and his photograph looks grand on the sideboard.

Then he thanked me for coming.

'Don't be silly. I'm delighted.' I said.

I shouldn't have said that. I should have said I was pleased, or that I was going to do it myself at the weekend. But I did say it, and the words are travelling through space without any acoustic attenuation, so that's that.

'It means a lot to me,' he said. 'I've always had mixed feelings about snow. Back before my brother became another Brussels sprout, a complete vegetable, we used to have great fun as boys. We had a proper toboggan for years. Then, one day, a new rector arrived in the parish. The poor fellow was as short as his sermons were long; so short, in fact, that he had to sit with the children in the front row of the cinema. My mother gave him the toboggan for the pulpit, so he could reach the microphone for the public address system. Afterwards, my brother and I used large trays on a steep slope in a private field nearby. The farmer never complained. We were Protestants, and he was known widely as a liberal.'

I could see two people, a man and a woman, walking towards us from the stile at the car-park. They were swinging a toddler between them. Has any artist ever thought of representing the Holy Family like that? And if not, why not? Because they looked lovely. They looked like the image of God.

'When I was seven, it snowed for a week,' Antony said. 'My father didn't mind. "Better to be snowed in than snowed under," he told us. But my mother caught me heaping slush into the copper gauge that measured rainfall. My father used to write the figures in a ledger, you see, and send the ledger up to the Government Offices in Dublin at the end of each year. So my mother asked me if this was the first time I'd ever added to the amount in the copper gauge, and, of course, I said it was. But it wasn't. She knew from my face. She knew the figures had been falsified for months. She was in such a rage that she got down on her hands and knees, and beat the bare maplewood floor with her hands. Then she made me stick out my tongue, as far as it would go, and she hit it twice with a broken car aerial.'

'What did your father do?' I asked him. 'Where was he all this time?'

'He was upstairs,' he said. 'He was ironing his newspaper before he read it.'

He thought this was hilarious. He thought the whole story was hilarious. He laughed so much that he got a bubble at the end of his nose, which embarrassed him terribly. The bubble at the end of his nose upset him more than the broken car aerial.

The couple with the toddler were passing by. And I knew them. I knew them both. It was the sixth-year who had given birth the time that the other Meggie was in hospital, having hers. She had poured boiling water over her writing hand to get out of doing her Leaving Certificate, but the other Meggie had arranged with the Department for a series of orals instead. It was her, all right. And the good-looking boy in the army surplus must have been her husband. The toddler was the outcome, then, of all their pain and apprehension, the vodkas in the bath, the bed-sits circled with an eyebrow pencil in the evening papers, the priest in the family summoned home from Wolverhampton for a furtive wedding in a rented dress. Why didn't I visit her in hospital? I know I never taught her, but still. There must have been some very bad reason at the time.

He said hello, the husband, as he passed us. He said, Hi. I think he's working in a panel-beater's on the north side, because there's a small, smudged card on the noticeboard of the staffroom that Meggie put up with a note about who he was, and why we should rally round him.

'How-di-doo-dee,' Antony said to the toddler. He had his soother on a piece of parcel-string inside the hood of his little anorak, and his nose was all glued up with stuff. You could have put his picture on the label of a tin of baby-food. It might be worth some money, too; plus you would get free baby-food until he was onto solids.

She never looked up. Of course, my hair is different now, a bit more Titian than before. But I don't think she was avoiding me. She was watching where she walked, keeping her eyes on the ground in front of her. She might even have been pregnant, and taking care. I shielded my face against the glare, and the father gathered the baby up in his arms, making sounds like a saw into his hood, and she passed without comment.

I was relieved, really. I was so afraid she'd stop and think that Antony was my brother. If she'd said that, I was going to tell him afterwards that, yes, I did have a brother once, but he died, and there was no point bringing him up because it was too sad for words.

'She's just over five months,' he said. 'Come the Whit weekend, there'll be a brand-new human being in the world. Somewhere between seven and nine pounds, and aged about thirty-five-and-a-half-thousand years, the love-child of an angel and a chimpanzee.'

'At least he stood by her,' I said. 'At least he played Scruples instead of Trivial Pursuit.'

But he laughed out loud until they must have wondered what on earth we were laughing about, and then he told me that he hadn't meant the boy in the army surplus. He had only meant what he said. Is it any wonder I find him hard to understand? On the other hand, his eyes were beginning to look like Donald Sutherland's.

Now why didn't I notice that before?

The man and the woman and the child were walking very slowly into the slowly falling snow. The snowflakes blinked around them, faster and faster, like the leaking blanks on the oldest archive footage, the runny white bits blobbing the white dress of the Tsarina as she turns on a white balcony under a white parasol to laugh at the haemophiliac child in his white sailor's suit; and then the snowfall of the frames blots everything out, and there is only the insect sound of the projector cooling.

They were gone. There was no sight nor sound of them. Everywhere was as quiet as the soundless laughing of the dead Tsarina under the soft tassels of her parasol, when she waved without separating her fingers; waved into the blizzard as the splices thawed.

That was what I thought; but I also thought: this would be good weather for a panel-beater. Antony thought so, too.

We went to a pub and had three hot whiskeys each. Three might be one too many for somebody driving, but I said nothing. At least he didn't suck the lemons. I would hate to have to worry about his drinking. His being free on a Wednesday afternoon is enough of a poser. Then again, maybe he works a roster with a team of gynaecologists. Also, he'd be called out a lot at weekends. Waters don't invariably break between nine and five. So perhaps this was a day off in lieu. I just wouldn't like to think of him feeding the ducks in Stephen's Green when he could be sectioning a few fee-paying clients. After all, you have to make a living to make a life. And his livelihood is a damn sight more lively than mine, God forgive me.

'Why don't you say "God bless me" instead of "God forgive me"?' he said.

This was over the second hot whiskey, but I was in great form because we had grabbed the bench beside the fire, and the man behind the counter had handed me Antony's gloves to bring to my husband.

'You're worse,' I said. 'You don't say either.'

'I say "Jesus" sometimes,' he said. 'I call on the Lord in the most unlikely situations.'

Actually, I can't imagine him saying 'Jesus'. He's more a 'Good God' man. Anyhow, I can't remember what I said, but it was ingenious.

'I live around here,' he said. 'As far as I can walk in a day is my spiritual home; and it agrees with me. I wipe my glasses with toilet paper, not with taffeta.'

He was speaking figuratively, of course. He does not wear glasses.

'It's an EPNS world,' he said. 'That's about the closest we can get to pure gold.'

The pub had put on background music. It was Dvořák's *New World Symphony*. Everyone has gone crazy about it since they used it in the slow-motion toilet cleanser ad. Even the music teacher has taught it to the brass band.

'But I believe in the spirit,' he said. 'The spirit is at work in my life; and, more importantly, the spirit is at play in my life. I carry a candle for Christ; I just don't know that I want to carry a cross for him. Crucifixion can take twenty minutes; carrying a cross can take twenty years.'

I shouldn't even be writing these things down. I'll stop now. There is so much unresolved anger. I will need to be Florence Nightingale.

'That's what I find so funny about you and about me,' he said. He didn't say 'you and me'; he slipped in the preposition to destabilise the phrase.

'What's so funny about you and me?' I said.

'Well,' he said, 'you're sort of cheese and onion; I'm more salt and vinegar.'

Then we stopped talking about God, and got down to brass tacks.

Was there anyone else? Now, of course, he didn't say it in so many words. He didn't say: Would you think it forward of me if I asked you whether you have a man-friend at present? And he didn't say: Are you before, during, or after an involvement with anyone else? I mean, you can't settle these things as the crow flies; and he didn't. But he led up to it. In fact, he led up to it in a way that made the Grand Old Duke of York look like a Roman road. In the end, though, he got there, and it boiled down to Was there anyone else?

I hadn't thought this through properly. It must have showed, because he went off to order another hot whiskey, which was nice.

What could I say? That my Buy Before date expired around the time President Nixon resigned? That I wouldn't mind him being kinky and smelling my feet if he actually cared, if he washed while I dried or dried while I washed, and rang me at work to ask about my steam-burn, and talked to me about the Reformation or what I should have said to the other Meggie, and gave up salt for my sake, and the baby's? And that I wouldn't mind the awful rugby internationals or the test cricket at three in the morning, with the smell of cheroots defeating the freesia, if he found me once upon a time, or twice upon a time, rinsing my hair into the bath with the shower attachment, and laid me down on the rubber-back carpet with my dressing-gown open and my pelvis angled like a wishbone, there, there, between the toilet and the beautiful, blue nudes of Henri Matisse; and made love to me, man and child, as if it were Venice and I was a woman he had brought there so her greens and reds and yellows would echo in the water like an avenue of lanterns.

I told him there had been someone else. Now it was over. It was water under the bridge.

What was his name?

Anthony. Anthony was his name. But it was not the same Antony. It had a H.

Strange.

No, there was nothing strange about it. Millions of men were called Anthony; especially if they were Catholics. Actually, they shouldn't talk about Tom, Dick, and Harry. Instead, they should talk about Anthony, Frank, and John. There were pages of the same name in the Directory. You had to take pot-luck, sometimes. Middle initials should be mandatory.

What did he do?

To me?

No. What did he work at?

Guess.

I wish, I wish, I wish that I'd thought this through. It was very remiss of me, really.

A gynaecologist?

Guess again.

It was a bit strange of him to say that, but he didn't know yet that Anthony was dead. I had just decided.

A solicitor?

At least, he assumes that I've always gone out with professional people, which is something. It never occurred to him that I might be dating a teacher.

What?

A marine biologist, I said. He worked on an off-shore oil-rig. He wrote poetry under an alias on an Amstrad computer. He could make the first verse move to the end of the poem, or the last verse move to the top, just by playing around with it. With the computer. It kept him occupied. You can't really smoke on an oil-rig.

What was his alias?

Luke Waters, I said. But you won't find them anywhere. They were never published. After his death, I destroyed them. They were too sad for words. I read them aloud to myself, then I burned them in the fire, like letters to Santa. But I was sorry afterwards.

He died?

He died. He died in a car crash in England. I was at a catechetics course called Beyond Catechetics, on the island of Inishbofin. When I got back again, he'd been brought home and buried. He was buried with his mother and father.

Had he any family left?

He had one brother, but the brother was dead as well. He was buried with the mother and father, too. Really, it didn't bear thinking about.

Meggie, he said. But he didn't say it that way.

I looked up at him.

I think you're fantastic.

Then we had chicken in a basket, and I offered him my breast, and he gave me his drumsticks, because I told him I loved drumsticks. I don't know why, but I did. I felt so new and possible again. I felt like a dried-out stole of seaweed when the tide comes up and up and in and over it, and the seaweed hisses and bristles with the wet of the water. That was how I felt; that was what I felt; that was where I felt it, and when I felt it. That was the why and wherefore of Snowday afternoon.

He dropped me off at the school, and who should I meet but the crowned principal? Leadership qualities blazed from every surviving capillary.

'Meggie,' he said, 'were you on about sex with the fifth years?'

'I was,' I said.

'Were you on about weird stuff?'

It was the cunnilingus he was thinking about. What possessed me to say it? When I showed them the Holocaust series two years ago, the parents' council were up in arms about the topless dancing in the Weimar night-club. Will I never learn? Of course, when I do, is the time to stop teaching.

'I was talking about a man and a woman making love.'

'Just straightforward straight sex?'

'Yes,' I said. 'A man doing things to a vagina.'

'I'm sorry,' he said. 'I got the wrong end of the stick.'

And off he went, with his hand inside his jacket like Napoleon Bonaparte. I think he likes to feel his credit cards. They're a kind of worry beads.

I was stopped beside a Black Maria at the traffic lights, so I rolled the window down and turned the radio up, in case there was some poor prisoner inside, trying to light a cigarette with handcuffs on. Actually, it was 'Tie a Yellow Ribbon Round the Old Oak-Tree' that they were playing, so the words were a wee bit off-beam, but maybe the melody cheered him up. I only hope it made the wardens feel that high.

My mother rang. Surprise, surprise; and here's another: the Tower of London is in . . . London. What I don't understand is why the dialling tone sounds like the opening notes of Beethoven's Fifth, whenever she's at the other end.

'*Babes in the Wood* isn't on,' she said. 'It's *Snow White and the Seven Dwarfs.*'

I had forgotten about my downrighter, but she reminded me.

'I worry about you,' she said. 'When you tell me lies, I worry about you. Your father was a terrible man for white lies, but at least they were white. They weren't off-white, and they weren't cream, let alone caramel.'

'I've gone to the dogs,' I told her. 'I have the makings of a bag-lady.'

'It's probably the change of life,' she said. 'All that jogging might have brought it on early.'

'I know,' I said. 'It would give you a lump in your throat, wouldn't it?'

And I put the phone down, God forgive me. One of these days the woman is going to die. She is that manipulative. Then I'll die a death, which is much worse. Her slippers will be parked under my television set till I go to my grave, and I'll have to donate my body to medical research to avoid being interred on top of her.

All the same, I was sorry I mentioned lumps. I thought of all the pills she has to take, the colours, the combinations, the tablets I break in half for her, and the plastic containers she keeps for storing stamps and thumb-tacks and American cents that she finds among her small change, because they would be useful if you were to go to New York and use the subway. Her pills have names like the names of Assyrian warlords in the Bible; the titles of Hittite princes circle her capsules; her tablets are the pink pellets of the Ten Commandments. It is a Babylonian captivity, and she did nothing to deserve any of it. If her father had done as my father did, if he had tattooed his left kneecap with her name, which is my name too, then she would have known there was one place that was set aside for her, one knee that would always bend at the sight of her name.

But she had taken the phone off the hook.

Well.

Xerxes is fine. In fact, he loved the tumble-dryer. He wants to tumble in it again, soon. His trunk has perked up no end, and his ears have gone beyond regal. They are imperial. Tonight I shall let him sleep with his head under my armpit, which is the way he likes best.

Wednesday 14 February

'There's a man with a gorgeous voice on the phone for you, Meggie,' said the other Meggie; and there was. But I wiped the receiver first. It stank of pipe-smoke. That would be the vice-principal.

Antony had to babysit a boy of five or six for a doctor friend who had one hundred and eighty-two parking tickets to answer for. He had parked wherever he liked in the run-up to emigrating to Hong Kong. Now he'd changed his mind about emigrating, but the police had not changed their mind about the one hundred and eighty-two parking tickets. He was in court at two o'clock. Antony would be in the Zoo. So would the boy. Would I care to examine the zebras, and decide whether they were black with white stripes or white with black stripes?

I told him I was doing *Animal Farm* at the moment, and I'd love to go.

Meggie, of course, was malarial with curiosity.

'Is he married?' she said.

'His wife died in childbirth,' I said. 'So did the child. It was too sad for words.'

'Well,' she said, 'when I heard his voice, I instinctively sucked in my tummy. Then I remembered I was six months pregnant. I doubt if a voice like that would have any interest in a married thirtysomething with a family.'

I hadn't seen a zebra since I left school. A cousin of mine who used a sun-ray lamp for his spots, brought me to the Zoo dance; but he drank himself into a rage when I wouldn't let him snap my elastic, and he ended up throwing lit cigarettes into the Capuchin monkeys.

'He does have a beautiful voice,' I said. 'It is almost like a voice-over.'

The funny thing is, I was wearing tights, not stockings.

'But is it real?' said the other Meggie. 'Is he Protestant, or is he just pretending to be? Is it pâté de foie gras or is it chicken liver?'

'He is Anglo-Irish,' I said. 'But the part of him I like the best is the hyphen.'

'So,' said the other Meggie, coming in so close I could see her bridge-work, 'has he deflowered you yet?'

'You should know,' I said to her. 'You're the one who always says you can tell from the way a woman walks whether she was stalked the night before.'

'He may not have picked your petals, Meggie,' she said, 'but he hasn't trimmed your thorns.'

I got up to go. I am always getting up to go, in that staffroom. It is the only way to be rid of people. There are times when I almost envy the deaf woman in career guidance. Nobody ever bothers her, as she cuts out her cartoons from the *New Yorker*, and pastes them into her scrapbook.

'I have a hunch,' said the other Meggie, 'there's great chemistry going on in your extra-curricular life.'

'I don't know about the chemistry, Meggie,' I said, 'but the biology is honours material.'

She could think of nothing to say, so, of course, the baby leapt in her womb promptly, and I had to feel here and to feel there until, quite by accident, I felt her navel, and it was the wrong sort. It's a bulge instead of a button. I'm sure she wears swimsuits instead of bikinis on the beach. But I didn't ask her. I let it go. It was reparation for talking to my mother about lumps last week.

The Zoo was the very same. The animals did not look one day older. Time had stood still since the day the teacher made us walk in a blindfolded Indian file around the precincts, smelling the hippo and the kangaroos, until we met a party of blind children with two albino guides, and the teacher sat by herself with her head in her hands, so still that the flamingos came up out of the water and picked through the chip-bags at her feet.

The little boy was a South-East Asian, with a name like the sound of a xylophone, but he spoke pure Swallows and Amazons English. When the keeper at the elephant house asked him where he was from, he said, 'Churchtown', and everybody laughed, and thought I was his mother, or his stepmother; and I tucked the label of his sweater down under the collar, because it was sticking up, and I carried his empty carton of pineapple juice until we found a litter-bin beside the monkey cages.

There were butts on the tarmacadam, but no ice-pop sticks. It was still too cold. I thought of my cousin throwing the cigarettes, of how he lit one after another, of how they sparked as they struck the bars, of how two went in, into the scampering dark inside; and I thought of the cries that were human, almost, like the cries from a dentist's chair, the low, clenched whimpering as the bits that were burning burned the pink part of their inner ear or the flat fat of their tongues.

One of the chimpanzees was watching television. It must have been a video, because I had seen the same quiz show three weeks before. I would have known the answers, but there was no sound, or the sound was turned down. Still, the chimpanzee clapped whenever the audience did, though he clapped more slowly, even ironically, as if he thought the whole thing had been fixed beforehand.

Antony ran his hand down over my bottom, and I tried not to tighten the muscles. I tried to be casual and Californian, of course. I wanted him to feel that I'm used to being felt, and it's cool, it's no hassle; but it's hard to have your bottom touched by a man, especially if the man is a gynaecologist and you've always thought of your behind more in terms of a mule than an ass.

The monkeys were holding their hands out at the bars. Right down a whole row of cages, fingers and thumbs uncurled into patient pink palms. And I wanted it to snow, slowly and suddenly, so that snowflakes would teeter into their hands, a whiteness turning to transparency, like a Holy Communion wafer.

There was no one around, apart from the monkeys. I put my hand on Antony's bottom, and moved it up and down a bit. But I don't know if he liked this, because he moved away then; and the little boy with the name like a xylophone twirled the monkey keyring I had bought him, and threw it high up onto the barred roof of the cage with the South-East Asian monkey; and when we left, the monkey was still trying to drag the keyring through the stained mesh of the wire.

We brought the boy to his father in the Four Courts. The wife, apparently, can kiss goodbye to the Greek islands this year. The closest she'll get to the Odyssey is reading *Ulysses* in the back garden. Actually, he seemed to find this terribly funny. The poor woman has already bought a kimono for Mykonos, and she took the label off, because it wasn't designer, so she's stuck with it. But he wasn't laughing when he found a parking ticket on his car outside the Courts. That makes one hundred and eighty-three. I think the Lord may be telling him to go to Hong Kong.

Antony said he wanted to buy me something.

'Don't be so silly,' I said. 'Why would you want to buy me something?'

But he insisted. He had to. I had been such a sport.

I'm not quite sure about being a sport. It's a bit too jolly hockey-sticks, really. At the end of the day, I would rather be a pet. But he did insist, and he went on insisting until I insisted that he stop. We were standing outside a very de luxe lingerie store, with all sorts of hairline fractures in black and burgundy, and I was afraid he might want to tog me out in something that looks very chic and very carnal with dry ice and strobe lighting, but makes you feel like the Abominable Snowman in the publicity of your own bedroom. It's not that I'm being ideological about it, either. A merry widow is perfectly kosher and table-for-two, though why it's called a merry widow is beyond me; I would have thought it's the winter wardrobe of desperate women. Besides which, you can't get a good night's sleep in a tight-fitting flimsy. The rapid eye movement is all on his side of the bunk. So give me comfy cottons any day.

'Here we are,' he said, but we were three doors down from the garter-belts, and he could have said '*Voilà*', because we were stepping into the French designer boutique where the girls are all the daughters of ambassadors, and two of them have fathers who were shot. In fact, I think one of them might have been eaten, the poor man; and Antony spoke to them in English, because he's too classy to care less about being fluent in French.

'Now,' he said, 'I'm going to have to ask you to take off your clothes.'

He smiled, and the girl smiled, and I laughed, which was hicky, but I couldn't help it. Spontaneity is such a curse. What I need is ten script-writers to laminate my ripostes before I leave the house each morning. And the funny thing is that I can wander round the classroom like a latter-day Pied Piper, and they laugh at everything. Even the brainy boys with glasses have erections if the zip at the back of my skirt slides down, God forgive me. But put me in an up-market outlet for the highest *haute couture*, and the coaches turn to pumpkins, and it's Hallowe'en again.

God of Abraham, God of Isaac, God of Jacob, God of Joseph, God of all the other big names in the Bible, don't let me become a blue-stocking. I ask this in the name of Jesus.

I'd have tried on tons, but it might have been common.

They had beautiful reds and pinks, but what can you do if you're Titian? There was an exquisite ivory blouse with a choice of pale blue or turquoise waistcoat, and a gorgeous, gorgeous, gorgeous, very straight, figure-hugging, black *diamanté* off-the-shoulder cocktail dress with accessories that would make you weep; but the price was a mix of miles and kilometres multiplied. You could almost donate it to the Third World as payment in kind.

What I chose was a lemony bo-peep. It looked the cheapest item in the shop, and there was a smudge on it which I made a bit worse by rubbing it.

'How about this?' he said, and he passed it through the curtain of the changing-room.

'Antony,' I said. How I said it was in a tone of astonishment. I honestly didn't think they made them any more. This crocus-coloured, full-length evening dress with scallopy shoulders had come straight from Mrs Brezhnev's trousseau. Professor Higgins put his head round the curtain.

'Aren't you going to try it on?' he said.

'Antony,' I said, 'does this remind you of your mother?'

'Don't confuse me,' he said. 'I'm confused enough already.'

So I did try it on, and he peeped round again. There were

mirrors to left of me, mirrors to right of me, mirrors before and behind. I felt like the Elgin Marbles.

'Gosh,' he said.

'It would be lovely with a beehive and long, white gloves,' I said. 'But I'd have to wear a different bra, or no bra at all.'

I eased the straps of the dress down over my shoulders as slowly as if I had sunburn, and the dress slid to my bra.

'A beehive is going back,' he said.

I opened my bra and took it off, and hung it on a hanger. It balanced beautifully, one cup on each side of the wire. It didn't tilt, and slip to the ground. I was so grateful.

'A beehive,' he said, 'is going back a very long way.'

I gathered the flowing folds of the gown from where they had run like water to my pleated waist, and I drew them up slowly over my stomach and the cove of my ribs and my bare, unbearable breasts, until I was decent again.

'A beehive,' he said. 'There's a word to conjure with.'

He had seen them. He had wanted to touch them; not to test them, not to handle or manhandle them with brisk, cellophane fingers, palpating for lumps; but to touch them, to squeeze them, to leave the marks of his fingernails around the wet stub of the nipple. He was not thinking of lactation then; he was thinking of milk and honey.

Men are like that.

'Do you know,' he said, 'you were never vaccinated?'

'My mother made them do it in the small of my back,' I said. 'That was before the bikini.'

Of course, he was mortified when I haggled over the smudge. He thinks the bazaar stops at the Bosphorus. But women are more used to the world, because they're more used by it. It all comes down to adding up figures, including your own. Take care of the pounds, and the pennies will look after themselves.

Where do the traffic wardens come from? We were being ticketed when we got to where the car was parked. That was because Antony had left it in a handicapped space, so he had to do a polio leg for the last hundred yards.

The man has me in stitches.

When he dropped me home, I kissed him, or he kissed me, or

we kissed each other at the same time. Then I put my tongue in his mouth. Somebody has to start the ball rolling.

His mouth has a lovely taste. I can still taste it.

There was no post, except for the census forms. They are not to be done yet. The whole nation is to fill them out during the commercials on Sunday week. Whoever Caesar Augustus is, he must be a majority shareholder in black biros. I think I shall do mine in mauve.

My mother didn't ring, so I got worried and rang her. But she's in great form. Her next-door neighbour had her purse snatched, one of the rabbit ears has snapped from its socket, and she has found a particularly promising lump, but she won't show it to the new GP because he has a pirate's ring in his ear.

I am going for the A post. I am. Fuck it, anyway; why not? God forgive me.

Xerxes is behaving very strangely. I think he might have met the little elephant with the pink bow in the dormer window of Number Four. He has gone very deep in the bed.

I am very near the world. I can almost smell it.

Hobbes was wrong. Life is not nasty, brutish, and short.

Friday 23 February

Antony is coming for dinner tomorrow. I have everything I need for shrimp teriyaki, except the shrimp. I do not quite understand about them having to be 'deveined', and when I complimented the home economics teacher on her outfit, she smiled and said: 'You must be entertaining again, Margaret.' I could have asked the man who teaches Business Organisation and something else, but he's so paranoid about being gay he might have thought I was probing.

Anyhow, I have the pineapple juice and the curried rice, the sherry, the wine, the port, and the brandy; and I shall have a Road-to-Damascus revelation about the main course sometime during the night.

I am not going to talk about the A post. Why do people from the Department of Education wear such awful aftershave? Is it because they are all ex-priests or because they're all pretending to be ex-priests, for the kudos? There were four of them, with four ashtrays in front of them. Actually, in strict fairness, one of them may have been a woman. He was wearing a skirt and earrings, and his hair was in a bun; also, his name was Marion. They gave me seven minutes and six seconds of their time. I had the stopwatch on the table.

The other Meggie is not herself. She has to see her doctor over the weekend. Her doctor is not Antony. His name is Benedict, and he has three point five children and a Labrador. He was the Commodore of some golf club, but he was ousted in a putsch when he nominated a Jew for membership. Now he's only an ordinary member, but he doesn't mind one bit. He says that Thermopylae was a victory in the long run.

He sounds a real shit to me.

At the lunch-break, I went over to her.

'Meggie,' I said, 'you're not yourself.'

'Meggie,' she said, 'I love you in Christ Jesus, and I hope you win the lottery and find happiness, but in the meantime would you piss off?'

So I did. I went off to the other end of the staffroom, and sat with the rude mechanicals and talked about somebody being relegated to the league table of the second division. Of course, it'll be rugby, rugby, rugby for the next two months. But one of the men was saying that his tiny premature child has been given little contact lenses because she was born before her eyes had developed; and another man said that a woman should cook her placenta, and eat it, because it was full of multivitamins.

I was absolutely fascinated by all of this, and forgot the time. When I went in search of the other Meggie to say sorry for anything I might have done to upset her, she was gone.

She had left her gloves behind, drying on the radiator.

I took two of her classes. I didn't mind doing it. I showed them *Animal Farm*, and we talked about how the cartoon ends in a more animated way than the book, and everybody laughed, and the girls wound their boyfriends' scarves around their necks; and I told them how there was hope, and the drum was always beating, beating away inside us, and it gave us heart, it was our heart, we must stop smoking, because we were human beings, the love-child of an angel and a chimpanzee.

It was the usual stuff, I know. But so are the readings at mass; so are they. Yet once in a blue moon, perhaps, somebody stops what she's doing, stops trying to read the headlines of the Sunday papers upside down, and listens for one momentous moment to the sound behind the organ, the tiny, toneless cheeping of a chick in a nest of twig-leaves and pale missal paper, high up, higher up, higher than even that, in the grim, groined vaulting.

The boy at the blackboard listed the points until there was no more chalk.

'Thanks, Anthony,' I said. 'You're a great man.'

The whole class hooted, because they call him Tony.

'Never mind them,' I said to him. 'Anthony is a fine name. Fine men have been called Anthony.'

We had started a group-discussion about what was posh, and what wasn't, and how posh came from port out, starboard home, when Sue-Ellen threw up. Then she threw up again. They were all thrilled, of course.

'Ham and eggs,' said one.

'Ham and eggs and cheese,' said another.

She was white in the face. I gave her a hug, and got stuff on my hair. I hope to God she's not pregnant, but I couldn't ask her, even in the loo. She wears a Band-Aid on her index finger so her father won't know she smokes. She's another ugly duckling in a world where ugly ducklings grow up into lame ducks. A dozen more computers in the computer room will change nothing. What she needs is a family. A mother and a father and two brothers are not the same thing at all.

'Have you a key?' I said. 'Are you sure you have a key to get in?'

She keeps the key inside her sock, for safety. That explains the limp.

'Have you bus-money?'

She has bus-money. She will go straight home. She will go to the neighbours and watch 'Neighbours'. The baby shaves her legs with his father's battery razor. She can fix their video, no bother.

The class was in an uproar. They were dancing on the desks. I put on *Animal Farm* again, just to shut them up. They lowered the blinds to see it better, and I picked the vomit up with my bare hands. There were no kitchen-gloves or clingfilm. I couldn't use the other Meggie's gloves; they looked too demoralised. So I made do. And, right enough, she'd been eating ham and hard-boiled eggs. But I wasn't disgusted. I wasn't even indifferent. Actually, I was quite happy. It made such perfect sense, really. It was so right, everything that had happened and was happening, that it was almost rightful.

When I looked up, and around me, and through the window under the short blind, it was as if I had been digging for roots in a wasteland, digging out some soft, spoiled onion like an eye, and then looking up, looking around, and finding that I was master gardener in the middle of a vast, landscaped garden, a loveliness that went in every direction.

The bell sounded, and the blinds went up, and the daylight was still clinging on to the things of this world. I realised that I was in the same place at the same time; I realised that the landscape and the wasteland were the two diminutives of the one name, a name we can never call, or call out, or call upon, because we remember it only when the mouth has had its fill of eating and speaking, of corned beef and adjectives. Then, as it springs to mind, as it sweeps to the tip of our tongue, as our lips part, we are joined at the mouth in a kiss.

And I think I felt joy for the time that it took for the classroom to empty around me. I am not quite certain what joy feels like, but I think I felt joy. I had to rub my eyes with my thumbs because they were filling up, though it might have been the chlorine I was putting down.

I suppose it was.

First I went to the bookshop. I bought *An Illustrated History of Warfare*, a novel by Wilbur Smith with rhinoceroses and naked women on the cover, a thriller about the Kremlin and the KGB with the Kremlin and naked women on the cover, a book about famous and infamous unsolved murders with naked women and a noose in silhouette on the cover, and *The Collected Poems of Sylvia Plath*, because I distinctly remember telling my Antony that the other Anthony, the Anthony with a H, wrote poems when he was feeling poetic, which is, of course, the wrong time to write poems. However.

The point is, I bought some books that you would not be surprised to find a man reading. Just for good measure, I went the whole hog and picked up a copy of *The Documents of Vatican Two* in the bargain basement. Actually, they are thicker than the Bible, those same documents. You could do somebody an injury with them.

The next stop was the supermarket. Shaving cream, men's deodorant, and powder for athlete's foot, I watched what other women were buying, and then I stocked up on toothpicks and liquid antacids. A big thing of talcum powder was my own idea. I thought of my father opening his shirt-button, each morning before he headed off to work, and shovelling loads of talc down inside his collar. My Antony is not like that at all, but the other Anthony was, or would have been.

Would you believe that I saw Leslie there? Leslie who gives her au-pair cat-food, and corrected me about the nappies? I had to wait till she was through the check-out before I could join the queue at the ten items or less. In the meantime, I had two tastes of wine and a cocktail sausage on a stick. The woman was a bit iffy with me. I was supposed to dip the sausage in the sauce first.

'I didn't know you were married, Miss,' said the girl at the check-out, as she rolled my shaving cream down to the boy who was packing. I had to look at her closely. She was one of mine, all right. It was the hair that threw me. It had gone all hedgehoggy.

'You're looking great,' I said.

'There is no art can tell the mind's construction in a face,' she said.

I haven't taught *Macbeth* for four years, so she must be twenty-one. Isn't she great to remember? She had the opposite of anorexia, and binged in the toilets. She was cute enough to eat quiet foods, though. If she was biting crackers, she used to flush while she broke and chewed. She has subtle, soft-grey eyes. An artist would give up, and paint her asleep.

'How do you feel about school now, looking back?' I said.

'I feel,' she said, 'that to call an ice-cap Greenland was a bit of a con, from the point of view of the settlers. But I suppose they wouldn't have gone to a place called Ice-Cap.'

'Was it that bad?' I asked her. I was thinking of the time I made her stand outside the door, and she stuck a hair-clip up a plug-socket, and the tips of her fingers were all black for a week.

'I wasn't thinking of school,' she said. 'School was only the departure lounge.'

Then the woman behind me said that she had an ice-cream for a children's party, and did we want it to melt it away on her?

And that was that.

The last port of call was the record-shop. I bought a Beatles compilation, because it had 'Here Comes the Sun', and Dvořák's *New World Symphony*, which everybody has been buying because of the toilet cleanser commercial. The girl had never heard of James Taylor.

Whenever I had to stop at the traffic lights, I bent back the book of documents about the Vatican Council. They look very read now. I signed it 'Anthony Sutherland', the way that the other Meggie writes. He was not the sort of Anthony who would write his qualifications after his name, but I put in 'St Johns' under-neath, because that could be Nova Scotia or Oxford.

I think I have done everything now. I even did the canopy of the fireplace, and then turned the mattress in case he thought it was me and not the hot-water bottle. All of the Dickens and *The Forsyte Saga* I brought upstairs, and put them in a shoe-box at the back of the press in the room where I iron. Then I filled the space on the shelf beside where he'll sit with Teilhard de Chardin and Anaïs Nin and a few *livres de poche*. Thank God I didn't give the other Meggie all my Sartre in French, the time she started at the Alliance Française. You never know when you'll need a challeng-ing philosopher to shed light on your life. But the best of all is a book in Hungarian, which is actually about brucellosis in cattle.

I cannot decide between plain old beef stroganoff and boeuf bourguignonne. Which would be better with stuffed grape leaves? Imagine being a housewife and having to make these decisions every night of the week.

I have put that strongly scented soap at the bottom of the cistern, so it should smell lovely at every flush. Or should I pour in some boiling water to soften it?

My mother is going in for tests on Tuesday, or Monday if they have a bed. I don't know what to think about this; about that. It has always been knights and bishops between us; now she's moving her queen. There was a pact that we had, that the queens would stay put. I don't know.

I sat in the bath for an hour. I've never been so clean. I'm as clear as a long-stem glass that's been steeping in hot suds before being rinsed under icicles. I shaved a lot of myself; I could wear a thong, almost. The bath was like flooded woodland, with floatings. Then I got hard skin off the side of my foot with the edge of the scissors.

Honestly, you would think that I was heading off to see my gynaecologist.

Am I?

Would he know, from being what he is, that I'm Titian everywhere, as well as my hair? And, if you've done a thousand episiotomies, would it mean that you might be thinking of needles and thread when it would not be at all appropriate, really? On the other hand, I was at school with a girl who was the daughter of a gynaecologist, and she was one of six, perhaps seven. Yet the other Meggie said that having your husband present at the birth of a baby is a more effective contraceptive than castration.

Why are my fingers so much colder than my breasts? When I touch them, it's like a dog's nose against my leg. They seem not to be part of the same body, my hands and my heart.

I am not going to hang the new underwear on the washing line. They are very pretty and girlish, but it would be crazy, if I hadn't worn them first. Besides, by the time he gets here, it will be so, so dark.

275

Sunday 25 February

The woman who was buying milk and the *News of the World* said I was quite right.

'More power to you,' she said. 'You're quite right. I wish I had the nerve to do it.'

Everybody was staring at me, and smiling; but I didn't mind. I got the papers, and Rolos, and salt. I had used up the salt I had, when I knocked over the sherry. That was because the pressure cooker had gone psychotic in the kitchen. But Antony calmed it down.

'If you can go out with curlers, or slippers, why can't you go out in your dressing-gown?' said the woman.

Everybody in the shop agreed.

'After all,' said the man behind the counter, 'this is a community, not a condominium.'

He lived in one, you see, for three years, in a place called Billings, Montana. He likes to weasle it into any conversation.

Off I went with myself, home again, home again, and I know that half the road saw me. Of course, by this time, half the road had heard about this man who looked like Donald Sutherland, standing beside me at the hall-doorstep, emptying an upside-down toaster onto the ground where the rose-tree used to be. They must have seen him kissing me at the car, as well, before he climbed in and drove off, with his lovely doe-skin gloves on the roof. God only knows what I looked like, chasing after him in my dressing-gown, especially when it opened on me and the whole world could see I was wearing a cami-top and cami-knickers.

There is no such thing as privacy anymore.

He loved the chicken casserole. There was nothing left. And it was a serves-six recipe. He is an absolute trencherman. He just devours what you put in front of him.

He fixed the toaster. I told you that.

He fixed the cassette recorder. He spoke into it, and when we played it back, it was as clear as a bell. 'Testing, testing.' For months now, it's been sounding like a recording of Orville and Wilbur Wright, all tinny and indistinct, a wasp in a chandelier. Now I can use it again.

The *New World Symphony* did not work out. What I need is a stylus.

You don't want to hear about this. You want to hear about that.

You want to hear about the other.

I thought so. All right. But I shall only write this once. Once, and once only.

It was not the *1812 Overture*. Neither was Napoleon. But lots and lots of lovely things happened in 1812 that the *1812 Overture* knows nothing about; and what happened late last night in one of the dormitory outskirts of this pretty little city was one of them.

So there.

I did not bay at the moon. I did not bite my lips until the blood ran. I did not hyperventilate. But it was so lovely after so long. Besides, tonight was his night. I wanted it to be his. My night will be next. The next night, or the night after, and the night after that, too. There are three hundred and sixty-five nights in the year, if you follow the Julian calendar; and I do.

My body was Braille to his blindness. He read me everywhere. There are so many parts of my body I have never touched, unless they are ill. They are sick from not being touched. But his tongue toured me. He opened me like a book, and smelled the pages.

'What is it?' he said.

I had just thought of my mother. I had to get out of bed and disconnect the phone.

'Would anyone ring at midnight?' he said.

'Questions, questions,' I said.

He talked to my ways in and my ways out. He loves my bottom; he loves her. The black sheep of the family has come up trumps. I cannot tell you what he calls her. It would be wrong, really. I would have to ask his permission first.

Then his face tightened. I was a blur to him. My face went out like a light. I was a body of smells, a body of softness. I brought him into me. I had never been so close to him; he was farther from me than his first smile at the night-school. His tongue skidded into my ear. His shoulders have muscles. I had never noticed.

Xerxes was watching from the top of the wardrobe, his pink trunk sticking straight up.

When he came, I calmed him. I smoothed his hair, and closed his eyelids with my tongue. When a man has made love to a woman, he's a little wary, because she's seen him lose control. He has to be calmed like a child, to be told by touch that he's strange still, inscrutable still, still Christ on a cross; but he's not quite sure of himself until he can have another erection, and that can take ages. It can take an hour.

I wonder is the principal impotent?

I can still feel him inside me. Antony, I mean. I had forgotten that, too: the feeling of being filled. I had forgotten how quickly you itch afterwards, and how warm the sperm is, and the lines of noughts and crosses on your breasts from the weight of their bodies. I had forgotten how wise and frisky the body is. Perhaps I should write that out, about the wisdom and the friskiness, and send it back to myself in a registered envelope, and then I'd have copyright on one good insight. Because the theologians and the pornographers only know the half of it, like the two families who have fifty per cent each of the secret formula for Coca-Cola.

How long do you feel a man inside you? It will be twelve hours in two hours' time.

When we slept, we slept spoons; my back against his chest and collar-bone, his wrist between my thighs. We nestled; we nested. It was nice. His feet, though, are as cold as anything. Cold, but not clammy, of course, with one very blue vein you can feel with your finger. I hope it isn't a varicose vein. Varicose veins are hereditary.

After he fell asleep, I was listening to him breathing. I held my breath until the right moment, and then I started breathing with him, in and out, as if we were singing together, or walking in step.

First he has to see his patients. They are mostly in the hospital, but he has others in the private nursing home. Then he drives up North, and gets the ferry across to Scotland. Why he can't just fly from Dublin is beyond me. I would organise him in no time at all, if he let me. Of course, I warned him about being careful, but he found this funny.

'There was a garden fête at the school when I was fourteen,' he said, 'and a dotty old dear set up a fortune-teller's stall. The proceeds were to go to a trust for the conservation of stately houses. It turned out that she was installing central heating in her own place. She stared at my hand for a long time, and told me how I'd die.'

'How?' I said. The night-nurse opposite had just pulled in, and she was taking a long time to lift a bale of briquettes out of her boot.

'I will be killed by a falling sandwich in the middle of Manhattan, and be enrolled for ever after in the *Guinness Book of Records*.'

He is giving one paper, and introducing another. The whole conference is about foetal distress. He'll be back on Thursday, lateish.

I should do the dishes. Most of the service with the swallows is in the sink. But if I wash them, my hands will smell of rubber gloves and Fairy Liquid, and not of him: of his hair, of between his legs. He washed his own hands twice, three times this morning, but that's different. He's a doctor. Doctors are always washing their hands. As well as that, he fixed the toaster.

My hands smell so lovely, like the Middle East. They smell of mint and watering-cans. I'll wash the dishes later.

Snowdrops, and then crocuses. Crocuses, then daffodils. Daffodils, and then tulips. The evenings will be stretching like a woman.

I want him to be here on the Sunday. Then I can write him down beside me on the census.

Monday 26 February

He hasn't rung yet. Of course, he might be tied up. There might be a wine and cheese somewhere, or they might have to sit and listen to a string quartet. At this very moment, he might be trying to extricate himself from some sozzled Egyptian delegate whose wife is taking Polaroids of the party-goers, to bring home to her cousins in Cairo.

A woman rang. She asked to speak to Liam. She had put the six in front of the seven, instead of behind it. That was at five past eleven. He might have been trying to get through. The stupid woman kept apologising. I think she wanted to have a conversation.

Meggie wasn't in today. Something is wrong, something is awry. I don't know what. I would have asked the principal, but what's the point? He has started to lift his eyebrows like Paul McCartney, whenever I loom large. None of the other women knows anything. The rumours range from measles to German measles, and back again. One of the Commerce teachers thought that she'd gone to London to audition for *Cats*. That was the high point of the bitching hour.

Her gloves have gone all brown on the radiator, under the map of the solar system. The palms of them are crisp and discoloured, as if they had the stigmata. I put them in her pigeon-hole, and looked at the pictures in a holiday brochure. The topless woman on Lanzarote wears the same slide in her hair on the surf of Cyprus. I bet you anything the photographs were taken on the Isle of Man.

Actually, it's different without the other Meggie. I feel a bit like Laurel without Hardy. Life is strange, and then stranger. That is the way of it, and the wayside.

I wasn't up to the third years, so I gave them a test on *Romeo and Juliet*, and how the two of them fall in love only because they're not supposed to, and how the difference between the two families goes on and on and on, because there's absolutely no difference between either of them. At the end of the class, I collected twenty-three scripts from the swinish multitude, of which twenty-one had to do with how Romeo and Juliet were bird-brains from a brat-pack movie, and two had to do with similarity as the source of all human conflict. One of the girls wrote a scathing attack on Shakespeare as a male chauvinist, and why wasn't the play called *Juliet and Romeo*?

But little Alec who uses the inhaler three times a day, and loves to shake his corkscrew ponytail whenever words like 'ride' or 'sod' or 'feckless' crop up in the literature, handed in a wire-spine piece of graph paper with the first letter of his name in an enormous, multi-coloured calligraph, a rainbow alpha out of some illuminated manuscript on Mount Athos. But this, alas, is the world of the word-processor, and not the world of the Word. There is nothing to be gained by brooding in a battery-farm.

My mother went in to hospital this afternoon. I got the last class off, to bring her. She wanted to take the bamboo that she painted before Christmas, so the bus-drivers would think she was blind, and slow down, and stop, to give her time to cross.

Upstairs, in her room, I was searching for a warmer nightdress in her chest of drawers, and I found a plastic, geriatric nappy. It couldn't be her size, though. It was too large; much too large. I held it against me; I was sure of it.

I am always losing her scent. She hides in the river.

We left at six, on the dot.

'Come on,' I said. 'We're late. The News is starting.'

She hadn't heard me. She was checking the back door, opening it to see if it was locked.

'We'd better go,' she said. 'We're late. I can hear the Angelus.'

The room is nice. It's roomy. She has eleven stations on the set; she has a remote control. She has a bedside table with her prayerbook, and a book about the Duchess of Windsor, and a net of bad mandarins. The chair farts when you sit down. The loo makes little sounds, like birds in a chimney. Outside the window, the golfers are teeing off into the dark. But the window-blinds are stuck, and stay up. So the room shows a film of itself on the window, of everything that happens, of tea poured and pillows turned, without sound, in silence, in shades of black and white. It is a film made with a small budget, and with semi-professional actors, under cover of darkness, a spool of samizdat. When the nurse comes in, you do not look at the door; you look at the film. You don't know whether she'll take the patient's pulse or open the buttons at her stopwatch, and start circling her nipples with her nails.

'I hate everything about hospitals,' she said. She had heard me committing thought-crime in the corner, putting away her clothes, sorting them, smoothing them. She'd brought enough to last a lifetime.

'I know you do,' I said. 'You know I know you do.'

When she switched her light off later, and went down into the bed, and slowly made it smell of her, she would close her eyes and be able to hear her parents practising their Irish grammar by gaslight, and the shrews scampering in the attic, and the water-tank filling like the silence after a gong.

Is it a fine day?

Yes. It is a fine day.

Will it be a fine day tomorrow?

It will be a fine day tomorrow.

Will it be a fine day yesterday?

When her mother took her soother, she started to suck her hair.

'I hate everything about them. Everything,' she said.

I filled out all the forms for her, and wrote her name in pencil wherever she had to write it in ink. She wanted me to stay, to meet the locum registrar. He is about fifty, he's not married, he wears a tiger's eye on his ring-finger, and he looks a bit like Gregory Peck, except for his nose, which might be from rugby.

They don't let little children in at night. There were three or four outside the hospital, two in red wellies and one in a balaclava, waiting while a man bought nail-polish remover for someone whose lower intestine had been incinerated that morning in the furnace behind the mortuary chapel. They were jumping in and out of the automatic doors, out of the darkness into the light, making the panels open and close, open and close, testing the distance they could go before the glass sprang back and the lobby boomed at them, with the split-second, squash court sounds of trolleys and tannoys and women taking off their stilettos and carrying them, walking barefoot in their nylons over the linoleum, like tourists on a fortnight's holiday, picking their way over the white-hot sand.

I do not think that God would tolerate our sufferings, if they were not so beautiful to look at.

Tuesday 27 February

Why Antony has not phoned is simple. Stupid of me. There is a two in front of my number now, just like there's a six in front of others. I keep forgetting, so why wouldn't he? The poor man is probably distraught at not being able to get through; and, of course, he can't send a telegram either, because there is no telegram service anymore.

God love him. He should be thinking about his paper, and his diagrams and slides and things, and, instead of that, he's wondering what I'm wondering. He'll be talking meconium and monitors, and all the women at the seminar will be doing a Humming Chorus out of *Madame Butterfly* whenever he runs his hand through his hair; but the still, small voice at the back of his head will be telling him: Good God above, she's going to think I'm a carpet-bagger.

I read this stupid, stupid article about erections. The angle decreases from eighty per cent in your teens to more like fifty per cent in your late forties. Have you ever heard such balderdash? How could anyone be so geometric about the good things of life? Honestly.

But there was an interesting piece about a woman in Arkansas who had her first child at fifty-two, and there is nothing the matter with the baby. Eight-and-a-half pounds he was. Then again, the woman who lives two doors down from the career guidance teacher's sister had a poor little boy with Down's Syndrome, God bless him; and she was a young one, maybe twenty, twenty-one. So it just shows you. I'm not Katharine of Aragon yet. I'm not even Patience, her maid.

There's the phone.

It was only my mother. A person's voice sounds different when they're lying down. She put on a very frail, feeble one, this time. Actually, she's as happy as a child at summer-camp, though she needs to be seen as Venice sinking. What she wants me to do is to switch on the lights for her neighbours on Friday, but I'll still be in class when it's getting dark. What they should do is buy some sort of timer thing for themselves. Anyway, it's a crafty dodge, getting the gentiles in, on the Sabbath. It's like my father swallowing raw eggs in a large brandy so that his hacking cough wouldn't annoy the people in the pew beside him, and then going up without a qualm to receive Holy Communion, God bless him.

I have a notion he will ring. I just hope he wasn't trying to get through while my mother was expiring with such gusto. Between her and the wrong number, the line's been blocked half the night.

When the kids pair off, they have this little ritual. They share their chewing gum. Leonora was chewing away in a slow, suggestive style during Yeats today, and just as I came to the sixty-or-more-winters-on-his-head bit, she took it out and put it on her boyfriend's tongue. Everybody started drumming their heels, and I had to laugh; but I brought it round to a smile, and then a sarcastic twitch.

Actually, it was very erotic, God forgive me.

It is twenty-four hours since I stopped feeling him inside me. Now I can only feel his absence. It is not as nice.

Leonora would be a lovely name for a girl. Leo, though, would be awful for a boy. Life is hard enough, without being gay as well.

There's the phone. Again.

It was not my mother. It was not my Antony. It was not a wrong number. It was the vice-principal.

'It's about timetables,' he said. 'We have an awful problem with the timetable.'

He has a problem with timetables. I have a problem with time. The other Meggie has a problem with eternity.

'What can you say?' he said. 'At times, there's nothing to say. At a time like this, the less said the better.'

Meggie's baby will not be born. It will be disinterred, and buried again somewhere else, with the skeletons and the signet rings of its great-grandparents. It will never kick her again; it will only trample her into the ground. It had the life-span of a laboratory mouse or a tin of pears. It was alive; now it's dead. And the little semi-colon in between, that tough and tiny waterway between the one and the other, like the Panama Canal between the Atlantic and the Pacific, will never see it throw a stone and watch the circles spread.

They say it's been dead for a week.

'You know Meggie,' the vice-principal said. 'She'll have another.'

But this one will not die. This one will never die. Die down or die away. It'll hang on in there, upside-down on the roof of her head, like a bat. She'll come at night and put it in her blouse and feed it. No one will ever know.

'I'd better go,' he said. 'Time and tide.'

He has been decomposing inside her suntan for seven days and seven nights, with his thumb in his mouth and his ankles crossed, drifting in the middle of a ghost bikini, while the sound-waves of a horn concerto moved like a cat's paw through the waters toward him.

'By the way,' said the vice-principal, 'do you happen to have the exact time?'

Ash Wednesday

Is it February or March? I don't know. Do I lose a day or gain a day? I don't know. I never buy the paper. I know that I'm a woman; I know I'm forty-one. You don't need the Milky Way to steer by. The North Star is enough. All the Swiss watches in the world will not stop the fall of night. There are moments in our life which are not momentary, and there are minutes which are not minute, and there are seconds which are second to none. The only thing that goes like clockwork is a clock, sometimes.

I am just trying to get into the party mood of Ash Wednesday. Actually, I took the ashes from my own fireplace early this morning, because I knew the chaplain would be giving them out at Assembly, and I was dead late.

The funniest thing happened at mass, but not in the sense of funny-funny, more in the sense of funny-peculiar.

I went to the little pre-fab oratory at the shopping centre on the way home. It was jam-packed. To make it worse, some of the women had wheeled in their trolleys, just in case some Artful

Dodger thought that the season of Lent was also the season of borrowing. But I caught sight of one of my second years, and I stood right beside her, without saying a word, until I shamed her into giving me her seat. Her eyebrows and her eyelashes are all singed from a chip-pan she was cooking scampi in. Her mother has sent her to thank the second person of the Blessed Trinity for saving her from a skin-graft.

The ashes on her forehead had smudged. They looked a bit like a burn. I wet the tip of my finger, and tidied them up. If I were her mother, I would have been twenty-seven when she was born, and her ears wouldn't be pierced. The boy who sang in the folk mass would teach her the guitar, and they'd smoke at her bedroom window, blowing the smoke through their mouths into the darkness of the garden, the busted, breathless trellis, the tinsel on the grass; the good, green rain. I'd call them down for punch and pancakes. I'd turn the radio way up. That would be the signal.

'Ta,' she said, when I'd made her all right.

She'll get four honours in her Intermediate. She won't be one of the also-rans. She'll be worse off. She'll be one of the runners-up.

Antony might have delivered her.

When we went up for Communion, she took some bubble-gum out of her mouth, and stuck it on her watch-strap. That was when I remembered I hadn't wiped my lipstick, and it was too late. In my whole life, I've never once received Holy Communion with lipstick on. I just wouldn't. It's not a question of right or wrong; it's more that it's not me. It's not like me.

It's not me at all.

I received in the hand, and went away with it, back to my place, where I could take a tissue from my handbag, before I put the host in my mouth; because I'd used the handkerchief in my cardigan pocket to clean the blackboard, and the chalk had been red and yellow as well as white. And then I was more confused, because, lo and behold, there was Leslie, Leslie with the cat-food and the husband who cried at Christmas, and she was making straight for me.

'Stick around,' she said. 'I'd love to have a good old natter.'

I think she'd been drinking. There was the slightish smell of I don't know what. Sherry, a hot port. I didn't know what to think. I didn't know what to say. I pretended I had the host in my mouth; I made a sign.

'Mum's the word,' she said. She really had been drinking. That was an awful thing to say, when you think about it. She must have a problem; she must be under pressure. Maybe the parents of the au pair found out about the cat-food, and flew in. Christ.

God forgive me.

The second-year had disappeared. I think her brother packs trolleys, and they walk home together, because you can't smoke on the buses anymore. I waited behind, after mass, for twenty minutes, until the oratory closed, and the guard with the Alsatian checked the benches for a tabloid or two that he could read during his shift. I wanted to be sure that Leslie had passed on or passed out. I can do without drunks who want to make a general confession. Then they never forgive you for having listened in the first place.

There was no one in sight. I made my own way home.

The man next door is putting up a fence, straight down the middle of the front garden. The left-hand side will be his half, and the right-hand side will be my half; and none of the children will be able to run across the grass anymore. The line is as neat as the polygons that rest on the map of Africa like a fishing net on the Gulf Stream. If the wind blows from the east, the leaves from the maple-tree will be his for the burning; if it blows from the west, they can squeak and shrivel on my patio.

The car-lights picked out Kenya on the planking. He has been chopping up tea-chests for the space between us. I went over and smelled them. Sure enough, they have the fragrance of a friendly cup.

It hit me when I hung up my coat. Every part of me prickled. It was like when you're leaving the pool, and the wind returns you to your body. My hand closed round it, found it, felt it, picked it out.

I had brought the host home with me.

Jesus of Nazareth had been in the car beside me all the time. I was sitting on the stairs in a hall that had to be seen to be believed, with the mystery of the world in the palm of my hand. I didn't know where I was. I was beside myself.

I was so happy. I was so happy, I was afraid. I was afraid to be that happy.

The car-keys had bashed it a bit. One of the sweeteners that I use instead of sugar had stuck to it, but I got it off with my nail. Then I smelled the inside of my coat-pocket, to see. It smelled the same as ever: of my hands, of what my hands touch, of chalk and windfalls.

I had never really looked at a host before. They are very delicate. They break at the wrong touch; they break at a touch, even. If you dropped them, they would not fall; they would flutter, like flakes of snow. Nuns make them. They are made by hand.

I wonder did the nun who made my host ever love a man, apart from Our Lord, apart from the God who mingled with the crowd, not like the Princess Elizabeth on VE day, but like the white doctor who changed his colour to black somehow, and went to live with blacks in Alabama? Because that was what God did, I think. He became naked so that we could be nude again.

Wouldn't it be terrible if my hands still smelled of Antony, while I was holding the host in them? Or would it?

I brought the Blessed Eucharist into the dining-room, God forgive me, and I placed it on a very clean napkin between the two scented candles that I bought for the dinner party with Antony. I hadn't any matches, so I lit them off a long shopping receipt that I screwed up and set fire to, in the toaster. Then I sat down and said some prayers. I balanced the Bible on its spine, and let it fall open; but, of course, it was at one of those enormous genealogies, so I did it again, and, this time, it fell apart at the woman at the well in St John. I read it from where the woman comes to draw the water in the first place, up to where she says: 'Come, see a man who told me all that I ever did. Can this be the Christ?'; and then I stopped, because I got a bit upset. I just find the gospels so beautiful and so sad.

I went to Holy Communion then, more than I have ever gone before in my life; and it was too late by the time I realised that I had completely forgotten to wipe the lipstick off my lips.

There is another world, and it is this one.

Would you believe I have a migraine? Antony gets them all the time. I think it's probably from the lights in the theatre. Ordinary people get headaches, I told him. Only geniuses get migraines. And he laughed, and said: 'Meggie.'

I am almost sorry I let everyone call me Meggie. I should have been Margaret, and kept Meggie till last, like the best wine. But Margaret is so spinterish.

I pressed the cassette to eject the tape, and instead I pressed the play button. Out came 'Testing, testing', and you can hear me banging away in the background, squeezing the oranges.

I can smell him on his side of the bed. Xerxes, of course, is having a crisis. He needs a lot of reassurance about the whole situation.

Why am I still so happy? Because I have passed the Why stage. I am not two-and-a-half any longer. I have arrived at the Yes stage. Yes is a much more interesting question than Why.

This is not a migraine. This is an earthquake. I am going down for some ice-cubes to put on my eyelids, like the pennies on the eyelids of the dead.

Thursday 29 February

It is on my way, so I stop.

It is on my way into town to buy a dressing-gown for my mother, so I stop.

It is on my way into town to buy a dressing-gown for my mother, and I make up my mind to leave a note for him on a Charlie Brown card, with a message that only he will understand; so I stop. I sit in the car, and write the note, and think about it, and bend the card at the crease, and flatten the crease with my fingers, and tear the card in two, and write a different note on the side with the picture of Charlie Brown.

My moonshine wants another rub.

Then I add two more full stops after the first one, to make them trailing dots.

The out-patients' clinic is full of pregnant women and their mothers. So many of them are smoking, although there are signs which say no, don't smoke, don't. Their children are as good as gold. One of them is playing with a magnet on a fishing rod, and the fishing rod catches little metal fish and a metal pencil-sharpener that are swimming in the lid of a biscuit-box.

There's a nurse. I can ask her. She can put the note in under the X-rays on his desk. He will be holding them up at the window, up to the light, when the small white envelope will slip out and fall down, onto the carpet-tiles. When he reads what I have said to him, his hands will remember me, how I opened my lips and held them open by the hairs, how the shadow of his shoulders slammed against the pebble-dash, and how we closed the chink in the curtain by weighting the ends with William Shakespeare's *Collected Works*.

'I'm terribly sorry,' the nurse said. 'It was in the papers.'

The child with the fishing-rod is crying, because its mother wants to use the biscuit-box as an ashtray.

'He was stone-cold sober,' the nurse said. 'He had his seat-belt on. That time between when it's light and when it's dark is the worst.'

Is it a boy or a girl, the boy or the girl with the fishing-rod? Is it?

'The funeral is tomorrow,' the nurse said. 'I'm going up myself. I think it's eleven. A dozen of us are going, to form an honour guard.'

When my cousin threw the lighted cigarettes into the monkey cages, I got down on my knees on the tarmacadam. On my hands and knees I got down. He was standing in his tuxedo, with two, three cigarettes in his mouth, his hands hiding the sputter of matches. My hair slopped like a cake. The monkeys were sobbing; it was a child's sobbing.

'Stop,' I said. 'Stop, please. Stop, please. Stop, please, stop.'

'At least he wasn't married,' said the nurse. 'There is that.'

Her stopwatch is ticking away. Why is it ticking away? It is ticking away, there, there, there on the blonde run of her breast. I can see it. I can hear it. Can she not hear it ticking, its tiny cricket calls?

'Dr Macready is taking over his list,' the nurse said. 'He's very nice.'

The mother with the biscuit-box for an ashtray takes the fishing-rod from the crying child, and breaks it in two.

'I can make another appointment for you,' the nurse said. Her eyes flitted down to the middle of me; to my Charlie Brown card; to the chalk on my ringless fingers.

'How far gone are you?' she said to me. 'Is it still early days?'

Outside the hospital, there are railings; and I wait there, at the railings outside the hospital, while a traffic warden puts a parking ticket under one of the wipers. When he goes, when he goes away, I sit in the car, I fold the ticket and put it in the glove-compartment with the Charlie Brown card. There are some people. There are some trees. There is a tree in the black visor of a motorcycle courier's crash-helmet. On the balcony of the council flat across the road, a boy is peering at the world with a long telescope made from the cardboard centres of toilet rolls.

I think I sat there. I think that was what happened. The lights went red, green, amber; red, green, amber. There is a rhythm, really. Red is for stop; red is the colour of blood. Blood is awful. You think: I don't want to die. I'll stop. Green is for go; green is the colour of trees and things. Trees and things are great. You think: I don't want to die. I'll go. Amber is for please stop now, don't go, please; amber is the colour of the whole street flashing amber from the windows and the wet slates as the sun sets on the other side of the television aerials and the gasometer. Amber is all the months that end in ember or ober. You think: I don't want to die. I don't want to die without him.

I went back to my house at some stage.

My mother rang me, you see, from her bed. She is well. When I heard her voice, I don't know, I was glad. I was as glad as if my luggage had been found again at an airport where nobody spoke any English.

'Tell me,' she said. 'I know. I know there's something I don't know.'

'I would like to be little,' I said. 'I would like to be that again.'

'What are you talking about?' she said. 'Is this another trip to the pantomime?'

'I'd like to be even smaller than that,' I said. 'I'd like to go back inside you.'

'You've been drinking,' she said. 'Your speech is slurred. Can you not hear yourself slur what you're saying? You're as bad as your father, but it's worse in a woman, much worse. It's poignant in a man; it's pathetic in a woman. Do you want to be pathetic? Do you want to end up freezing the sherry in the ice-cubes, so they come out yellow? And he thought I didn't notice; he thought it was great gas; he did the laughing hyena routine.'

'Listen to me,' I said.

'No,' she said, 'you listen. I got through the change of life without an aspirin. You want an off-licence. You should be ashamed. How would you feel if you found out that the operator was listening to you? You'd sober up pretty fast. You'd want the ground to open up and swallow you, that's what. I've seen the alcoholics on the fourth floor; I've seen them go to their lectures. It would put the fear of God into you.'

'Mummy,' I said.

'Stop it, stop it,' she said. 'What would your Protestant doctor friend think, if he could see you in this state? You'd never see his face again.'

'I want to start from the beginning,' I said. 'I want to be conceived. I want to be thistledown drifting inside you, picking my way on the wall of your womb.'

She started to cry.

'You want to kill me,' she said. 'I don't know why you want to, but you want to.'

'Then I want to be passed as a heavy period,' I said. 'I want to be blood in a pedal-bin.'

There was nowhere in the house I could be on my own. I had shown him every room, even the room where I do the ironing. My cami-top is still on the clothes-horse. So I went downstairs, and I put my head in the washing machine, because it was cold, and clean, and used to being wet with every sort of mess.

Friday 1 March

Meggie was sitting in the staffroom. She wants to keep going. She wants to correct copybooks and supervise detention, and argue with the substitute teacher who poured the flat Seven Up into the rubber plant. This is the way she has chosen; this is the choice she has made. She doesn't want to sit at home with the Mothercare catalogues and the big bump of her belly, a globe gone bad on her, a fatness flattening to the shape of an atlas now.

'Meggie,' I said, in the way that he had said it to me. She thought it was for her, the one tear finding its way home, oozing out of my eye as slowly as the glue from a chipped egg-shell.

'Don't,' she said.

The Art teacher who's emigrating to Australia at Easter was roaming round the staffroom in a kangaroo suit, and everyone was howling, and stuffing Bon Voyage cards in his pouch. The poor girl who's replacing him on Monday morning was looking a bit lost and left out, or maybe she was trying to look that way for the sake of decorum.

'I understand,' I said to Meggie. 'I understand a little. A little is lots.'

'Please,' she said to me, 'please, don't. I don't understand you, and you don't understand me, and the Sunday-school stuff about people understanding other people, and everybody becoming upstanding in their understanding of other people, it's all for the birds, Meggie. I know that, and you know that. We've been around, the two of us. We've been through things, we've seen through things. We know the ropes, and the knots in the ropes. We understand. The priests look great in their vestments. That's the height of it. There's no point in the two of us blowing the kiss of peace at each other. Is there?'

Her face was running like a watercolour left out in the rain. I bent down to her to kiss her on the mouth.

'Is there?' she said.

At the last moment, the very last moment, I wasn't sure; and I moved my lips to the tip of her nose, and kissed her there.

I was leaving for class when the chaplain stopped me.

'Better luck next time,' he said.

He smelled of altar wine. I love that smell. Anglicans receive under both species. Antony used to turn the sheet-music for the organist. He used to wait for the organist to nod, and then turn the page. If he turned two, there'd be an awful stink. The choir would heave like a hawthorn in a cross-wind.

'Don't take it to heart,' he said. 'You look like you're at your own funeral. It's only an A post, for God's sake. Do you know how much an A post is worth, after tax? After tax, an A post is worth about six hundred smackers. What's six hundred smackers? Is it even ten pounds a week? In Dar-es-Salaam, of course, ten pounds a week would be jackpot territory; but in Dublin, it's what, a packet of cigarettes a day, or maybe soup and a salad in a takeaway.'

I have always known that someday, someday in the dark of my life, I will need to hate another person, so that the twelve hours of darkness in each day will not increase and multiply out of all control; and I had always thought it would be Meggie. But where is she now when I need her more than ever and most of all? Life is so clever. I think that life invented us just to show off, to dance on a handkerchief in front of the dreadful universe.

He looked at me, as if I were a prescription he couldn't make out. The poor man means no harm.

'You're in another world, Meggie,' he said. 'That's bad theology.'

God looked at the world, and saw that it was good; not happy. I never noticed that before. He knew the whole time. He knew from the word Go.

'Keep the faith,' said the chaplain, and he walked away, into another part of the world. By the time he stopped at the next table, there were light-years between us. Motes and the steam from coffee and the smoke from cigarettes floated in the light of the staffroom skylight like the great, migrating gases that cool and contract, and become stars, I suppose, and shed light on things that aren't worth leaving home for, or writing home about.

My hand was so far from my body, even, that I didn't think I could reach it. I pulled it from the shoulder, and after a while it came.

It was ten o'clock; then it was five past ten. The nurses would be stepping out of the taxi. The one I spoke with would be handing the taxi-voucher in through the driver's window. She would be signing for it, perhaps. The others would be wrapping their capes around them in the cold, and asking each other if you genuflected in a Protestant church. They would decide to do whatever the family did. The brother was high up in Europe.

I think I was reading a book in the classroom. The print was tiny. The heating was off. The girls had leggings under their skirts. I wore my scarf and I wore my coat. I could see my breath in front of me, as I read. It disappeared up.

It was half-past ten. My life strained at an anti-clockwise angle. I was reading Dickens. I was reading *Hard Times*. That was it. That was what I was doing. I was doing it well. The different voices, the different accents. My Bounderby was the best Bounderby I have ever done. They laughed, the children. They laughed, and showed their bad, bungled teeth; and their legs jigged up and down under the desks.

I bent the book back until the spine squeaked, and a page split neatly from its stitching. Mrs Sparsit, ma'am, I said. It was a quarter to. The organist would be playing a voluntary, and the rector would be vesting in the vestry, slipping his surplice on, over a shirt that smelled of wood-preservative from creosoting the slide-down door of a garage. He mightn't even know what he looked like, the strong, slim body in the coffin, mightn't have met him. He was beautiful. He was beautifully co-ordinated, except for his socks. He laughed greatly. He could see through things, and into them. He had a cormorant's eye. His ear curved like a question-mark; he listened. He listened with Van Gogh's ear. His hair was so fine, and fair, you could have used it for paintbrushes, to paint a man and a woman walking through the snow while the snow fell, or a man and a woman going in and out of each other on a bed in a bedroom, parting, imparting, a shoreline, the suction; those noiseless oyster-catcher cries she made to please him, as the dense, decent stench of the sea, iodine, brine, washed and wetted the sheets where she slept with an elephant.

I did Louise in my own voice. I could not think of any other accent. It was almost eleven. The clock in the classroom was ticking like a slow, slow turnstile. The mourners would be leafing through the Book of Common Prayer, and trying to remember how many years it had been since they read such beautiful English. They would take it with them to Portugal, and read it on the beach.

'The factory hands could be fired if they whistled while they worked,' I said. 'Women who were pregnant went down into the mines. They carried canaries, like lanterns. Their waters broke in the thin tunnels, while the coal was carted off to warm the backsides of the men who made history what it is today.'

'Miss,' one of them said. 'What about *Animal Farm*?'

'*Animal Farm*,' I said. 'What about *Animal Farm*?'

'You said,' they told me. 'You said.'

'What did I say?' I said. Whatever I said, I take back. Whatever I did, I didn't mean. Whatever I meant, I didn't do.

Whatever.

It was five to eleven. The two hands of the clock folded in prayer.

'You promised,' they said. 'You promised to show us *Animal Farm* or *Romeo and Juliet*. You said we could look forward to putting our feet up. You marked the day down in your diary, in case you'd forget it.'

I told them the video had gone wonky.

'The video has gone wonky,' I said. 'It won't work for me now.'

They told me there was another.

'There's another,' they said. 'The principal has one; the chaplain has one.'

'The principal has two,' somebody said.

'I can't work those,' I said. 'I'm used to what I'm used to.'

But the boy called Anthony put up his hand; his thoughtful, tired-out hand. He could work them. He could work anything. Would I let him go? Would I let him go and get them? If I let him go now, there would still be time to see everything, before the bell went, before it was too late.

'If I let you go,' I said, 'you'd never come back to me. I'd never see you again.'

He pulled at his leather pencil-tie, like a bell-rope. He was mad with me.

'Jesus,' he said; and the class laughed.

'What was that?' I said.

'What was what?' he said.

'What you said,' I said. 'And take the chewing-gum out of your mouth before you answer.'

I could not call him Anthony. There are names that are too sad for words. There are words that are too sad for names.

'Good God,' he said. 'That's all. Good God.' And the class laughed longer, and louder.

'It's a lie,' I said. 'The cartoon of *Animal Farm* is a lie. It's a lie, because it lies about the ending. If you lie about the end, then you lie about the middle, too; and you end up lying about the beginning, as well; and then you're back where you started, aren't you? And it's too late to do anything about it.'

The way they make the clocks now, they are quiet, except for the ticking, of course. Nothing happens when the hour strikes; nothing at all. And I realised that the church-bells have stopped, too; stopped going, going, going, like they did when I was small, or smaller. Is that because everyone can afford a wristwatch now, or because they are building churches without spires and steeples at ninety degrees to the ground we walk on? They are very expensive, of course, are spires; and you can walk into the sea with a wristwatch, and it will still work; it will still go on.

I have never been to a Protestant funeral.

'We could watch *Animal Farm* until the cows come home,' one of the girls said; and they howled at that.

Is he wearing his wristwatch in the coffin? Do Protestants wear shrouds, like us? I knew a Catholic who was buried in his ordinary clothes, in a shirt and a pair of trousers and a blazer, but without underwear, I think; without a vest or his underpants.

'Where the cows come home,' said the girl, 'is where the cartoon goes away from the book, a bit.'

He placed his wristwatch on the bedside table, and then he was naked. It had left a pink pinch-mark on the skin, like when you peel a piece of bandage; and the tight top of his shorts had drawn a line across his stomach, like the ring around the bath, and I told him so, and he said I was a right monkey.

'This is not Disneyland,' I said to her. 'This is Ireland. This is it. The lollipop lady's gone; the zebra crossing's gone; the main road's gone. There's heavy traffic on no hard surface; and feet. Feet taking steps, whatever steps are necessary, before they hit the ground. There's nothing down to earth, you see, about being here, down here, on earth.'

A service without a mass would be short, wouldn't it? And they use 'The Lord is My Shepherd'. They use 'The Lord is My Shepherd' in the graveyard. It is in all the horror films, and they pay a man to take all the leaves off all the trees, so that the scene will look like winter. It must take him an eternity to tear them off, one after the other, the mountain ash, the maple, until they're only sticks in the ground, scrawls in the rush-hour failing of the light. His hands would smell of them, like the inside of a teapot, for ages; or until he bought chips on the way home.

'What are we doing?' I said.

'Dickens,' they said. '*Hard Times.*'

There were twenty-seven or twenty-eight of them in the class. Two of them will be dead in five years' time. Six will have left for England or America. Ten will never find work. Two will have abortions; two will not. One will go to jail. Two of the girls will lose children; one of them will have a handicapped child, and call it Madonna. Five of their faces will wizen like party balloons, on a diet of ashtrays and anti-depressants, and sedatives with feminine names, the names of wild-flowers found in the Arctic only. And one of their wrists will be scarred, from the bracelet to the elbow, with a sum of pale slashes, like the chalk-marks that a prisoner makes to mark the passage of time.

'Miss,' they were saying. 'Miss.'

Not one of them is wearing glasses. That is how good their eyes are, nowadays.

'We're still here, Miss,' Anthony said. 'We'll be here for another year and a half.'

At their debs' dance, I'll have to make sure that every girl gets danced with by one member of staff and two boys, not counting her escort. I'll look the other way in the loo, when they use a trick diaphragm as a vodka measure. I'll organise espressos for the ones who've vomited, for the ones about to. I'll dance with the chaplain when the music is fast and I don't have to touch him. The nun always gets her priest at the fancy-dress.

'I think you're a tonic,' I said to them.

Their paths will never cross. Their paths will be full of crosses.

'I think you're fantastic,' I said.

If you ring the speaking clock, a woman tells you. It is never a man; it is always a woman. That is because the person who is calling is anxious and naked; he cannot rest, he does not know, he needs to hear her voice, telling him: rest, rest now, I am here, I am here beside you, at the signal it will be zero, zero, and forty seconds. Her voice is civil but strange, as a woman's voice should be, reciting the statistics of a massacre to a man she has never met.

'Thank you,' he says. 'Thank you very much, Miss.' He has been drinking his duty-free whiskey out of a plastic glass that smells of dental floss; he does not realise that he was listening to a recorded announcement. He sits on the candlewick bedspread and reads the pages aloud, timing his lecture on foetal distress against the stop-watch on the pillow.

When he fell asleep and he was breathing through his mouth, I put his wristwatch on the carpet, because it was ticking so loudly through the wood of the bedside table that I could not get it out of my head.

'Miss,' said a girl, 'if we can't have *Animal Farm*, can we have *Romeo and Juliet*?'

It would be over now.

'*Romeo and Juliet*?' I said.

'Yes,' said a boy. 'Romeo and Olivia Hussey.' And all the other boys made plop noises with their thumbs in their mouths, and the girls were delighted, and told them to drop dead.

One mourner would be giving his business card to another mourner, as they left their smelly hymnals in a stack at the back of the church; and the other mourner would take it, and be cross that he had none of his own, and he would decide to have them printed, even if it cost a bit. The nurses would be looking at the Holy Communion Service in the prayer-book, and saying how much it was like the mass, really, except that when Protestants said body and blood, they didn't mean flesh and blood, did they? They meant a breaking of bread, and not a breaking of hearts. And the poor priest in the vestry would be disrobing, or would he, among the mouse-traps and the mutton-chop portraits of the rectors before him, and he would be wondering about the smell from the two-bar electric fire at his feet. That was something he should think about; that was something he should think about very seriously.

They wouldn't cremate him. They wouldn't do that. They wouldn't.

'Come on, Miss,' they said. 'We can fast-forward the bold bits.'

'We've no time,' I said. 'We've no time left.'

Anthony looked at the clock.

'We've loads of time,' he said. 'It's only gone eleven.'

'Please,' said another boy. 'If we start now, we can see everything.'

'Be a sport, Miss,' said one of the girls.

I always thought that the Wherefore in 'Wherefore art thou, Romeo?' meant Where. Where are you? But it doesn't. It means Why.

I didn't know that, and me a teacher.

'Why not?' I said; and the whole class cheered.

At lunch-time, I went to the office, to tell the principal I was going home because I wasn't myself. I would be myself on Monday. I would be more like myself than ever. But he'd gone; he'd gone to a meeting. His secretary told me. She speaks slowly, as if she were counting the words in a telegram. Otherwise, she forgets to say One instead of You.

'Tell him,' I said, 'that I'm not a hundred per cent.'

'One understands,' she said. 'One had one's own, this morning.'

'It isn't that,' I said.

'It never is,' she said.

Actually, I think she is on something. Her laughter is inappropriate. She eats raisins all day long. She keeps jump-leads in her locker, but she charges for their use, a pound at a time.

'There's nothing wrong with me,' I said.

'I see,' she said. 'One's heading off for the weekend.'

'Yes,' I said. 'Yes, I am.'

'Paris,' she said, 'is not very gay, this weather. Snowstorms and a strike at the airport, or so one hears.'

'I'm not going to Paris,' I said.

'Very sensible,' she said.

'I'm going home,' I said.

'They'll be thrilled to see you,' she said. 'One won't say a word to the Friend and Father of all Mankind, when he does return from his meeting to resume the revolutionary struggle, and his Argyll socks go creepity, creepity, creep across my carpet.'

She was on the verge of tears about something. I made my excuses, God forgive me.

'I'll make it a hat trick for the Three Monkeys,' she said, as I went away; and then she was more upset, because she had said 'I' and not 'One'.

Monday, a bad day. Tuesday, a better day. Wednesday, a half-day. Thursday, a whole day. Friday, a good day. Saturday, a great day. Sunday, a mass day. That was my week, week in, week out, for years. At the weekends, I met God; always at his place, never at mine. We had an arrangement. Only at the weekends. He was not to ring me at home; he was not to contact me at work. He was not to leave messages. There was a place and a time, for everything.

Now he's broken the rules. Now he wants more. He wants more than my lips and my tongue. He wants me. He has started writing letters. He has begun to phone the school. He has broken into my home, to search for me, to search the toilet-cistern for a string of seed-pearls, to search through slips and blouses in the laundry-bin for a gold bracelet, to search the solid grease in the chip-pan for two diamond earrings. I go in, I turn on the light, and everything is upside-down in my life.

Yet I thought it would last. I didn't want it to do more than that. It would have been enough if it had lasted, and gone on lasting. It would have been more than enough. I thought it would be safe, safe for the two of us, Meggie and Antony, because it was second-rate, because there was an elephant involved, and a vein that might have been varicose, and hair that was thinning, and a gum-boil in the mouth that I offered him, to kiss, to kiss again, and again to kiss, while my nose got noisy because I had not blown it for ages.

I blew it in the bathroom, with the two taps running, to muffle the sound.

'Are you running a bath?'

He was calling from the bedroom, calling from the bed. He had Xerxes on his lap. They were getting acquainted, you see. It was awkward. Xerxes knew nothing about gynaecology, and Antony knew nothing about elephants. It would be ages before they divided the left-hand side of my mattress between them. In the generous meantime, they talked about me.

'No,' I said, 'I'm drowning a spider.'

But he didn't hear me, over the noise of the water.

'You sound like you're running the rapids,' he said.

And I dropped the strip of toilet-paper into the toilet-bowl, and flushed it, and the water whisked it off, off and away, down through the dirty Venice of one pipe after another, a ghetto of drains, the transit camp of tears, toenails, and snowflakes, into the sewage treatment farm they plant the poplars round.

Saturday 2 March

It was dark when I awoke.

I sound like Dante Alighieri, or is that how you spell it? One of these days I am going to buy myself a proper dictionary. The one I have doesn't give 'priapic', or 'pusillanimity', and that is just two. I know it is for youngsters, of course, but still.

Anyhow.

It was nearly four when I got up. *The Cruel Sea* was on. It is about the sea, and things. Actually, I thought that the set was on the blink, sort of, because there was no colour until the toilet cleanser ad with the *New World Symphony* came on, at the break. Then I realised the film was in black and white, which is strange, because *Gone With the Wind* was made before the Second World War, and it's all in colour. Or is it?

Of course it is. Her dress was lemon. You don't get lemon in black and white. Period.

I have had a few scoops, and why not? Anyway, I need the ship's decanter for port, and I've nothing to decant his whiskey into, except tupperware. So there. Plus I still knew every single answer on the quiz show, bar one about the year Prince Philip and the Queen got married. Which was, I have forgotten. But eleven out of twelve was not bad, with my brain cells dying at the rate of about fifty thousand per glug.

The name of Dennis the Menace's dog is Gnasher.

There are no penguins at the North Pole. Not one.

Egypt.

The Latin for left is sinister.

He was born and died on April 21.

It was Churchill who said the bit about the beaches, etc.

The Ides of March. Any fool knows that, for God's sake.

The Bridge of Sighs is in Venice.

Tommy Cooper.

John F. Kennedy. But I don't believe a word of it. Not one solitary syllable. Besides, the poor man is dead now; and so is Marilyn Monroe. Let them rest in peace. Nobody knows what they went through. Nobody. They might not even have known themselves.

The last one was about the eskimos. They have forty words for snow, but none for wilderness. I knew that one, too.

To be honest, though, and I have nothing against eskimos, it sounds a bit naive.

When the phone rang, I thought it was my mother. It's hard to break the habit of making enormous assumptions, based on overwhelming probabilities; it seems to be bred into us, into the most unnatural recesses of our nature. Perhaps it's a part of original sin, this bone-marrow belief of ours that one and one makes two, and that water will flow from the tap if you turn it, in a house which will still be there, its spice-racks, its carpet-rods, when you stand at the door, and slip a key that fits into a keyhole that matches.

Meggie put her child's name down for a private, fee-paying Benedictine secondary school two days after her urine was positive, when the future boy soprano and captain of the minor league cricket team was the size of an eyelash floating over her pupil.

'He could be anything,' she said. 'He could be an astronaut. I haven't decided.'

He has. He's an astronaut's suit, drifting through the dead stars of space. And Antony's fingers have blackened, as if he'd been changing a typing ribbon for a secretary who didn't want to mess her ivory blouse. She likes his aftershave so much, she asks him: Did Meggie get you that? And he says: Who else?

It was one of my past pupils, on the phone. She wants me to go to her wedding; not to the church, or the dinner, but the disco afterwards. I said I'd be thrilled; she said she was thrilled; she said her husband-to-be was thrilled, too. I was thrilled for them both. It means a present, of course, but I was thinking I could give them *The Collected Poems of Sylvia Plath*. I might even give them *The Documents of Vatican Two*. There is heaps on the sacramentality of sexual love, which they could use as a pillow-book.

God forgive me.

Prostitutes in Florence had to wear their clothes inside out. That was the law. They'd put their coats on first, and then their dresses over their coats; and, after that, they'd put their slips on, if they wore slips, I suppose, slips and whatnot; and, finally, they'd wear their underwear, whatever that was like, because this was long ago, in an age when the churches and the chapels were being decorated by all the geniuses, and the whole of Europe was Catholic to a man.

Nothing has changed. In one way or another, we're all Florentine prostitutes. The health clubs and the hair salons function as our pimps. We give them their percentage.

That's why I loved him. A consultant gynaecologist could have gone out with a woman half his age, and no one would have thought twice. He liked me, I think, because both of us had been brought to the party by a friend, and our facial muscles were sore from smiling at jokes we didn't understand.

Maybe everyone's the same, everyone at the party. In which case, whose party is it? And do any of us know the host?

Then the phone rang again, and this time, this time, I had the strangest feeling. For a moment, a moment that went on and on, like the ricochet of a shout, I thought that perhaps, perhaps I'd been terrified, terrorised, by something imagined, something imaginary, a mean trick of the night, the trees and their heavy breathing, the lightning tour of the car-lights through my room.

It rang, and I could not lift it.

He had been delayed. He had stayed over. The car had given up on him. He had sold it to a Morris Minor enthusiast. He had crossed by ferry, come down by train. His brother in Belgium had had another coronary; he might die. They were reconciling. The doctor who had died had the same name, almost, just like me and the other Meggie. That was why. That was why everyone was so confused. It was chaos in the hospital. He had been looking after the dead man's patients. He had not slept. He had not slept a wink. They would have to put a notice in the paper, an announcement about the mix-up, about the names being similar but not the same, not his name, not him, not Antony.

It rang, and I moved towards it. I reached it, reached down to it; touched it. My fingers spread and settled. We would talk about this all our lives, and laugh, laugh ourselves sick; we would never, ever talk about it, and only look at each other, when the same thing happened to our eighteen-year-old daughter. She would not want to talk about it, either; and I would understand. Our tears would drop and dribble into the common fund.

'Speaking,' I said.

It was only a woman. She wanted to speak to Liam. She had put the six in front of the seven, instead of behind it.

'I'm terribly sorry,' she said. 'I really am terribly, terribly sorry.'

Sunday 3 March

My head has been at me. It will not go away; the migraine, I mean. I feel that my skull is supporting the weight of a veil as long as a train that is trailing. The light is so strong I can see the bones in my hand.

I was seven. I was once seven. They gave me a pamphlet at Montessori. If there was an atomic war, it said, I should stand with my back to the blast. I was to shut my eyes. Afterwards, I was to rinse the cutlery before using it.

'Sister,' I said, 'what do I do if two bombs go off, one behind me and one in front of me, at the very same time?'

'Lie down on the ground,' she said, 'and hold on to the earth, as if it was a cliff.'

When they gave her radiation for her brain tumour, she cut off her hair with a bacon scissors before it began to fall out. Then she burned it, strand by strand, like letters from a trousseau drawer.

The man who does the weather says it might snow. He put arrows all over his map, until he ran out of them. I shall have to make allowance for that. I shall have to leave ten minutes earlier in the morning, because the cars will be moving like a cortège. And I must make an appearance. Because, if I go on making an appearance, each morning, every morning, I may someday make a reality. If I try to be on time for my appointments, perhaps I will be late for my disappointments; so late, even, that I may miss them all together. And I shall try to look forward to tomorrow, even when it has decayed into today.

The census. The census is tonight. Right across the country, wherever there are lights and locks and aerials, in bungalows, bed-sits, maisonettes, cottages, flats, farms, and family homes you can tour with a ticket for two adults, children no charge, there are men and woman puzzling over their vital statistics like a problem in higher mathematics. But for me it is so straight-forward. It is as simple as two plus two, really.

My name is Meggie.

My husband's name is Antony. There is no H in it. It is spelled the same as Antony and Cleopatra.

Felicity is my firstborn child. She is seventeen. She is not crazy about her name, but it's too late to do anything about it now.

Hannah is in the middle. She is eleven. She has started to babysit for pocket-money; if it is after ten o'clock, she has to be driven home. I will not negotiate on that.

Antony is the baby. He is only nine. There is less than two years between him and Hannah. I could tell you stories about how Antony got started, but it is too private. Suffice it to say, he was not planned. His father thought it was a bad idea to call him by his name; he thought it would make his Oedipal complex more complex than ever. But I insisted. The poor little man has a hearing problem which may, or may not, get worse. He follows me around the garden when I'm gathering windfalls in a Moses basket; and he keeps asking me, do I love him? Do you?

I take him into my arms, like clean washing. I inhale him, the good laundry.

He was a man who brought people into the world. That is not the worst way to have wasted your life. A forty-year-old infant said that, if she lived to be a hundred, she might never see anything more beautiful than the road outside her window, when she waved him off in her dressing-gown, and he drove away with his doe-skin gloves creeping along the roof of his car, like something out of *The Twilight Zone.* Because nothing had prepared her for such loveliness, and nothing now remained to be seen. It was time for the other senses. The balance of her mind had been disturbed by a moment of temporary sanity.

I feel him in me like a phantom limb. My toes itch at the end of no leg.

I am so tired. I am not sleepy at all. My eyes are too heavy to close. The lashes of my eyes are tearing like stitches.

He was wrong. It is nasty, brutish, and long.

Why has my mother not rung?